ONE TINY

LIE

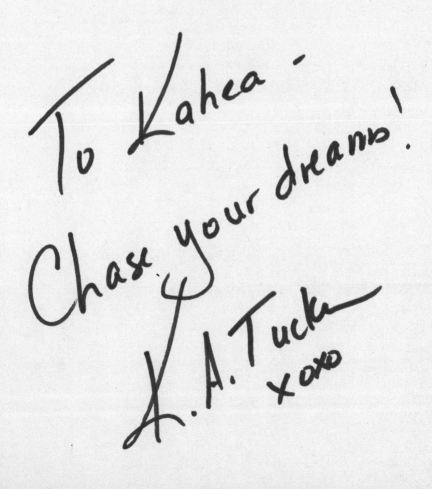

To Kahea –
Chase your dreams!
K. A. Tucker
xoxo

ALSO BY K.A. TUCKER

Ten Tiny Breaths

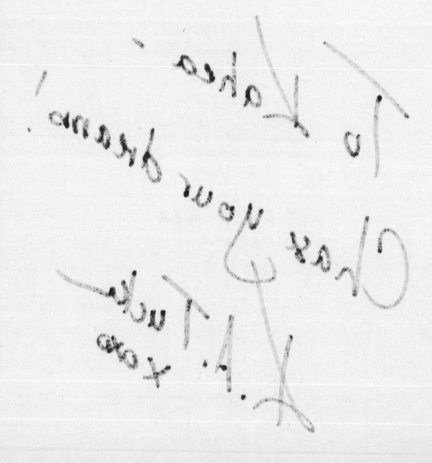

ONE TINY LIE

a novel

K.A. TUCKER

ATRIA PAPERBACK

NEW YORK LONDON TORONTO SYDNEY NEW DELHI

ATRIA PAPERBACK
A Division of Simon & Schuster, Inc.
1230 Avenue of the Americas
New York, NY 10020

First Atria Paperback edition January 2014

ATRIA PAPERBACK and colophon are trademarks of
Simon & Schuster, Inc.

For information about special discounts for bulk purchases, please contact Simon & Schuster Special Sales at
1-866-506-1949 or business@simonandschuster.com.

The Simon & Schuster Speakers Bureau can bring authors to your live event. For more information or to book an event contact the Simon & Schuster Speakers Bureau at 1-866-248-3049 or visit our website at www.simonspeakers.com.

Manufactured in the United States of America

10 9 8 7 6 5 4 3 2 1

Library of Congress Cataloging-in-Publication Data
Tucker, K. A. (Kathleen A.)
    One tiny lie : a novel / K.A. Tucker.—First Atria Paperback edition.
        p.   cm
    1. Promises—Fiction. 2. Life change events—Fiction. I. Title.
PR9199.4.T834O54 2014
813'.6—dc23
                                            2013014510

ISBN 978-1-4767-4047-8
ISBN 978-1-4767-4048-5 (ebook)

To Lia and Sadie
Your lives are always yours to live

To Paul
For daddy day care

To Stacey
A true writer's agent

I walk away.

I walk away from the voices, the shouts, the disappointment.

I walk away from my deceptions, my mistakes, my regrets.

I walk away from all that I am supposed to be and all that I cannot be.

For all of it is a lie.

chapter one

■ ■ ■

TOO PERFECT

June

"Livie, I think you're completely fucked up."

Chunks of cheesecake fly out of my mouth and splatter against the deck's glass panel as I choke on my fork. My sister has a twisted sense of humor. I automatically attribute her declaration to that. "That's not funny, Kacey."

"You're right. It's not."

The way she says it—her calm, gentle tone—sends a strange ripple through my stomach. Wiping off the gob of cheesecake from my bottom lip, I turn to search her face, looking for a tell—something to expose her game. I see none. "You're not serious, are you?"

"As a heart attack."

A bubble of panic rises into my throat. "Are you on drugs again?"

She answers with a flat glare.

I don't take that as truth, though. I lean forward and peer into her face, looking for the signs—the dilated pupils, the bloodshot whites—the traits of a user that I came to recognize when I was twelve. Nothing. Nothing but crystal-clear blue eyes staring back at me. I allow myself a small sigh of relief. At least we're not heading back down that road.

With a nervous giggle and no clue how to respond, I bide my time with another mouthful of cake. Only now the mocha flavor has turned bitter and the texture is gritty. I force it down with a hard swallow.

"You're too perfect, Livie. Everything you do, everything you say. You can do no wrong. If someone slapped you across the face, you'd apologize to them. I can't believe you don't deck me for some of the stuff *I* say. It's like you're not capable of getting angry. You could be the love child of Mother Teresa and Gandhi. You're . . ." Kacey pauses as if searching for the right word. She settles with, "Too fucking perfect!"

I cringe. Kacey tosses F-bombs around like some people toss pennies. I got used to it years ago, and yet each one of them feels like a punch to the nose right now.

"One of these days, I think you're going to crack and go all Amelia Dyer on me."

"Who?" I frown as my tongue works the last bits of mealy cake off the roof of my mouth.

She waves a dismissive hand at me. "Oh, that woman in London who murdered hundreds of babies—"

"Kacey!" I glare at her.

With an eye roll, she mutters, "Anyway, that's not the point. The point is that Stayner has agreed to speak to you."

This is getting more ridiculous by the second. "What? Bu . . . I . . . but . . . *Dr.* Stayner?" I sputter out. *Her PTSD therapist?* My hands are starting to shake. I place my plate down on a side table before I drop it. When Kacey handed it to me and suggested that we watch the Miami Beach sunset from our deck, I thought she was being sweet. Now I see she was masterminding a crazed intervention that I don't need. "I'm not suffering from PTSD, Kacey."

"I didn't say you were."

"Well, then, where is all of this coming from?"

She doesn't give me a reason. She gives me the mother lode of guilt trips instead. "You owe me, Livie," she says in an even tone. "When you asked me to go into inpatient therapy three years ago, I did it. For you. I didn't want to, but—"

"You *needed* it! You were a mess!" That's putting it lightly. The drunk driving accident that killed our parents seven years ago sent Kacey spiraling down into a rock-bottom haze of drugs, one-night stands, and violence. Then, three years ago, even rock bottom fell out from under her. I was sure I'd lost her.

But Dr. Stayner brought her back to me.

"I did need it," she admits, pursing her lips. "And I'm *not* asking you to commit yourself to inpatient therapy. I'm asking you to pick up the phone when Stayner calls. That's all. For me, Livie."

This is completely irrational—downright insane—and yet I can see by the way Kacey's fists are balled by her side and she chews her bottom lip that she's not messing around. She's genuinely concerned about me. I bite my tongue and turn to stare out at the setting sun's last rays dancing over the water. And I consider it.

What on earth could Dr. Stayner have to say? I'm a straight-A student on her way to Princeton and, after that, med school. I love children and animals and old people. I've never had the urge to pull wings off insects or fry them with a magnifying glass. Sure, I'm not big on attention. And I tend to sweat profusely around attractive guys. And I'll probably stroke out on my first date. If I don't melt into a puddle of sweat before someone even has a chance to ask me out.

All that hardly means I'm two steps away from becoming the next mass-murdering psycho. Still, I do like and respect Dr. Stayner, despite his peculiarities. Talking to him wouldn't be unpleasant. It would be a quick conversation . . .

"I suppose one phone call won't hurt," I mumble, adding, "and then we need to talk about this psychology degree you're working on. If you see red flags waving around my head, then I'm beginning to doubt your long-term career success."

Kacey's shoulders sag with relief as she settles back against her lounge chair, a contented smile touching her lips.

And I know I've made the right choice.

■ ■ ■

September

Sometimes in life you make a decision and you find yourself questioning it. A lot. You don't regret it, exactly. You know that you *probably* made the right choice and that you're *probably* better off for it. But you do spend a lot of time wondering what the hell you were thinking.

I still wonder why I ever agreed to that one phone call. I wonder it daily. I'm definitely wondering it right now.

"I'm not suggesting you star in a *Girls Gone Wild* video, Livie." He's already switched to that smooth, authoritative tone that he uses for coercion.

"How would I know? Three months ago, you suggested I have a conversation with an orangutan." *True story.*

"Has it been three months already? How is old Jimmy doing?"

I bite my tongue and take a deep breath before I say something snippy. "Now's not a good time, Dr. Stayner." And it's not.

Truly. The sun is shining, the air is warm, and I'm carting my pink suitcase and a cactus through a picturesque setting toward my dorm along with a thousand other confused students and flustered parents. It's move-in day and I may still vomit from the bumpy plane ride. One of Dr. Stayner's guerilla-tactic calls is definitely not what I want to be having right now.

And yet, here we are.

"No, Livie. Probably not. Maybe you should have rescheduled your therapy session with me, knowing you'd be on a plane to New Jersey this morning. But you didn't," Dr. Stayner calmly points out.

Looking from left to right to ensure no one overhears this conversation, my shoulders hunch in and my voice drops as I whisper, "There's nothing to reschedule because I'm not in therapy."

Okay. So that's not entirely true.

It hasn't been entirely true since the pleasant June evening when my sister ambushed me with cheesecake. Dr. Stayner phoned me the very next morning. In typical Stayner fashion, his first words to me weren't "hello," or "nice to talk to you again." He simply said, "So I hear you're a ticking time bomb."

The rest of the conversation had gone smoothly. We chatted about my flawless academic career, my lack of love life, my hopes and dreams, my future plans. We spent a bit of time talking about my parents, but he didn't dwell on it.

After I hung up, I remember smiling, sure that he would tell Kacey that I was fine and well adjusted and she could continue her witch hunt for the mentally unstable elsewhere.

When that same Chicago number appeared on my phone the following Saturday morning at ten o'clock sharp, I was more than surprised. But I picked up. And I've been picking up every Saturday at ten a.m. ever since. I've never seen a bill or a patient record or the inside of a psychiatrist's office. Both of us have danced around the word "therapy," but we have *never* used it before this conversation. Perhaps that's why I refuse to acknowledge Dr. Stayner for what he is.

My therapist.

"Fine, Livie. I'll let you go. We'll resume our *chat* next Saturday."

I roll my eyes but don't say anything. There's no point. I'd get farther dragging a mule through a hay field.

"Make sure to have a shot of tequila. Break dance. Whatever it is you youngsters do nowadays during frosh week. It'll be good for you."

"You're recommending addiction and life-threatening dance moves for my well-being?" It was pretty obvious from that second phone call that Dr. Stayner had decided to take on the task of "treating" my awkward shyness with a weekly course of absurd, often embarrassing, but ultimately harmless assignments. He's never admitted to what he was doing, never explained himself. He just expects me to comply.

And I always do.

Maybe that's why I should be in therapy.

The surprising thing is that it *has* worked. Three months of harebrained tasks has actually helped calm my nerves around crowds, free my inner thoughts, and arm me with enough confidence that sweat doesn't instantaneously erupt from my pores when an attractive man walks into the room.

"I suggested tequila, Livie. Not crystal meth . . . And no, I'm not *recommending* tequila because you are only eighteen and I am a doctor. That would be highly unprofessional. I'm recommending that you go and have *fun!*"

I heave a resigned sigh but smile as I say, "You know, I *was* normal. I think that *you've* turned me into a head case."

My ear gets a blast of laughter. "'Normal' is boring. Tequila, Livie. It makes wallflowers into butterflies. Maybe you'll even meet"—he gasps for dramatic effect—"a boy!"

"I really have to go," I say, feeling my cheeks flush as I climb the concrete steps to my stunning Hogwarts-style residence hall.

"Go! Make memories. This is a happy day for you. A victory." Dr. Stayner's voice loses that playful lilt, suddenly turning gruff. "You should be proud."

I smile into the phone, happy for the moment of seriousness. "I am, Dr. Stayner. But . . . thank you." He doesn't say the words but I hear them. *Your father would be proud.*

"And remember—" The lilt is back.

I roll my eyes at the phone. "I got it. 'Girls Gone Reasonably Frisky.' I'll do my best." I can hear his chuckling as I press "End" on the call.

chapter two

■ ■ ■

JELL-O SHOTS

This must be what Cinderella felt like.

If, instead of gliding gracefully around the dance floor of the royal ball, she was flattened against a wall at a college house party, getting jostled by drunks from all angles.

And, instead of dazzling everyone in a glamorous ball gown, she was furtively tugging on her toga to ensure all vital body parts were covered.

And, instead of a fairy godmother granting her every wish, she had an obnoxious older sister forcing Jell-O shots down her throat.

I'm just like Cinderella.

"A deal's a deal!" Kacey yells over the DJ as she hands me a tiny cup. I accept it without a word and tip my head back, letting the slippery orange substance slide down my throat. I'm actually enjoying these things. A lot. Of course, I won't admit that to my sister. I'm still bitter that she blackmailed me into making my first night at college also my first night to get drunk. Ever. It was this or have her walk into my residence hall wearing a T-shirt with my face on it and a slogan that reads, "Liberate Livie's Libido." She was serious. She actually had the damn thing printed.

"Stop being such a sourpuss, Livie. You have to admit, this is fun," Kacey shouts, handing me two more shots. "Even though we're wearing bedsheets. I mean, seriously. Who throws toga parties anymore?"

She keeps on talking but I tune her out, sucking both shots back in quick succession. That's how many in the last hour? I'm feeling fine right now. Relaxed, even. But I've never been drunk before, so what do I know? These can't be too potent. It's not like it's tequila.

Freaking Stayner! I should have known he would enlist Kacey in his dirty work. He's been doing it all summer. Of course, I have no solid proof for tonight's escapade. But if Kacey busts out a bottle of Patrón, I have my answer.

With a sigh, I lean back against the cool wall and let my gaze drift over the sea of heads. I'm not exactly sure where we are, aside from the spacious basement of a booming house party just outside campus grounds. A well-planned one, too, complete with a DJ catering to a crowd of people—some dancing, most stumbling—in the center of the big open space. Regular house lights have been replaced with colored, flashing ones and a strobe, making the place look more like a club than a home. I'm assuming the owners normally have furniture in here. Tonight, every single piece has vanished. All except for a bunch of tables lining the perimeter, supplying red plastic cups for the kegs of beer tucked underneath and holding trays of these delicious shots that I can't seem to get enough of. There must be hundreds. Thousands. Millions!

Okay. I might actually be drunk.

A short, curvy body sails past me with a fluttering wave, instantly making me smile. That's Reagan, my new roommate, and the only other person here besides my sister whom I've talked to. Each year, students are entered into a draw and assigned dorms. Freshmen get the added bonus of random roommates. Even though we only met today, I'm pretty sure I'm going to love Reagan. She's bubbly and outgoing and talks a mile a minute. She's also very artistic. After we moved our stuff into our room, she made a sign for the door with our names in calligraphy, surrounded by hearts and flowers and x's and o's. I think it's really sweet. Kacey thinks it screams "lesbian couple."

The second we stepped through the doors, Reagan was gone, chatting up a group of guys. Considering she's a freshman, she seems to know a lot of people. Mostly male. She's the one who suggested we come tonight; otherwise we would have ended up at one of the many campus-organized events that I had every intention of going to until Kacey hijacked my plans. Apparently, Princeton students living off-campus is rare, and therefore these house parties should never be missed.

"All right, Princess. Drink this," Kacey says, producing a bottle of water out of thin air, adding, "I don't want you puking tonight."

I take the bottle and let the fresh, cold liquid pour into my mouth. And I imagine projectile-vomiting my fajita dinner all over Kacey. It would serve her right.

"Oh, come on, Livie! Stop being mad at me." Kacey's voice is getting that whiny twang to it, a sign that she is sincerely feeling guilty. And then I start feeling guilty for making *her* feel guilty . . .

I heave a sigh. "I'm not mad. I just don't get why you're on a mission to get me drunk." It was drunk driving that killed our parents. I think that's one of the main reasons I've avoided anything to do with alcohol up until now. Kacey barely touches the stuff too. Though she seems to be making up for it tonight.

"I'm on a mission to make sure you have fun and meet people. It's frosh week of your first year of college. It's a once-in-a-life-time thing. It should involve copious amounts of alcohol and at least one morning with your head in the toilet." I answer her with an eye roll, but that doesn't dissuade her. Turning to face me, she throws her arms over my shoulders. "Livie. You're my little sister and I love you. Nothing about your life has been normal these past seven years. Tonight, you are going to live like a normal, irresponsible eighteen-year-old."

Licking my lips, I counter with, "It's illegal for an eighteen-year-old to drink." I know my argument is futile against my sister, but I don't care.

"Ah yes. You are right." Sliding a hand under her toga to reach into the pocket of her shorts, she pulls out what looks like a driver's license. "And that's why you are twenty-one-year-old Patricia from Oklahoma if the cops show up."

I should have known my sister would have all her bases covered.

The music begins to pick up tempo, and my knees move along with the beat. "You're going to dance with me soon!" Kacey shouts as she hands me two more shots. How many is that now? I've lost count but my tongue feels funny. Wrapping her arm around my neck, my sister pulls me down so we're cheek-to-cheek. "Okay, ready?" she says, holding her phone out in front of us. I hear, "Smile!" as the flash goes off. "For Stayner."

Aha! Proof!

"Cheers!" Kacey taps her Dixie cup into mine and then tips her head and sucks it back, quickly followed by the other. "Oh, blue ones! I'll be back in a sec!" Like a golden retriever chasing a squirrel, Kacey tears off after a guy balancing a large round tray on his shoulder, oblivious to the heads turning as she passes. Between her fierce red hair, striking face, and muscular curves, my sister *always* turns heads. I doubt she even notices it. She definitely isn't uncomfortable about it.

I sigh as I watch her. I know what she's doing. Aside from getting me drunk, of course. She's trying to distract me from the sad part about today. That my dad is not here on the one day that he should be. On the day that I start at Princeton. This was always his dream, after all. He was a proud graduate and he wanted both of his girls to go here. Kacey's declining grades after the accident didn't allow for that possibility, leaving it to me. So I'm living his dream—my dream, too—and he's not here to see me do it.

I take a deep breath and silently accept whatever fate—and by fate I mean Jell-O shots—has in store for me tonight. I'm certainly less nervous than I was when I first stepped through those doors. And the buzzing atmosphere is pretty cool. I'm at my first college party. There's nothing wrong with it or with me being here and enjoying it, I remind myself.

With a shooter in my hand, I close my eyes and let my body just feel the throbbing beat of the music. Let loose, have fun. That's what Stayner always tells me. Tipping my head back, I squish the bottom of the Dixie cup and bring it to my lips, sliding my tongue out to accept the wiggly mess into my mouth. I feel like a pro.

Except for one amateur mistake—I should never have closed my eyes.

If I hadn't, I wouldn't have looked like an easy drunk chick. And I would have seen him coming.

The tangy orange flavor has just touched my taste buds when a strong arm hooks around my waist from the front and pulls me away from the safety of my wall. My eyes fly open wide as my back presses against someone's chest, one muscular arm snaking around my body. In the next heartbeat—not mine, because mine has stopped beating altogether—a hand seizes both my chin and the Dixie cup against my lips and tilts my head back so it's facing up and at an angle. I catch a whiff of musky cologne a split second before a guy leans over and his tongue slips against mine, twirling around and coaxing it a little before drawing the Jell-O away. It all happens so fast that I have no chance to think or react or put my tongue back in my mouth. Or bite the intruding tongue off.

It's all over in a second, leaving me shooterless, breathless, and gripping the wall for support as my knees shake. It takes me a few seconds to regain composure, and when I do, my brain processes the loud roar of approval behind me. I spin around to find a group of tall, brawny guys—all in togas strategically wrapped to show off well-defined chests—cheering and slapping the guy on the back as if he's just won a race. I can't see his face. All I can see is a mess of dark brown—almost black—hair and the solid ridges of his back.

I'm not sure how long I'm standing there with my mouth hanging open, staring, but one of the guys in the group finally notices. He casts a furtive look at the Jell-O thief, jutting his head in my direction.

What the hell am I going to say? Without being too obvious, I frantically search the room for my sister's fiery red hair. Where is she? Gone, leaving me here to deal with . . . My breath catches as I watch the Jell-O thief turn with slow, leisurely movement to face me dead-on.

This guy's tongue was in my mouth? This guy . . . this tall, giant Adonis with wavy hair, tanned skin, and a body to tempt a blind nun . . . had his *tongue* in my *mouth*.

Oh God. The sweat is back! All those weeks of speed dating for nothing! I feel the trickles—multiple ones—run down between my shoulder blades as his coffee-colored eyes do a quick scan down and up my body before settling on my face. And then one side of his mouth curves up and he offers me an arrogant smirk. "Not bad."

I'm still not sure what my first words would have been to him. But then he had to go and say those two little words with that cocky little grin . . .

So I haul back and punch him in the jaw.

I've only punched one other person before. My sister's boyfriend, Trent, and that was because he broke Kacey's heart. It took weeks for my hand to heal. Since then, Trent taught me how to throw a punch, with my thumb wrapped around the outside of my knuckles and my wrist tilted downward.

I really love Trent right now.

I hear the howls of laughter from around us as the Jell-O thief rubs his jaw, wincing and adjusting it this way and that to test it out. That's how I know that it hurt. If I weren't so rattled by the fact that this guy had just forcefully French-kissed me, I'd probably have a giant grin on my face. He deserved it. He didn't just steal my shooter. He stole my first kiss.

He takes a step toward me and I instinctively retreat, only to find my back pressed up against the wall once again. A sly smile creeps over his mouth, as if he knows that I'm cornered and pleased by it. Closing the distance, his arms stretch out, his hands pressing up against the wall on either side of my face, his broad body, his towering height, his entire presence effectively boxing me in. And I suddenly can't breathe. This is suffocating. I try peering around him, looking for my sister, but I can't see anything past flesh and muscle. And I don't know where to look because no matter where I do, he's there. Finally, I hazard a glance up. Heated eyes as dark as midnight bore into my face. I swallow, my stomach doing several full somersaults.

"That's one hell of a swing for someone so . . ." He moves one hand down and closer to my arm. I feel a thumb graze along my bicep. "Female." I shiver responsively and a visual flashes through my mind—a shaking rabbit, cornered by a wolf. He cocks his head and I catch curiosity flitter past. "So you're shy . . . but not too shy to punch me across the face." There's a pause, and then he offers me another crooked smile laced with arrogance. "I'm sorry, I couldn't help myself. You looked like you were really enjoying that shooter. I had to taste it for myself."

Swallowing, I manage to pull my arms up and across my chest in an attempt to force some barrier between his chest and mine. My voice decidedly shaky, I say, "And?"

The grins widens, his eyes dropping to stare at my mouth for so long that I don't think I'm going to get an answer out of him. But I finally do. One that comes after he licks his bottom lip. "And I could go for another one. You game?"

My body instinctively presses against the wall as I try to meld into it, to get away from this guy and whatever lewd intentions he has.

"All right, that's enough!" A wave of relief sweeps over me as a delicate hand slips between us, landing against the Jell-O thief's bare chest and pushing him back. He submits, slowly retreating, arms raised as if in surrender. He turns to rejoin his friends.

"Way to start off, Livie. I think that should keep Stayner off your back for a while," Kacey says, barely able to get the words out through her laughter. She's laughing!

"It's not funny, Kacey!" I hiss. "That guy *forced* himself on me!"

She rolls her eyes but then, after a long pause, she sighs. "Yeah, you're right." Reaching over, she pinches the guy's arm without hesitation. "Hey, buddy!"

He turns back toward us with a scowl, mouthing "fuck" as he rubs his arm. The scowl lasts only a second before he sees Kacey's glare. Or rather, her face and her body. And then that stupid grin is back. Huge surprise.

"You do that to her again and I'll sneak into your room and rip your balls off while you sleep, *capisce?*" she warns with a pointed finger. Most times my sister's threats involve the mutilation of testicles.

The Jell-O thief doesn't respond at first. He simply stares at her and my sister levels him with her own glare, completely unfazed. But then his gaze flickers back and forth between the two of us. "You guys sisters? You look alike." We get that a lot so I'm not surprised, though I don't see it. We both have the same light blue eyes and pale skin. But my hair is jet black and I'm taller than Kacey.

"Pretty and smart. You've got a real winner on your hands, Livie!" Kacey shouts extra loud so both of us can hear.

He shrugs and the cocky grin is back. "I've never had two sisters. . . . " he begins with a suggestive arched brow.

Oh. My. God.

"And you never will. Not *these* two sisters, anyway."

He shrugs. "Not at the same time, maybe."

"Don't worry. When my baby sister gets laid for the first time, it won't be with you."

"Kacey!" I gasp, my eyes darting to his face, praying that the loud music drowned out her words. By the flash of surprise I detect there, I know that it didn't.

I grab hold of her arm and tug her away. She's already sputtering apologies. "Jeez, Livie. I'm sorry. I guess I'm drunk. Loose lips . . ."

"Do you know what you just did?"

"Painted a big virginal bull's-eye on your back?" Kacey confirms with a scrunched-up face.

With a cautious glance over my shoulder, I find him back with a group of guys, chuckling as he sips on his beer. But those piercing eyes stay on me. When he catches me looking, he reaches over to take one of his friend's Dixie cups. He holds it up, making a show of his tongue sliding over the top before quirking his brow and mouthing, "Your turn?"

My head whips back around and glare at my sister. I snap, "I should have just let you wear that damn T-shirt!" I may be inexperienced and naïve in some manners, but I know full well that a guy like *that* discovering an eighteen-year-old virgin is his idea of finding that ever illusive pot of gold at the end of a rainbow.

"I'm sorry . . ." She shrugs, glancing back at him. "Gotta admit he's hot, though, Livie. He looks like a Mediterranean underwear model. There'd be no coyote-ugly situation in the morning there."

I sigh. I don't know why Kacey seems hell-bent on getting me to trade in my "V-card." For years, she never cared. In fact, she seemed happy that I didn't date in high school. But lately she's been driven by this notion that I'm sexually repressed. I swear I'm beginning to loathe her choice to go into psychology.

"Just look at him!"

"No," I refuse stubbornly.

"Fine," she mutters, grabbing four shooters off a platter that a stocky guy in a kilt—a kilt, at a toga party?—carries past. "But if you were planning on giving it up anytime, I'll bet *that* would be a memorable way to do it. I'm sure he'd quickly get you up to speed on all that you've missed these past few years."

"Including gonorrhea and crabs?" I mumble, staring at the two blue shooter cups in my hand. I'm thankful for the dark as I feel my cheeks flush deeply. Bringing the one to my mouth as I had before, I let my tongue skate across the top of it, mentally reliving the seconds of that—I refuse to acknowledge that as my first kiss—that *thing* he did to me.

"Bottoms up!" Kacey sucks hers back in rapid succession.

I follow her lead with the first. With the second one at my mouth, I stupidly hazard a sideways glance, assuming he's moved on to another unsuspecting victim. But he hasn't. He's there, sur-rounded by a few girls, one with her hand against the tattoo on his chest. But he's still watching me. Still smiling. Except now it's this strange, dark smile, as if he has a secret.

I guess he does. *My* secret.

A nervous thrill fires through me as my cup sits frozen at my lips.

"That's Ashton Henley!" someone yells into my ear. With a start, I turn to find Reagan next to me, a beer in one hand and a shooter in the other. She's so short that she needs to be on tiptoes to reach my ear.

"How do you know who he is?" I ask, embarrassed to be caught ogling.

"He's the captain of the Princeton Heavyweight rowing team. My dad is the coach," she explains, her speech slurring slightly. Her hand waves around the room in a wide spiral. "I know a lot of these guys." That explains her social ease, I guess. "And I think you've caught his attention, roomie," she adds with a sly wink.

I shrug and give her a tight smile, wanting to change subjects before we give him the satisfaction of figuring out we're talking about him. But as I glance around the room at the little pock-ets of females and see the glances in his direction—some furtive, some downright obvious—I'm sure there's no shortage of atten-tion on this Ashton guy.

Reagan confirms that a second later. "And he's pretty much the hottest guy at this school." She takes a sip of her beer. "And also, a giant ass."

"That much, I gathered," I murmur, more to myself than to her. I suck back my shooter, intentionally turning my back to him, hoping he'll redirect his predatory stare to a willing recipient.

"And a bit of a man whore."

This just keeps getting better and better. "I'm sure he'll have no trouble finding someone to . . . whore it up with." Someone who isn't me.

I'm not sure if I'm officially drunk or Kacey is a magician, but she does a twirl and two more shooters land in my hand. The music has picked up tempo and volume and now I feel it vibrating through my entire body, making my hips sway of their own accord to the beat.

"It's fun here, isn't it?" Reagan shouts, her straight honey-blond hair flipping around as she jumps, throwing her arms in the air and screeching, "Wooh!" She has a ton of energy. Like one of those kids who gets dosed with Ritalin. "All these people, the excitement, the music. I love it!"

I smile and nod as I look around again. And I have to admit, this is fun. "I'm glad I came!" I yell, bumping shoulders with Kacey. "Keep me out of any more trouble tonight, though. Please," I warn as I suck both shots back.

Kacey answers with a laugh, hooking an arm around mine and throwing the other arm around Reagan, who happily joins in the revelry. "Of course, baby sis. Tonight, Princeton is going to party Cleary style."

I giggle, my sister's giddiness temporarily pushing everything else away. "I don't even know what that means."

With one of her notorious evil grins, my sister says, "You're about to find out."

chapter three

■ ■ ■

THE BEAST

There are about five seconds of calm and blissful ignorance after I crack my eyes open. Five seconds when I stare at the white ceiling looming not far from my face, as my eyes adjust to the dim light, as my brain just sits idly, waiting for the neurons to start firing.

And then the avalanche of confusion hits.

Where am I?

How did I get here?

What the hell happened?

I roll my head and find my sister's face only a few inches away. "Kacey?" I whisper.

She moans, and my nostrils catch her rank breath. I cringe and turn away. Too quickly, it would seem, as a sharp, stabbing pain pierces my brain. I cringe a second time.

We're in my dorm room. That much I can quickly deduce by the cramped space and a few personal belongings. But I don't remember coming home.

What *do* I remember?

My hand slides feebly up to my face to give it a good rub while I pick through my foggy memory, trying to piece together the night . . . Bits of blurry images flicker so faintly that I'm not sure they're real. Shot after shot. After shot. Orange, blue, green . . . Kacey and me doing the robot on the dance floor? I groan and immediately wince at another throb of pain in my head. *God*, I hope not. From there . . . nothing. I remember nothing. How can I not remember *anything*?

Kacey moans again and I'm assaulted with another wave of that foulness. Swallowing several times, I accept that my breath can't be much better and that I would kill for a bottle of water. I push my sheets off my body with slow, uncoordinated kicks.

And I frown as I take in my exposed flesh. *Why am I . . . Oh, right*. I was wearing that stupid toga last night. That doesn't explain why I'm in nothing but panties now, but my head hurts too much to think about tha . . . *Whatever*. It's only my sister. And Reagan, but she's a girl.

I struggle to sit up, groaning as I push my hands back through a mess of knotted hair, squeezing my temples to relieve some of the pressure. And why does my head feel ready to burst! I think if someone walked in here with an axe, I'd stretch my neck out for a clean cut.

There's already a vile taste in my mouth when a surge of nausea hits me. I need water. *Now*. With shaky arms and legs, I rock my body around and down, not wasting time with the ladder and hoping I don't step on Reagan's head. If I can just make it to the mini fridge and chug a bottle of cold water, I'll feel better. I know it . . .

A second later, as my feet hit Reagan's plush white shag rug by the bed, I get my second shock of the morning.

An ass. A *male* ass. And it's not just an ass. It's everything. There's a very large, very naked guy sprawled out on Reagan's bed, his legs and one arm hanging off the edge. By the mess of honey-blond hair poking out from beneath the covers in the corner, I can see that Reagan is buried somewhere in there.

I can't stop staring. I'm standing there in nothing but underwear, the room is spinning, my mouth tastes like I drank sewer water, and I'm frozen, focused on this naked man in front of me. Partly because he's the last thing I ever expected to see when I climbed down. Partly because he's the first naked man I've ever seen. Partly because I'm wondering what the hell he's doing here.

And . . . what is that on the top of his left ass cheek? My curiosity overtakes my shock as I step forward cautiously, hesitant to get too close. It looks like . . . a tattoo. It's red and puffy. I've seen pictures of fresh tattoos and that's what they look like. Like, really fresh. It's a fancy scroll font and it reads "Irish." *Irish?* I frown. Why is that word jogging my memory . . . ?

The floor creaks as my weight shifts, startling me. I abruptly back away. The sudden movement makes the crammed room spin. *Water. Right. Now.* With wobbly legs, I stumble toward the fridge and my robe that hangs on a hook by the door. Unfortunately, our dorm rooms are tiny and, let's face it—I'm an ox in a closet when I'm nervous. My back slams into Reagan's dresser, hitting it hard enough to knock over an array of her glass perfume bottles. I hold my breath, hoping the loud noise isn't enough to wake up the naked giant.

No such luck.

My heart stops beating as I watch the guy's head roll over to face out. He cracks open his eyes.

Oh. My. God.

It's the Jell-O thief. It's Ashton.

Memories start washing over me like violent waves.

They start at the stolen Jell-O shot but they don't end there. No . . . they go on and on, each jarring flashback slamming into me, weakening my knees and tightening my stomach. Music and strobe lights and Ashton, leaning into me on the dance floor. Me, yelling at him, my hand slapping the arrogant smirk on his face. My hand, smacking his chest once, twice . . . I don't know how many times. And then I'm not smacking him anymore. My hands are resting on his bare chest, my fingers tracing the lines of a fist-sized Celtic sign and the curves of his muscle with intrigue. I remember dancing . . . fast, slow . . . my fingers curled in his hair, his hands squeezing my waist tightly, pulling me into him.

I remember the cool night air teasing my skin and a brick wall supporting my back as Ashton and I . . .

I gasp, and my hands fly to my mouth.

His eyes, first narrow and struggling against the light, widen in surprise as they rake over my entire body, resting on my chest. I can't move. I can't breathe. I'm the terrified rabbit again, two seconds before knowing it's going to be eaten by a wolf. A rabbit in nothing but her floral panties.

I unfreeze just long enough for my arms to wrap around my chest, concealing my nakedness.

The movement seems to break Ashton's trance because he groans, running his hand through his dark hair. It's already standing in every direction possible but somehow he makes it even messier. His head rolls to the side to see Reagan peeking out from under the covers, just waking, the stages of confusion to recognition flittering through her eyes. "Fuck . . ." I hear him mumble, pinching the bridge of his nose as if in pain.

"We didn't . . . ?" I hear Ashton ask her in a low voice.

She shakes her head, strangely calm. "No. You were too drunk to make it back to your house. You were supposed to sleep on the floor." She sits up slightly to take in his present attire, or lack thereof. "Dude, why the hell are you naked?" Her words remind me that he is still very naked. My eyes glance across his long form again, a strange stirring in my belly at the sight of it.

He drops his forehead into the pillow. "Oh, thank God," I hear him mumble, ignoring her question. With surprisingly graceful movements, he rolls out of the bottom bunk and stands. Air hisses through my teeth as I inhale, shifting my wide eyes to the window, but not before I get a full frontal show.

Chuckling, he asks, "What's wrong, Irish?"

Irish.

My head snaps back. "What'd you call me?"

He smirks, his hand resting on the ladder rung, seemingly comfortable in his current lack of covering. "You don't remember much from last night, do you?"

The way his intense dark eyes settle on my face makes my stomach slide down into my leg. I have to clench my muscles before I lose bladder control right here. "If it explains why we're all in a room together and you're naked . . . then no." The words fly out of my mouth, two levels higher than normal and wobbly.

He takes a step forward and I instantly shift back, trying to squeeze into the space between the wall and the dresser. I'm so light-headed, I'm sure I'm going to pass out. Or throw up. All over the bare chest that I just barely remember groping last night.

There's a plain white sheet resting on the dresser beside me. I curl my body toward the wall as I reach over and grab it, pulling it down to cover my front. He takes another step and I lean against the dresser for support, willing my eyes to stay level but panicking the entire time. If he moves any closer, *that thing* is liable to brush up against me.

"Don't worry. We agreed last night that I'm not marriage material," he says.

I tighten my grip around the sheet and my chest and set my jaw stubbornly. "Well, at least I was still semi-coherent, then."

I can't seem to peel my focus away from his rich brown eyes. They're boring into my face but there's something unreadable behind them. I wonder if he remembers kissing me. I wonder if he regrets it.

I sense him about to edge just a tiny bit closer. And then I can't control it anymore. I burst out, "Can you please point that thing somewhere else!"

Throwing his head back to howl with laughter, he holds his hands up in surrender and backs away. "Reagan, don't tell anyone. Especially your dad," he calls out over his shoulder.

"No worries there," Reagan mutters, rubbing her face.

"What the fuck?" I hear Kacey mumble as she comes to. She sits up and peers down at Ashton—all of him—before her gaze darts to me standing there. Her eyes widen momentarily. "Oh, no . . . please tell me you two didn't . . . ," she says with a groan.

I hug my body tight as I stare at her pleadingly. *I don't know! I don't know what we did!*

"No, they didn't!" Reagan calls out.

Air explodes out of my lungs in relief, and then I wince. Even that rattled my pounding head.

I'm not the only one relieved. The deep frown on my sister's face relaxes. With that out of the way, she takes another look at him, dropping her gaze low. "You wanna cover your junk, buddy?"

He grins, holding his hands out. "I thought you liked me like this?"

She responds with a smirk of her own, her eyes dropping meaningfully downward. "I've got better things waiting at home for me." She flickers her hand toward the door. That's Kacey. Cool and confident when faced with a random penis.

Shaking his head but chuckling, he says, "Fair enough." He turns to hold my gaze for a long moment, an unreadable expression on his face, before his eyes drop to the sheet I'm clutching for dear life. "I believe this is mine," he says at the same time he yanks it out of my grip, leaving me exposed once again. My arms fly to cover my chest as I watch him close the distance to the door in four strides. Throwing it open, he strolls out into the hall.

Which is exactly when a student and her mother pass by, suitcases in hand. Ashton isn't fazed by their hanging mouths as he walks past them, taking his time wrapping the sheet around his lower half. "Ladies," he says with a half-salute. But then I hear him bellow, loud enough for I'm sure half the floor to hear, "Sorry, but I don't do one-night stands, Irish!"

I'm left standing in the doorway with my arms hugging my boobs, hoping against all hope that a piano will come crashing through the ceiling to end the most mortifying moment of my life.

That's when I feel the warning stir in the pit of my stomach, moving up my esophagus. I know what's about to happen. And there's no way I'm going to make it to the bathroom in time. My mouth flies to cover my mouth as I frantically scan the room for something. Anything. Including the gold and beige planter holding Reagan's ficus. I dive for it just as a night's worth of Jell-O shooters rises.

I was wrong. *This* is the most mortifying moment of my life.

■ ■ ■

"I should have just let you wear that T-shirt," I moan, my arm flung across my forehead. After poisoning my roommate's plant with high doses of stomach acid and toxins, I crawled back into my top bunk with Reagan's hangover stash—Advil and a gallon of isotonic liquids—where I've remained, drifting between unconsciousness and self-pity. The few hours of sleep have helped with the monstrous headache. The puking helped with the nausea. Nothing has helped with the shame.

Kacey giggles.

"It's not funny, Kacey! None of this is funny! You were supposed to keep me out of trouble!" I shift, and the movement reminds me of the discomfort in my back. "And why is my back sore?"

"Maybe it was the brick wall Ashton had you pinned against while he was diving for second base?" Kacey murmurs with a devilish smile.

"I don't remember anything!" I yell, but my cheeks flush. Basically, all I do remember about last night involves touching or leaning against or kissing Ashton. "Why him?" I cry out, my hands covering my face as another burst of embarrassment colors my face.

"Oh . . . Livie girl. Who knew a few dozen Jell-O shooters would unleash the beast hiding within?"

Livie girl . . . My brow furrows, another eerie wave of familiarity settling over me. It's what our dad always called me, but why does that remind me of last night?

"Here . . . This may help." Kacey hands me her phone.

With a shaky hand and a sinking stomach, I start flipping through the photo album. "Who are all of these people? And *why* am I *hugging* them?"

"Oh, they're your best friends. You love them," she explains with a matter-of-fact raised brow. "At least, that's what you kept telling them last night."

"I did not!" I gasp. And then I pinch my lips together with my hand as more hazy memories swarm me. I did. I remember saying that word. A lot. Why couldn't I just lose my voice? Or have someone cut my tongue off for me? The thought of a tongue brings me back to Ashton and I groan. Did I tell him that I loved him too? Is that why this happened?

I go back to flipping through the pictures to distract the blush from creeping up my face. There's a close-up of a guy with a kilt and a bagpipe, his arm around Kacey. I flip to the next to see Kacey pointing intentionally at his kilt, her eyebrows arched questioningly. "What's he doing at a toga—" I begin to ask but then flip to the next picture and gasp.

"That's called 'going traditional,'" Kacey explains.

With a deep frown and a shaking head, I keep moving through the pictures and I feel my face lose more blood by the shot. Kacey and I are hugging in most of them. In some, we look like we're trying to seduce the camera with wagging tongues and wild eyes. Every once in a while, Reagan's big grin shows up alongside us.

"Oh no . . ." It's funny how just a photo can trigger a memory. That's exactly what happens when the picture of myself pointing to a sign that says "Inky's" appears. "Ohmigod!" I've said that at least ten times this morning. "Oh God, oh God, oh God . . ." I mutter frantically as I flip through the next pictures, hoping my mind is playing tricks on me. Nope! Sure enough, there I am, straddling a chair, holding my hair and the top of my toga to the side as a burly man in black leather pants and covered in ink grips a tattoo gun behind me. I stare at the picture, my mouth hanging open. That explains why my back is so sore. "How could you let this happen, Kacey!" I hiss, hysteria kicking in.

"Oh, no you don't," Kacey interjects, snatching the phone from my hand. She quickly finds a video file and hits *play* before shoving the phone back in my face. I'm all smiles in it, though my mouth and eyes look a little droopy. "I will not hold my sister, Kacey Cleary, accountable for my actions when I wake up!" I declare with resounding clarity.

I hear Kacey's excited voice as she responds. "Even though I warned you that you would not be happy about this in the morning, right? And that you would try to blame me?" She doesn't slur when she's drunk either.

"That's right!" My hand flies up in the air and the artist stops for a moment to place my arm back down and order me not to move. He goes back to work and I say, "I demand the right to have a tattoo because I, Olivia Cleary"—I jab myself in the chest with my thumb like a caveman, earning another pause and annoyed glance from the artist—"am a super *badass*."

My hand holding the phone falls to the side of the bed as I rub my eyes. "How could that guy tattoo me in good conscience? I mean, look at me!" I thrust the phone in her face. "I was drunk! Isn't that illegal?"

"I don't know about illegal—it probably is—but it's definitely frowned upon," Kacey admits.

I cringe, my stomach curling. "Well, then, how did—"

"He's a friend of Ashton's."

I throw my hands up in the air. "Well, that's just great! Because *he's* reputable. What if they used dirty needles? Kacey!" My eyes widen. "People catch HIV and hepatitis from those places! How could you let—"

"It's a legit, clean place. Don't worry," Kacey muttered in that calm but annoyed tone she uses on the rare occasions that I get hysterical. "I wasn't as drunk as you. I knew what was going on."

"How? You had a shot in your face every time I looked at you!"

She snorts. "Because my tolerance for booze is *slightly* higher than yours. I promised Stayner I'd stay lucid."

"Stayner." I shake my head. "What kind of psychiatrist masterminds his patient getting blitzed to the point of tattoos and random make-out sessions?"

"The completely unorthodox and therefore brilliant kind?" Kacey responds with a severe stare. Her response doesn't surprise me. In my sister's eyes, Dr. Stayner can turn water into wine. "And he didn't have anything to do with that, Livie. He just told you to go have fun. You did all this on your own."

"And you knew I'd be furious today," I say with a resigned sigh.

She shrugs. "The tattoo is pretty. I promise you'll like it when you see it."

I pretend to study a mark on the ceiling for a moment as I clench my jaw stubbornly. I've never held a grudge against my sister. Never. This may be a first.

"Oh, come on, Livie! Don't be mad. Don't pretend you didn't enjoy last night. You told me it was the best night of your life. About a thousand times. Besides"—she rubs her shoulder and I know she's not even aware of it—"we deserve to have some harmless fun together after what we've been through."

My eyes catch the long, narrow surgical scar along her arm. A scar that puts all of this into perspective. "You're right," I murmur, my finger trailing the thin, white line. "It's nothing." There's a long pause. "You said it was pretty?"

She flips through the rest of the pictures until she finds one of the finished product: *Livie Girl*, in delicate scroll writing between my shoulder blades. It's no more than four inches wide. Now that the initial shock has subsided, my heart swells seeing it. "Pretty," I agree, staring at the beautiful calligraphy font, wondering if my dad would agree.

"Dad would love it," Kacey says. Sometimes I swear my sister has a channel into my brain. And every once in a while, she seems to know exactly what to say. I smile for the first time this morning.

"I washed it for you last night. You'll need to clean it a few times every day for the next two weeks. There's a bottle of Lubriderm over there." She waves a lazy hand toward a desk. "Wearing light clothes will help with the tenderness."

"Is that why I woke up practically naked?"

She snorts and then nods.

My hand moves to rub my brow. "It's all making sense now." Drunken, idiotic sense. I study the picture again. "Is it supposed to be that red and puffy?"

"Yeah, there was some blood."

I groan at the thought, my hand pressing against my still-queasy stomach.

"I think there's another planter over there."

I groan again. "I'll need to replace that later today for Reagan."

We lie in silence for a long moment. "How did you end up on the top bunk, by the way? That really sucks," she says. Some of the dorm rooms have bunks. Some of the rooms are too small to separate the bunks into two individual beds. We ended up in one of those rooms.

"Reagan's afraid of heights, so I gave her the bottom. I don't mind."

"Huh . . . I guess that makes sense. She's so short. Almost a dwarf."

I turn to shoot a scathing glare at my sister. Reagan is right below us. Sleeping, but *right below* us!

There's another long pause before Kacey continues with that devilish little smile. "Well, I hope she doesn't mind your rampant sex life. It could be lethal for her if this thing isn't stable."

Sudden tittering tells us Reagan is in fact awake and listening. "Oh, don't worry. I know the rules," she calls out in a groggy voice. "I have a red sock we can hang on the doorknob when Livie's in here with Ashton—"

I yank the covers over my head because I know exactly where this is going and my cheeks are flushing furiously. Somehow I've ended up with my sister's mini-me as a roommate. Unfortunately my sheets aren't soundproof, and I have no problem hearing Kacey's continued teasing. "No need, Reagan. Livie likes witnesses."

"I noticed. From what I hear, so does Ashton. And I'm okay with that because that body is to die for! He has the most incredible chest. I could run my tongue down it all night long. Just like Livie did—"

I burst out in nervous giggles, both horrified and delirious. "I did not. Stop!"

"Not until you admit that you enjoyed messing around with him last night."

I shake my head furiously.

"His ass is hard too. I've copped a feel before. Not the two-handed grip that Livie had on him, though," Reagan continues.

"STOP!"

My raised voice only feeds Kacey's amusement. "I can't wait until the first time she has a two-handed grip on his—"

"Okay! I enjoyed it! Immensely! Stop this conversation now, please! I don't ever want to see him again."

"Until the next time you're drunk."

"I'm never drinking again!" I declare.

"Oh, Livie . . ." Kacey rolls over to snuggle against me.

"No, I'm serious! I'm like Jekyll and Hyde when I drink."

"Well, Dad did say there's always a bit of crazy in even the most reserved of the Irish. You sure proved that last night."

Irish.

"Ashton called me 'Irish.' Why?"

"I don't know, Livie. You'll have to ask him the next time you guys get drunk and make out."

I roll my eyes but don't bother to respond. Something is nagging at me still.

Irish.

Irish.

My eyes pop open. I pull the cover off my face. "Did Ashton get a tattoo on his butt that says 'Irish'?"

There's a long pause. And then Kacey bolts up, her eyes wide and bright, her mouth hanging open. "I totally forgot about that!" She and Reagan are suddenly howling with laughter. "How did I forget about that?" Jutting a finger in my face, she says, "*You* dared the cocky bastard!" She's clapping her hands with a level of giddiness I rarely see from Kacey. Or even from a four-year-old hopped up on sugar. She raises one up to me and, after a long pause, I give her a reluctant high five. "You think *you* have regrets, Livie? Wait until he figures out why his ass is sore . . ."

Reagan is laughing so hard that I'm sure there must be tears running down her face, and it's infectious. Soon the entire bunk bed is shaking as we laugh at the gorgeous rowing team captain and his inked ass.

And as much as I hate to, as hard as it is to do, I have to admit to myself . . . yeah, last night was fun.

Every second of it.

■ ■ ■

By three o'clock that afternoon, I'm feeling a lot better. Enough that the smell of coffee and fresh pastries didn't turn my stomach when we grabbed a quick bite at a quaint local café. But now the hangover has been replaced with melancholy.

I'm saying goodbye to my sister today.

Of course there are texts, and phone calls, and email, and face time, and I'll see her when I fly down for our friends Storm and Dan's wedding in a few weeks, but . . . it's not the same. I remember the two months away from her while she was in Dr. Stayner's care. I felt like someone had ripped a chunk of my heart out. Outside of that time, I've seen her face every single day of my life.

Every. Single. Day.

Even when she was in the ICU after the accident, even when she was messed up with alcohol and drugs, even when she was working those crazy hours tending bar at Penny's, I still always peeked in on her asleep in her bed, just to get a glimpse of her face. To prove to myself that she hadn't died on me too.

Knowing this day would come hasn't made it any easier. Now, standing here, I'm sure I'm losing something. It's as if I'm saying goodbye to a part of my life that I'll never get back.

"Well . . . ," Kacey says, looking up at me with glassy blue eyes and a tight smile as we stand next to a taxi. My sister doesn't cry much. Even after everything we've gone through, and how far she's come, she normally manages to use inappropriate humor to shrug off any threats of sadness. Now, though . . . now I see a single tear trickle down her cheek. "Little sis," she mumbles, sliding her hands around my neck to pull me down so our foreheads meet. "You did it, Livie."

I smile. "*We* did it." It would have been easier for her had she left me with Aunt Darla and Uncle Raymond three years ago. Heck, it would have been expected. She didn't have to burden herself with a mouth to feed. I think a lot of other siblings in her situation would have simply walked out the front door and never looked back. Not Kacey, though. "Thanks to you—" I start to say. She cuts me off with her typical stern brow.

"Oh, no. No thanks to me, Livie. I'm the train wreck of a sister who somehow, miraculously, didn't derail your future with my mountain of shit." She closes her eyes as she whispers, "It's me that owes you. Everything." She pulls me tight to her in a hug. "Remember, I'm never too far. You let me know if you ever need me and I'll be here in an instant. Okay?"

"I'll be fine, Kacey."

"And even when you're not, I'm still here. Okay?"

I nod, not trusting my voice.

I hear my phone chirp, indicating an incoming text. Thinking it's Storm—because she's the only one aside from Kacey who texts me—I check my phone.

Tell me you did one out-of-character thing last night?

"You have got to be kidding me!" I burst out.

"What's going on?" Kacey asks with a frown, leaning in to peek over my shoulder at the screen.

"What kind of doctor *texts* his patients?" I mean, non-patients.

"You have about five minutes to respond before he calls you. You know that, right?" Kacey says.

I nod. I've learned that Dr. Stayner is a very patient man . . . unless he wants answers. "What should I tell him?"

She shrugs and then grins. "I find shock value works best with him."

"Well, I definitely have enough material for that." She waits with arms crossed as I type:

I drank enough Jell-O shots to fill a small pool, and then proceeded to break out every terrible dance move known to mankind. I am now the proud owner of a tattoo and if I didn't have a video to prove otherwise, I'd believe I had it done in a back alley with hepatitis-laced needles. Satisfied?

My stomach tightens as I press "Send." He keeps telling me to leverage that inner sarcasm he knows is in my head.

Ten seconds later, my phone beeps again.

That's a good start. Did you talk to a guy?

I stare wide-eyed at my phone, processing his reaction—or nonreaction—to my night of scarring debauchery.

That gives Kacey a chance to grab my phone out of my hand.

"Kacey, what are you doing!" I chase her around the cab as her fingers furiously type; she's cackling the entire time. I don't know how she can run and text, but she does. Not until she's hit "Send" does she slow enough to toss my phone to me. I fumble as I catch it and quickly check to see what my sister has done.

> Not only did I talk to a guy but I've now seen two penises, including the one attached to the naked man in my room this morning when I woke up. I have pictures. Would you like to see one?

"Kacey!" I shriek, smacking her against the shoulder.
It's a moment before the response comes.

> Glad you're making friends. Talk to you on Saturday.

There are a few seconds of silence, during which my shock outweighs anything else, and then we burst out laughing, lifting the entire mood of this goodbye.

"Okay, I've got to go now or I'll miss my plane," Kacey says with another tight hug. "Go forth and make thy mistakes."

"More than last night?"

Kacey winks. "I didn't see you making any mistakes last night." Opening the taxi door, she waves at me before climbing in. And she keeps waving from the back window, her chin resting on the headrest, as the taxi disappears around the corner.

chapter four

■ ■ ■

REGRET

I'm sure most girls do everything in their power to stage a run-in with Ashton Henley after getting drunk and making out with him on a random street corner.

But I am not most girls.

And I have every intention of avoiding him for the rest of my Princeton career.

Unfortunately for me, fate has decided that forty-eight hours is all I get.

After standing in line at the bookstore for hours, I'm rushing back to the dorm to unload twenty pounds of textbooks before I can join the late-afternoon campus tour. This 250-odd-year-old campus, with acres of stunning Gothic-style architecture, is rich with history that I want to see in person. I don't have time for diversions.

Of course, that's the perfect time for an ambush.

"What do ya got there, Irish?" A hand swoops in and grabs

the course registration paper that's tucked in between my chest and my books. I suck in a breath and shiver as his finger grazes my collarbone.

"Nothing," I mutter, but I don't bother with more as there's no point. He's already intently reviewing my course list and is chewing a very full bottom lip in thought. So I just sigh and wait silently, taking the opportunity to notice things I couldn't when I was drunk and it was dark. Or when I was naked and cornered. Like how, in the late-afternoon sunlight, Ashton's shaggy hair has more brown in it than black. And how his thick brows are neatly groomed. And how his eyes have the tiniest green speckles within the brown. And how his impossibly long, dark lashes curl out at the ends . . .

"Irish?"

"Huh?" I snap out of my thoughts to find him staring down at me with that smirk on his face, implying he said something to me and I missed it because I was too busy gawking.

Which I did. Because I was.

I clear my throat, my ears burning with the rest of my face. I want to ask him why he keeps calling me that, but all I can manage is, "Pardon?"

Thankfully, he doesn't tease me. "How's the tat?" he asks as he slowly slides the paper back to where he got it from, his finger once again grazing my collarbone. My body, once again, shivering and tensing at his touch.

"Oh . . . great." I swallow, hugging my books closer to my chest as I avert my gaze in the direction of my residence. At the groups of students milling about. Anywhere but at the breathing reminder of my night of scandal.

"Really? Because mine is annoying the hell out of me."

"It *is* kind of itchy," I admit, glancing back to see Ashton's mouth stretched into a wide grin, displaying dimples that are smack dab in the middle of his cheeks and deeper than Trent's. Deep enough to make my breath hitch now. Deep enough that I remember admiring them in my drunken stupidity. I'm pretty sure I stuck my finger into one. And possibly my tongue.

"At least your itch is on your back," he says with a sheepish look. His skin is so tanned that it's hard to tell, but I'm sure I see a slight flush in his cheeks.

A giggle escapes me before I can hold it back. He joins in with a soft chuckle. And then I'm hit with a flash of us—facing each other and giggling. Only my fingers are entwined in the hair at the nape of his neck and his tongue is flicking one of my earlobes. I abruptly stop giggling and pull my bottom lip in between my teeth.

"Of all the dumb things to do," he murmurs, shaking his head. "At least it's small."

I'm still trying to push the previous image of us out of my head as I hear myself agree with him, not thinking. "Yeah, I could barely read it until I really leaned in—" My stomach hits the ground like a bag of rocks, taking all the blood from my face with it. Did I just say that out loud? No, I didn't. I wouldn't.

By the twinkle in his eyes, I know without a doubt that I did. I think I'm going to be sick. "It . . . I wasn't . . . I really need to get going." I start sidestepping around him as a bead of sweat trickles down my back.

Stepping with me and nodding toward my books, he says, "You're taking a lot of science classes." Escape plan thwarted. What is he doing? Why is he chatting me up? Is he hoping for a repeat? Would I want one?

My eyes flitter across his appearance. Yes, I'll admit it. He's beautiful. As Reagan pointed out, he may well be one of the hottest guys on campus. I've been here four days. I have nothing to base it on, and yet I'm confident that it's true. And I've had too many face-flushing memory flashes in the last few days to try to deny that I didn't enjoy that night.

But . . . no, I don't want a repeat. I mean, when I look at him, all I see is *wrong*. He doesn't even look like a Princeton student. Not that there's one specific type of person at Princeton; there isn't. From what I've seen, it has a wonderfully diverse student body. Nothing like the sweater-vest-spoiled-brat stereotype portrayed in countless eighties movies.

But Ashton just doesn't fit in my mental image of Princeton. I don't know if it's his faded jeans that hang slightly too low, or the thin gray shirt with sleeves pushed halfway up his arms, or the tattoo snaking up his inner forearm, or the frayed leather cuff around his wrist . . . I don't know what it is.

"Irish?"

I hear him call my name. *Gah!* Not my name. *His* name for me. By that crooked smirk on those full lips, he's caught me staring again and he's enjoying it.

I clear my throat and abruptly force out, "Yup. All science. All but one." An English lit class. It's impractical, useless for my medical career, but it will satisfy Dr. Stayner's "suggestion" to pick one course that I would otherwise skip right over in the course calendar.

"Let me guess. Pre-med?"

I nod, smiling. "Pediatrics. Oncology." Unlike so many students who toil over what to do with their lives, I've known my chosen career since the day my friend Sara Dawson died of leukemia. I was nine. The decision came quite easily. I cried and asked my dad what I could have done. With a gentle smile, he reassured me that there was nothing I could have done for Sara, but that I was bright enough that I could grow up to be a doctor and save other kids. Saving kids sounded like a noble life. A goal that I've never questioned or wavered from since.

Now, though, as I look at Ashton's scowl, you'd think I told him my dream was to work in a sewage plant. There's a pause, and then he changes topic completely. "Look, about Saturday night . . . Can we just pretend it never happened?" he asks, sliding his hands into his pockets.

My mouth drops for a second as my brain replays those words. The words I've been playing over and over in my own head for the last three days. Can I? I'd like to. It would make it easier if I could just press a Delete button on all the images that still blaze in my head, making me suddenly blush and lose focus on . . . everything. "Sure," I say with a smile. "Well . . . as long as we can get my sister and Reagan to pretend as well."

One arm lifts to rub the back of his head, pulling his shirt tighter against his chest, enough that I can see the curves. The ones I had my hands all over. "Yeah, well, I figure your sister can't cause too much trouble, being from out of town."

"No, she can't," I agree. *She can just randomly text me pictures of a chubby bald man holding a tattoo gun to your ass, like she did yesterday.* I promptly erased it, but I'm sure that's not the last of them.

"And Reagan won't say a word," I hear Ashton say. Dropping his arm to his side, he looks off in the distance, muttering more to himself, "She's good like that."

"Okay, great, well . . ." Maybe I can just put all this behind me and get back to being me. Livie Cleary. Future doctor. Good girl.

Ashton looks back at my face, his eyes dropping to my lips for a second, likely because I'm chewing on the bottom one so much I'm about to gnaw it off. I feel as though I should say something more. "I hardly remember it, so . . ." I let my voice drift off as I deliver that lie with a degree of coolness that surprises me. And impresses me.

His head tilts to the side and he looks off again, as if deep in thought. Then an amused grin touches his lips. "I've never had a girl tell me that before."

A tiny smile tugs at the corner of my mouth as I look down to study his sneakers, feeling like I've finally scored a point. Livie: one. Mortifying conversation: a million. "I guess there's a first time for everything."

His low, throaty laugh pulls my attention back up to see twinkling eyes. He's shaking his head as if thinking of a private joke.

"What?"

"Nothing. It's just . . ." There's a pause, as though he's not sure whether he should say it or not. In the end, he decides to, delivering my pinnacle of humiliation with a wide grin. "You had a lot of firsts that night, Irish. You kept pointing each one out."

I can't keep the strangled sound from escaping, as if I'm dying. Which I might be, given my heart just stopped beating. I don't know whether my arms slackened or I actually threw them in the air to cover my gasp, but somehow I've lost the death grip I had on my textbooks. They end up scattered all over the grass. Right next to the last shred of my dignity.

I practically collapse to collect my books as I rack my brain. The problem is, I don't remember talking to Ashton a whole lot. And I certainly don't remember pointing out all my—

That stupid vault opens up in my brain, just enough to let another explicit memory slip out. A flash of that brick wall against my back and Ashton against my front and my legs wrapped around his waist and him pressing against me. And me, whispering in his ear that I've never felt that before and how it's harder than I thought it would be . . .

"Ohmigod," I moan, clutching my stomach. I'm sure I'm going to be sick. I'm going to become an exhibitionist vomiter.

My heart is back to beating—racing, actually—as a new level beyond mortification slams into me. I sounded just like the actress in that awful video of Ben's that Kacey made me watch over the summer. Literally. I accidently walked in on those weirdos watching it one night. Kacey took that as an opportunity to pin me down on the couch while Trent, Dan, and Ben howled with laughter at my flaming cheeks and horrified shrieks.

My sister is the Antichrist. This is all her fault. Hers and Stayner's. And those stupid Jell-O shooters. And—

"Irish!" My head snaps up at the sound of Ashton's voice. It takes me a moment to realize that he's crouching in front of me, holding a textbook, a curious look on his face. His hand cups my elbow and he pulls me to my feet. "You're in your head a lot, aren't you?" he muses, holding my textbook out.

I'm not sure how to answer that, so I don't. I simply purse my lips for a moment, accept my book, and say quietly, "Consider Saturday night forgotten."

"Thanks, Irish." He rubs his forehead with his fingertips. "I didn't want that getting out. I regret it. I mean . . ." He cringes as he looks at me, as if he bumped into me and is checking to see if I'm hurt. I hear the slightest exhale, and then he takes a few steps backward. "See you around."

I offer him a tiny nod and a tight-lipped smile. Inside, I'm screaming at the top of my lungs, "Not a chance in hell!"

■ ■ ■

"Dammit," I mutter, arriving at the rendezvous location for the tour ten minutes late. I glance around but see nothing that resembles a tour group. They're gone, off to learn about the historical significance of this foremost college, and I am stuck here, replaying the entire conversation with Ashton over and over again. Each time, those words—his words—suspend in my thoughts.

I regret it.

He regrets me. The man whore regrets messing around with

me. Enough to track me down and ask that I not tell anyone. He even felt bad when he let that fact slip. That's what that cringe was.

It was one thing when *I* was regretting *him*. I mean, I did something stupid and completely out of character. I gave away a whole pile of firsts to a guy I don't even know. Who's probably had a hundred drunken one-night flings that went farther than the one the other night did with me.

Who regrets me.

I take a seat on the steps and stare vacantly down at my hands. Every rational bone in my body is telling me to stop thinking about it, but I can't. I swallow several times, but the dryness in my throat won't abate as I run through all the reasons why Ashton might regret me. Does he find me that unattractive? Was waking up on Sunday one of those "coyote ugly" mornings Kacey always talks about? I know I must have looked terrible, with my hair a wild rat's nest and my eyes bloodshot and my breath harsh enough to wilt daisies.

Maybe it was my "skill level"? I sure as hell know I'm not experienced, but . . . was I *that* bad?

I'm so wrapped up in trying to comfort my ego that when I hear a guy say "excuse me" nearby, I keep my focus on the ground, dismissing him entirely, hoping he's talking to someone else. His next words, though—not so much the words but how he says them—make my head snap up, searching for the owner.

"Are you okay?"

I know my mouth is hanging open as I watch him take a seat next to me on the step, but I don't care. I just nod in awe as I stare at the deep green eyes and pleasant smile.

"Are you sure?" he asks with a soft chuckle. His chuckle is just as pleasant as his smile.

"Are you from Ireland?" I blurt out before I'm able to control it. Closing my eyes, I try to explain myself by stumbling over my words. "I mean . . . I thought . . . you have an accent . . . you sound Irish." *And* you *sound like a moron, Livie.*

"I'm Connor," he says. "And I am. I'm originally from—"

"Dublin," I interrupt as a bubble of excitement grows inside me.

He nods once, beaming as if pleased. "I moved to America when I was twelve."

My grin widens. I can't stop. I must look like an idiot.

"And do you have a name, miss? Or should I just call you Smiley?"

"Oh, yes, right." I purse my lips to get my face under control and I thrust out my hand. "Livie Cleary."

His eyebrow shoots up as he accepts my hand. His is warm and strong and . . . comfortable.

"My dad grew up in Dublin. Your accent . . . you sound like him." My dad had moved to America when he was thirteen, so he'd lost the thickness of the brogue, but it was still there, slipping in and out of his words gracefully. Just like Connor's.

"You mean your dad is charming and smart as well?"

I giggle as I drop my gaze momentarily, biting my tongue before I accidentally correct him with the past tense. *Was* charming and smart. Two minutes into a conversation isn't exactly the time to be bringing up my dead parents.

There's an easy silence between us and then Connor asks, "And why are you sitting here, all by yourself, Miss Cleary?"

I wave a dismissive hand in the air. "Oh, I was supposed to take the historical tour but I missed it. I got delayed with . . ." My thoughts drift back to my previous conversation, taking a part of my comfort with it. "An asshole," I mutter absently.

Connor does a quick scan around us and asks with a smile. "Is the asshole still around?"

I feel my face turning red. "You weren't supposed to hear

that." Ever since that week when Stayner made me inject a variety of swear words—of my sister's choosing—in every sentence that came out of my mouth, I've found my vocabulary unintentionally more colorful. Especially when I'm upset or nervous, though I find that I'm suddenly neither, right now. "And, no. I hope he's far away." Deep in a well, with a slew of girls he doesn't regret to keep him occupied.

"Well"—Connor stands and holds out a hand—"I doubt my tour will be nearly as educational but I've been here for three years, if you're interested." I don't even hesitate, accepting his hand. Right now, there isn't a thing I'd rather do than walk around the Princeton campus with Connor from Dublin.

■ ■ ■

It turns out that Connor from Dublin knows surprisingly little about Princeton history. He does, however make up for it with enough embarrassing personal stories. My sides hurt from laughter by the time we reach a secluded, medieval-looking courtyard outside my residence hall, one I didn't know existed and am glad that I've discovered because it looks like a perfect place to study. " . . . and they found my roommate in nothing but black socks right *here* the next morning," Connor says, pointing to a wooden bench, an easy smile on his face.

Somewhere between our meeting spot and now, I started to appreciate just how attractive Connor is. I hadn't really noticed it immediately, but it was probably because I was still so ruffled after seeing Ashton. Connor is tall with sandy blond hair—tidy but stylish—and smooth, tanned skin. His body is lean, but I can tell by the way his pressed khaki pants fit him as he walks and how his button-down checked shirt stretches across broad shoulders that he's fit. Basically, he's the guy I've always pictured myself walking around this campus with someday.

But I think it's Connor's smile that makes me gravitate toward him. It's wide and genuine. There's nothing hidden behind it, no deception.

"How do you pass your classes? It sounds like all you do is party," I ask as I lean against the bench, pulling one knee up on the seat.

"Not as much as my roommates would like me to." Just hearing his easy chuckle makes me sigh. "The parties are over once classes start. Until after midterms, anyway. To each their own, but I want to go home with an excellent education, not a failed liver and an STD."

My eyes flash toward him in surprise.

"Sorry." His cheeks flush slightly, but he quickly recovers with a grin. "I'm still a bit annoyed with them. They threw a bloody toga party on Saturday. We're still cleaning up the house."

My body instantly tenses. Toga party? The same toga party where I was wasted and making out with Ashton? I swallow before I manage to ask in strained whisper, "Where did you say you lived?" I have no clue where that party was, so knowing the address makes no difference. What *does* make a difference is whether Connor was there to witness my spectacle.

He slows to look at me with a curious expression. "Just off campus, with a few other guys."

Just off campus. That's what Reagan said when we headed out that night. Maybe there was more than one toga party that night?

"Oh yeah?" I try to make my voice sound light and relaxed. Instead I sound like someone's choking the life out of me. "I went to a toga party on Saturday."

He grins. "Really? Must have been my house. Not many people throw toga parties anymore." With an eye roll, he mutters, "My roommate, Grant. He's cheesy like that. Did you have fun?"

"Uh. Yeah." I watch him from the corner of my eye. "Did you?"

"Oh, I was in Rochester for my cousin's wedding," he confirms, shaking his head. "Kind of sucked that it was the same weekend, but my family's big on . . . family. My mom would have killed me if I missed it."

I let the air release from my lungs painfully slowly, just so it's not obvious how relieved I am that Connor wasn't there. Although if he had been, he probably wouldn't be talking to me right now.

"I heard it got pretty wild, though. Cops shut it down."

"Yeah, there were some drunk people there. . . ," I say slowly and then, wanting desperately to change the subject, I ask, "What's your major?"

"Politics. I'm pre-law." He watches me closely as he talks. "Hoping for Yale or Stanford next year, if all goes well."

"Nice," is all I can think to say. And then I catch myself staring at those friendly green eyes and smiling.

"And you? Any ideas what you're going to major in?"

"Molecular biology. Hoping for med school."

A rare frown furrows Connor's brow. "You know you can still apply to med school with a humanities major, don't you?"

"I know, but sciences are easy for me."

"Huh." Connor's eyes appraise me curiously. "Beautiful and smart. A deadly combination."

I duck my head as a blush creeps into my cheeks.

"Well, here we are." He gestures toward my hall. "Gorgeous building, isn't it?"

I tip my head back to take in the Gothic architecture. Normally, I'd agree. Now, though, I find myself disappointed because it means my tour, and my time with the smiling Connor, is over. And I'm not ready yet.

I watch as he backs away, sliding his hands into his pockets. "It was nice to meet you, Livie from Miami."

"You too, Connor from Dublin."

He kicks a loose stone around with his shoe for a few awkward seconds as I stand and watch. Then he asks, almost hesitantly, "We're having little party over at our house this Saturday, if you're interested. Bring that wild roommate you talked about, if you want."

With my head tilted and my lips pursed, I say, "But I thought you said the parties were over once classes started."

His eyes search my face, a thoughtful gleam in them. "Unless it's an excuse to invite a beautiful girl over." Then his cheeks redden and his gaze drops to the ground.

And I realize that, on top of being good-looking, Connor is about as charming as they come. Not sure how to answer, I simply say, "See you Saturday."

"Perfect. Say, eight o'clock?" He rhymes off a street name and house number and, with one last, wide grin, he takes off at a slight jog as if late for something. I lean against the bench and watch him go, wondering if he was just being nice. And then, as he's about to slip behind a building, he slows and turns to look back in my direction. Seeing that I'm still watching, he blows a kiss my way and disappears.

And I have to press my lips together to keep from grinning like an idiot.

This day is definitely looking up.

chapter five

■ ■ ■

DIAGNOSIS

While I've attempted to experience as many of Princeton's campus-coordinated events as possible as a way of immersing myself in the spirit and culture, Reagan has decided to immerse herself in as many beer-and-vodka-coordinated events as exist. And she's decided that I need immersing along with her. It's because I want to please my lively roommate that I ended up at dorm parties every night this week and in bed each morning with heavy eyelids. That, and I also hoped I'd run into Connor again. In the back of my mind, there was a fear of running into Ashton, too. In the end, hope won out over fear.

Unfortunately, I never saw Connor. But I also didn't see Ashton. I did meet a few more freshmen, though, including a Korean girl named Sun who's as new to the whole partying scene as I am and sort of attached herself to me on Thursday night.

I honestly don't know how Reagan is going to survive the heavy workload of classes here. Her books sit in a pile on her desk, unopened. Not even a flip-through. I'm starting to believe that she's not a student, that Kacey and Dr. Stayner have some-how planted her here. I can almost picture them cackling while they hatched this plan. Student or not, though, I'm happy to have Reagan as a roommate. Except when she puppy-dog-eyes me into drinking with her.

■ ■ ■

Ceaseless knocking on our door wakes me up.

"Kill me now," Reagan moans.

"I will, but can you get that first?" I mumble, burying my head under my pillow, pushing a textbook with exceptionally sharp corners out from beneath me. I had managed to sneak out of the dorm party two floors up and come back to get some read-ing done late last night. The clock read three a.m. the last time I had checked. Now it reads seven. "It has to be for you, Reagan. I don't know anyone on campus," I rationalize, curling my body up tighter.

"Shhh . . . they'll go away," she whispers. But they don't. The knocking increases in strength and urgency, and I'm starting to get concerned it will wake up half the floor. As I lift myself to my elbows, ready to crawl out of my top bunk and answer it, I hear Reagan's defeated groan and rustling sheets. She makes a point of stomping to the door. She throws it open with a quiet curse and something about Satan.

"Wake up, sleepyheads!"

I bolt upright so fast that the room starts to spin. "What are you doing here?" I ask in a high-pitched voice as I turn to see the distinguished-looking man in a well-tailored suit step into the room. I haven't seen Dr. Stayner in person in two and a half years. He looks basically the same, if not for a bit more gray in his hair, which he has a bit less of, in general.

He shrugs. "It's Saturday. I told you that we'd talk today."

"Yeah, but you're *here*. And it's *seven a.m.*!"

He glances at his watch with a frown. "Is it really that early?" And then he shrugs and throws his arms up in the air, his eyes lighting up with genuine excitement. "What a beautiful day!" As quickly as they lifted, his arms drop and his calm tone returns. "Get dressed. I have a conference in the city that I have to get back to by noon. I'll meet you in the lobby in thirty minutes."

Before turning to leave, he spots a disheveled but curious-looking Reagan in a rumpled tank top and pink pajama bottoms. He holds out his hand. "Hi, I'm Dr. Stayner."

She accepts it with a weary frown. "Hi, I'm Reagan."

"Ah, yes. The roommate. I've heard so much."

From whom? I haven't talked to him since . . .

I sigh. *My freaking sister.* Of course.

"Make sure Livie socializes, will you? She has a tendency to focus too much on school. Just keep her away from those Jell-O shooters." Not waiting for a reaction, he walks out as briskly as he walked in, leaving my new roommate staring at me.

"Who *is* that?"

Where do I begin with that answer? Shaking my head as I swing my legs out of bed, I mumble, "I don't have time to explain right now."

"Okay but . . . He's a doctor? I mean, is he . . ." She hesitates. "*Your* doctor?"

"For better or worse, it would seem." I want nothing more than to pull the covers over my head for a few more hours, but I know that if I'm not down there in thirty minutes, he's liable to march down the hall shouting my name at the top of his lungs.

"What kind of doctor is he? I mean . . ." She's twirling a strand of her long hair around her fingers. Nervous Reagan is a rare sight.

I open my mouth to answer but stop, an impish idea coming

to me. I still owe Reagan for the vodka shot she practically forced down my throat last night. . . Pressing my lips together to hide my smile as I rifle through my dresser for a pair of jeans and a shirt, I say calmly, "Oh, his focus is primarily schizophrenia."

There's a pause. I don't look, but I'm sure her mouth is hanging open. "Oh . . . well, is there anything I need to worry about?"

Grabbing my toiletry bag, I walk over to the door but make a point of slowing as my hand closes over the knob, looking up as if deep in thought. "I don't think so. Well, unless I start to . . ." I wave my hand dismissively. "Oh, never mind. That probably won't happen again." With that, I quietly slip out the door. I make it about four feet before I burst into giggles, loud enough that someone moans, "Shut up!" from a nearby room.

"I'll get you for that, Livie!" Reagan shrieks through the closed door, followed by her howls of laughter.

Sometimes humor does make it better.

■ ■ ■

"I knew the text was from Kacey," Stayner says as he tips his head back to drain the last of his coffee—the largest cup of it that I've ever seen. I on the other hand have let mine grow cold, barely touching it as Dr. Stayner coaxed out every last embarrassing detail from my first week on campus.

He's big on talking things out. I remember Kacey cursing him for it in the beginning. My sister was broken back then. She refused to discuss anything—the accident, the loss, her shattered heart. But, by the end of that intense inpatient program, Dr. Stayner had dragged out every last detail there was to know about Kacey, helping her heal in the process.

She warned me about him too, back when the calls started. *Livie, just tell him what he wants to know. He will find out one way or another, so make it easier on yourself and just tell him. He probably already knows anyway. I think he uses Jedi mind tricks.*

In the three months of our nontherapy sessions, I've never had a truly difficult conversation with Dr. Stayner, nothing that I found too painful, too tragic, too hard to bring up. True, he's asked me to do things that still give me heart palpitations, like bungee jumping and watching a back-to-back marathon of the *Saw* movies, which gave me nightmares for weeks after. But our actual conversations—about Mom and Dad, about what I remember of my childhood, even about my uncle Raymond and why we left Michigan—were never difficult or uncomfortable. Most of them were pleasant.

Still, two hours talking about my drunken make-out session and everything that has ensued since has left me drained and my face smoldering. I knew I'd likely be questioned about last Saturday night. I planned on glazing over the more embarrassing moments, but Dr. Stayner has a way of drawing out every last detail.

"You've come far in our few months together, Livie."

"Not really," I counter.

"You're going on a date with a guy tonight, for Pete's sake!"

"It's not really a date. It's more of a—"

His dismissive wave quiets my objection. "Three months ago you would have blown the guy off for a textbook without even thinking twice."

"I guess." I push back a strand of hair that has blown across my face with the light breeze. "That or just dropped to the ground, unconscious."

Dr. Stayner snorts. "Exactly."

There's a pause, and I cast a sidelong glance. "Does that mean my therapy is over? I mean, look at me. I've practically become an exhibitionist. And if I don't cut back on the partying soon, you'll have to admit me to an alcohol abuse program."

Dr. Stayner bursts out in a round of loud, boisterous laughter. When his amusement dies down, he spends a few moments staring down at his cup, his index finger running along the rim.

And I start to get nervous. Dr. Stayner is rarely quiet for this long.

"I'm going to let you live your college life the way you need to live it," he says quietly. "You don't need me telling you what to do or how to have fun. You need to make those decisions for yourself."

I flop back against the bench with a sigh of relief, a strange calm washing through me. As quickly as Dr. Stayner planted himself into my life, he's stepping right back out. "I guess Kacey was wrong," I say more to myself, the declaration lifting a weight off my shoulders that I didn't realize was there.

There's that soft laughter again. "Oh, your sister . . ." He drifts off as a group of cyclists speed past. "When Kacey was first admitted into my care, I wondered about you, Livie. I truly did. I questioned how you turned out so well, all things considered. But I had my hands full with Kacey and Trent, and you seemed to be motoring along on a clear path. Even when Kacey came to me in the spring with her concerns, I was skeptical." He pulls his glasses off to rub his eyes. "It's the people like your sister—the obviously shattered ones—who make my job easy."

I frown, his words puzzling. "But I'm not like her, right?" I catch the waver in my voice.

Dr. Stayner's shaking head answers me before his words do. "Oh, no, Livie. You are surprisingly alike in many ways, but you are not alike in those sorts of matters."

"Really? I've always seen the two of us as polar opposites."

He chuckles. "You're both stubborn as mules and sharp as whips. Of course your wit is a tad more sugarcoated than hers. Your sister wears her temper on her sleeve, but . . ." He purses his lips. "You've surprised me a few times with your outbursts, Livie. And I'm not easily surprised."

I watch those same cyclists cross along another path as I take in his words, a tiny smile touching my lips. No one has ever compared me to my sister quite like that before. I've always been the studious, responsible one. The trustworthy one. Cautious, calm, and levelheaded. My sister's the firecracker. I've secretly envied her for that.

And I think back on the past summer, jam-packed with things I never thought I could do, and a whole lot of other things I never even considered doing. Kacey had been there with me for a lot of it, eagerly embarrassing herself along with me. "This summer was interesting," I admit with a smile. I turn to look at the graying doctor and I ask him the one question he'd never answered before, hoping that he will now. "Why did you have me doing all those crazy things? What was it really about?"

He puckers his lips as if deciding what to say. "Would you believe me if I said it was purely for my own entertainment?"

"I might," I answer truthfully, earning his chuckle. "I mean, I get the speed dating, but I don't see how line dancing or prolific cussing has helped me. I'd think it would have the opposite effect. You know . . . extreme psychological scarring."

Dr. Stayner looks skeptical. "How could line dancing possibly *scar* you?"

I raise an eyebrow. "Have you ever been to one of those places before? With my sister?"

He rolls his eyes. "Oh, you're being dramatic. It couldn't have been that—"

"She had a microphone!" I exclaim. "She tried to hold an impromptu auction to sell me off for a date!" Thank God Storm was there to get her under control . . . My hand flies up as I remember the best part. "Oh! And then she spiked my drink." Dr. Stayner starts chuckling as I shake my head. "I noticed right away, of course. Otherwise *who knows* what would have happened." I settle back against the bench as I mutter more to myself, "I probably would have made out with a cowboy or a mechanical bull, or something. Had my ass branded, maybe . . ."

His head falls back with raucous laughter and after a few moments I can't help but giggle along with him. "Oh, Livie," he says, pulling his glasses off to wipe the tears from his eyes. "It was never about *what* I asked you to do. It was about your exuberance tackling each and every single task." He turns to look at me with amazement in his eyes and a slight chuckle in his voice. "I was waiting for you to tell me to go to hell but you kept answering the phone, taking each and every one of those *crazy* requests I made, and delivering with excellence!"

I cock my head to the side as I regard him. "You knew they were *crazy*?"

"You didn't?" He shakes his head at me, and then a sad smile transforms his face. "I learned a lot about you over the summer, Livie. Between the wild-goose chases and our talks. That's what this summer was about. Information gathering." He pauses to scratch his cheek. "You are one of the kindest souls I've ever met, Livie. You respond to human heartache so acutely. It's like you absorb others' pain. Despite your extreme shyness, you will do just about anything not to fail. You don't like to fail tests and you most certainly don't like to fail people. Especially those you care about and respect." His hand goes to his heart and he bows his head. "I'm touched, truly."

I dip my head as I blush.

"I also learned that while you are accepting and open-minded of others and their faults, you are exceptionally hard on yourself. I think doing something wrong would make you physically ill." Dr.

Stayner steeples his fingers in front of his face for a moment. "But my biggest discovery? The reason that I wanted to talk to you in person today . . ." He sighs. "You seem to be governed by a life plan. It's ingrained in your daily routines; it's almost like a religion for you. It has dictated the choices you have made so far and those you plan to make in the future. You don't question it, you don't test it. You just do it." Running his finger along the rim of his cup, he goes on to say with an even, slow voice, "I think your parents helped create that plan and you are holding on to it for dear life as a way of holding on to them." He pauses, and then his voice grows soft. "And I think it's stifling your growth as your own person."

I blink repeatedly, trying to process how this conversation turned so quickly from talk of mechanical bulls to my stifled growth. "What are you saying?" I ask, my voice a touch strained. Is this a diagnosis? Is Dr. Stayner diagnosing me?

"I'm saying, Livie . . ." He pauses, his mouth open to say something, a pensive expression on his face. "I'm saying that it's time for you to find out who you really are."

I can do nothing but stare at the man in front of me. Who I am? What is he talking about? I know who I am! I'm Livie Cleary, daughter of Miles and Jane Cleary. Mature and responsible daughter, driven student, loving sister, future doctor, kind and considerate human. "But, I . . ." I struggle to find the words. "I know who I am and what I want, Dr. Stayner. That's never been in question."

"And don't you think that's a little strange, Livie? That you decided at the age of nine that you wanted to go into pediatrics, specializing in oncology, and you have never even considered another life? Do you know what I wanted to be when I was nine?" He pauses for only a second. "Spider-Man!"

"So, I had more realistic goals. There's nothing wrong with that," I snap.

"And did you ever wonder why you avoided boys like the plague up until now?"

"I know exactly why. Because I'm shy and because—"

"Boys suck the brains out of girls . . ."

"And make them crazy." I finish my father's warning with a sad smile. Dad started warning me of that around the time that Kacey's hormones started raging. He said my grades would suffer if I fell into the same trap.

"I think your reaction to the opposite sex is less about your shyness and more a subconscious mindset to avoid straying from this life plan you believe you must follow." Subconscious mindset? Unease slips through my stomach like a snake, sending shivers up my spine. Is he saying that Kacey is right? That I'm . . . sexually repressed?

I lean forward and let my chin rest in the palm of my hand, my elbows set against my knees, as I think. How could Dr. Stayner find fault in who I've become? If anything, he should be pleased. He said it himself! I turned out so well. I know my parents would be proud. No, there's nothing wrong with who I am.

"I think you're wrong," I say quietly, staring at the ground. "I think you're looking for things to diagnose me with. There's nothing wrong with me or what I'm doing." Sitting up straight, I take in the campus surrounding us—this beautiful Princeton campus that I've worked hard to make sure I attend—and I feel anger surge. "I'm a straight-A student going to Princeton, for Christ's sake!" I'm borderline yelling now and I don't care. "Why the hell would you show up at seven a.m. on a Saturday after I just started college to tell me my entire life is . . . what . . ." I swallow the sudden lump in my throat.

Dr. Stayner takes his glasses off and rubs his eyes yet again. He remains completely calm, as if he expected this reaction. He told me once that he's used to being yelled at, so not to ever feel guilty about it. I sure as hell don't think I'll be feeling guilty after the bomb he just dropped on me. "Because I wanted you to be aware, Livie. Fully conscious and aware. This doesn't mean you should stop doing what you're doing." He shifts slightly so that he's facing me. "You're a smart girl, Livie, and you're an adult now. You're going to be meeting people and dating. Working hard to achieve your goals. And, I hope, going out and having some fun. I just want to make sure you're making your choices and setting your goals for *you* and not to please others." Sliding back against the bench, he adds, "Who knows? Maybe Princeton and med school are what you really want. Maybe the man who makes you happy for the rest of your life is also the one who your parents would have handpicked for you. But maybe you'll find out that's not the right path for you. Either way, I want you to make your choices with your eyes wide open rather than on autopilot."

I don't know what to say to all of this so I stay silent, staring at nothing, confusion and doubt settling heavily on my shoulders.

"Life has a funny way of creating its own tests. It throws curve balls that make you do and think and feel things that are in direct conflict with what you had planned and don't allow you to operate in terms of black and white." He gives my knee a fatherly pat. "I want you to know that you can call me anytime you want to talk, Livie. Anytime at all. No matter how trivial or silly you think it is. If you want to talk about school, or guys. Complain about your sister"—he says that one with a crooked smile. "Anything at all. And I do hope you call me. Regularly. When you're ready to talk. Right now I assume you want to pour that coffee over my head." Standing up with a big stretch, he adds, "And all conversations will be confidential."

"You mean you won't be enlisting my sister to do your dirty work anymore?"

Rubbing his chin, he smiles as he murmurs, "What a good little minion she has become."

"I guess you considered the whole doctor-patient confidentiality thing optional?"

He peers down at me with an arched brow. "You were never my patient, were you?"

"And now I am?"

He smiles, holding out his hand to guide me up. "Let's just keep it loose. Call me when you want to talk."

"I can't pay."

"I don't expect a dime from you, Livie." Almost as an afterthought, he slides in, "Just your firstborn child."

Normally I'd give him an eye roll at the very least for a joke like that. But not now. I'm not in the mood for any jokes. The weight that I've worn on my back for three months as I wondered what Dr. Stayner might discover about me, which lifted just twenty minutes ago, has now crashed back down onto my back, crippling me under its heft.

I'm sure he's wrong.

But what if he isn't?

chapter six

■ ■ ■

IF VERSUS WHEN

The almost two-hour commute from the Princeton campus to the Children's Hospital in Manhattan gives me plenty of time to stew over Dr. Stayner's surprise visit and outrageous diagnosis. By the time I get to the front desk to sign in for my first volunteer session, I'm more rattled than I was to begin with. I'm also convinced that he might be losing his magic touch as the brilliant psychiatrist. Either that or he's insane and no one has caught on yet. Maybe both.

"Have you ever worked with children in a hospital before, Livie?" Nurse Gale asks as I follow her swaying hips down the long corridor.

"No, I haven't," I answer with a smile. I've spent enough time in hospitals, though, that the sounds of beeping machines and the mixture of medicine and bleach filling my nostrils instantly brings me back seven years to the days of forced smiles, and Kacey with tubes and bandages and a hollow stare.

"Well, I hear your reference glows in the dark," she jokes as we round the corner and follow the signs toward the playroom, my quick tour of the hospital coming to an end. "You're a natural magnet for children."

My eyes roll before I can stop myself. Not at the nurse—at Stayner. Back in June, when I mentioned to him that I had applied for a volunteer position at this hospital but hadn't heard back from them, he casually mentioned that he had a few friends there. The next week, I received a phone call for a brief interview, quickly followed by an offer for a position on Saturday afternoons in the Child Life program—playing with young patients. I jumped at the opportunity. Of course I saw Dr. Stayner's fingerprints all over it but it only made me appreciate him more, knowing that when I apply for med school, having this volunteer position on my application will show that I've been committed to pediatrics for years. It had seemed like he was helping me achieve my goals at the time. Ironic now, given that he basically thinks I'm a preprogrammed drone who shouldn't be here in the first place.

I push all of that away, though, because I know what I want and I know that I belong here. So I nod politely at Nurse Gale and say, "I think they're a magnet for me too."

She stops at a door and turns to give me a pensive smile. "Well, you just be careful about what kind of attachments you make, you hear, sweetie?" With that, we step into a bright and colorful playroom with a handful of children and other volunteers. My shoulders immediately relax as I hear the infectious laughter. It's like a shot of Valium through my veins.

I know I've never been quite normal. As a child, I was always the one rushing to the teacher when someone needed a Band-Aid, or stepping in between a squabble to mediate. As a teenager, I looked forward to my volunteer days at the YMCA, or the pool, or the library. Really, anywhere that involved these tiny humans.

There's just something so uncomplicated about small children that I gravitate toward. Maybe it's their infectious giggles or their shy hugs. Maybe it's their brutal honesty. Maybe it's the way they cling to me when they're scared or hurt. All I know is that I want to help them. All of them.

"Livie, this is Diane," Nurse Gale says, introducing me to a stocky, middle-aged woman with short, curly brown hair and kind eyes. "She's a part of our Child Life program. She's supervising the room today."

With a wink, Diane gives me a quick five-minute tour of the bright playroom and explains what her role is. When she's done, she points out two boys sitting side by side with their backs to me, cross-legged, in front of a pile of LEGOs. They're the same size, except the one on the right is leaner. He's also completely bald, whereas the boy on the left has short, sandy brown hair.

"These two are yours today. Eric? Derek? This is Miss Livie."

Identical faces turn to regard me. "Twins!" I exclaim with a grin. "Let me guess . . . you're Derek." I point to the one on the left, the one with the full head of hair.

He gives me a wide grin displaying missing front teeth, instantly reminding me of Storm's daughter, Mia. "I'm Eric."

I roll my eyes dramatically. "I'm never going to get this right." Why do parents feel the need to name their identical twins rhyming names? I don't say that out loud, though. I only smile.

"Derek's the bald one. He's easy to remember," Eric confirms with a shrug. "But soon I'm going to be bald too. Then you're screwed."

"Eric," Diane warns with an arched brow.

"Sorry, Miss Diane." He diverts his attention to a Hot Wheels car next to him, a sheepish look on his face. And my chest tightens a notch. *Both* of them?

"Are you here to play with us?" Derek asks quietly.

I nod. "Is that all right?"

His little face suddenly brightens with a smile and I see that he's also missing his two front teeth.

Shifting my focus to his brother, who's now smashing two cars together, I ask, "And you, Eric? Are you okay with that?"

Eric looks over his shoulder at me and says with another shrug, "Sure. I guess." But I catch the tiny smile as he turns back, and I know without a doubt that he's the imp of the two.

"Okay, good. First I'm just going to go over a few things with Miss Diane, okay?"

Their heads bob in unison and they go back to their LEGOs.

With my eyes still on them, I take a few steps back and drop my voice. "Cancer?"

"Leukemia."

"Both of them? What are the odds of that?"

She just shakes her head and sighs. "I know."

"How—" I swallow, unsure how to finish that sentence, a lump forming in my throat. "How bad?"

Diane crosses her arms over her chest. "Their chances are great. Well . . ." Her eyes flicker to Derek briefly. "Their chances are good," she corrects herself. Offering me a pat on my forearm, she says, "You're going to see a lot while you're here, Livie. Try not to lose sleep over it. Best you just focus on the here and now and leave the rest to medicine and prayer."

I have to remind myself to smooth my furrowed brow as I walk over to where the boys are. Sitting down cross-legged on the floor opposite them, I clap my hands. "Who wants to show me how to build one of these cool houses?" Neither, apparently, because that's when I get hit with a barrage of questions—one after another, the two of them tag teaming like they've rehearsed it for hours.

"We're almost six years old. How old are you?" Eric asks.

"Eighteen."

"Do you have parents?" Derek's voice is so soft next to his brother's that I barely hear him.

I simply smile and nod, not elaborating.

"Why did you come here?"

"To learn how to build with LEGOs, of course."

"What do you want to be when you grow up?"

"A doctor. For kids like you."

"Huh." Eric pushes his little car around. "I think I want to be a werewolf. But . . . I'm not sure yet though. Do you believe in werewolves?"

"Hmm . . ." I twist my mouth as if considering it. "Only the friendly kind."

"Huh." He seems to consider that. "Or maybe I'll be a race car driver." He gives an exaggerated shrug. "I don't know."

"Well, lucky for you that you have lots of time to decide that, right?" I feel the little kick my subconscious gives my stomach, warning me to get away from this line of conversation.

Thankfully, Derek is already moving toward a new direction. "Do you have a boyfriend?"

"No, not yet. But I'm working on it."

His little bald brows bunch together. "How do you work on a boyfriend?"

"Well . . ." My hand crosses over my mouth to keep from bursting out with laughter. With a quick glance over to my left, I see that Diane's lips are pressed tightly together as she helps another patient paint. She's within earshot and she's trying hard not to laugh. "I met someone who I like and I think he might like me too," I answer honestly.

Derek's little head bobs up and down slowly as he mouths, "Oh." He looks ready to ask another question, but his brother cuts him off.

"Have you ever kissed a boy?"

"Uh . . ." I stall for just a second, not expecting that question. "I don't kiss and tell. That's a good rule. You should remember it," I say, and I fight against the blush.

"Oh, I will. Dad says one day I'll want to kiss girls, but I'm only five so it's okay not to want to now."

"He's right, you will. You both will." I look at them both in turn with a wink.

"Unless we die," Eric says matter-of-factly.

I pull my legs to my chest and hug them, the position somehow comforting against the sudden tightness inside. I've been around a lot of kids and I've heard a lot of things. I've even had several conversations about death and heaven. But, unlike that idle child chatter sparked by curiosity, Eric's words send a chill through my body. Because they're true. These two little boys in front of me may never kiss a girl, or become race car drivers, or learn that werewolves—friendly or otherwise—don't exist. They may miss out on all that life has to offer them because, for some cruel reason, children are not immortal.

"You're pressing your lips together tight, like Mom does," Eric says, snapping two LEGO blocks together. "She always does that when we talk about dying."

I'm not surprised. God, what that poor woman must face, watching not one but both of her little boys get pumped with rounds of chemicals, not knowing if it will be enough, wondering what the next few weeks, months, or years will bring!

A painful lump swells in my throat just thinking about it. But I can't think about it, I remind myself. I'm here to make them *not* think about it. "How about we make a rule," I begin slowly, swallowing. "No talk of dying during our playtime. Only talk about what you're going to do when your treatment is over and you go home, okay?"

Eric frowns. "But what if—"

"Nope!" I shake my head. "There is no 'what if.' Got it? How about we don't plan on dying. We plan on living. Deal?"

They look at each other and then Eric says, "Can I plan on not kissing a girl?"

The heavy cloud in the room suddenly evaporates as I burst into laughter, on the verge of tears for so many reasons. "You can plan whatever you want as long as it involves you growing old and wrinkly. Shake on it."

Their eyes light up as they slip their little hands into my proffered one in turn, like we're making a secret pact. One that I think I need as much as they do.

I help the twins build a battleship, an aircraft carrier, and a torture chamber—Eric's idea—out of LEGOs. They chatter back and forth, bickering occasionally, exactly as I would expect twin brothers to act. It's so normal that I almost forget that both of these boys are in a hospital with cancer. Almost. But that unease in my chest lingers, and no amount of giggles seems to dissolve it.

I'm surprised when four hours has passed so quickly and a nurse pokes her head in to tell the boys it's time for them to tidy up and get back to their room. "Are you coming back again?" Eric asks, his eyes wide with the question.

"Well, I was thinking about coming back next Saturday, if that's all right with you."

He gives an indifferent shrug, but after a moment I catch the sidelong glance and the grin.

"Okay then," I stand, ruffling his hair. "See you next weekend, Eric." Turning to Derek, who's offering me a shy smile, I now notice the redness around his eyes and his slouched posture. Four hours in here has tired him. "See you next weekend, Derek, right?"

"Yes, Miss Livie."

With a small wave to Diane, I slowly make my way out to the hallway where a woman with dirty-blond hair pulled into a messy ponytail stands.

"Hello," she says. "I'm Connie—their mother." Her eyes— shadowed with darkness from lack of sleep—flicker toward the boys, who are arguing over which box a specific piece of LEGO should go in. "I was watching you with them. I . . ." She clears her throat. "I don't think I've seen them smile so much in weeks. Thank you."

"I'm Livie." I offer her my hand. Hers is rough and strong. I notice that she's in a waitress uniform, so I suspect she just got off work. I'd imagine she's working a lot these days with the medical bills she's facing. That's probably why her skin looks drawn and the most she can offer me is a sad, worn smile. The thought makes my heart ache for her, but I push it aside. "Your little men are lovely."

I see the infamous pursed lips as she stares through the window at them again, seemingly lost in thought. "They're still babies to me," she whispers, and I watch her blink back the sudden glossiness in her eyes. "Will you excuse me?" I watch her as she walks into the room, replacing the pinched face with a beaming grin full of hope and happiness.

"So?" I hear Nurse Gale ask from behind me. "How was your first day?"

"Great," I murmur absently, watching the boys as they each grab one of their mother's outstretched arms. She's a small woman but she manages both of them at once, squeezing them tight. Even when Eric starts wiggling out of her grasp, she doesn't relent, holding on for another moment, her lids pressed together firmly. Squeezing them like she never wants to let them go. And I can't help but wonder if every hug feels like one of the last hugs she'll have.

What if it is? What if I show up one weekend to find one of them . . . gone? It's not as if I've come in blind, not expecting that. But now there are little faces and voices attached to that possibility. I suppose I'll cry. I'll have to accept it. And I'll move on. But if I do this, if I become a doctor, how many more times will I stand in a window and watch parents cling to their children? How many more times will I make deals that fall through? Will I ever become immune to this sick feeling in my stomach?

Standing here with all of these thoughts swirling through my head, my eyes suddenly widen in shock. I realize that this is the first time in nine years that I've ever considered becoming a doctor as an "if" versus a "when."

chapter seven

∎ ∎ ∎

SMALL WORLD

"How's Princeton?"

"A bit overwhelming," I admit with a sigh. "I got lost trying to find my classes on Thursday and Friday. Ended up walking in just as the professors introduced themselves. Almost went epileptic." I'm never late to class. I knew this campus was huge but I hadn't realized quite how big. I've mapped out the routes to the rest of my classes to avoid all potential seizures in the future.

"Yikes. But, you had your volunteer thing today. How was that?" Kacey's last words are blurred by Mia's shrieks and what sounds like our friend Ben's maniacal laughing in the background.

"It was good. There are these two boys—"

"Hold on, Livie." I hear muffling, like she's covering the receiver with her hand. "Guys! I'm talking to Livie. Can you just . . . vamoose!" A second later, screams of "Hi, Livie!" flood the phone as they run by, making my heart swell and then immediately constrict. Uncovering the phone, Kacey says, "Sorry, Livie. You know how Saturday nights get."

I smile wistfully. Yeah, I know exactly how Saturday nights get. The eight-person dinner table in the spacious kitchen is never enough for everyone. It's always us plus Trent and usually a few friends from Penny's. Occasionally our old landlord, Tanner, comes. Right now, Storm is probably clearing the table and Dan is washing dishes—if he's not out arresting Miami's criminals. It's a mishmash of misfits and yet . . . it's family. It's home.

I sigh as I glance around at my tiny dorm room. It's clean and nice, but I wonder when the novelty of it will wear off—when it will feel like I belong here.

"So, how was the hospital? You met two boys?" Cupboard doors slam in the background, which tells me that Kacey's on tidy-up duty while she talks to me. She's a tornado when she steps in the kitchen.

"Yup. Twins. Eric and Derek."

"Seriously?" I can almost hear my sister's eye roll.

I snort. "I know. They're really cute."

"And are they . . ." She doesn't say the words. She doesn't have to, and my stomach clenches tightly all the same.

I swallow. "Prognosis is good." I don't know that, but I say it anyway because it will make both of us feel better. The long commute home gave me a chance to decompress and evaluate. I acknowledged that the first day in a children's hospital with sick—possibly dying—kids was bound to pull on a few heart-strings. Of course it'll get better. I'll probably also freak out the first time that I face a cadaver in med school. Everyone does. It's normal. It doesn't mean I'm not meant to be there or that I can't hack it. By the time I arrived back at my dorm room tonight, the cloud hanging over me was all but gone. My bitterness with Stayner, though, had increased tenfold.

Kacey sighs. "Well, that's good." I hear the screech of the oven drawer opening and I grin, knowing what's coming next.

Sure enough, there's a loud slap, followed by a yelp. I'm laughing as Kacey shrieks, "Dammit, Trent!" because I know that he caught her bent over and distracted and Trent just can't seem to stop from slapping her butt playfully every chance he gets. A few seconds later, there's a noisy kissing sound near the phone and Kacey's giggle.

"Hi, Livie," a deep male voice says.

"Hi, Trent," I say, smiling at the two of them and how completely enamored with each other they still are, even after three years. It's heartwarming, knowing that two individuals with such a train wreck of a past can thrive together. Hearing it in the middle of the night is not so heartwarming. Dan has had to bang on their door more than once to tell them to keep it down. I usually can't make eye contact with Trent the next day, which amuses Kacey to no end.

"How's school going?"

"Good. Classes only started on Thursday but they're good so far."

"Yeah?" There's a short pause. "And have you made out with any other guys?"

I gasp as I hear jostling on the other end, followed by a loud slap and Trent's laugh moving away.

"Sorry," Kacey mutters.

"How could you tell him that?" Trent has become a big brother to me. A giant man-child brother who loves to tease me almost as much as my sister does. It's a hundred times more embarrassing when he does it. "I'm never going to hear the end of this! He's going to tell Dan now and then they're going to gang up on me!"

"Relax, Livie!" Kacey's voice cuts in. "He's not going to say anything. Else. I had to explain why I had pictures of a guy's ass on my phone, though, so he wouldn't think I cheated on him."

"Oh," I say, biting my lip.

"But don't worry. I'll thoroughly beat him tonight for you." She says that last part extra loud and I know it's for Trent's benefit. He's probably grinning at her right now.

"Great," I mutter, rolling my eyes. My sister is the opposite of sexually repressed.

"So . . . have you run into that guy? What was his name?"

"Ashton. Yes," I admit reluctantly.

"And . . . how'd it go?"

I sigh. "About as good as a lit match near a pool of gasoline."

"Wow."

I fill her in on the conversation.

There's a loud clatter as Kacey throws whatever she had into the sink. "What a douche bag! The next time I fly up there, I'm going to tear that guy's balls off as promised."

"No you're not. It's fine. I'm over it. Reagan and I are going out with some friends tonight. I'm just waiting for her to get back from the bathroom and then we're on our way."

"Oh, good. I knew I liked that chick." I hear the patio door slide open and the sudden breeze against the receiver, followed by Kacey's small groan. I can tell she's easing herself into one of the lounge chairs on the back deck. "Well, I hope you have fun. Maybe lay off the Jell-O shots, seeing as I'm not there to control the repressed beast when she reveals herself."

"Funny." I bite my lip, hesitating. Do I just come out and tell her what Dr. Stayner told me? I don't know how she'll take it. Probably not well. I don't want her worrying about me because there's nothing to worry about. Dr. Stayner is wrong.

Before I get a chance to decide, Kacey starts up again in typical Kacey fashion. "But if you do go on another wild bender, make the guy wrap it up."

"Jeez, Kacey. You sound like a dude," I hear Trent say in the background.

"What! I'm just making sure my virginal sis thinks about these things when she lets the beast loose again."

"What beast? Livie has a beast?" I hear a second male voice chirp. Ben, Kacey's good-looking bouncer-turned-lawyer friend. "Damn. I need to meet it. I love beasts."

And it's official. Even a thousand miles away, my sister has still managed to make me want to die. I groan, my face falling into my hand. "Why did I wait until college to drink, Kacey? I should have gotten this out of my system years ago. Why would you let me wait?"

"Hey, I tried. Remember? If spiking your iced tea isn't sisterly love, then I give up."

The door opens and Reagan walks in, tossing her stuff on her dresser. She promptly taps her watch and then gestures to say she'll be in the hall.

I nod, holding up a finger to indicate one minute. "Kace. I've got to go. Say hi to everyone. And tell them that I miss them."

"Will do, Livie. We miss you tons. It's not the same without you."

Again, I have that nagging feeling that I should be telling her what Dr. Stayner said to me, but I don't know how. I know he's not right, but . . . what if he is? I know she'll believe him. Maybe that's why I don't want to tell her. Because what will she say? What will she tell me to do? Probably the same thing she always says: Go live and let yourself make mistakes. "Hey, Kace?"

She must be able to sense the serious tone in my voice because her playful lilt disappears. "Yeah, Livie?"

"How do you figure out the right way to live your life?"

There's a long pause. So long that I check the screen of my cell phone to see if the call is still connected.

"Trial and error, Livie. That's the only way that I know of."

■ ■ ■

"It looks pretty quiet," I say as I follow Reagan along the interlock driveway up to the front porch, which is attached to a stately two-story modern Craftsman-style house and surrounded by towering oak trees. One week ago I was walking along these same stones and feeling these same butterflies. Only this time it's different because I do know someone inside.

Connor. And it's a weird excited-nervous feeling that's stirring inside my stomach this time.

"It's early," is all Reagan says, jogging up the steps like she's been here a thousand times. She reaches out and opens the front door.

"Reagan! Shouldn't we knock or—"

"Gidget!" I hear a male voice bellow. Peering over Reagan's head, I see a guy sauntering down a long hall toward us, his bare feet slapping the hardwood floor.

Under my breath, I whisper, "Who is that?" I remember her saying that she knew a lot of people going to the party, but does she know the guys who live here? Does she know Connor? I mentioned Connor and she didn't say anything except, "I'm in!"

"How could you forget Grant?" Reagan announces rather loudly, flashing one of her giant smiles. Subtlety doesn't seem to be in Reagan's nature.

He slows as he approaches, a crestfallen look passing over his face. "You don't remember me?" he asks, his hands lifting to cover his chest as if his heart is in pain.

"I . . .uh . . . ," I sputter, shooting a glare in Reagan's direction as my cheeks flush. They both burst out in laughter.

With a boyish grin, he extends a hand. "Hi, I'm Grant. Glad you ladies could make it."

I offer a shy smile as I take it. "Livie."

"You'll always be Irish to me," he says with a wink and then turns to head back down the hall that stretches to the very back of the sizeable house.

He called me Irish.

Why did he call me Irish?

I don't remember him.

Why don't I remember him?

Ohmigod. He saw me like that. He must know Ashton. Does he know what I did with Ashton? Is he going to tell Connor that I'm a maniac when I drink? Has he already told Connor? What if Connor doesn't want anything to do with me now?

This is a disaster.

Reagan grabs my forearm and squeezes. "Livie, you're not blinking. It's creeping me out."

"Sorry," I mumble. *It's nothing,* I tell myself.

We start following Grant back, past a spacious but unoccupied living room on the right. "Reagan has won my undying love, but I'm willing to date around while she sows her wild oats," Grant calls out over his shoulder.

"I think you'll be dating until you're old and gray, then," I warn with a sidelong glance at her.

He stops walking and spins around, flashing Reagan a wide grin. "She's worth it. Would you ladies like something to drink?"

Before I can request water or a Coke, Reagan is already placing our order, holding up two fingers. "The usual, Grant. Thanks." I have a feeling *the usual* is coming from the selection of glass liquor bottles on the kitchen counter I see up ahead. And Grant obviously knows Reagan well if he knows what "the usual" is.

"Anything for you, Gidget," he says with another winning smile as he turns a corner.

I grab her arm to stop her from following. "Did you know that Grant lived here, Reagan?"

Her brow furrows. "Oh, yeah. Of course."

I feel my eyebrow arch and I know it's probably halfway up my forehead. "So then you knew that he was Connor's roommate . . ."

"Uh-huh," she says absently, wiggling from my grasp and speeding toward the kitchen.

Why is she being so evasive?

"Hey, Livie!" I hear. I turn to see Connor coming down the set of stairs, his face beaming. I sigh with relief. Okay, so he doesn't appear to be regretting this invitation . . .

He confirms that a second later as he wraps his arms around my body, enfolding me in a warm hug, as if we're old friends rather than two people who just met. "So glad to see you again," he murmurs into my ear, sending a shiver through me.

"You too," I giggle, melting into him with ease.

With a gentle hand on my back, he leads me into a large galley-style kitchen full of dark woods and stainless steel. I never saw any of this the night of the party, seeing as we entered the basement through the back of the house. I'm more than surprised that a bunch of college guys live like this. The back wall is basically all windows, overlooking the secluded wooded backyard.

"Did you meet Tavish?" Connor asks, gesturing to a stocky guy about my height with red-tinged hair leaning against the counter, inhaling a piece of pizza.

"Call me Ty." He wipes his hand on his jeans and then offers it to me.

"Dude! This is America. We're not barbarians here. Wash your hands before offering it to the ladies," Grant mutters as he hands me a drink, waggling his eyebrows. He has a very pleasant, friendly smile.

"Bile yer heid!" Ty roars at Grant in a thick Scottish accent that I assume is fake, given he didn't have it a moment ago. I have no idea what he said but Grant's chastising must have worked because Ty goes to the sink to wash the pizza grease off.

"If you ever need a little man in a kilt, Ty's your guy," Connor says with a wry grin.

"A kilt?" I repeat in a high-pitched voice as I remember the picture on my sister's phone.

"Ty's all about the traditions. Aren't you, Ty?" Reagan chirps from behind me, giggling. She flipped through the pictures too, so she knows exactly what I'm remembering.

He responds with a loud belch and a grin.

"Man, Ty. Ease up," Connor says with a laugh, shaking his head. To me, he says, "He's a small-doses kind of guy. And a no-doses kind of guy when he's walking around in that thing. You don't want to witness it. It's not pretty, trust me."

Reagan howls with laughter as my cheeks burn and Connor chatters away, clueless.

Connor quirks his brow at her. "What's so funny, Reagan?"

"Oh, nothing . . ." An impish grin flashes across her face and then it's gone. "Good to see you, Connor."

He walks over to give her a hug. "Good to see you too, Reagan. Though I don't know if Princeton is ready to handle you . . ."

She only winks in response.

Folding my arms over my chest, I ask, "So how exactly do you all know each other?" I shoot my sneaky little roommate a pointed glare. She quickly ducks behind Grant, avoiding eye contact.

"Reagan's dad coaches my rowing team. Didn't she tell you that?"

"She left out a few details." I know that Reagan's dad is the coach of a rowing team but she neglected to mention that she even knew Connor, let alone that he was on that team. Again, I glance over my shoulder. Reagan is leaning up against Grant, half hiding, watching me with a pained expression.

"We're also all members of Tiger Inn. A Princeton eating club. You've heard of those, right?"

"Kind of like a frat, right?"

Connor shrugs. "Way more relaxed than a frat, but we do bicker."

I quickly pick through my limited knowledge of Princeton's social scene to avoid sounding like a dumbass. "Bicker . . . that means pledge, right?"

"Right. You can't bicker until spring of your sophomore year, but you should start getting to know the various houses." Grabbing my hand, Connor pulls me toward another room.

"So you're on the rowing team?"

"Yeah, all four of us. Come on." Connor tugs me forward. "Come meet Ash."

My brain has just enough time to process, my stomach has enough time to drop, and my legs falter as we step into the den. I'm sure my face is displaying the perfect mix of shock, embarrassment, and horror. There, stretched out in an oversized armchair, beer in one hand, remote in the other, is the tall, lean form with dark brown eyes and shaggy hair that I've sworn out of my life.

Ashton "I Regret You" Henley.

"This is Ashton, our captain, though for the life of me I can't figure out why," Connor says in a playful manner, seemingly oblivious to the fact that I know exactly who Ashton is and am about to collapse.

I can't speak as I stare at that face, as I watch those eyes shift from me to Connor to Connor's hand holding mine, taking a long sip of his beer as he does so.

"Irish," he finally offers in a flat tone. I notice his jaw is clenched. This is probably as comfortable for him as it is for me. His regretful night—the girl he wants to forget happened—is standing in his house.

"Wait a minute . . ." Connor's hand slips out of mine. *Oh . . . here we go . . .* A finger points toward me as Connor's head cocks to the side. He stares wide-eyed at his roommate. "*This* is the girl who dared you to get that tattoo?"

I close my eyes and take several deep breaths, silently saying goodbye to any chance I might have had with Connor. When I open them again, the two of them are staring at me.

"Well, how about that!" Connor throws an arm around my shoulders and squeezes me to him. "You're famous around here!"

I feel the color drain from my face. "Famous?" I manage to squeak out. As what? The robot-dancing, face-sucking virginal boozehound? I turn around to find that Grant and Reagan have snuck up behind us. I throw a set of extra-sharp daggers directly at Reagan's face for setting up this ambush. Her mouth clamps on her drink as she quickly ducks behind Grant.

I turn back to face the guy I want to impress and the guy I want to forget, and I silently wonder how today could possibly get worse.

"Ashton. Babe—we've got to get going if I'm going to get to the airport in time." I hear the voice before the blond appears through another entrance into the room with her purse and coat slung over her arm. Leaning over the back of his chair, she lays a long kiss on his lips.

Connor leans toward me in ignorant bliss. "That's Ashton's girlfriend, Dana."

chapter eight

■ ■ ■

MAN WHORE

I've given up on talking by this point. I know that whatever comes out of my mouth will be idiotic gibberish because I tend to speak that way when I'm nervous or shocked or upset. Right now, standing here, watching Ashton and his girlfriend kissing, the perfect storm of all three brews inside me.

Dana pulls away from Ashton at the sound of her name. "Hi, Reagan! Hi . . ."

"This is Livie," Connor says.

She offers me a warm smile. "Hi, Livie. It's nice to meet you."

I try to smile back. I think that I succeed. I'm not sure; it could have looked more like the sneer of a rabid animal. I'm too busy trying to calm the screaming inside of my head.

That asshole *cheated* on her. With me!

My eyes dart to his face, to see that he's staring at me with a strange expression. It's not his usual arrogance. It's not guilt, which it *should* be. No, I know exactly what it is. Desperation. He's pleading with me not to say anything. He doesn't want his girlfriend to find out. It all makes sense now. This is why he wants to keep what happened between us quiet. But then . . . why would I be *famous*?

I sneak a peek at Connor to see him smiling at me. It's a warm smile, not the amused smile of a guy who knows that I messed around with his roommate and am now being introduced to said roommate's unsuspecting girlfriend. Either he doesn't think there's anything wrong with what happened—making him a complete ass and *so* not the nice guy that I thought he was—or he doesn't know.

I don't get it. But everyone is staring at me, waiting for me to respond to Dana. I swallow and then do my best to force out a pleasant, "Hi, Dana. Nice to meet you too." It must have sounded passable, because she smiles and nods before she grabs hold of Ashton's arm and yanks at it. "'Kay, seriously, Ash. Get that gorgeous butt up so we can go or I'll be late."

He complies, sliding out of his chair with ease to tower over her. Her loose curls spill back as she tilts her head to gaze at him. The way that her eyes sparkle—like Kacey's do when Trent is in the room—I can tell that Dana is head-over-heels in love with him.

I want to be anywhere but in this room with this sweet, unsuspecting girl and her lecherous boyfriend right now. "Connor, where's your bathroom?" I ask, trying to keep my voice steady.

With a nod to the left, he says, "There's one through that doorway, around the corner. First right."

"Oh, I'd give that one an hour," Grant warns from behind us. "Ty was in there. It's not suitable for ladies. Or most humans."

"It's that damn chili your mama made!" Ty bellows from the kitchen.

Shaking his head at his roommate, Connor says, "Third door to the right, upstairs. You want me to show you?"

"No, I'll find it, thanks." I pat his arm as I turn to dash out of there.

"It was nice to meet you, Livie," Dana calls out.

"You too," I throw back with a smile, rushing to the stairs. I hope that wasn't too rude but I can't help it. She's super-nice and that's making me want to scream.

I hear Ashton behind me say, "I'll meet you out by my car in five. I've got to change and grab my wallet."

He's following me.

Blood rushes to my ears. I speed up, taking the steps two at a time, determined to get behind a locked door before I have to face him. And I would have made it if my toe hadn't snagged the lip of the top step, sending me sprawling out onto the hardwood floor, flat on my stomach.

My face burns as I scramble to my hands and knees, still determined to hide. I hear a soft chuckle behind me as two hands grab my waist and yank me to my feet effortlessly.

"Jeez, Irish," Ashton mutters. I bristle as I feel his hand touch the small of my back.

"I'm fine from here," I mutter angrily, twisting away from him as I hurry toward the bathroom.

He follows suit, increasing his speed behind me. "I doubt that," he says, but he doesn't laugh. When I reach the third door to the right, Ashton grabs my hip and practically shoves me into the spacious room. I spin around to close the door but it's too late. He's already maneuvered his way in, shutting the door behind him. And locking it.

"What are you—" I start to say in a biting tone but his hand clamps over my mouth.

"Shut up." He pushes me backward until the edge of the granite countertop hits my tailbone, keeping his hand on my mouth the whole time. I briefly consider biting it but I restrain myself. I'd probably draw blood, I'm so angry. Livie the Biter. God knows that would only add to whatever stories are already circulating about me.

He's staring down at me, those deep brown eyes intense and thoughtful. My nostrils catch that light musky cologne of his. It instantly triggers memories from last Saturday. Memories that just won't leave me alone.

I look away from him as my heart starts racing and I feel the first trickle of sweat down my back. I just want to get away and I can't. He's trapped me. The entire situation is overwhelming and I have to fight to keep my knees from buckling. Or maybe it's just Ashton that's overwhelming me. Everything about him. I swallow repeatedly.

"If I move my hand away, will you keep quiet and let me explain something?" he says with a warning glare.

My brow furrows. What is there to explain? That he got drunk and cheated on his girlfriend? But at this point, I just want to get away from him, so I bob my head.

The second his hand drops from my mouth, my anger flares again. "How could you do—" My words are cut off as Ashton grabs my waist and spins me around to face the mirror. I'm about to twist my torso against him to get away, but then I look up at our reflection and find his dark stare pinning me with its strength. My breath hitches.

"How do you know Connor?" His voice is strangely calm. I tense as his hand lifts to brush my long black hair off to the side, his fingers grazing my neck.

"I met him the other day," I answer involuntarily, distracted. "Didn't he mention it?" *What is he doing?*

"No." His index finger tugs gently at the back of my shirt, pulling it down far enough to expose my tattoo. "Small world," he murmurs as his finger runs horizontally along the writing. He exhales slowly, his breath sending shivers down my back and legs, stiffening my entire body.

I set my jaw. "Unfortunately."

His finger stops moving as searing eyes flash toward mine in the mirror. When he looks back to my tattoo, I catch the little smirk. His finger starts running back and forth along the ink on my back again, the motion drawing the breath out of my lungs and making my face redden. "Now you see why last Saturday needs to stay between us?"

"It should never have happened in the first place," I say, my voice cracking as his muscular arm reaches toward the bottle of lotion on the counter, pumping a small amount onto his fingers. With a pinched brow, I watch as he brings it toward me and, with the most gentle of touches, begins to smooth it over my freshly inked skin. I close my eyes as I swallow, taking a moment to enjoy the cool, soothing cream. That damn thing has been driving me insane all week. I'm diligent about caring for it, but I have to admit that my hands don't feel nearly as good as his.

I hate admitting that.

"Feels good, doesn't it," he murmurs with a huskiness in his voice that makes heat blaze through my body.

"Yes," I hear myself murmur. *Wait* . . . My eyes fly open to find his trained on my reflection. *Dammit, how does he do that!* "No!" I snap, wiggling my way free of him and spinning around. I move toward the door, but Ashton's giant hands land on my waist. He roughly lifts me up and sits me on the counter to face him. "Stop being so fucking stubborn and listen, Irish," he snaps, his hands squeezing my sides, his thumbs pressing into my hip bones.

It's his tone that makes me flinch, though. "Connor is my best friend. We've known each other for four years. I know him well." He pauses, his eyes skating over my face. "I know he seems really easygoing, but . . . I can tell you that Connor wouldn't like knowing that you and I hooked up. Even if it was for one night. Even if we didn't fuck." I gasp at his crudeness, but he continues without apology. "So if you want anything to happen with him, you should probably stay quiet."

I frown. "I don't get it. I thought he knew—"

"No, he doesn't," Ashton confirms with a shake.

"Nothing?"

Ashton's hands slowly slide from my waist over my hips, down the sides of my legs, squeezing them slightly, to settle on my knees as he steps away. "Nothing."

A strange heat spikes in my thighs with his touch but I clench my teeth, more focused on answers. "Well, then why am I *the famous* Irish?"

"Oh." Dipping his head, he chuckles. When he looks up at me, it's with a private smile. "Because I've never taken a dare before." Seeing my confused look, he adds, "The tattoo. On my ass."

I feel my cheeks flush, but my focus quickly moves to my curiosity. "Why did you, then?"

His voice is soft when he speaks again. "I had my reasons." The way his eyes settle on me then—a hint of a secret behind them—instantly dries my mouth. "And I'm asking you now—again—not to say anything. For Dana. She doesn't need to get hurt."

The way he says her name, I immediately sense the reverence there. He does care for her. Maybe he was as drunk as I was . . . "Shouldn't you tell her, though? I mean, it's . . ." My voice drifts off, looking for the right word. Despicable. Evil. Wrong.

"It's complicated," he snaps. "And none of your business. And if you don't want to keep quiet for Dana's sake, do it for Connor. If you're planning on hooking up with him." Unlocking the door, he opens it and steps out. But stops abruptly. "One more thing . . ." He looks over his shoulder at me and my stomach clenches. "Tell Reagan that I'm going to kill her." With that, he heads down the stairs.

"Not if I don't kill her first," I mutter to the reddened face in the mirror.

■ ■ ■

"I couldn't tell you!" Reagan whines, pleading with big, wide doe eyes. "You never would have come!"

"That's not true," I mutter stubbornly. But she's right. I wouldn't have. And then I wouldn't be sitting out on the back deck, waiting for sweet, unsuspecting Connor to bring me my Jack and Coke. My third one tonight, thanks to my frazzled nerves. "And what about Dana?" I hiss. "You didn't think I needed a warning about that?"

She cringes. "I wasn't sure how to bring it up, seeing as your head looked ready to explode from everything else that happened that night. And if you actually liked Ashton, then—"

"I don't," I blurt out, a little too quickly.

I see the flicker of a smile touch her lips, but she smooth it over quickly. "Good, because you're not a fuck-buddy kind of girl and he's not boyfriend material. Clearly."

With a sigh, I murmur, "I get why you didn't tell me last weekend. My head probably *would* have exploded. But you didn't think telling me *before* I walked into this house was a good idea?"

She has the decency to look sheepish as she places her empty cup onto a side table. "Probably . . . I'm sorry. When you told me that you met Connor and wanted to come here today, I hoped you wouldn't care anymore. Once you saw Ashton, I mean."

I glare at her. "And what about when I met his *girlfriend*?"

"She was supposed to be back in Seattle for school already!" Reagan groans, dropping her face into her hands. "I'm sorry! I'm a terrible friend. An awful roommate. I just don't do well with uncomfortable situations."

"Me neither. Especially the one I just got thrown into back there."

"Gidget!" The back door opens and a grinning Grant steps out to hand Reagan her drink. When he sees the morose look on her face, he quickly turns and ducks back inside without a word. I can almost see the guilty tail tucked in between his legs.

"So Grant was in on this too?"

"He won't say a word. Seriously." She looks at me with pleading eyes. "Please don't hate me, Livie."

Setting my jaw stubbornly, I stare out into the darkness of the expansive backyard as I think through it. None of this is Reagan's fault. I'm the one who made out with Ashton. I'm the one who met Connor and wanted to come here. I'm the one who's bitter with Ashton for cheating on his girlfriend. I'm the one who keeps letting fleeting memories of kisses and touches creep into my mind. I need to stop thinking those things about Ashton and start focusing on the gorgeous blond Irish guy who *is* available. Maybe I can make some new memories and prove Dr. Stayner wrong while I'm at it. "I don't hate you, Reagan," I say with a sigh. "I may still kill you in your sleep, but I'll think of you fondly while I'm doing it."

She exhales noisily. "Give me fair warning though? I've always wanted to eat the tequila worm before I die. Should I do that tonight or wait?"

I half snort, half giggle, her joke defusing the tension. "Why does Grant call you 'Gidget'?"

Shaking her head at the silly nickname, she mutters, "It's after that character from the fifties and sixties. You know, *Gidget Grows Up, Gidget Gets Married*. There's a slew of books and movies on her. Even a television show. Apparently the author came up with the name by mashing *girl* with *midget*. And, well," she gestures to herself, a knowing smirk on her face. "It's a good thing I don't have a height complex."

I giggle softly at her confidence. It's refreshing. "I have yet to ask Ashton why he's calling me Irish. I feel like every time I see him, I'm too busy swallowing my tongue to get the question out. Do you think Grant knows?"

Reagan shakes her head. "I asked. He doesn't. Only Ashton knows."

There's a long moment of silence, during which Reagan gulps back her drink. I don't know how that tiny body can hold so much alcohol. Then she says, "Connor's into you."

I flush, glancing over my shoulder and into the kitchen window to see him talking with Grant and a new guy. "He is?"

Her head bobs up and down. "Oh, yeah. I can tell. He can't take his eyes off you. He's probably imagining what he's going to do to you later."

"Reagan!" I shake my head as she grins. She's as bad as my sister.

She takes another long, noisy sip as my thoughts unintentionally drift back to Ashton. "She seems nice."

"Who?"

"Ashton's girlfriend."

"Oh . . ." Reagan pauses and then murmurs, "Yeah. Too nice for him. I feel guilty every time I see her. If he could just learn to keep it in his pants . . ."

Wait . . . "He cheats on her, a lot?" It wasn't just with me?

She shrugs. "I hear things. A lot of things. He has quite the appetite. His heart and his brain are two separate entities that don't commingle. Ever. Poor, sweet Dana doesn't have a chance in hell of satisfying him."

"I'm sure no one does," I murmur, silently relegating him to top spot on the man-whore totem pole.

■ ■ ■

When we reenter the house, there are a dozen new people in the kitchen and adjoining family room, taking up the right side of the house, opposite the den. More people are at the front door, trickling in.

"You guys good?" Connor appears with my drink. "Sorry, I was going to bring it out, but you looked like you were having a serious conversation."

"We were, but . . ." I glance over at Reagan, who's fluttering through the room with waves and nudges and smiles. Grant trails two feet behind her, his eyes glued to the back of her head, a goofy expression on his face. And I smile to myself, wondering if Reagan has any clue that Grant is seriously crazy about her.

"But what?"

The sound of Connor's Irish intonation brings me back to him, to his beautiful green eyes and his easygoing smile. "Girl stuff," I say as I clink his glass.

The smile never slips from Connor's face, even as I catch his eyes flickering to my lips for a second before lifting back up to ask, "How were your first few classes?"

I open my mouth to answer when the stereo blasts on. We both turn in time to see Ty strut out in his kilt, rubbing his hands up and down over a puffed-out chest as he surveys the crowd.

"He likes to accidentally flash people when he sits down."

I lift a brow. "Accidentally?"

Shaking his head, Connor admits, "No. Come on." He grabs my hand and leads me back out to the deck where I just stood with Reagan, shivering against the chilly night air.

Connor must notice my involuntary shudder, because he slips

his arm around my shoulder and pulls me toward him so that I'm tucked against his broad chest. "Better?" he murmurs, his one hand rubbing up and down my arm. "Okay, *now* tell me how your classes were."

I let myself soak up Connor's body heat for a moment as my nose absorbs the scent of his cologne—light and clean, with hints of lavender. And I silently marvel at how *comfortable* this is.

I tell him about the two science classes I had on Thursday and Friday and the ones I have next week. I tell him all about the volunteer job at the hospital and about the twins, rehashing their interrogation.

"Derek and Eric are twins?"

I roll my eyes and giggle. "I know."

He takes a sip of his beer and then his arm moves back, pulling me tighter. "So, what makes you want to go into pediatrics?"

"It's just something I knew I wanted to do since I was young. I can't picture myself doing anything but that." Stayner's words from this morning slink into my thoughts and I instantly chase them out.

"That's noble. And sweet," Connor says. Letting my head tilt back a bit, I feel his head turn, his lips brush my forehead as he murmurs, "And hot."

I swallow and duck back down, knowing my face is red again. "What about you, lawyer?"

I get jostled lightly as Connor shrugs. "I come from a long line of lawyers. Me and Ashton both, actually. It's a family tradition. Are your parents doctors?"

I shake my head, smiling wistfully. "My dad was a high school principal and math teacher. My mom was a music teacher."

There's a long pause. "Was?"

Taking a deep breath, I pull away from Connor, enough to see his serious expression. "Yeah . . . *was*." I take a long chug of

my drink. And then I tell him everything—about the car accident, about Kacey almost dying, about all the people who *did* die
that night. About Trent. Everything.

As I talk, I feel his arm slide around my shoulders and tighten.
I feel his other arm wrap around my body, his hand cupping the
side of my head, his thumb grazing my cheek, pulling me even
closer than I was before, until I close my eyes and let my head
melt against his chest, feeling his rapid heartbeat, cocooned in
his warmth. Protected.

We stand like that through an entire song, not talking, swaying silently to the beat, until Ty barrels through the door, visibly
more drunk than he was only twenty minutes ago. "Now I remember you!" he bellows, holding his hand out and wiggling his
fingers. "Come on. Lemme see that picture. I need to make sure
it's flattering."

"Oh no . . ." I groan, shrinking back.

Connor laughs unsuspectingly as he gives Ty a playful shove.
Taking my hand, he leads me back. "Let me show you the rest
of the house." Connor keeps me close as we weave through the
house and he introduces me to people. I think I remember a few
of them. I pray they don't remember me. Or that I likely told
them that I loved them. And I sure as hell hope they don't remember me with Ashton.

Once I've seen the entire main floor, Connor leads me upstairs. "That's Grant's room," he says with a head nudge to the
left. "Across from him is Ty." As we pass by the bathroom, he
murmurs, "You've already seen that." I nod, biting my bottom
lip as I glare at it, as if the room itself did something heinously
wrong. At the end of the hall are two doors opposite each other.
"That's Ash's," he says, a lazy hand waving to the open door on
the left, revealing a king-sized bed and dark gray linens. I in-

stantly picture Ashton's body stretched out over those sheets as he was the morning in my dorm room, and my stomach muscles tighten.

Opening the closed door to the right, Connor leads me into a large bedroom with a double bed and two giant windows. "This room's mine," he says, turning on a small lamp.

I'm in Connor's bedroom. Did he bring me up here for a reason? My eyes skim over the space, settling on the bed for a moment. Does he think we're going to have sex tonight? I clear my voice and offer, "Nice house," as I spin around, noticing the door was left slightly open.

Connor is leaning against a wall, watching me intently. "My parents own it. They bought it two years ago so I could get off campus for my junior and senior years. Almost everyone lives on campus around here, but I was finding it a bit too much. And the guys jumped at the chance to move in with me. They pay next to nothing for room and board, so it was worthwhile for them." Stepping forward to push a thick lock of my hair back behind my ear, he murmurs, "Relax, Livie. I didn't bring you up here with any expectations." His hand moves to cradle my chin. "Just one hope . . ." Leaning down, Connor's lips slowly close over mine, moving as if coaxing a response. It feels safe and warm and nice.

That doesn't mean I'm not petrified that I'm doing it all wrong, that Connor will regret me as well. When he breaks away, I wonder if my one drunken night was enough to teach me the basics. With my bottom lip tucked under my teeth, I look up to see eyes a darker shade of green and more glossy than normal.

"I'm just . . ." I frown. "I'm not very experienced."

Placing a gentle kiss on my forehead, he murmurs, "That's okay. To be honest, I really like that you're different." Does *different* translate to *virgin*? With a second kiss on my brow, his hands lift to hold my face on either side as he murmurs, "Let's keep things slow and easy." *Slow and easy.* What does that mean?

"Okay." I use my drink as a diversion, bringing it to my lips to take an extra-large gulp, thankful that Mr. Jack Daniel's is helping to keep me calm.

"So, I hear you got a tattoo last weekend?"

The quick change of topic is appreciated. I still groan and roll my eyes, of course. "Looks like it. Do you have any?"

Connor's hands fall from my face to ruffle the top of his head. "Nah, I hate needles. Ash keeps trying to get me out with him but I refuse."

"Go drinking with my sister and you'll end up with one whether you like it or not," I mutter wryly, but inside I'm mentally taking inventory of Ashton's tattoos, ones I've seen sober and the other ones that I somehow remember—a bird on the inside of his right forearm, the Chinese script on his right shoulder, the Celtic symbol over his left pectoral, *Irish* on his butt . . .

And my face is burning again. *Dammit.*

"What are you thinking about?"

"Nothing! Do you want to see it?" I blurt out, intent on diverting his attention from me and my perverted mind.

"Sure. I mean, it isn't anywhere . . ."

"Yeah. I mean, no. I mean, it's on my back so, yes, you can see it." I shake my head at my flustered self as I quickly turn around and sweep my hair to the side. I stretch the back of my shirt down. "See it?"

"Yeah." There's a long pause as he looks at it. He doesn't touch it, though, and I wonder whether he wants to or not. This is so unlike the caveman-style manhandling earlier with Ashton. I'm seeing very quickly that Connor is his opposite in so many ways. I don't get how they're best friends. "What does it mean?"

"Just something my dad used to call me," I smile wistfully.

"Well . . ." Connor's hand gently takes mine and my shirt falls back into place. He sweeps my hair back the way it was, smoothing it gently, before his hands settle on my shoulders. I sense him leaning forward until his mouth is close to my ear. "It's beautiful," he whispers, his voice decidedly husky, his thumbs sliding back and forth over my back with a hint of pressure. And I know that, despite not having expectations, Connor definitely has ideas.

I think this is the part when my brain is supposed to vanish. It's supposed to be sucked right out of my head by the sexy guy breathing in my ear. At least, that's what I've always assumed was supposed to happen. When you're in a bedroom with a hot guy for the first time and he's all but saying, "I'm horny and I'm yours," you're not looking for an escape route. You're looking for a way to lock the door so you can tear his clothes off and do all kinds of things that don't involve your brain.

But the problem is my brain is still intact, and it's telling me I want to go back to leaning against his chest and feeling his warmth. I can even handle another kiss. Maybe. Though, if I'm being honest with myself, something about that doesn't sit well with me either right now.

Is this proof that I'm repressed? Maybe I need to get drunk again. Maybe then it will sit well.

Or maybe I just need time to ease myself into this.

Or maybe I should just give up now and join a convent.

The volume of the music suddenly spikes, rattling the glass in the window. With a sigh of reluctance, Connor takes my hand and mumbles, "I'm sorry. We'd better go downstairs. Ty's going to bring the cops here if I don't go put a leash on him."

I feel my shoulders sag with relief, my face stretching out into a contented grin as we leave his room, knowing that I'm getting the time that I need. Until I see Ashton's bedroom door closed and a red sock hanging on the doorknob. I remember Reagan talking about "the code."

"I thought Dana went home."

Connor shakes his head, looking over his shoulder at me with a knowing stare. "She did."

chapter nine

■ ■ ■

GAMES

Students trickle into the cold lecture hall for the Monday mid-morning class as I make my way down to the front. The entire first row is empty but I don't care, picking a seat near the professor's podium, my stomach a bundle of nerves as I anticipate a semester of difficulty. I briefly considered dropping this English lit course out of spite, seeing as Dr. Stayner was adamant that I do things based on what I want—not on what others want—and this is clearly what someone other than me wants.

Everyone assumes I'm a genius and grades just fall onto my lap because I ace the hard classes like calculus and physics. It's true that those grades come easier to me than they do to most. The material is straightforward, black-and-white, right and wrong. I'm all about the clear-cut choices.

Subjects like philosophy, and history, and the English lit class that I'm about to begin, though . . . they just don't make sense to me. If there's a formula to find a right answer, I can nail it. But in classes like these, all I see are degrees of rightness and wrongness, and I've had to work hard to uncover those. In the end, I always get my A—I've never received anything but an A in anything, including gym—but those grades certainly never fell into my lap.

The door to the side of the chalkboard opens and a graying man in a black turtleneck and wire-rimmed glasses enters, carrying a stack of books and papers to the desk at the front. I smile. Finally, one thing that's consistent with how I always pictured Princeton to be.

"Hey, Irish."

The Ivy League's walking contradiction takes the seat right next to me. His tall frame fills out his space and encroaches on some of mine.

"What are you doing here?" I hiss, turning to see Ashton in dark jeans and a sky-blue shirt. I'm starting to recognize it as his typical style—flawless but careless. And he can pull it off, too, because he has a body that would make leopard-print tights look hot.

Sitting up straight in his chair, he looks around the room. "This is Professor Dalton's English lit class, right?"

"I know what class this is!" I bark, and then temper my tone, catching the professor's eyes flicker up at us from his podium. "Why are *you* here?"

"I'm a student and I'm here to take his class," he answers slowly, his expression somber. "Some of us are here for a serious education, Irish. Not just to party."

I glare at him, fighting the urge to punch him in the face again. There's a mischievous twinkle in his eye, which is quickly followed by the crooked smile I've come to know as Ashton's trademark flirt move. One that obviously worked on me when I was drunk but will definitely not work on me when I'm sober and annoyed.

"You're a senior."

"You seem to know a lot about me, Irish."

Gritting my teeth, I simply stare at him, waiting for his answer. Finally he shrugs, making a display of opening up his notebook and clicking his pen a few times. "Had a course to burn and this one was open."

"Bullshit!" The word bursts out of my mouth before I can stop it. This time the professor looks up from his notes to stare at us directly, and I feel my cheeks burn under the scrutiny. When he looks down, I turn back to Ashton.

"Relax, Irish. At least you know one person in the room now."

He has a point, I think, as I look around at a sea of unfamiliar faces. "And I suppose you're going to sit beside me every single class?"

"I don't know. You seem like an angry student. I'm not sure I want the prof associating me with you."

I shift away from him intentionally, earning a derisive snort. "So the fact that you saw my schedule has nothing to do with picking this course?" I ask.

"What? You think I'm taking this just because you're in it? Why would I do that?" There's a playful quirk in his brow.

Good question. But I still know it plain in my gut: he's here because I am. I just don't know why. "How'd you get in, anyway? I thought there was a wait list for this."

I see his fingers running back and forth over that worn leather band around his wrist. "I know one of the ladies in the registrar's office."

"Perhaps the one you had over on Saturday night?" I blurt out, the image of that stupid red sock still burning in my mind, reconfirming how *wrong* he is.

He pauses and then turns to look at me, cocking his head. "Are you jealous, Irish?"

"Of what? That you're such a douche bag that you drop off

your girlfriend and have another woman in your bed within hours?"

"I didn't have anyone in my bed," he says defensively, his tongue sliding over his bottom lip slowly. I fight the urge to look down at it.

"You didn't?" I sigh with relief. And then I realize that I just sighed with relief. Why am I sighing with relief?

He shakes his head, clicking his pen a few more times. "Up against the wall . . . in the shower . . ."

I start gathering my books in order to change seats before the professor begins, but Ashton's hand lands on top of mine, holding it in place. "What does it matter? You were with Connor in his room anyway, weren't you?"

"No, I . . ." Heat creeps up my neck. "We were just talking." I shake my head. I don't know why it matters, really. What he does behind his girlfriend's back is sleazy, but he's right—it's none of my business. He'll get what's coming to him eventually. "It doesn't matter, Ashton. I just thought you regretted messing around on your girlfriend."

"I never said *that*," he answers softly, releasing his grip of my hand and shifting in his seat as the professor affixes a microphone to his collar, ready to begin the lecture. "I said I regretted messing around with *you*."

My jaw clenches as my pride takes another hit. "That makes two of us," I mutter, hoping that came out convincing, knowing that it doesn't make me feel any better.

"Nice skirt, Irish," he murmurs, his eyes now very obviously on my thighs. I instinctively smooth the simple black skirt, wishing it were longer.

I struggle to keep focus for the next hour, Ashton's words weighing on me. I grab onto bits and pieces of what Professor Dalton says, sometimes even an entire point. And then a brush against my knee or my elbow makes me jump. I adjust in my seat. I squirm. Several times I glare at him, but he either doesn't notice or doesn't care. And he doesn't take notes, I notice. I see him scribble a few lines on a page, but I doubt they have anything to do with this lesson.

By the time the class wraps up, I'm ready to run up the stairs. Or stab him in the leg with my pen.

As the professor writes our first assignment on the board, I hear Ashton mumble, "Now I remember why I never wanted to take this class."

"There's still time to drop it," I snap back.

Mock horror twists Ashton's distractingly beautiful face. "And not enjoy your pleasant company twice a week for an entire semester? Heavens, no!"

I shake my head with resignation. "Okay, seriously, Ashton. Back off."

"Or what?"

"Or . . . I'm going to tell Connor."

"No, you won't," he says softly.

"Why? Because you think he won't want me after? I have a feeling you're wrong." I don't have that feeling at all. In fact, I have the feeling that Ashton is right. But I also have the urge to have the upper hand on him. For once, dammit!

Leaning to the side until his shoulder presses against mine, he murmurs, "No . . . because you're in love with me."

A strangle gurgling sound escapes my throat.

Upper hand gone.

My heart hammers in my throat. I'm really not sure how to respond to that but my gut says that I have to, partly to defend myself, partly because I know he likes embarrassing me. It takes a few swallows to form words. "If loving you means wanting to rip your balls off, then . . ." I turn to lay what I hope is a steely gaze

on him. His face is inches away from mine but I don't back off.
"Yes. I'm madly in love with you."

Kacey would be so proud.

I'm not sure what I expected in response. I've never threatened anyone like that before. Maybe a flinch, maybe a shift away
from this crazy girl who talks of maiming his genitals? Definitely
not that damn smirk again. And I think he may have leaned in
even closer. "I love getting you all riled up, Irish." He grabs one of
my books and scribbles something on the inside cover, and then
tucks in a folded piece of paper. "I just remembered . . . I already
took this course three years ago. I aced it. Call me if you need help
with your papers." With that, he scoops his notebook up. I turn
in my seat and watch as he bounds up the stairs, earning glances
from pretty much every female and a few guys in the class, before
the prof officially releases us.

I shake my head as I flip open the book to read "Irish loves
Ashton" with a big heart and a phone number scrawled across the
inside of the front cover. "Dammit," I mumble. He just defaced
a two-hundred-dollar textbook with this nickname I *still* haven't
asked about. On the plus side, he's no longer in the class.

Curious to see what the note says, I unfold it.

*The only thing I regret is that it ever ended. And I'm the one
who's jealous. Insanely so.*

My heart rate skyrockets.

■ ■ ■

*"Nice skirt," he says as his hands slide up my bare thighs, sending fire
shooting upward. I'm standing in front of him as he sits on the edge of
his bed. And I'm shaking. Strong fingers curl around the backs of my
thighs and squeeze, dangerously close to where I've never been touched*

before. My body's reacting to him, though. My heart rate is racing, my breathing quickening, and I feel myself getting wet. Sliding his hands up, he hooks his thumbs under the band in my panties. He pulls them down until they fall to the ground on their own. I step out of them.

"Come here." He gestures to his lap and I comply, letting him guide my one knee to one side of him and the other to the other side so that I'm straddling him, my hands gripping his shoulders, marveling at their strength. He pushes my skirt up to pool around my waist and I'm instantly self-conscious. "Look at me," he orders and I do, watching his dark eyes bore into mine, holding them there. Never shifting. I hold that stare as he reaches around to settle one hand on the small of my back. I hold that stare as his other hand moves up my inner thigh. My breath hitches as he touches me. "Don't look away from me, Irish," he whispers as his fingers push inside, first one, then another . . .

I wake with a gasp, the textbook lying across my stomach sliding off and making a loud noise as it hits the ground. *Ohmigod.* What the hell was that? That was a dream. I just had an afternoon nap with a dirty dream about Ashton. *Ohmigod.* I sit up in bed and look around. I'm alone. Thank God I'm alone! A strange discomfort stirs between my thighs. It feels . . . frustrating? Is *this* what Storm and Kacey are always talking about?

I wish I had time to sort this out. But someone is knocking on my door. That must be what woke me up in the first place. If the dream hadn't been interrupted, would I have had dream sex with Ashton? No . . . my brain doesn't even know how to conjure that up.

Maybe if I weren't so frazzled, I would have looked in the mirror. That would have been smart. But Ashton and apparently anything to do with Ashton turns me into a primate.

And so I simply throw open the door.

"Connor!" I exclaim with way too much enthusiasm, my eyes widening in surprise.

I see his eyes shift down and I follow them to appraise my pair of ratty Lululemons and my dad's old Princeton sweatshirt—three sizes too big for me. "What are you doing here?" I stealthily drag my fingers through my hair. I don't need a mirror to tell me that it's a wild mess.

He steps in with an easy smile, one hand coming from around his back to reveal a large pot of green leaves. "Here."

I tilt my head and frown as I examine it. "Clover?"

"To remind you of me while you're in here, being a good student."

"Wow." I swallow as my cheeks burn. *Yes, that's what I was doing in here. Being a good student.* "Thank you." I try to slow my breathing and act normally.

"How are classes so far?"

"Busy. I'm already swamped with English lit."

"Are you liking it?"

"It's . . . interesting." A hand unconsciously brushes against the folded note in my pocket. The one permanently creased from all the times I've folded and unfolded it, running my fingers along the edges, trying to puzzle it out. Trying to make sense of my reaction to it and why it's made me so giddy when it should make me angry. It's as though Ashton telling me that he doesn't regret what happened has now given my brain license to flash inappropriate memories from that one night at an alarmingly more frequent rate, leaving me flushed and scattered and unable to focus. Even Reagan has noticed.

"I won't keep you, then." I squeal as, grabbing my waist, Connor lifts me up onto the top bunk. Considering I'm about 125 pounds, that's not easy. Then again, I shouldn't be surprised, I realize, noting the definition of his arms in that gray-striped shirt he's wearing today. He's not quite as tall or broad as Ashton, but he's built almost as well.

Ashton . . . my thoughts always veer back to Ashton.

Sliding his hands from my waist, Connor rests them on my knees. "We're going out tomorrow to Shawshanks. It's a local bar. Do you want to come?"

"Sure." I smile and nod.

"Are you *really* sure? I mean, Ty's going to be there."

"In his kilt?"

"Nah, they won't let him through the door in that," Connor chuckles, shaking his head as if remembering something. "Well, not again, anyway."

"Well, I can handle Ty."

"Yeah? And what about Ashton?"

My stomach does a flip. What does he mean? What does Connor know? What—

"I know you don't think too highly of him after last Saturday night. I saw the look on your face. You know, after he dropped Dana off . . ." His words drift off like he doesn't want to come right out and say it.

"You mean when he was being a philandering pig?" I don't know why I said it. Maybe saying something so mean out loud will remind me of why Ashton is all wrong and I should burn up that damn piece of paper and threaten my subconscious with a lobotomy. I bite the inside of my lip. "Sorry. I didn't mean that. Exactly."

Connor gives my knee an affectionate squeeze. "Well, I'm happy that you don't find him as appealing as every other female on this planet seems to find him. But he's not that bad. He just doesn't think with his brain most of the time." Stepping up onto the ladder rungs until he's level with my face, he leans in to kiss me. This time I feel his tongue slide over my bottom lip, gently finding its way in to curl around mine. Never forceful, never insistent. Just . . . nice. "See you tomorrow, Livie," he murmurs. Then, hopping off and shooting me a broad smile and a wink, he leaves my dorm room.

I flop back on my bed, holding my clover, closing my eyes as I think about Connor. *Yeah, I know my parents would love him, Dr. Stayner.* I'm not oblivious. I know they'd pick him out of a hundred-man lineup just because of his smile. That's okay. He's the guy they'd want. He's the kind of guy every girl wants.

I hear a beep and a click and, a second later, Reagan walking in, out of breath from her jog. "I just passed Connor. He was looking happy. Was that one of your rampant sex sessions?" she jokes between pants, gripping her side like she's in pain.

"He's really sweet, Reagan." I roll onto my stomach, resting my chin on my arms. "Did you know how sweet he is?"

"I did. I've heard he treats his girlfriends really well."

Huh . . . I don't know why but, for some stupid reason, I haven't even pictured Connor with anyone else. I've pictured Ashton with *everyone* else and it's made me nauseous. But Connor's a gorgeous, smart senior. He's obviously had girlfriends. And, let's be smart about this, Connor has also had sex. Probably a lot. I wonder how slow he's willing to go with me. "How many girlfriends do you think he's had?"

"Two or three since being here." Reagan kicks off her shoes. "He was single all of first year. God, did I ever have a massive crush on him back then!" She makes a face. "I also had braces and a fat ass. That's what you get for being short and curvy. If I don't keep jogging . . . look out!" She pulls her T-shirt over her head and throws it onto the heap on the floor with her other clothes. Reagan isn't the neatest person in the world. I don't mind, though. It suits her wild demeanor. "You know, you should start jogging with me!"

"I'm not the most coordinated person," I warn with a grimace. "I'm liable to take you out."

She shrugs. "That's okay, I know how to tuck and roll."

"Maybe. One day." Maybe I'll like jogging. I won't know unless I try.

Until then, I can work on calming the butterflies that are swarming inside my stomach, now that I know I'm seeing Ashton tomorrow night.

No, Connor, I don't find your best friend appealing. Not at all.

chapter ten

■ ■ ■

JEALOUSY

Everyone knows Connor. At least it seems that way as we follow the server through the pub. To my left, a guy waves. To my right, another guy fist-pumps. We pass by a table with four young women. "Hey, Connor!" one calls out. He flashes them a smile and a polite nod and continues on. That's when all four sets of eyes settle on me and I morph into that frog in my tenth-grade science class. The unfortunate one beneath my scalpel. I shift discreetly to avoid their gazes and end up bumping into Connor. "Sorry," I murmur. But he just displays those perfect white teeth to me. He doesn't seem bothered that I'm on his heels. He's never bothered.

The attractive fortyish server shows us to a table for six and takes a handmade *Reserved* sign off it. "Thanks, Cheryl," Connor says.

She pats him on the shoulder. "What can I get you two?"

"A Corona for me and a Jack and Coke for Livie. Right, Livie?"

I just bob my head, clenching my teeth and fighting the urge to announce publicly that I'm only eighteen and this establishment should know better than to serve me alcohol. I have the fake ID my sister gave me but I'm terrified to use it. I think I may pass out if she asks me to pull it out of my wallet.

Cheryl doesn't card me, though. She simply nods and walks away, her eyes dropping to get a good look at Connor's butt as she passes.

"Tonight should be a good night. We've got front-row seats for the band," Connor says, gesturing to the stage directly in front of us.

"I thought you said they didn't reserve tables here."

Connor's head ducks and I catch those dimples again. "We tip Cheryl well, so she takes care of us. She likes us." *Yes, I know which part of you she likes . . .* I wonder what kind of tips Ashton gives her, but I bite my lip before I make another philandering pig comment. He is Connor's best friend, after all. And a philandering pig.

Unzipping my jacket and hanging it over my chair, my eyes drift over Shawshanks. It's a large, open space, full of dark wood and stained glass. One wall—entirely brick—displays an eclectic assortment of artwork hung haphazardly. Near the back is a wall-to-wall bar with at least twenty brass beer taps on display. A four-tiered shelf behind the bartender gives patrons countless liquor options to choose from. On the other end—the end we're seated at—is a stage and dance floor.

"They bring great bands in," Connor says, noting my gaze over at the instruments.

"Is that why it's packed here?" Every table is taken, most of them by college-aged people.

Connor gives a half-shrug. "Once schoolwork really kicks in, it slows down a bit. People get pretty focused. But there's always a party somewhere, someone letting off some steam. Usually at the eating clubs. We'd be at Tiger Inn tonight if they hadn't shut down the taproom to fix a leak. Here." He gestures to a chair. "Take this seat before—"

"—Tavish gets here!" Ty's boisterous voice booms in my ear as two stalky arms wrap around my waist. He lifts me off the ground and swings me in a circle—past an approaching Grant and Reagan—to settle me back down facing the stage. Before I can regain my footing, Ty slithers into the chair I was about to fill. "And takes the best seat in the house!" he finishes.

"Hey!" Connor barks and I note the irritation in his voice, a rare scowl marring his normally contented face.

"It's okay. Seriously." I give Connor's forearm a squeeze for good measure just as Grant leans in to kiss my cheek and smack Ty upside the head simultaneously.

"Hey, Livie!" Reagan calls out, unzipping her own jacket.

"Hi, Reagan. Missed you at the dorm," I say, swallowing nervously as my eyes do a furtive glance around the room, looking for Ashton. I'm not sure how to act around him now. I can't even guess how he's going to act around me.

"I couldn't make it back in time, so I met up with Grant and we came together." Reagan shoots a secretive look to Grant as she takes a seat next to him.

"Oh yeah?" Biting the inside of my mouth to keep my grin in check, I ask, "How was your politics class?" Reagan is embracing an assortment of classes: in three different conversations, she's told me she's thinking of majoring in Politics, Architecture, and two days ago, History of Music. I don't think Reagan has a clue what she wants to do after Princeton. I don't know how she sleeps at night with that level of ambiguity.

"Very political," she answers dryly.

"Hmm. Interesting." Interesting, because one of her classmates, Barb, swung by our dorm room to drop off photocopies of notes for Reagan, who couldn't make it to class. Reagan is obviously lying but I don't know why. I suspect it has something to do with the lanky guy next to her. If I wanted to get back at her for . . . oh, everything . . . I'd call her on it in front of everyone. But I don't.

"Who's playing tonight?" Ty asks, banging the drink menu noisily against the table.

"Dude, that doesn't make the waitress come any faster and it makes you look like a complete dick," Grant mutters, snatching the thing out of his hand.

Apparently it does work, though, because Cheryl appears within seconds to place our order on the table. "What can I get the rest of you?"

Ty's face looks ready to split, he's grinning so wide. "What was that you said, Grant?"

"I said 'nice gut.' Eat another bag of chips."

Ty's grin doesn't falter as he slaps his stomach in response. There's nothing resembling a gut there. I take a sip of my drink as I survey each of them with curiosity. None of the guys have an ounce of flab on them, anywhere. Their bodies are all very different—Ty being on the shorter side and thick, Grant tall and lean, Connor that perfect balance of height and build—but all are equally in shape. I'd imagine it's due to the grueling workout schedule Reagan's dad has them on.

"What's everyone drinking?"

I hate that my heart skips a beat at the sound of that voice. I hate it because I'm usually also hit with the memory of his mouth on mine. It lingers like a sugary aftertaste, one I can't seem to rid myself of—even with Connor sitting next to me. Tucking a strand of hair back behind my ear, I glance discreetly over my shoulder to find Ashton, his eyes scanning the crowd slowly, one hand absently scratching the skin above his belt. His shirt is lifted just high enough and his jeans are hanging just low enough that I can see the V-shape of his pelvis beginning. My breath hitches, recalling those same ridges in my room less than two weeks ago. Only he didn't have a stitch of clothing on him then.

"You okay, Irish?"

As soon as I hear the name, I know I've been caught staring. Again. With a furtive glance over at Connor, I'm relieved to see that he's occupied with Grant. I tilt my head back up to find Ashton's knowing smirk.

"I'm fine," I say, sliding my straw into my mouth, taking an extra-long sip of my drink. The Jack in it is potent, which is good because it means that warm tingle will start flowing through me quicker. And I'm going to need all the warm tingle that I can get tonight if Ashton's going to be here. I'm also going to turn into an alcoholic if this keeps up.

"Hey, why did we start calling you Irish, anyway?" Ty asks as Ashton's beautiful frame glides into the seat beside me. He sits with his legs bent and spread out, unconcerned that he's encroaching on my space, that his knee leans against mine.

Good question. One I don't necessarily have the answer for. I'm about to swallow my mouthful of drink and explain that Cleary is an Irish name, but Ashton butts in before I can get the words out to announce in a loud voice that the entire table and likely the surrounding ones can't miss, "Because she told us that she wants to fuck an Irishman."

Caramel-colored liquid explodes from my mouth, spraying all over the table, catching Reagan's and Grant's shirts as I start to choke. And I pray that I'll choke to death. And if that doesn't work, then I pray that someone slipped Drano into my glass so I can start convulsing and be done with this horror.

My prayers aren't answered, though, and soon I'm left with nothing but burning cheeks as I listen to Ty bellow with thunderous laughter, turning half of the bar our way. Even Grant and Reagan can't keep a straight face as they wipe my drink off themselves. I can't meet Connor's eyes. He hasn't said a word. What if he believes it?

With teeth gritted so tightly that I think they may crack, I turn toward Ashton, intent on stabbing him with my glare. He's not even looking at me, though. He's busy reading the menu. And smiling, clearly proud of himself.

I don't know what I expected from him tonight, but a comment like that wasn't it. If I don't leave right now, Connor will witness me turn into a female version of Tarzan and leap onto his best friend's back. Through a clenched jaw and to no one in particular, I say, "Be back in a sec." My chair makes a loud screeching sound as I push it back and escape to the restroom.

Once there and safely locked inside my stall, I lean my forehead against the cool door, thumping against it a few times. Is this how it's going to be from now on? How am I going to deal with him? I'm used to being teased by my sister and Trent and Dan and . . . well, all of them, really. They get a kick out of making me blush because I've always been so uncomfortable when it comes to this stuff. Why, then, does it make my blood boil when Ashton does it?

Maybe he wants me to lose my cool in front of Connor. If the note is true and he's jealous of his best friend, then convincing Connor that I'm a nut job would effectively scare him away. No . . . that just seems like too much work for a guy who has a girlfriend and one-night stands waiting in the wings. *Dammit!* I'm thinking too much about this. I'm analyzing and overanalyzing, moving on to obsessing. This is why I've avoided guys up until now. They make you crazy.

And this is also why I need to stop thinking about Ashton and focus on "slow and easy" Connor.

My eyes sting as I dig my phone out of my purse to I text my sister:

Ashton is an ass.

Her response comes almost immediately:

A giant ass.

I quickly text back, playing the game we've played since we were young—still childish, only now more colorful:

A giant leprous ass.

A giant leprous ass that plays his penis like a banjo.

I giggle with the visual in my head as I type:

A giant leprous ass who plays his penis like a banjo while singing "Old McDonald."

The responding text is a picture—one of Ashton leaning over in the tattoo artist's chair, the man with the ink gun at work. Ashton's face is twisted into a hideous, exaggerated wince.

I burst out in a fit of giggles, the tension sliding off my shoulders. Kacey always knows how to make things better for me. I'm still giggling, typing out a response to her, when a door squeaks open. I clamp my hand over my mouth.

"Did you see who's here?" a nasally female voice asks.

"If you're talking about Ashton, then . . . how could anyone miss him," another voice drawls as the sound of water rushing from a tap fills the room.

My ears perk up. I hit "Send" on my text to Kacey, telling her that I love her. Then I set my phone on *silent*.

"He's sitting at a table with two girls, though," the second voice continues.

That's when I know for sure. They're talking about my Ashton. I mean . . . not *my* Ashton, but . . . My cheeks heat. I probably shouldn't be listening to this. But it's too late; I can't leave now. I'm one of *those girls*.

"So what? He was here with a girl the last time I was here and I still went home with him," the first voice murmurs haughtily, and I picture her leaning forward to apply lipstick in the mirror. She moans. "God, that was such a great night."

Now I'm downright uncomfortable. The last thing I want to hear are details about Ashton's dirty exploits. I wonder if he chased this one into a classroom and defaced her books with hearts and his number, too.

Either she hasn't noticed that there's someone in the stall or she doesn't care, because she continues. "We did it out on the back deck. Out in the open. Anyone could have seen us!" she whispers excitedly. "And you know me . . . I'm pretty respectable . . ." I roll my eyes and decide that Ashton likely didn't have to do much chasing at all. "But with him . . . Oh my God, Keira. I did things I never thought I'd do."

Sure thing, whore.

My hand flies over my mouth as the words register in my head, shocking myself with my viciousness. For a second, I'm afraid that I might have said it out loud.

I guess I didn't, because the nasally voice adds, "I don't care who he's here with. He's leaving with me tonight."

I close my eyes and hug my arms to my body, afraid to sneeze or cough or shuffle my feet too loudly because they'll know I was listening, and then they'll see me sitting with him when I go back out there. And they'll know I was eavesdropping.

Thankfully, they're only there to reapply their makeup and fawn over Ashton's earth-shattering sex skills, so they vacate the bathroom shortly, leaving me to escape the stall and wash my hands. And wonder if this mystery girl will succeed. Probably. My gut tightens at the prospect.

"There you are." Reagan plows in through the door. With a deep sigh, she pats my back. "He's never going to let up if you react like that. You need to start dishing it back."

"I know, Reagan. I know. You're right. I'm just not good at that." It's surprising, given that I grew up with the queen of comebacks. But if I don't learn to handle him, "slow and easy" Connor is going to run "fast and hard" away from me.

"Just laugh it off." She gives my arm an affectionate squeeze as we head out the door.

Then I remember the picture of Ashton that Kacey just sent me. I know it's juvenile but I hold my phone up, a vindictive thrill making me smile. "Take a look at this, Reagan." By the time we arrive at our table, tears are streaming down our cheeks, we're laughing so hard.

Connor's green eyes flicker with a mixture of surprise and amusement as he holds out my chair for me. "What's so funny?" If Ashton's earlier comment affected him one way or another, I can't tell.

"Oh, nothing," I say casually, downing what's left of my drink and picking up the fresh one that someone ordered while I was gone, intentionally ignoring Ashton's watchful gaze.

"Show him, Livie," Reagan announces with an impish grin, adding, "You know what they say about payback . . ."

Grinning, I hold my phone up.

I've never heard three grown men howl like Connor, Grant, and Ty do when they see the picture. Clapping his hands, Ty bellows, "We need to get that blown up and put on our wall!" Then he mimics the look on Ashton's face, making a low guttural sound and pointing to his roommate, who has no clue what's happening because I intentionally hold it out of his view.

A bulging arm stretches out in front of me to grab my phone but I'm ready for it, hitting the power button and tucking the phone into my pocket. Drawing my straw into my mouth, I take my time sucking back my drink. The guys are still laughing as I place it down and fold my hands over my knee. I hazard a glance in Ashton's direction to see that playful twinkle in his eyes as he chews the inside of his mouth. Thinking about all the ways to get even, no doubt. Part of me is downright terrified of what's about to come out of his mouth because it will likely make me shrivel up into a fiery ball of humiliation.

"Hi, Ashton." Looking over my shoulder, I find a gorgeous Latina woman batting long, made-up lashes at Ashton. I instantly recognize her voice as the one from the bathroom, only now she's got the "come-home-with-me" sultry tone dialed to max.

Ashton doesn't turn to acknowledge her right away. He takes his time, slowly twisting in his chair, his arm coming up to rest on the back. When he's finally facing her, his eyes graze over her curvy, fit body.

I roll my eyes, the desire to slap him upside the head over-powering.

"Hello?" Ashton finally says and, by the inflection at the end, I can't tell if it's a do-I-know-you hello or a why-are-you-bothering-me hello. She must be wondering that too, because her tongue darts out to nervously lick her red lips. "We . . . met last year. I'm over there if you want to swing by for a drink later." She gestures to our left with a flirty flip of her long, curly black hair, but I notice that her voice is a tad less sultry, a touch more unsure now.

Nodding slowly, he gives her a polite smile—not his flirty smirk—and says, "Okay, thanks." Then his arm slips down and his body shifts so he's facing our table again. He takes a sip of his drink as he checks his phone.

I look behind us to see the girl leaving quietly, her exhibitionist ego that much smaller than when she arrived.

I should feel bad for her. He wasn't outright mean, but he certainly wasn't friendly.

I know I should feel bad for her.

But I don't. I don't want him going home with her. Or anyone.

So instead, I feel a bubble of relief surge inside my chest. A bubble that makes me blurt out a stupid thing like, "I heard her talking about you in the bathroom." As soon as the words leave my mouth, I regret it. Why the hell would I tell him that?

"Oh yeah?" Ashton's eyes flicker to me. "What'd she say?" From the way his eyes twinkle with a spark of recognition, I see that he does remember her, and that he has a good idea about what she would have said.

I take another very long sip of my drink. Ashton's gaze drops down to my mouth and I stop, lifting the glass to hide my lips. His smile widens. *He enjoys making me uncomfortable.* The guy is so damn confident, it makes me sick. I have no interest in aiding that by telling him the truth. "That she's had better."

Where did that come from? My subconscious evil twin?

I guess it's the right answer, because another round of laughter explodes at the table. This time Grant is the one smacking his hands against the table noisily, threatening all of our drinks. Try as I might, I can't help the wide, stupid grin that I feel stretching over my face as I watch Ashton's cheeks brighten.

Finally. I may still die from embarrassment tonight, but at least I'll go down swinging.

I have no clue what to expect next. Ashton's shining eyes are so hard to read most of the time, aside from knowing they mean trouble. So when his hand latches onto my knee and slides up and down my thigh—not too high to be completely inappropriate, but enough that uncomfortable heat shoots through me—I assume an agonizingly slow torture, like stringing me up naked in front of a crowd.

"I knew you had it in you, Irish," is all he says, though. Leaning over the table, he calls out, "So, Connor . . . do you think you can make it through a few drinks without pissing in my shoes tonight?"

My head whips around in time to catch Connor's brow arch with a flash of surprise, his cheeks turning rosy. He clears his voice and peeks at me as he mutters, "That was Ty."

A hand slaps the table. "I do not, nor have I *ever,* urinated in anyone's shoes!" Ty exclaims indignantly.

"Oh, yeah? What about my boots?" Grant counters with a bitter edge to his voice.

"Those ugly red fur things? They were asking for it."

"I had no winter boots for a week during exams because of you, fuckhead! I almost froze to death!"

"Speaking of freezing to death, remember the time Coach found Connor buck naked and ass up in one of the boats the morning of the big race?" Ashton reminisces, stretching in his seat, his arms lifting to hold the back of his head as he grins. "You almost got kicked off the team."

"Oh, I heard about that!" Reagan folds her hands over her mouth to cover her gaping mouth. "Man, was my dad pissed."

I'm giggling as I glance at Connor, who winks at me before retorting, "Not nearly as bad as the time you were handcuffed, stripped, and robbed by that transvestite in Mexico."

I manage not to spray anyone but myself as my drink explodes from my mouth a second time.

Ashton reaches over and yanks my glass out of my hand, his fingers skating across mine, sending a shock through my body.

Every touch from him seems to have that effect. "Someone get Irish a bib."

The guys spend the next two hours highlighting stories of their drunken debauchery—most involve waking up in public places naked—as I allow myself to relax. And believe that maybe being around Ashton won't be so unbearable after all. By the time the band begins their set, we're all feeling the effects of alcohol and every last piece of dirty laundry has been hung on display—Ashton's and Connor's in particular. They seemed to be trying to match and raise each other all night. .

It's hard to talk over the band, so we sit back and listen. Connor's arm is thrown over the back of my chair, his thumb strumming against my shoulder with the beat of the music. It's a local alternative band, playing mainly covers but a few of their own songs. And they're really good. I'd be able to focus if Ashton's leg didn't keep brushing up against mine. Short of throwing my legs over Connor's lap, I can't seem to get away from it.

When the band takes its first break and the boring satellite radio music comes back on, Connor leans over and says into my ear, "I hate to do this, but I've got to head out now. I have an early class tomorrow."

Glancing at my watch, I'm shocked to see that it's close to midnight. With a big bubble of disappointment rising, I reach back to grab my jacket.

Connor's hand on my shoulder stops me. "No, you don't have to go. Have fun." He's slurring slightly.

I scan our table to see that everyone has a full drink in hand. Ashton is flipping a paper coaster around in his fingers as he talks to Grant and Reagan. No one else seems ready to go.

Ashton doesn't seem ready to go.

A tiny surge in my heart tells me I'm not ready to go either.

"You sure?" Maybe I'm slurring too.

"Yeah. Of course." He presses a kiss against my cheek and then stands to pull his jacket on. "See you guys. Make sure Livie gets home all right." He stops as if remembering something. I catch his gaze roll over at his best friend and then settle on me. Gripping my chin with his thumb and index finger, he leans down and places a sloppy kiss on my lips. I feel the prickles at the back of my neck and I instantly know Ashton is watching. "Just don't drink too much," Connor whispers in my ear. I roll my tongue to gauge the degree of numbness in response. "You don't want to wake up with any more tattoos."

I watch him leave, hyperaware of Ashton's brown eyes still on me. A ripple of discomfort flows through me and I decide that now is probably a good time to stop drinking, and it has nothing to do with waking up with tattoos. It's also a good time to use the bathroom. For the fiftieth time.

I'm returning to our table when the band is kicking off their next set with a slow song. The open floor space in front of them is packed with people, some swaying to the music, others there to get close to the edgy-looking lead singer. Ty is busy shooting lascivious smiles at Sun, whom I ran into here tonight and made the mistake of introducing to our table. Ashton seems content just sitting and listening to the music, his hands interlocked behind his head, a strange, peaceful smile on his face.

I see her approach from the other side of the room.

The sultry Latin exhibitionist is closing in on our table again. If her ego was bruised by Ashton's polite brush-off earlier, it has quickly recuperated and is now gearing up for the second attack. I can't help but think that Ashton must really be *that* good if a knockout like her, who could probably seduce the Pope, is willing to take another run at him.

I hope he shoots her down.

What if he doesn't?

She's only a few steps away from our table, approaching it from the opposite side. I don't know why but I rush forward to reach it before she does, tripping over my own feet as I do. I recuperate quickly, but Ashton is facing me and sees the entire thing. It elicits a wide, genuine grin. "Irish, what's the rush?" he asks just as her long fingernails glide intimately across his bicep. "Come dance with me, Ash." The sultry is dialed back up again. Man, she's sure of herself! I wish I could be that sure of myself.

I hold my breath as recognition flitters across Ashton's eyes. I know he heard her and I know that I don't want him going anywhere with her. I watch as one arm slides out from behind his head to clamp onto my wrist. "Maybe next time," he calls over his shoulder as he stands. Before I know what's happening, his towering body presses up against me and he's ushering me toward the dance floor.

Adrenaline blasts through my veins.

Once safely in the sea of bodies, I expect that he'll let go of me, the dodge successful. Just like he manhandled me that day in the bathroom, he again smoothly whips me around, pulling my body close against him. He takes my hands and settles them around his neck and then those fingers of his slide down my arms, down my sides, all the way to my hips.

The music is loud enough that conversation is difficult. Maybe that's why Ashton leans so close that his mouth grazes my ear to say, "Thanks for saving me." It sends a shiver through me. "And you don't need to be nervous around me, Irish."

"I'm not," I lie, and I hate that I sound breathless but if he doesn't stop whispering in my ear, I'm going to . . . I don't know what I'm going to do.

His hands squeeze me, tugging on my hips, bringing me

flush against him—against what I should not be feeling right now. *Ohmigod*. Ashton's actually turned on. This is all wrong. My hands slip down to press flat against his chest and yet I can't will my body to push away as it responds the exact same way I remember from my dream.

"Do you know why I call you Irish?"

I shake my head. I assumed it was because, in my drunken stupor, I divulged my background. Something now tells me there's more to the nickname than that.

"Well," he says, with a lascivious grin, "admit that you want me and I'll tell you why."

With a stubborn shake of my head, I mutter, "Not a chance." I may have left my pride on the dance floor that night, but I certainly won't do it again tonight.

Ashton's perfect full lips pucker slightly as he stares down at me with intense, thoughtful eyes. I have no clue what he's thinking, aside from the obvious. Part of me wants to ask outright. The other part is telling myself that I'm an idiot for tripping into this situation. Literally. Then, when Ashton's thumbs start to stroke over my hip bones and my heart begins to pound against my rib cage, I'm convinced that I should have let the sultry exhibitionist have her way with him because now I've really gotten myself into trouble.

That's why his next words surprise me. "Connor asked that I make you like me," Ashton casually says, easing his tight grip on my hips so that I'm not pressed directly against his erection, allowing me to breathe again. His mouth twists as if from something sour. "Since he really likes you." Then he sighs, looking over my head, as he adds, "And I'm his best friend." As if he's reminding himself of that.

Right, Connor. I swallow. The mention of Connor and his feelings for me while my hands are still flattened against his best friend's chest, the one that I pawed repeatedly not even two weeks ago, fills me with guilt.

"So?" Serious dark eyes lock on my face. "How do I do that, Irish? How do I make you like me?" His question is already dripping with innuendo but when he uses that tone—one that is crackling with desire—my mouth instantly dries. And I remember exactly why I probably *did* throw myself at him the first time. And I'm about to do it again.

I try to summon the willpower to turn and walk away. With a deep exhale, I slide my hands back to his neck and match his intent gaze. I'm speechless. Utterly speechless. I bite my bottom lip. His eyes drop to my mouth, his own lips parting a touch. I quickly manage to croak out without thought, "Stop embarrassing me?"

He nods slowly as if considering it. There's a pause. "What if I'm not trying to and I still embarrass you? You embarrass easily."

Case in point, my cheeks flush and I roll my eyes. "Just tone it down."

Ashton's hands shift up and back slightly, his fingers spreading out along my sides and back, his pinkies just above the border of inappropriate ass touching. "Okay. What else? Come on, Irish. Lay it on me."

I chew the inside of my mouth, thinking. What else do I say? Stop looking at me like that? Stop touching me like that? Stop being so sexy? No . . . if I'm being honest, those things aren't bothering me right now. Probably because I'm drunk.

"Of course, we could go back to your room and—"

"Ashton!" I smack his chest hard. "Stop crossing the line!"

"We've already crossed that line." His arms suddenly surround and crush me against him, until I can feel every part of him. For just a second, my body responds of its own accord, drawn by the electricity surging through to the very ends of my nerves.

Finally my brain manages to break the magnetic pull. I pinch a muscle in his shoulder hard enough that he flinches as he releases his grip.

He's not ready to let me go just yet, though, his hands settling on my hips again. "Feisty. Just how I like you, Irish. And I'm kidding."

"No, you're not. I *felt* it." I tilt my head and cock one eyebrow to give him a knowing stare.

That only makes him laugh. "I can't help that, Irish. You bring out the best in me."

"*That* defines you?"

"Some would say . . ."

"Is that why you . . . with so many women?"

An amused smirk touches his lips. "What is it you can't say, sweet little Irish? Is that why I fuck so many women?"

I wait for the answer, curious as to what he's going to give.

The strangest look passes over his face. "It's an escape for me. Helps me forget when I want to forget . . . things." With a smile that doesn't touch his eyes, he adds, "You think you have me all figured out."

"If pompous, philandering, narcissistic ass is what I'm thinking, then . . . yeah." I need to stop drinking. Loose lips syndrome has officially taken over. Next, I'll bring up my dirty dream.

He nods slowly. "If I don't mess around, would that make you feel better?"

"Well, it'd certainly make your girlfriend feel better," I mutter.

"What if I didn't have a girlfriend?"

I don't notice that my feet stop moving until his do as well. "You . . . broke up with Dana?"

"What if I said that I did? Would it matter to you?"

Not trusting my voice, I simply shake my head. No, in my head I know it wouldn't matter because he's still all wrong.

"Not at all?" His eyes drift to my mouth as he asks in a tone so gentle, so vulnerable, so . . . hurt, almost.

My body involuntarily reacts to him, my hands curling tighter around his neck, pulling him closer to me, wanting to comfort and assure him. What exactly do I feel for him?

The slow song has ended and moved on to a high-tempo rock song, but we're still standing chest to chest.

I know I shouldn't ask, but I do it anyway. "What you said in that note. Why?"

He looks away for a moment and I watch his jaw clench. When he meets my eyes, there's resignation there. "Because you're not a one-night girl, Irish." Leaning in to place a kiss on my jawline, he whispers, "You're my forever girl."

His hands slip away from me and he turns. With my heart pounding in my throat, I stand there and watch as he calmly walks to the table to grab his jacket.

And then he walks out the door.

chapter eleven

■ ■ ■

ATTRACTION

You're my forever girl.

I can't shake his words. Since the moment they escaped those perfect lips of his, they've hung over me. They followed me all the way home in a drunken stupor, they crawled into bed with me, and they lingered there all night to greet me the moment my eyes opened in the morning.

Moreover, I can't shake the way I've felt since he said them. Or even the way he made me feel the entire night. I can't articulate what that feeling is; I just know that it wasn't there before. And it's still here now, even though I'm sober.

I'm attracted to Ashton Henley. *There.* I've admitted it. Not to him or Reagan or anyone else, but I may as well admit it to myself and learn to deal with it. I'm attracted to my drunken one-night stand, who also happens to be an unavailable whore and my kind-of boyfriend's roommate and best friend. *Wait.* Is he available? He never answered my question. But I guess a whore is always available, so it's a moot point.

Lying here, staring up at my ceiling, I have sorted out one thing, though. My body is staging a mutiny over my mind and my heart, and consuming alcohol is like handing it a set of knives.

Reagan's moans interrupt my silent berating. "Jack bad . . ." As usual, she didn't pace herself, matching Grant drink for drink. Grant, who has at least a hundred pounds on her. "I feel like a horse's ass. I'm never drinking again."

"Didn't you say that last time?" I remind her wryly.

"Hush now. Be a good roomie and support my self-deception."

I don't feel much better, truth be told. "Alcohol really is the devil, isn't it?" My fanatical Aunt Darla may not be so crazy after all.

"And yet it makes the nights so much fun."

"We don't need alcohol to have fun, Reagan."

"You sound like an after-school special."

I groan. "Come on. We should probably get to class."

"Uh . . . which one?"

Rolling my head to the side, I can see that the red digital clock on the dresser reads one p.m. "Shit!"

■ ■ ■

"Still angry with me, Livie?" Dr. Stayner asks in that smooth, unperturbed way of his.

I kick a loose stone as I make my way to my train. "I'm not sure yet. Maybe." That's a lie. I know that I'm not. But that doesn't mean that I won't be again by the time I hang up the phone.

"You never could hold a grudge . . ." Kacey was right. He can read minds. "How are you?"

"I skipped class yesterday," I admit, adding dryly, "Doesn't sound like part of my autopilot master plan, does it?"

"Hmm . . . interesting."

"Well." I roll my eyes and confess, "Not really. I slept in. It wasn't intentional."

He chuckles. "And how do you feel, now that it happened?"

I frown. "Strangely, okay." Twenty-four hours after a mini meltdown—one where I texted my lab partner in a panic and he assured me at least five times that the prof didn't notice that I was missing and that I could borrow his notes—I'm oddly unbothered.

"You mean, like missing a class is not the end of the world?" There's a soft chuckle again.

I smile into the phone, defeated by his ease. "Maybe not."

"Good, Livie. I'm glad that you will survive this heinous offense. And how was your first day of volunteering at the hospital?" I catch the shift in his inflection. I recognize it well. It's the one where he already knows the answer but is asking me anyway.

"Livie? You there?"

"It was good. The kids are sweet. Thanks for setting it up."

"Of course, Livie. I'm a firm believer in gaining experience where you can."

"Even if I don't belong there?" I retort, my words laced with bitterness.

"I never said that, Livie, and you know that."

There's a long pause and then I blurt out, "It was hard." He waits silently for me to elaborate. "It was harder than I thought it would be."

He seems to know exactly what I mean without me saying it. "Yes, Livie. It's hard for grumpy old men like me to walk those halls. I knew it would be especially tough on you, given your nurturing spirit."

"It will get better, though, won't it? I mean," I say as I dodge a woman who's stopped in the middle of the sidewalk, looking confused, "I won't feel so . . . sad every day that I'm there, will I? I'll get used to it?"

"Maybe not, Livie. Hopefully, yes. But if it doesn't get easier, and if you decide that you want to head in a different path, find another way to help children, that's okay too. You're not failing anyone by changing your mind."

I chew the inside of my mouth as I consider that. I have no intention of changing anything and it's not as if he's encouraging me to give up. I know that. It's almost as if he's giving me permission, if I should so choose. Which I'm not doing.

"Now tell me what's going on with these boys who are chasing you."

Boys? Plural? My eyes narrow as I glance around, surveying the people in the area. "Are you following me?"

I have to wait a good ten seconds for him to stop howling with laughter before I can continue. I know what I want to ask him, but now that I'm talking to him, I feel stupid. Should I be asking the renowned PTSD therapist about something so trivial? So girly? I can hear Dr. Stayner sipping something on the other end of the phone as he waits quietly. "How do you know when a guy likes you? I mean, *really* likes you? Not just . . ." I swallow as my cheeks redden. I might start to choke on my words soon. "Not just in a physical way?"

There's a long pause. "It's usually by the things he does rather than the things he says. And if he does them without making a show of it, then he's got it bad."

You're my forever girl.

Just words. There, Dr. Stayner has confirmed it. I shouldn't be hung up on what Ashton said to me while drunk because they're just words. It doesn't mean there's anything there aside from a case of raging hormones. I feel my heart sink a little with that realization. But at least it's an answer and not the unknown.

I should stick with Connor. He's what feels right.

"Thanks, Dr. Stayner."

"Is this about that Irish fellow you met?"

"No . . ." I heave a sigh. "Ashton."

"Ah, the Jell-O thief."

"Yeah. He also happens to be Connor's best friend and roommate." And he may or may not have a girlfriend, but I leave that part out. It's already complicated.

"Well, that's quite the pickle you're in, Livie."

My only response is a grunt of agreement.

"How would you feel if this Ashton fellow was interested? More than physically, I mean."

I open my mouth, but I realize I don't have an answer aside from, "I don't know." And I don't, truthfully. Because it doesn't matter. Connor is perfect and easy. Ashton is far from perfect. I know now what Storm and Kacey mean when they call someone "sex on a stick." That's what Ashton is. He's not a forever guy. Connor is a forever guy. Well, I think he's a forever guy. It's just too soon to tell.

"Have you at least admitted to yourself that you're attracted to Ashton?"

Dammit! If I answer him truthfully, it makes it that much harder to deny. It makes it more real. "Yes," I finally grumble reluctantly. *Yes, I'm attracted to my kind-of boyfriend's man-whore best friend. I'm even having dirty dreams about him.*

"Good. Glad that's out of the way. I feared it would take months before you stopped being so stubborn."

I roll my eyes at the know-it-all doctor.

"You know what I would do in the meantime?"

My mouth twists, curious. "What?"

"I'd wear my hair in pigtails."

At least five seconds pass before I can get around my shock to ask, *"What?"*

"Boys with crushes on girls can't control themselves around pigtails."

Great. Now I'm being mocked by a psychiatrist. *My* psychiatrist. I see the station up ahead and, checking my watch, I know that the train will arrive shortly. The one that takes me to Children's Hospital so I can focus on things that matter. Shaking my head, I say, "Thanks for listening, Dr. Stayner."

"Call me anytime, Livie. Seriously."

I hang up, not sure if I feel better or worse.

■ ■ ■

"Now can you tell us apart?" Eric stands side by side next to a paler-looking Derek. He's rubbing his smooth scalp. Both of them are grinning.

I purse my lips to keep from smiling as I pull my brows together tightly. My eyes shift from one to the other and back again, scratching my chin as if I'm truly confused. "Derek?" I point to Eric.

"Ha, ha!" Eric's scrawny arms shoot out in a funny little dance. "Nope! I'm Eric. We win!"

Tilting my head back, I smack my forehead. "I'll never get you two right!"

"We shaved my head this morning," Eric explains as he skips over to me. "It's really smooth. Touch it."

I oblige, running my fingers over the faint hairline that I can still see. "Smooth," I agree.

He scrunches his nose. "It feels weird. But it'll grow back, like Derek's always does."

Like Derek's always does. My stomach muscle spasms for just a second. How many rounds of treatment has that poor kid endured? "It definitely will, Eric," I say, forcing a smile as I walk over to the table and take a seat. "So what do you want to do today?"

Derek silently takes a seat beside me. By his slower movements, I can tell he doesn't have the energy of his brother, who just started his treatments this week, according to Diane. "Draw?" he suggests.

"Sounds like a good plan. What do you want to draw?"

His forehead creases as he thinks hard. "I want to be a policeman when I grow up. They're strong and they can save people. Can I draw that?"

With a deep inhale, I smile. "I think that's a great idea."

As the boys get to work, I scan the playroom. There are several other kids here today, including a little girl in an entirely pink ensemble—pink pajamas, pink fuzzy slippers, pink handkerchief covering what I assume is a hairless head. She clutches a pink teddy bear under one arm. Someone—likely another volunteer— trails behind her as she floats from toy to toy, casting furtive glances over in our direction.

"Hi, Lola!" Eric calls out and then, leaning in to me, whispers, "She's almost four. She's okay. For a girl."

"Well, then, we should invite her to sit down with us," I say, raising an eyebrow and waiting.

Eric's eyes widen when he clues in that I'm suggesting he do the asking. A shy smile curves his mouth as he watches her out of the corner of his eye.

It's his brother, though, who turns around and says in that soft, raspy voice, "Do you want to sit with us, Lola?"

Eric scrambles to take the seat next to me, edging in a little closer, watching Lola like a hawk as she gingerly picks her way to the empty seat between him and Derek. "Feel my head, Lola," he says, leaning forward to point his smooth scalp in her face.

Giggling, she shakes her head and folds her hands under her arms, recoiling slightly.

Derek doesn't find it amusing, though, and glowers at his brother. "Stop telling people to touch your head."

"Why?"

"Because it's weird." Derek's eyes flicker over to Lola and the glower vanishes instantly. "Right, Lola?"

She just shrugs, her eyes flickering back and forth behind the two brothers, not saying anything.

Giving up on his attempt to impress Lola with his smooth scalp, Eric occupies himself with his picture, drawing a tank. His brother, though, slides a sheet forward and, holding out his box of crayons, offers, "Here, do you want to draw a picture with me?"

And that's when it hits me. Derek has a crush on little Lola. I share a look with the middle-aged volunteer who trailed her here. She winks, confirming it.

The boys and Lola color for an hour straight, using up a stack of paper as they draw themselves as everything from a policeman to a werewolf to a scuba-diver to a rock star and the entire time, I can't take my eyes off Derek as he dotes on Lola, helping her hold her crayon properly, drawing parts of her picture that are harder for a four-year-old than for an almost-six-year-old.

I watch while my heart melts and aches at the same time.

At the end of the hour, when Lola's volunteer reminds her that she needs her rest, Eric, who's busy coloring the wheels on his dump truck, hollers, "'Bye, Lola!" Derek, though, takes the picture he drew of himself as the policeman and quietly gives it to Lola for her room.

And I have to turn away before they see the tears welling.

chapter twelve

■ ■ ■

HOMESICK

"Can you believe this?" Kacey's chin settles on my shoulder from behind as we stare out onto the ocean together, our matching plum-colored silk bridesmaid dresses fluttering in the light breeze. "I still remember them going on their first date. Storm was petrified. And now here they are, getting married and having a baby."

We turn in unison to look at the stunningly beautiful couple as the photographer captures them with the sun setting in the background. Storm may be six months pregnant, but other than the cute, round bump on her abdomen and her gigantic breasts—a product of raging hormones mixed with silicone implants—she looks exactly like she always has. A Barbie doll.

A Barbie doll who, along with her adorable little daughter, stumbled into our lives when we needed it most. It's funny how some relationships can be so accidently forged and yet so perfectly matched. When Kacey and I took off to Miami, we ended up in a run-down apartment building, living next door to a bartender/entertainer and struggling single mom to a five-year-old girl. Storm and Mia. They welcomed us both into their lives without reservation, without apprehension. Because of that, I've never thought of them as neighbors or friends.

In some strange way, they've always been family.

All of them are, I admit, looking at the small crowd gathered after the sunset beach wedding outside our house. It's the biggest mixed bag of people you could imagine—our old landlord, Tanner, as awkward as ever holding his date's arm while he scratches his belly absently; Cain, the owner of the strip club where Storm and Kacey used to work, sipping on a glass of liquor as he watches Storm and Dan, a strange, proud smile touching his lips; Ben, the former bouncer at Penny's who's become a close friend to all of us, arm-in-arm with a cute blond lawyer from his firm. I have to admit, that's a welcome sight, as he's been dropping not-so-discreet hints about wanting to date me since the day I turned eighteen.

"I wish you were staying longer," Kacey moans. "We've been so busy, we haven't had a chance to talk. I feel like I don't know what's going on in your life anymore."

That's because you don't, Kacey. I've told her nothing. It's status quo as far as she's concerned—school's great, I'm great. Everything's great. I'm not telling her the truth: that I'm just plain confused. I spent the plane ride down convincing myself that this will all blow over. I need to adjust, that's all. And while I'm adjusting, I'm not taking any attention away from Storm and Dan's day.

"Kacey!" Trent's hands are cupped around his mouth as he calls my sister.

"Oh, gotta go!" She squeezes my elbow, a devilish grin curling her lips. "Make sure you're back at the house in fifteen, for their first dance." I watch her as she takes off, skipping barefoot through the sand toward a stunning Trent in his fitted tux. The first few times I met him, I couldn't be in the same room as him without sweating profusely. But, at some point, he turned into nothing more than my sister's goofy soul mate. And right now, they're up to something. I'm not sure exactly what, but by the whispers I've caught, it involves a bottle of champagne, the silver stage hoop from Penny's that Storm used to use in her "act," and an embarrassing video montage of the happy couple.

Trent and Kacey are perfect together.

I hope I have that one day, too.

I turn back toward the setting sun. And I breathe. In and out, slowly. I breathe and I relish this beautiful moment, this wonderful day, pushing all my worries and fears away. I find that it's not hard to do. The sound of waves and Mia's laughter as Ben chases her around serve as an anchor to keep me grounded.

"How is college, Livie?"

The voice surprises me and sends prickles down my spine. Turning, I find those coffee-colored eyes staring out at the ocean next to me. "Hi, Cain. It's good." Family or not, I'm still not a hundred percent comfortable around my sister's old boss. He's never done anything to warrant my unease; in fact, he's one of the most respectable men I've ever met in my life. But he's an enigma of sorts. He has that timeless look to him, both youthful and wise beyond his years. When Kacey first met him, she thought he had to be in his early thirties, but a slip of his tongue one night told us he'd just hit twenty-nine. That means he opened his first adult club in his early twenties. No one knows where he got the money. No one knows anything about his family, his background. All we know is that he makes a lucrative living off the sex trade. But according to Kacey and Storm, all he seems to want is to help his employees get on their feet. He has never crossed the line.

Although most of the dancers wouldn't mind if he did. I'm

not surprised. Cain is not only good-looking; he exudes masculine confidence—his well-cut suits, perfectly styled dark hair, and intimidating, reserved demeanor only add to his appeal. And underneath all that? Well, let's just say that the few times he's come over to enjoy the beach with us, I've noticed Dan and Trent stand a little closer to their women. Kacey says that Cain has a fighter's body. All I know is that, between the striking face, the hard muscles, and a multitude of interesting tattoos, I've been caught staring more than once.

"I'm glad. You know your sister is so proud of everything you've accomplished."

My gut tightens. *Thanks for the reminder . . .* I sense his eyes on my face now and I blush. Without looking, I know he's studying me. That's Cain. You feel as though he can look right through you.

"We all are, Livie. You've grown into one remarkable woman." He takes a sip of his drink—likely cognac, seeing as that's his alcohol of choice—and adds, "If you need any help, you know that you can call me, right? I gave you my number."

Now I do turn to look at him, to see his genuine smile. "I know, Cain. Thank you," I say politely. He said the same thing a month ago, at my farewell party. I was busy crying my eyes out alongside a hormonal Storm. I'll never take him up on it but I appreciate it, all the same.

"When do you head back?"

"Tomorrow afternoon," I say with a sigh. Not necessarily a happy sigh. The last time I left Miami, I was sad, but I had all of that nervous excitement for college to help me get on the plane. Now, I don't have the same excitement.

At least, not for the *classes* part of college.

chapter thirteen

•••

FALLING

"Your dad throws this party every year?" I ask as Reagan pays for the cab with her credit card and we hop out. Either Princeton rowing coaches get paid very well or Reagan's family has money through other means, based on the two-story house we pulled up to. It's a mix of stone and brick, with steep roofs and a matching turret. English-style gardens break up a perfectly groomed lawn and the driveway forms a large loop at the front door. A dozen or so cars are already parked around the circle, including Connor's white Audi.

"Like clockwork. Kind of a 'welcome-back-slash-we're-gonna-win-the-big-race-slash-I'm-gonna-work-your-ass-over-the-winter' gathering." I trail her as we walk around the side of the house to an equally beautiful backyard. About fifty well-dressed people mingle with drinks in hand, accepting appetizers from the servers in tuxes floating around. The crowd is predominantly male, but there are some girls around. Girl-friends, Reagan confirms.

I instinctively smooth my gray pencil skirt. Reagan described the party as "dressy but modest." I didn't bring a lot of dressy clothing suitable for the still-warm temperature, so I'm limited to a fitted skirt and a violet-colored sleeveless silk blouse with a deep dip in the back that, unfortunately, shows off my new tattoo. Reagan assured me that her parents won't think any less of me if they see it. I kept my long black hair down, all the same.

I quickly scan the group, looking for Connor. I don't know if Ashton will be here. I'd think that, being the captain, it's expected, but . . . it's also expected not to sleep around on your girlfriend, and Ashton hasn't figured that one out yet.

"Oh, Reagan! How are you?" a female voice cries out. I turn to see an older version of Reagan dash toward us, her arms extended, and it makes me smile. They're identical in height, figure, smile . . . everything.

"Great, Mom," Reagan says calmly as her mom plants a kiss on her cheek.

"How are you doing? How are classes? Have you been going out?" she asks in a quick, hushed voice. She seems a little frantic, as if she doesn't have much time to talk but needs to get information out of her daughter.

"Yeah, Mom. With my roommate. This is Livie." She directs her mom's attention to me.

"Oh, it's so nice to meet you, Livie. Call me Rachel," she says with a warm, polite smile. "My, you are pretty. And so tall!"

Heat crawls up my neck. I open my mouth to thank her, but her attention has already turned back to Reagan. "And how is the dorm? Are you getting any sleep in that tiny bed? I wish they'd make them bigger. They're not fit for people!"

As she prattles on, a snort escapes me and I quickly cover my face and pretend to cough. *Somehow your daughter's bed fits two.*

Reagan answers with a broad grin. "It's not bad. More comfortable than I had expected."

"Okay, good. I was afraid you wouldn't sleep well."

"Mom, you know I'm sleeping well. I talked to you yesterday. And the day before. And the day before . . . ," Reagan patiently says, but I catch the note of exasperation.

"I know, dear." Rachel pats her shoulder. "I have to go now. The caterers need some direction." With that, Reagan's mom sails off like a wisp of smoke in the air, swift but graceful.

Reagan leans forward. "Excuse her. I'm an only child and she's a little overprotective. And high-strung. We're weaning her off her antianxiety medication." In the next breath she starts to ask, "Are you hungry? Because we can go over there and—"

"Reagan!" a man's voice booms, cutting in.

Reagan's eyes light up and she grabs my hand. "Oh, come meet my dad!" I can barely keep up with her as she takes off toward the house at a brisk, excited pace. She's more like her mother than she wants to admit. The only time she slows down is when Grant appears out of nowhere to hand each of us a drink. "Ladies," he says with a curt bow, and then disappears as quickly as he came, giving Reagan a quick wink as he turns. One sip tells me it's loaded with Jack and I'm relieved. There's been an edge lingering at my nerves since leaving the hospital today.

Reagan continues on, cutting through a crowd of guys—grinning at them as we pass—until she reaches the covered patio area near the house, where a giant man with a gray, neatly trimmed beard and round belly—her father, I presume—stands next to Connor.

"Hi, Daddy!" Reagan squeals, leaping into his arms.

He lifts her off the ground, chuckling as she places a kiss on his cheek. "There's my baby girl."

I slide into Connor's outstretched arm for a hug as I watch
Reagan and her dad, a twinge of envy sparking in my chest.

"You look beautiful," Connor murmurs, placing a chaste kiss
on my lips.

"Thank you. You look great too." And he does. He's always
dressed well, but now he's wearing dress pants and a crisp white
dress shirt. As he smiles at me with that dimpled grin, air slowly
leaves my chest in relief. I'm noticing I'm more relaxed when
Connor is around. He just has an air about him. Easy, calm, supportive.

This is right.

"How was the hospital today?"

I tilt my head side to side as if I'm undecided. "Good. Hard
but good."

He gives my forearm a light squeeze. "Don't worry about it.
It'll be fine. You'll do great."

I force a smile as I turn back to Reagan and her father, glad
that someone has confidence in me.

"How has your first month been? Nothing too wild, I hope?"
Reagan's dad asks her.

"Nope, my roommate keeps me in check." Reagan turns to
point to me. "This is Livie Cleary, Daddy."

The man turns to regard me with kind blue eyes. He offers his
hand. "Hello, Livie. I'm Robert."

"Hi, sir . . . Robert. I'm Livie Cleary." I fumble over my words.
A nervous giggle escapes and I shake my head. "Sorry, Reagan
just told you that."

Robert chuckles. I see his eyes shift to a focal point behind
me. "Oh, thank you," he says, reaching to accept a drink.

A tall, dark figure appears to take a spot next to Robert. One
with impossibly long eyelashes and piercing brown eyes that
make my heart stutter. "You're welcome," he says politely.

Ashton is always gorgeous, even in the most basic of clothes. But tonight he has clearly respected Coach's dress code. His hair is styled in a way that looks neat and tidy while still sexy. Instead of jeans and sneakers, he's wearing black tailored pants and dress shoes. Instead of a threadbare T-shirt, he's in a midnight-blue shirt, perfectly fitted and pressed. Watching him take a sip of his drink, I see the worn leather band peeking through. That's the only thing that resembles the Ashton I've known up until now. He looks like he just stepped off the pages of *GQ* magazine.

And I don't know if it's because of this transformation or because I've finally accepted that I'm attracted to Ashton, but the discomfort that I've always felt around him is beginning to fade—or morph—into something entirely different and not at all unpleasant. Although still completely distracting.

Robert's jovial voice interrupts my thoughts. "I can feel it, boys. We've got a winning team this year." He slaps a large hand over his captain's shoulder.

Ashton responds with a genuine smile, full of respect. One I've never seen on him before.

Turning to me, Robert says, "So, Livie, you're one of Princeton's newest crop along with my daughter."

My eyes meet Ashton's before I manage to turn and focus on Robert and it makes my heart jump. "Yes, sir," I say, clearing my voice.

"And how are you liking it so far?" His gaze shifts to my waist. And that's when I remember that Connor is standing with his arm loosely around me. "None of these scoundrels bothering you, I hope?"

I smile shyly at Connor, who gives me a sly grin back. "No scoundrels," I reply, sipping the last of my drink. How did I finish it that fast? Before I can stop myself, my eyes flicker to Ashton to see his focus settled on my chest. I instinctively cross my arms, earning a wide grin from him as he brings his glass to his lips. *Maybe one scoundrel.*

"Good. They're fine young men," Robert says with an affirming nod. Then we hear a holler as Ty stalks around back in his kilt, and Robert adds, "Maybe a bit wild at times, but then what college kid isn't. Right, Grant?"

I swear, either Grant has empty-drink radar or he's watching us like a hawk, because he suddenly appears from behind to hand Reagan and me fresh Jack and Cokes. "Right, Coach."

"No alcohol in that drink, right, Cleaver?" Robert's full eyebrow is halfway up his forehead with the question.

"Not a drop," Grant says, his goofy grin replaced with a mask of sincerity.

"Of course not, Daddy," Reagan echoes sweetly.

Robert looks down at his doting daughter, who can pull off the innocent, virginal schoolgirl act better than any real one I've ever met. Better than . . . well, me, I guess. I can't tell if he believes her. All he'd have to do is lean in and sniff her drink to know that it's more booze than mixer. But he doesn't press it. "So what will you be majoring in, Livie?"

"Molecular biology."

By the way his eyebrows spike, I can tell he looks impressed.

"Livie's going into pediatrics," Connor chirps proudly.

"Good for you. And what made you choose Princeton?"

"My father went here." The answer rolls off my tongue with ease. It's as good an answer as any. In truth, I could easily have gone to Harvard, or Yale. I had acceptance letters from all of them, given my school counselors made me apply. But there was never any debate over which one I'd choose.

Robert nods as if expecting that answer. I guess he hears that a lot. It's not uncommon for several generations to attend Princeton. His brow creases as he ponders this. "What year?"

"1982."

"Huh . . . I was '81." His hand moves to scratch his beard as if he's deep in thought. "What did you say your last name was again?"

"Cleary."

"Cleary . . . Cleary . . ." Robert repeats over and over as he rubs his beard with his fingers, and I can tell he's racking his brain. I take another long sip of my drink as I watch. There's no way he knows my dad, but I like that he's trying.

"Miles Cleary?"

I choke on a mouthful of liquid and my eyes widen in surprise.

Robert seems proud of himself. "Well, how about that!"

"Seriously? You knew him? I mean—" I try to temper my excitement.

"Yes." He nods slowly, as if memories are quickly filling his brain. "Yes, I did. We were both Tiger Inn members. Went to a lot of the same parties. Irish fellow, right?"

I feel my head bobbing up and down.

"Friendly, easygoing." He chuckles lightly, and I see a hint of something like chagrin pass over his weathered face. "We dated the same girl for a short period of time." Another chuckle, and his creased cheeks flush with whatever memory that brought up. One that I'm sure I don't want to hear about. "Then he met that gorgeous dark-haired gal and we didn't see much of him anymore." His eyes narrow just a touch as he peers at my face, studying my features. "Looking at you, I'd say he married her. You look like her."

I smile and nod, averting my gaze to the ground for a moment.

"That is so cool, Livie!" Reagan squeals, her eyes wide with excitement. "We should have them over next time they're in town!"

Robert is already nodding in agreement with his daughter. "Yes, I'd love to reconnect with Miles."

"Umm . . ." Just like that, my brief balloon of excitement is deflated by reality. Yes, it would have been great to see my dad and Robert together. To have my parents over here. To watch my dad's easy laugh. But that's not going to happen. Ever. I feel Connor's arm squeeze me, pulling me tightly to him. He's the only one who knows. Now everyone will know. "Actually, he and my mom died in a car accident when I was eleven."

There's a standard "face" for that news when you deliver it. Shock, followed by some paling of the skin, followed by a lifted brow. Usually a single, small nod. I've seen it a thousand times. Robert's face follows precedent to a T, with an additional why-didn't-you-know-that-about-your-roommate glare in his daughter's direction. It's not her fault, though. I never told her. I didn't avoid telling her; it just didn't come up in conversation. "I'm . . . I'm sorry to hear that, Livie," he offers gruffly.

I try to console him with a gentle smile and reassuring words. "It's okay, really. It was a long time ago. I'm . . . good."

"Well . . ." There's that awkward silence, the reason why I generally avoid sharing this about myself in groups of people. Then Grant, who's still lingering, saves the day by switching topics to the upcoming race, freeing me from being the center of attention. Freeing me to glance up at Ashton for the first time since the conversation about my parents began.

I expect that standard face. But I don't find it there. I find his eyes locked on me with the most peculiar expression on it. A tiny smile touches his lips; lightness floats in his gaze.

There's no other way to describe it other than . . .

Peace.

■ ■ ■

"So this is what all the fuss is about."

Grinning proudly, Connor clasps my hand as we walk along Prospect Avenue—or "the Street," as it's known by everyone at Princeton—and up the steps to the impressive Tudor-style building with brown clovers decorating the front. It's Thursday night. A line already snakes outside the entrance, but Connor flashes his club ID card and gets us past with no trouble.

Pushing the heavy door open for me to pass, he gestures dramatically toward the interior. "Welcome to *the best* eating club!" Sounds of laughter and music hit me immediately.

"I imagine you all say that about your respective clubs," I tease, taking in the floor-to-ceiling dark wood paneling and antique furniture as we move through. Last Saturday, after Robert had confirmed that my dad was a member here, Connor promised to give me a tour. My nerves have been swirling ever since. "It's nice." I inhale deeply, as if the act will somehow help me sense Miles Cleary's presence lingering within the walls.

"You haven't seen anything yet." Connor smiles and holds a muscular arm out. "Tour guide at your service."

Connor shows me around the various floors of the newly expanded and renovated club, highlighting the stunning dining hall, a library, and an upstairs lounge. He saves the basement for last—an open, dimly lit garagelike space called "the taproom."

"It's not too bad in here, now," Connor says, clasping my hand as we take the stairs down. "By midnight, we won't be able to move. This is the biggest and best taproom at Princeton." He grins, adding, "And I'm *not* just saying that because I'm a member."

"Not doubting you," I murmur as I take in the scene. Plenty of laughing, smiling students—both male and female—mill around with beer in hand. A few are carrying plastic swords and masquerade ball masks. Connor says they were likely at a theme party elsewhere earlier.

The only furniture I can see are a few large green-and-white wooden tables with the eating club's logo. Somehow, I'm not surprised to find Ty at one, yelling to someone as he pours beer from a pitcher into plastic cups laid out in two pyramid shapes on opposite ends of the table.

"Hey, buddy!" Ty slaps Connor on the back with his free hand. Dipping his head toward me, he bellows in his fake Scottish accent, "Irish!" making me giggle. There's just something about Ty that's so easy. He's crass, loud, and sometimes downright perverted, but you can't help but like him. I can picture him getting along well with Kacey. Maybe that's why I feel so comfortable around him. In some strange, kilt-flashing way, Ty reminds me of home.

Connor gives Ty's shoulders a tight squeeze. "We all come here to eat most days but Ty practically lives here. He's part of the officer corps. Probably why this place is so wild. I don't know how he passes a single class."

Jutting his chin toward a textbook that's laid out open on a chair nearby, Ty's face is a mask of confusion. "I don't know what you mean. I get some of my best work done here." Tossing the empty pitcher to the ground, Ty holds up two Ping-Pong balls. "Ready?"

Connor shrugs, looking to me. "You in?"

Scanning the table again and the balls, I ask, "What is this . . . beer pong?"

Ty bangs his pint glass down to announce with a grin full of mischief, "A Beirut virgin! I love it!" He jabs a pointed finger at me. "Never call this beer pong. And no wussing out or I'll kick that beautiful butt through the door!"

"Why do I have the feeling that I'm screwed," I grumble,

taking in all those cups of beer. But I also know that Ty's threats are not idle, and trying to escape will likely involve humiliation in front of the entire club.

"Crazy Scotsman," Connor mutters under his breath, but his eyes are twinkling. Roping his arm around my waist, he starts chuckling. "Don't worry. I'm good at this game. You're safe with me."

I give his forearm a light squeeze before he lets go, an ounce of relief washing over me with the reminder. I know I'm safe with Connor. If I were with Ashton, it would be a very different story. He'd probably lose just to get me plastered. Either way, my gulps will be the smallest sips known to mankind.

"What is this, two-on-two? Who's your partner, Ty?" Connor asks.

"Who do you think?" comes the giddy response a second before a wagging honey-blond ponytail and a grin appears.

"Reagan! Thank God. Save me from this."

"No can do, roomie." She pats my back with a lazy hand while accepting a full pint from Grant with the other, shooting him a playful wink. I'm thrilled to see Reagan here tonight. Since the conversation at her parents' house, she's been unusually quiet around me. She may be mad at me for not mentioning my parents. I can't tell and she hasn't brought it up. But tonight she seems normal, and I'm glad.

Everyone's here except . . . Tucking a strand of hair behind my ear, I discreetly survey the room, looking for that tall, dark form.

"He has a big test tomorrow," Reagan murmurs with a knowing smirk. "He's not coming."

"Oh." I leave it at that, though I can't ignore the disappointment creeping through me. And then I silently scold myself. I'm here with Connor. *Connor. Connor.* How many times do I have to repeat that name before it sticks?

"Okay, Gidget!" Ty calls out. "Get over here. Connor and the virgin are goin' *down* tonight!"

My face flushes as heads turn in my direction. "I've never played this game before!" I clarify in a loud voice, though Ty's not wrong in any regard.

"Heads, we start," Ty announces as a coin flies up into the air. They win the toss and a crowd quickly forms. Apparently, Beirut is a spectator sport. I soon find out it's because you get to watch people get really drunk. Really fast.

Connor explains the basic rules—if your opponents sink a ball or you completely miss the table with your ball, you drink. Well, there are two problems with these rules for me. One: our opponents are outstandingly good, and two: I am outstandingly bad.

Even with Connor's talent at sinking balls, it's not long before Ty and Reagan are in the lead. And when alcohol-induced relaxation spreads through my limbs, my aim gets even worse, to the point that people step away from the table when it's my turn, to avoid a ball to the groin.

"You really aren't getting better at this with practice, are you?" Connor teases, pinching my waist.

I stick my tongue out in response, slyly studying Connor's ripped arms and perfectly shaped backside in a rare pair of jeans as he assesses the table, a look of concentration on his face. Almost brooding, but not quite. It's attractive. Enough so that I'm annoyed when it's interrupted momentarily by a cute blond placing her arm on his bicep. "Hey, Connor." Her smile is unmistakably flirtatious.

"Hey, Julia." He flashes those winning dimples at her but then he's immediately back to the game, studying the shot, obviously disinterested in her. Obvious enough for me and certainly for Julia, who appears crestfallen.

By the time we reach the last cup—Ty and Reagan winning—I've given up on following along. I just drink when Grant—the self-appointed referee—yells the order at me.

Connor lays a kiss on my cheek and murmurs, "You're a trouper. I think you need to get outside for some air. Come on." With an arm wrapped around my waist, partly for affection but also for support, I'm sure, Connor leads me up the stairs and through an exit to a quiet space.

"This is nice." I inhale the cool, crisp air.

"Yeah, it's getting hot and sweaty down there," Connor murmurs, his hand pushing my hair off my face. "You having fun?"

I'm sure my grin speaks for itself but I answer anyway. "Yes, this is a lot of fun, Connor. Thanks for having me here."

Planting a kiss on my forehead first, Connor then turns to lean against the wall next to me. "Of course. I've been dying to bring you. Especially now that we know your dad was a member."

I smile wistfully as I lean my head back. "Was your dad a member?"

"Nah, he was part of Cap and Gown. Another big one."

"Didn't he want you to join that one?"

Slipping his fingers in between mine, Connor says, "He's just happy that I ended up at Princeton."

"Yeah." *Just like I'm sure my dad would be . . .*

Connor appears deep in thought. "You know, I never appreciated how good I had it with my dad growing up until these last few years." There's a long pause and then he adds, "Until I met Ashton."

I had been so distracted by Beirut and the girl hitting on Connor that I'd actually managed to stop thinking about Ashton for a while. Now he's back and I feel uneasy. "What do you mean?"

Connor sighs, his face twisting as if he's deciding how to

answer. "I've been around Ash when his dad comes to see a race. He's a different person. I don't know how to explain it. The relationship is just . . . strained. That's the impression I get, anyway."

Curiosity gets the better of me. "Well, haven't you asked him?"

A snort answers my question before his words do. "We're guys, Livie. We don't talk about feelings. Ashton's . . . Ashton. I know you think he's a dick, but he's a good guy when he wants to be. He's had my back more times than I care to admit. You remember that story about me in the boat? You know . . ."

"Ass up? Yes, I remember." I giggle.

Dropping his head with a sheepish grin, Connor admits, "I think Coach would have kicked me off the team if it hadn't been for Ashton. I don't know what he said or did, but he bought my pardon somehow. I know I joke about Ash being a lousy captain but he's actually a good one. A great one. The best we've had in my three years here. All the guys respect him. And it's not just because he gets more action than all of us combined."

That earns my eye roll. I'm hating the idea of Ashton with anyone—girlfriend or otherwise—more each day, and that comment created a stomach-wrenching visual.

"Anyways, sorry for bringing Ashton up. I love the guy but I don't want to talk about him. Let's talk about . . ." He rolls around to grasp my waist with his hands. Leaning down, he slides his tongue into my mouth with a kiss that lasts way longer than anything we've ever done before. I find I don't mind it, though. I actually enjoy it, allowing my hands to rest against his solid chest. God, Connor really does have a nice body and, clearly, other girls have noticed. Why are my hormones only beginning to appreciate this tonight?

It's probably the beer.

Or maybe they're finally starting to accept that Connor could be *very right* for me.

■ ■ ■

"I did warn you," I remind her as I stretch my calf muscles.

"You can't be that bad."

I make sure she sees my grimace in response. Outside of required track and field at school, and that time Dr. Stayner had me chasing live chickens at a farm, I've avoided all forms of running. I don't find it enjoyable and I usually manage to trip at least once while doing it.

"Come on!" Reagan finally squeals, jumping up and down with impatience.

"Okay, okay." I yank my hair back into a high ponytail and stand, stretching my arms over my head once more before I start following her down the street. It's a cool, gray day with off-and-on drizzle, another strike against this running idea. Reagan swears that the local forecast promised sunshine within the hour. I think she's lying to me but I don't argue. Things have still been kind of strange between us since her dad's party. That's why, when she asked me to go running with her today, I immediately agreed, slick roads and all.

"If we take this all the way to the end and turn back, that's two miles. Can you handle that?" Reagan asks, adding, "We can stop and walk if you flake out."

"Flakes are good at walking," I say with a grin.

She sniffs her displeasure. "Yeah, well, you probably lose weight when you sneeze."

It takes a few minutes but soon we manage a good side-by-side pace, where my long, slow strides match her short, quick legs well. That's when she bursts. "Why didn't you tell me about your parents?" I can't tell if she's angry. I've never seen Reagan angry.

But I can tell by the way she bites her bottom lip and furrows her brow that she's definitely hurt.

I don't know what else to say except, "It just never came up. I swear. That's the only reason. I'm sorry."

She's silent for a moment. "Is it because you don't like talking about it?"

I shrug. "No. I mean, it's not like I avoid talking about it." Not like my sister, who shoved everything into a tomb with a slow-burning stick of dynamite. Since the morning I woke up to find Aunt Darla sitting by my bed with puffy eyes and a Bible in her hand, I've just accepted it. I had to. My sister was barely alive and I needed to focus on her and on keeping *us* going. And so, at eleven years old and still half dead from a flu that saved me from the car accident in the first place, I got out of bed and showered. I picked up the phone to notify my school, my parents' schools. I walked next door to tell our neighbors. I helped Aunt Darla pack up our things to move. I helped fill out insurance paperwork. I made sure I was enrolled in the new school right away. I made sure everyone who needed to know knew that my parents were gone.

We run in silence for a few moments before Reagan says, "You know you can tell me anything you want to, right?"

I smile down at my tiny friend. "I know." I pause. "And you know you can tell me anything, right?"

Her wide, cheery grin—with those cute dimples just under her eyes—answers for her.

I decide that this is the perfect time to divert the topic completely. "Like you can stop pretending that you and Grant aren't together." I manage to grab hold of Reagan's arm just in time to keep her from diving into the pavement. When she has regained her balance, she turns to stare wide-eyed at me, her cheeks flaming. "I thought you were impervious to blushing, Reagan."

"You can't say anything!" she hisses, her ponytail wagging as she checks to her left and right, her eyes narrowing at the bushes as if someone might be hiding behind there. "No one knows, Livie."

"Are you serious? You think no one knows?" I watch with great satisfaction as her blush deepens. "I think *everyone* knows. Or at least suspects." Connor made an offhand comment the other day about Grant chasing Reagan around. I've even noticed Ty shaking his head at them a few times and if he's clued in, then the rest of the world must be.

She bites her lip in thought. "Come on. We can't just stand here." We start back up at a light jog. "I guess it's been brewing for a while. I've always liked him and he's been flirting with me for the past year. Then I ran into him at the library one night. There was a quiet corner. No one was around . . ." She shrugs. "It just kind of happened."

"In the library!" I squeal.

"Shhh!" Her hands wave in front of her as she runs, giggling.

"But . . ." I feel my face scrunch up. "Where?" I've been to that library plenty of times. I can't think of any corner dark and secluded enough to do anything in besides read.

She grins impishly. "Why? Want to get your freak on with Connor?"

"No!" Just thinking of suggesting that to Connor makes me scowl at Reagan.

That doesn't dissuade her, though. With a quirked eyebrow, she asks, "Ashton?"

I feel the burn crawl up my neck. "There's nothing going on between us."

"Livie, I saw you two at Shawshanks the other night. I see the looks you give him. When are you going to admit it?"

"What? That I have a roommate with an overactive imagination?"

I get an eye roll. "You know that the more time passes, the harder this is going to get, right?"

"No, it won't, because nothing is going on between us!" Remembering, I ask, "Hey, did he break up with Dana?"

She shrugs. "I haven't heard anything, but with him, who knows. Ashton's a vault."

"What do you mean?"

"I mean, he could have a dozen brothers and sisters and you'd never know." Reagan breaks to chug a mouthful of water from her bottle. Wiping her arm across her mouth, she continues, "My dad makes a point of knowing his team. You know—their families, their grades, their majors, their plans after college . . . He thinks of them all as *his* boys." Thinking back to the big, burly man from the weekend and all the pats on the back and the questions, I can see what she means. "But he knows very little about his own captain. Almost nothing."

"Huh . . . I wonder why." Small alarm bells start ringing in my head.

"Grant thinks it has something to do with his mom dying."

My feet stop moving. They just stop. Reagan slows to jog in place.

"How?" I ask, taking a deep breath. Meeting other people who lost their parents always strikes a chord deep within me. Even complete strangers can instantly become friends through that kind of familiarity.

"No, clue, Livie. I only know because I was eavesdropping on him and my dad one night in our study. But that's all that my dad managed to get out of him. He has a way of evading topics. I mean . . . you've met Ashton. You know what he's like."

"Yeah, I do." With a growing pain in my stomach, I also know that not talking about things like that normally means there's a reason. A bad reason.

"Come on." She gives my butt a slap and starts moving forward again.

I'm forced to join her, though I don't feel like running anymore. I want to sit and think. Vaguely remembering what Connor told me at Tiger Inn, I ask, "Have you met his dad?"

"At the fall race. He's usually there with a woman."

"A wife?"

"I've seen a few different ones over the past four years. Maybe they're wives. Who knows? Then again, Ashton fell from that tree, so . . ." She turns to give me a pointed stare.

"And what's he like?"

"He seems normal enough." There's a pause. "Though I get a weird vibe around them together. Like Ashton's very careful about what he says and does."

So Connor's not the only one who senses something off . . .

"Anyway, so what if he did?"

"So what if he did . . . what?" I repeat slowly, not understanding.

"What if he broke up with Dana?"

"Oh." Reagan may avoid awkward situations, but she doesn't hold back on asking the hard questions. I like that about her. Right now, though, I could do without the interrogation. "Then nothing. I'm with Connor. I think."

"Yeah, what's going on with you two anyway? Have you . . ." She raises her brow suggestively.

I only shake my head and mutter, "You're as bad as my sister. No. We're taking it slow and easy."

"Sounds boring if you ask me," she mutters dryly. "I'll bet you'd take it hard and fast with Ashton."

"Reagan!" I give her a playful shove and she starts giggling. But the thought has my stomach doing cartwheels. What if I were with Ashton instead of Connor? *No.* Impossible.

"You just seem so different around Ashton. And anything to do with Ashton."

I snort. "Angry?"

She grins. "Passionate."

Desperate to get the topic off me, I ask, "So are you and Grant together?"

Deftly leaping over a puddle, Reagan says, "I'm not sure yet. We're pretty casual. Not ready to throw a label on it. Yet." She ducks her head, a shy smile touching her lips. "I'm crazy about him, though, Livie. If I see him with another girl, I'll probably go apeshit and kill them both."

I frown, trying to picture Grant with someone else. I can't, what with the way he trails Reagan like a lovesick puppy. And then I wonder if Connor is seeing other girls because we haven't put a label on anything. What if he is? Does "slow and easy" mean "open to date"? If I saw him with another girl, would I also go apeshit? The girls introducing themselves at Tiger Inn made me realize that Connor could probably have his pick of women, but it didn't really bother me. An image of Ashton kissing Dana flashes through my head and my stomach instantly falls. I know it's not right but I recognize that now for what is was, aside from shock. Jealousy. It bothered me. As did hearing that girl at the bar talk about him. And then touching his arm after.

Reagan's sigh pulls me out of my head and back into our conversation. "Whatever it is, we have to keep it under wraps until Grant is done with school."

My responding frown tells her I don't understand why.

"My dad! Aren't you listening? Oh, Livie." She gives an exasperated look. "Sometimes I wonder where your head is . . . My dad isn't crazy about him."

"Why?"

"He thinks Grant doesn't take life seriously. Grant's afraid he'll kick him off the team if he finds out."

"But . . . he's going to Princeton. How much more serious can he get?" I say with a disbelieving snort.

"Serious enough not to do it in the library with the coach's daughter," she mutters, picking up her speed.

Fair enough.

The rain has started up again. It's a light, cool drizzle and it doesn't take long to soak through my navy shirt. But I don't mind it at all. The route Reagan has chosen is a tranquil street through a Pleasantvillesque neighborhood of pretty houses and manicured lawns and large trees, just starting to change colors. It feels good to be away from campus. I feel as though a weight has fallen off my shoulders. Maybe I'm spending too much time there, letting it become a bubble. I let the quiet environment envelop me as I enjoy my escape, focusing on my breathing, surprised that I'm keeping up with Reagan as well as I am.

And I think about Ashton. I wonder about his life, about his parents, about his mother. I wonder how he lost her. Was the cause of death sudden, like a car accident? Or was it an illness, like cancer? Thinking back to our conversation that first week, to his reaction when I told him that I was planning on going into pediatrics and specifically oncology, I have to think that it was cancer.

We haven't reached the end of the street when Reagan hollers, "Let's turn around. I'm getting cold and we have almost a mile back home." She crosses the street to retrace our steps on the other side. "Do you think you can manage a bit faster? This rain sucks."

"Maybe you shouldn't trust that weather station anymore," I call out wryly, sucking back a mouthful of water. My mouth is so parched that my tongue hurts, but I don't want to overdo the liquids for fear of cramps.

"What weather station?" She glances over her shoulder to give me an impish wink as I speed up, trying to catch her. That only makes her run faster. Too fast for me, I decide, keeping a few paces behind, gazing out on the quiet road ahead. It's long, with bumps and dips that we'll need to navigate through, and I need to direct my focus or I'm liable to trip over my own feet.

On the opposite side of the street—the route we were just on—I spot a lone figure jogging. Another insane person out in this weather. My eyes flicker back and forth between the road and the silhouette as I continue. Soon, it's close enough that I can identify a male. Even closer, I see dark, shaggy hair.

It's Ashton.

With evenly paced steps, sleek movements, and a stony face, Ashton runs like a well-trained athlete. One in a drenched white T-shirt that clings to every ridge of his chest. And I can't peel my eyes off of him. My heart is already pounding from the run but now I feel an adrenaline rush coursing through my body, giving me a boost of energy. I feel like I could run ten miles today, like I could leap over cars, like I could—

My hands just barely stop my face from smashing against the sidewalk.

I guess I made enough noise in my fall to alert Reagan, because she screams my name and rushes back. "Are you all right?"

I wince as I pull myself up, a sharp pain shooting through my ankle, a sting in my palm. "Yeah, I'm—" My words end in a hiss as another pain jolts me. "I must have tripped over that ridge in the sidewalk."

She walks over to inspect the concrete and frowns. "You mean this small, imperceptible hairline crack?"

With a curse under my breath, I mutter, "I warned you."

"You did. Now what are we going to do?" Biting her bottom

lip in, she slides her phone out of her hoodie pocket. "I'll see if Grant is around. Maybe he can pick us up."

"That was impressive, Irish!" Ashton calls out between breaths as he crosses the street toward us. Reagan looks up at him in surprise—as if she hadn't noticed him running this way. I watch as her eyes drop slightly and widen. *Exactly. How on earth could you not have noticed* that *running down the street, Reagan!* She fixes me with a knowing stare, telling me that her dirty little sex-in-the-library mind has connected the dots that led to my tumble. "Hi, Ashton," she offers with a playful lilt, still looking at me.

He gives her a quick nod before crouching down on one knee. While he inspects my ankle, I listen to his ragged breaths and swallow the sudden pooling saliva in my mouth. How is there pooling saliva in my mouth? A minute ago I was parched! The pressure from his fingers, though gentle, makes me flinch, bringing me back to reality.

"Can you stand?" he asks, those gorgeous brown eyes full of concern.

"I don't know," I mumble, and struggle to get to my feet. His hands are at my waist in an instant to help me. It's immediately obvious that I'm not going to be jogging or even walking home. "I think it's sprained." I've sprained my ankle enough times to know the feeling.

"I'm calling Grant," Reagan announces, holding up her phone.

Suddenly I'm off the ground, cradled in Ashton's strong arms, and he's walking down the street, his hands somehow searing my skin through my clothes. "I'm not standing out here in the rain, waiting for Cleaver to show up," Ashton throws back.

"Where are we going?" I ask, knowing that our dorm is a mile back in the opposite direction.

Focusing straight ahead, he murmurs, "I'm taking you back

to my place, Irish." By his crooked lip, I know that the innuendo is intentional. But it quickly slides away and he murmurs in a softer tone, "Put your arm around my shoulder. It'll make this easier."

I obediently lift my arm and drape it around the back of Ashton's neck, resting my hand on his shoulder, my thumb settling next to a tear in his collar. I can feel his muscles strain under my weight. I wonder how long they can hold me.

Reagan must too because she runs up beside us to exclaim, "It's far, though!"

"Half a mile, tops. Go." He jerks his chin forward and then winks at her. "You don't want Grant seeing that ass get fat again, do you?"

Mentioning the legendary fat ass is motivation enough. Sticking her tongue out at him and shooting me a pointed look, she takes off down the street at an even faster speed than before. Leaving me alone with Ashton.

"Sorry about the sweat, Irish. You caught me in the middle of a long run," he murmurs, brown eyes darting to me before shifting back to the road.

"That's okay. I don't mind," I say, my voice cracking. And I don't, I realize, even though his body is drenched head to toe. I'm not sure if it's from rain or sweat. His hair is plastered to his head and face, but it still manages to wisp out at the ends in that sexy way. I see a droplet of water running down his cheek and I feel the urge to reach up and wipe it away but I'm not sure if that's too intimate, so I don't. But my heart still starts pounding harder than it ever was while I was running.

"Stop staring, Irish."

"I wasn't." I turn to look down the street, my cheeks burning, embarrassed to be caught. Yet again.

He jostles my shoulders slightly as he adjusts his grip.

"Do you need to put me down?"

He smirks. "Eight years of rowing makes carrying you pretty easy."

"I guess." Eight years. That definitely explains his ridiculously fit upper body. "You must really enjoy it."

With a sigh, he murmurs, "Yeah, it's relaxing, being out on the water, focused on an end goal. It's easy to shut everything else out."

Ashton's head jerks to the side. I see another raindrop running along his cheek and realize that he's trying to shake if off since he can't brush it away.

"Here," I murmur, reaching up to help him. Dark eyes flash to me with a scowl and my hand instantly recoils. I must have misread that. I shouldn't have . . . But he's not scowling at me, I soon recognize. He's scowling at the nasty red scrape across my palm that I earned with my fall. Distracted by my ankle and by Ashton, I had forgotten about it.

"You should really think about never running again, Irish," he mutters.

"And you should think about wearing more clothes while you run," I snap back, my anger flaring without warning, followed quickly by heat crawling up to my hairline.

"And why is that?"

Running my tongue over my teeth to buy myself time, I decide to ignore his question. "I could have waited for Grant."

"And died from pneumonia," he retorts in exasperation, adjusting his grip once again. The movement shakes my leg, which shakes my foot, which shoots a pain up my leg. But I fight the urge to wince because I don't want to make him feel bad.

Ashton settles into a quiet, fast-paced walk with his eyes straight ahead, and so I assume all conversation is over.

"I'm sorry about your parents." It's so quiet I almost miss it.

I peek at him from the corner of my eye to see him staring straight ahead, his face a mask.

I'm sorry about your mom, too.

It's on the tip of my tongue but I bite it back. Reagan was eavesdropping, after all. She's not supposed to know. *I'm* not supposed to know. Not unless he tells me.

So I don't say anything. I simply nod and wait in silence for him to make the next move. He doesn't, though. There's another extremely long, awkward pause, where neither of us talks. Where Ashton stares straight ahead as he walks, and my eyes shift back and forth between his face and the turning colors of the trees. Where I soak up his body heat, I'm acutely aware that I'm covered in his sweat. Where I feel his heartbeat and try to synchronize my own heartbeat against it. And then acknowledge that that is utterly ridiculous.

I can't handle this silence.

"I can't believe Reagan's dad knew them," I say casually, adding, "and that he recognized my mother in me. I didn't know that we looked that much alike."

Ashton's brow furrows deeply. "You remember what she looks like, don't you?"

"Yeah. But my parents lost all of their childhood and college pictures in a flood one year, so I never got to see her at the age I am now."

I sense my fingertips rubbing across warm skin and realize that at some point in my reverie, my hand staged a mutiny against my common sense and slid under the collar of Ashton's shirt. I watch my fingers still drawing little circles as if of their own free will. And, seeing as I'm feeling all kinds of brave today and seeing as it's a fairly innocuous question that a person who didn't know the answer would ask, I decide to ask it, keeping my voice casual and light. "What about your parents?"

There's a pause. "What about them?" He tries to sound bored but by the way his arms constrict around me, the way the muscles in his neck spasm, I know immediately that I've hit a nerve.

"I don't know . . ." Turning to look out on the road, I murmur casually, "Tell me about them."

"There's not much to tell." The bored tone has switched to annoyed. "Why? What has Reagan heard?"

Keeping my focus ahead, I take a deep breath and decide not to lie. "That your mother's . . . gone?"

I feel Ashton exhale. "That's right. She's gone." It's very matter-of-fact and doesn't invite further questions.

I don't know what makes me push my luck. "What about your father?"

"He's not . . . unfortunately." The contempt is unmistakable. "Leave it alone, Irish."

"Okay, Ashton."

■ ■ ■

By the time we reach their house, I've asked Ashton at least five more times if he wants to rest his arms and he's told me at least five more times to shut up about him needing to put me down.

And we've said nothing else.

He marches right past Reagan—freshly showered and drowning in a pair of Grant's sweats—and a curious Grant, and upstairs, past the communal bathroom, to the bathroom within his bedroom. He gently sets me on the counter.

The corresponding groan tells me he should have put me down long ago.

"I'm sorry," I mutter, guilt washing over me.

Reagan and Grant appear in the doorway as Ashton stretches his arms in front of his chest and then over his head with another groan.

"Look at those big, strong muscles," Grant says with an exaggerated lisp, reaching out to squeeze Ashton's biceps.

"Fuck off, Cleaver," he snaps, swatting his hand away. He grabs a towel from the hook and starts patting my hair and face with it.

"What! I was going to go pick you up, but Reagan said you two wanted to—" Reagan's sharp elbow to Grant's ribs shuts him up mid-sentence.

"Here. Tea." Reagan hands me a steaming mug.

One sip tells me it's not just tea. "You spiked the drink of an injured person," I state flatly, the alcohol burning in my throat. "Who does that?"

"It's better than what a lame horse gets," Reagan answers as she unlaces my shoe and slips off my sock. Air hisses through my gritted teeth. "How bad is it? Should we take you to the hospital?"

I see the purplish bruise around my instep and my swollen ankle. "No, it's just a sprain, I think."

"You're not a doctor yet, Irish," Ashton murmurs, leaning over to study it, and I see that the back of his shirt is like a second skin. Every ridge, every curve, every part of him is visible. Perfect. Where my body protected the front of him, his back took the brunt of the rain. If he's cold, though, he doesn't let on. "Let's ice it for now but if it gets worse, I'm taking you to the hospital." I nod, noting how Ashton takes over the situation, as if I have no say in the matter.

"These should help you." Grant holds up a set of crutches. Seeing my frown, he explains. "They're Ty's. He sprains his ankle at least twice a year with a party injury. It's good that he's short. They should be about the right height for you."

"He won't mind?"

"Nah, he won't need them until November. Like clockwork," Grant says, and then peers down at my foot. He smiles.

I'm suddenly self-conscious. "What?"

With a shrug, he says, "You have sexy feet, Irish." His words are quickly followed by a grunt as Reagan playfully smacks his chest.

"Stop ogling my roommate's feet!"

"Fine, let me ogle yours."

"Eww!" she squeals, ducking under his arm to tear out of the room, Grant chasing her.

"Bring some ice up!" Ashton hollers behind them, followed by, "The idiot's going to get kicked off the team," in a low mutter.

I watch him as he searches through the vanity cupboard and resurfaces with a first-aid kit in hand. "Not if the coach doesn't find out. They're happy together."

Ashton freezes. It's a good four seconds before his hands start moving again, pulling out antiseptic and bandages. "Do you want to call Connor to let him know you're here?"

Connor. "Oh, yeah." I hadn't even thought about calling him. I kind of forgot about him . . . Not kind of. Completely. "He's working on that paper at the library, right? I don't want to disturb him."

Cradling my injured hand in his, he looks up to ask me quietly, "Are you sure?"

And I get the feeling that he's asking me something entirely different. Am I sure about Connor, perhaps.

The atmosphere in the room feels thicker suddenly, as my lungs work hard to drag air in and push it out, those dark eyes of his searching mine for an answer. "I think so," is all I can manage.

He shudders, and I remember again that he's sopping wet. "You need to change. You're going to get sick," I murmur, my eyes pointedly on his shirt.

Setting my injured hand down, he reaches back over his shoulders and pulls his shirt forward and over his head. Tossing it to a corner, he turns back to take my hand. And I'm facing the chest that I've not been able to dislodge from my brain for weeks. The one that instantly makes my breath hitch. The one that I've never had a chance to stare at so blatantly while sober. And I do stare now. Like a deer caught in headlights, I can't seem to turn away as I take in all the ridges and curves.

"What does that mean?" I ask, jutting my chin toward the inked symbol over his heart.

Ashton doesn't answer. He avoids the question completely by sliding his thumb across my bottom lip. "You have a bit of drool there," he murmurs before turning his focus back to the scrape across my palm, allowing my face to burn without scrutiny.

"It's not as bad as it looks," I hear myself mutter as he shifts my palm over the sink. The leather band around his wrist catches my eye, the one he doesn't seem to take off. Ever. Reaching over to tap it with my free hand, I ask, "What's this for?"

"A lot of questions today, Irish." By the way his jaw clenches, I know it's another answer hidden in his vault.

Reagan was right. He doesn't talk about anything personal. With a sigh, I watch him unscrew the cap off the antiseptic and hold my hand out. "It doesn't even—" The word "hurt" was supposed to come out of my mouth. Instead, a string of obscenities to make a lifelong sailor proud shoot out. "What the fuck are you doing? Shit! You don't pour it on like that, you fucking jackhole! *Fuck!*" I'm seething in pain, the sting agonizing.

Ashton isn't paying any heed, turning my hand this way and that to examine it closer. "Looks clean."

"Yeah, because you just bleached the shit out of it!"

"Relax. It'll stop stinging soon. Distract yourself by staring at me while we wait for this to settle down. That's how you got yourself into this mess to begin with . . ." Amused eyes flash to

mine for a second before dropping back to my hand. "Nice combination there, by the way. 'Fucking jackhole'? Really?"

"I meant it in the nicest possible way," I mutter, but it isn't
long before I'm fighting my lips from curling into a smile. I guess
it *is* kind of funny. Or it will be when I can walk again . . . Determined not to give in to temptation, I let my eyes roam the small
bathroom, taking in the tiles in the glass shower stall, the soothing off-white walls, the white fluffy towels . . .

And then I'm back to Ashton's body because, let's face it,
it's so much more appealing than tile and towels. Or anything
else, for that matter. I study the black Native American–style
bird on his inner forearm. It's big—a good five inches long,
its details intricate. Almost intricate enough to hide the ridge
beneath it.

The scar.

My mouth opens to ask but then firmly shuts. Peering up
at the sizeable Chinese script on his shoulder, I can see another
ridge skillfully covered. Another hidden scar.

I swallow the nausea rising in my throat as I think about the
day my sister came home with a giant tattoo of five black ravens
on her thigh. It covers one of the more unpleasant scars from that
night. Five birds—one for each person who died in that car that
night. Including one for her. I didn't know what it meant at the
time. She didn't tell me until two years ago.

With a heavy sigh, my eyes shift to the symbol on his chest
once again to study it more closely.

And see another ridge so expertly concealed.

"What's wrong?" Ashton asks as he unwraps a bandage.
"You're pale."

"What—" I catch myself before I ask what happened, because I won't get an answer. I avert my gaze to my scraped hand

to think. Maybe it's nothing. It's probably nothing. People get tattoos to cover scars all the time . . .

But everything in my gut tells me that it's not nothing.

I watch him affix the bandage over the scrape. It's no longer stinging, but I'm not sure whether that's due to time or the fact that my mind is working on overdrive, twisting and turning the puzzle pieces to see how they fit together. But I'm missing too many. Simple things like that leather band . . .

The leather band.

The leather band.

It's not a leather band, I realize, peering closely at it.

I grab Ashton's hand and hold it up to inspect the thin dark-brown strap—the stitching around the edges, the way the two ends meet with little snaps—to see that it likely was a belt at one time.

A belt.

A small gasp escapes my lips as my eyes fly from his arm to his shoulder and finally land on his chest, at the long scars hidden beneath the ink.

And I suddenly understand.

Dr. Stayner says that I see and feel others' pain more acutely than the average person because of what I went through with Kacey. That I react to it more intensely. Maybe he's right. Maybe that's why my heart drops and nausea stirs in my stomach and tears trickle silently down my cheeks.

Ashton's low whisper pulls my attention to his face, to see the sad smile. "You're too smart for your own good, you know that, Irish?" I catch his Adam's apple bobbing up and down. I'm still holding his wrist, but he doesn't pull away from my grasp. He doesn't pull away from my stare. And when my free hand reaches up to settle on his chest, over the symbol, over his heart, he doesn't flinch.

I want to ask so many questions. *How old were you? How many times? Why do you still wear it around your wrist?* But I don't. I can't, because the image of a little boy flinching against the belt beneath my fingertips brings the tears on faster. "You know you can talk to me about anything, right, Ashton? I won't tell anyone," I hear myself whisper in a shaky voice.

He leans in to kiss away one tear on my cheek and then another, and another, shifting toward my mouth. I don't know if it's the intensity of this moment—with my heart aching for him and my body responding and my brain completely checking out—but when his lips settle at the edge of mine and he whispers, "You're staring at me again, Irish," I automatically turn to meet them.

He responds immediately, wasting no time closing his mouth over mine, forcing it open. I taste the salt from my tears as his tongue slides in and curls against mine. One hand comes around to grip the back of my neck as he intensifies the kiss, pushing my head back to get closer, deeper. And I let him because I want to be close to him, to help him forget. I don't worry about how I'm doing, whether I'm doing it right. It has to be right if it feels like this.

My hand never moves from his chest, from the heart that races beneath my fingers, as this single kiss seems to go on forever, until my tears are dry and my lips are sore and I've memorized the heavenly taste of Ashton's mouth.

And then he suddenly breaks free, leaving me panting for air. "You're shivering."

"I hadn't noticed," I whisper. And I hadn't. I still don't.

All I notice is this pounding heart beneath my fingers and the beautiful face in front of me and the fact that I'm struggling to breathe.

Scooping me into his arms, he carries me out to his room, setting me down on his bed. With purpose, he marches over to his dresser, pushing his door shut as he passes. I don't say anything. I don't even look around the room. I simply stare at the definition of his back, my mind blank.

He walks over to drop a simple gray shirt and pair of sweatpants beside me. "These might fit you."

"Thank you," I mumble absently, my fingers running over the soft material, my mind reeling.

I can't explain the next few moments. Maybe it's because of what happened a month ago and what just happened in the bathroom, but when Ashton demands, "Arms up, Irish," my body obeys like a well-trained soldier moving in slow motion. I gasp as I feel his fingertips curl under the bottom of my shirt and lift the damp material up, up . . . until it's sliding over my head, leaving me in my pink sports bra. He doesn't gawk at me or make some remark to make me nervous. He quietly unfolds the gray shirt next to me and pulls the collar over my head and then slides it down over my shoulders. My arms aren't in it yet when Ashton kneels in front of me. Swallowing, I watch his face as his hands glide under the shirt to the back of my bra, deftly unhooking the clips, all while his eyes are on mine. Pulling it out to toss on the floor, he waits for me to ease into the sleeves.

"Stand," he says softly, and again my body responds, putting one hand on his shoulder for support to protect my sprained ankle. The shirt is at least five sizes too big and it hangs halfway down my thighs. So when his hands reach up to seize the waistband of my pants and tug them down, I'm not exposed. But he's still on his knees and his eyes are still locked on mine. They never wander. Not as my pants reach the floor. Not as his hands glide back up, gripping my thighs as they climb under my shirt to my underwear. A second gasp escapes me as his fingers hook under the elastic band. He pulls them down until they simply fall to the ground. With a sharp intake of air, he squeezes his eyes shut tightly for a moment before opening them.

"Sit," he whispers, and I do.

He breaks his gaze just long enough to gently slip my damp clothes off around my injured ankle. Unfolding his track pants, he eases them around my ankles and pulls them up as far as he can. "Stand, Irish." I do as asked, using him for support again as he slides them up and ties the drawstring tight. Never once touching me inappropriately.

And if he had tried, I don't think I would have stopped him.

When he's done, when I'm dressed and breathless and un-sure of what happened but still standing there in front of him, he reaches down to take my hand. He lifts it up and places it flat over his heart, just as I had done earlier. Only he holds it there, his hand covering mine completely, trembling from cold or something else, his heart pounding too. I look up into sad, resigned eyes.

"Thank you."

Swallowing my ball of nerves, I whisper, "For what?"

"For helping me to forget. Even for a little while." Giving my knuckles a kiss, he adds, "This can't work, Irish. Stick with Connor."

My stomach drops as he releases my hand. Turning, he walks toward the bathroom, his body rigid, his head bowed forward slightly, as if in defeat.

I'm afraid if I don't ask now, I'll never be able to again. "What does a 'forever girl' mean?"

His feet falter as he reaches the doorway, one hand on the handle, the other coming up to seize the frame, the bulge in his bicep tightening. His body sways forward into the bathroom and I assume I'm not getting an answer.

"Freedom." He shuts the door behind him.

My forever girl. My freedom.

All I can do is grab the crutches that are laid out on the bed and hobble out of there. I need time to think, and thinking around Ashton isn't possible.

This can't work, Irish. Stick with Connor.

Dammit. Connor.

I forgot about him. Again.

chapter fourteen

■ ■ ■

JUST SPIT IT OUT

"I went jogging. You know, trying out something new. Having fun."

"Oh yeah? And did you have fun?"

"I'm on crutches, Dr. Stayner. I sprained my ankle."

"Hmm. Well, that doesn't sound like much fun. But neither is jogging."

"No, it's pretty much the opposite of fun." Between ice packs and classes and a few awkward shower moments with Reagan, the last week and a half has been a nightmare. I missed my volunteer hours last Saturday because I was in too much pain. I would be missing this week as well if Connor hadn't offered to drive me.

"How is everything else?"

"Confusing."

"Which boy is confusing you?"

"Which one do you think?" I mutter as I watch for Connor's white Audi. I told him I'd wait for him on this park bench so he could just pull up to the curb and let me hop in. I'm still so thankful that he's taking an entire Saturday away from his schoolwork for me. I know he has a giant paper due next week.

And I don't deserve him after what I let happen with Ashton. His best friend.

I've chalked it up to temporary insanity. A momentary lapse in judgment brought on by a simultaneous full-scale Ashton assault on both my heart and my libido.

Once I escaped the situation, Grant drove Reagan and me back to the dorm, where I struggled between icing my foot, pretending to study, squirming under Reagan's penetrating stare, and setting my memories of the afternoon on repeat.

And I've continued doing basically that—missing some classes in the process—for the past eight days. I've steered clear of Ashton. He hasn't come looking for me, which is good, because I can't handle seeing him while I'm dealing with the overwhelming shame I feel around Connor. Connor swings by to check up on me every day, bringing me flowers and cupcakes and a "get well" bear. It's as if he has a "how to make Livie explode with guilt after secretly making out with my best friend" list and he's checking the boxes off one by one. Guilt that makes my teeth grit to keep from blurting out my string of indiscretions, guilt that makes me pepper him with kisses—so many kisses that my lips have started to swell.

The problem is that no amount of kisses I share with Connor can match the intensity of the one I shared with Ashton. It's the reason that I almost came clean.

But I can't do it. I'm too scared. I'm too weak. I'm afraid that I could be throwing away a great thing—*the* thing—for one heat-of-the-moment kiss that will never happen again anyway. Connor did say "slow and easy," after all. That could easily be interpreted as "open." If I say it enough times in my head, I might start to believe it.

Or I could pretend that the incident with Ashton never happened. Block it out completely.

"Care to tell me what happened?" Dr. Stayner asks casually. "No judgment here, of course."

Sighing, I mutter, "I can't." I'm afraid that if I start talking, I'll divulge Ashton's secret. I promised him that I wouldn't tell anyone.

"Okay . . . well, how can I help?"

"You can't. I just need to stay away from him. I think he's broken. Like Kacey broken."

"I see. And you, being the person that you are, have gotten emotionally involved before you realized it."

"I think that's what this is . . ." When my heart aches every time I think of him, when I play out a dozen scenarios for how Ashton became the way he is, when I want to hunt his father down and scream at him? Yeah, I'm pretty sure that's what it means.

"That, coupled with your attraction to him, helps things get out of control quickly, especially if you're carrying on this relationship with his best friend."

I dip my head in embarrassment because, once again, my mind-reading shrink has in two sentences summed up a week of inner turmoil. "I can't let myself get sidetracked by a hot guy and his issues. It's too distracting. I need to just avoid him for the next . . . year."

"That will be difficult, given that he lives with Connor."

"Better than the alternative," I mutter under my breath, rubbing my forehead.

"Hmm . . ." There's a long pause, and then I hear Dr. Stayner clap his hands. He must have me on speakerphone. "That's it! I know what your task is for this week."

"What? No task, Dr. Stayner. You said no more. You said—"

"I lied. You will find five of Ashton's redeeming qualities."

"Have you not been listening to me?"

In true Dr. Stayner fashion, he ignores my question. "As part of your task, you will say what you're thinking at all times. The truth. Don't overanalyze, don't choose your words. Just spit it out. And if he asks you a question, you have to answer it honestly."

"What? No. Why?"

"Let's call it an experiment."

"But . . . No!" I sputter out.

"Why not?"

Because what I'm thinking about around Ashton usually involves his body parts! "Because . . . no!"

"I expect a full report in a month's time."

"No. I'll barely even see him this month. I have exams. I'm busy."

"I'm sure you will."

"No."

"Work with me."

I set my jaw stubbornly. "I've always worked with you, Dr. Stayner. This time I'm saying no. It's a bad idea."

"Good. One month."

"You can't make me."

"Oh no?"

I purse my lips as I inhale deeply. "I could lie to you."

"And I could show up at your dorm with a straitjacket and your name painted on it."

I gasp, feeling my eyes widen. "You wouldn't . . ." He totally might.

"Let's not find out, shall we? One month, Livie. Get to know him."

"What about Connor?"

"I didn't say jump Ashton's bones as part of the 'getting to know him' process."

I cringe. "Ohmigod."

"Sorry, that's what my boys say. Is that not cool?"

"Nothing about this conversation is cool, Stayner," I moan. "I should go. Connor will be here any minute."

"Just trust me on this one, Livie. Just one more time. It's a good idea."

"Uh-huh." With goodbyes, we hang up our phones. My face falls into my palms as I wonder how I got myself into this. I'm not doing it. I refuse. He can come with a straitjacket. It'll fit me flawlessly by then. The ironic thing is that I blurt out things I shouldn't half the time I'm with Ashton but it's never intentional. If I said *everything*...

A horn honks.

I look up, expecting to see the white Audi. But there's a sleek black four-door with shiny silver rims instead. The driver side opens and a tall, dark figure in a trendy fall leather jacket and aviator sunglasses steps out and stalks around the car to open the passenger door. "Irish! Get in."

And I decide that Dr. Stayner is an evil wizard with a crystal ball and puppet strings attached to his fingers. He has somehow masterminded this entire situation. He's definitely cackling in his office right now.

Cars are honking behind Ashton's car. "Come on." There's a touch of irritation in his tone.

"Dammit," I mutter, making my way to the waiting car, keeping my gaze on the tan leather interior as I hand my crutches to him. His fingers graze mine as he takes them, sending an electric current through my arm. By the time I've eased into my seat and secured my seat belt, Ashton is sliding into the driver side and my pulse is racing.

"How's your ankle?" he asks as he pulls into traffic, his eyes shifting to my legs. I'd decided to wear a short pleated skirt because nylons are easier on my ankle than socks and pants. Now, as a flash of me straddling Ashton and a skirt around my waist hits me, I'm wishing I were in a one-piece snowsuit.

"Better. I've started to walk on it a bit." The car is a sauna compared to the crisp air outside, I note, shimmying out of my jacket. "Mild sprain. Like I thought."

"Connor said you went to the hospital?"

Oh, yeah. Connor. "What are you doing here?" I blurt out and then take a breath. "I mean, what happened to Connor?"

He shrugs. "He has a paper due on Tuesday, so I told him I'd drive you. Are you okay with that?"

"Oh. Of course. Thanks." And I'm a big fat jerk now. I would have missed another week with the twins if it weren't for Ashton. He's being nice. He'd already proven that he's capable of that by carrying me half a mile in the rain. Now he's driving me all the way into Manhattan.

"No big deal, Irish," he murmurs, following the signs to the highway.

I quietly play with my coat zipper as I wonder what Dana would say about all of this. Would it bother her? Are they even still together? He never did confirm or deny it. Should I ask him?

I glance over at Ashton to find him staring at my chest.

"Watch the road!" I snap with a start as heat crawls up my neck, folding my arms over myself.

With a smile of amusement, he says, "So you're allowed to stare at me but I can't even look at you?"

"That's different. I'm not naked."

"I wasn't naked when you did a nosedive on the sidewalk, either."

I shift my body away from him to stare out the window, shaking my head. *I can hear you laughing from here, Dr. Stayner.*

"Hey." Ashton's hand rests on my forearm. "I'm sorry, okay? I'm just . . . I haven't seen you in a while."

I realize how good that simple gesture feels and how much I've missed him. I nod, and look up to see sincere brown eyes on me. "Watch the road," I warn again, softer this time and much less irritated.

I get the trademark crooked smirk that I'm finding less arrogant and more playful now. He gives my arm a tiny squeeze before letting go.

"Thanks for giving up your Saturday for me."

"It's nothing," he murmurs, checking his side-view mirror as he changes lanes. "I know it's important to you." He adds with a hint of hesitation, "I have an appointment later, so I was going to be in Manhattan anyway."

"An appointment?"

A crease furrows Ashton's brow. "You looked upset back there, before I picked you up. Why?"

Avoiding my question. I heave a sigh.

"Uh, nothing. Just had a weird phone conversation." I busy myself with folding my jacket over my lap.

"Who's Dr. Stayner?"

My hands freeze. "*What?*"

"You just mumbled, 'I can hear you laughing from here, Dr. Stayner.' Who's Dr. Stayner?"

"I . . . uh . . . he's . . ." *I said that out loud! I'm already blabbing my thoughts without realizing it! Puppet strings! Gah! Ohmigod. Did I just say this out loud too?* From the corner of my eye, I check Ashton's expression. He's glancing between me and the road with a quirked brow. *I can't tell. I need to stop thinking. All thinking must stop!* "Relax, Irish! You've got crazy eyes. Kind of freaking me out now."

I can't tell. I don't think so. Forcing myself to take a few deep breaths, I will my eyes back into my head.

"By your reaction, I'm guessing he's a psychiatrist?"

Kacey was right—you're not just a pretty face.

"You think I have a pretty face, Irish?"

I slap my hand over my mouth. I did it again!

When his laughter dies down, Ashton lets out a heavy sigh. "So . . . you're in therapy?"

Do I want Ashton to know about Dr. Stayner? How do I even answer his question? Technically I'm not in therapy but, yes, Dr. Stayner is a psychiatrist. One that I may or may not have on speed dial. In any case, explaining Dr. Stayner and the last four months will make me sound like a wack job.

"It's a really long drive to New York," he warns me, strumming his fingers over the steering wheel.

I shouldn't have to explain anything to Ashton. It's none of his business. He has his secrets and I have mine. But maybe this is an *in*. Maybe talking about my issues will help him talk about his. And, given all the time I've spent trying to puzzle him out, I need an in . . .

"Yes, he's my psychiatrist," I say quietly as I stare out at the road. I can't meet his eyes right now. I don't want to see judgment there.

"And why are you seeing a psychiatrist?"

"My unruly sex drive?"

"Irish . . ." The way he says my nickname makes me glance in time to catch him lift in his seat and tug at his jeans slightly, as if to make himself more comfortable. "Tell me."

Maybe there's some negotiating to be had here. "Only if you tell me why you call me Irish."

"I told you I'd explain that, but first you have to admit that you want me."

My mouth clamps shut. No, there's no negotiating with Ashton.

"Seriously, Irish. Tell me about your shrink." There's a pause. "Unless you want explicit details about *my* unruly sex drive and how you can help me with it." He says it in a gravelly tone, the one that makes my mouth instantly dry and my thighs warm, as images of the first night and last week and my dream collide into one embarrassingly hot mess in my head. Damn Ashton! He knows exactly how to make me squirm. He enjoys it, too, laughing softly as my face turns red. Suddenly talking about Dr. Stayner doesn't seem so embarrassing at all.

"You won't tell anyone?"

"Your secrets are safe with me." By the way his jaw tightens, I instantly believe him.

"Okay. Back in June, my sister had this crazy idea . . ." At first my explanation is full of stilted sentences. But as I get further into it—as Ashton's cute chuckles grow more frequent, hearing how I spent my summer with Kacey swan-diving off a bridge and grocery-shopping in matching Oscar Mayer wiener costumes— it gets easier to talk, easier to divulge, easier to laugh about it.

Ashton doesn't interrupt me once. He doesn't make me feel stupid or crazy. He simply listens and smiles and chuckles quietly as he drives. He's actually a great listener. That's a redeeming quality. *One down, four to go.*

Shaking his head, Ashton murmurs, "This guy sounds like a lunatic . . ."

"I know. Sometimes I wonder if he's even licensed."

"Why do you keep talking to him, then?"

"He's cheap?" I joke feebly. In truth, I've asked myself that question a thousand times. There's only one answer I can come up with. "Because he feels it's important and I owe him for my sister's life. You don't understand what . . ." My words drift as I swallow the sharp lump in my throat. "My sister was in the car accident that killed my parents. It was bad, Ashton. Four other people died. And she almost did." I pause to study my entwined fingers in my lap. Talking about it is still hard for me. "In a way, she *did* die that night. She was in the hospital for a year before she was strong enough to be released . . ." I can't help the derisive snort and shake of my head, still bitter with the doctors who discharged her. *Strong enough* . . . What was she strong enough for? Lifting bottles and bongs to her lips? Pleasing more guys than I ever want to know about? Beating the hell out of a bag of sand? "My sister was lost for a long time. Years. And then Dr. Stayner—" I swallow as tears well in my eyes, trying to keep them at bay. A few slip out anyway. I rush to wipe them away but Ashton's hand somehow beats me, his thumb brushing against my cheek quickly and gently before it pulls back to rest on his thigh again. "Dr. Stayner brought her back to me."

There's a very long but easy silence as I gaze out at the blue skies above and the bridge that will take us to Manhattan. "Wow, we're already here," I murmur absently.

"Yeah, you wouldn't shut up," Ashton mutters dryly, but he throws me a wink. "So that was who you were talking to before I picked you up?"

"Yeah."

"What was so weird about it? What were you talking about?"

I sigh heavily. "You." I notice his one hand grip the steering wheel tightly when I admit that and I quickly confirm, "I didn't tell him anything about . . . that." My eyes flitter to the leather strap around his wrist. "I promised you I wouldn't."

His Adam's apple bobs with his swallow. "Well, then why were you talking about me?"

I look out the window with a groan. "This is so embarrassing."

"More embarrassing than what you've already told me?" Ashton leans forward in his seat, fully intrigued, a curious smile on his face.

"Maybe." Do I tell him? I stall by scratching my neck and tucking my hair behind my ears, and rubbing my forehead until Ashton finally grabs my fidgeting hand and rests it on the low console between us.

I clear my throat and I can't help but notice that my hand is still in his. When he sees me looking at it, he squeezes tight.

"I'll let go when you tell me."

"And if I don't?"

"Then good luck explaining to Connor why we're holding hands."

"Holding hands is the least of my worries," I mutter, before I look him straight in the face and admit, "I'm supposed to find five good qualities about you."

His face twists up into an *is-that-all* look. "Why is that embarrassing?"

Looking up at the ceiling, I mutter, "Because I also have to tell you everything I'm thinking."

There's a long pause. Ashton adjusts himself in his seat, sliding his pelvis down so he's slouching more, his leg bent a little more steeply. And then a wide, mischievous grin spreads across his face. "This is going to be fun."

I'm already shaking my head in response. "No, it's not, because I'm not doing it."

"What?" Ashton sits up straighter, glancing at me with wide eyes. "You have to!"

"No . . ." I pry my hand out of his and fold my arms over my chest. "I don't."

"Well, then, how are you going to know what my five best qualities are?"

"I'm sure you'll tell me," I answer in a wry tone.

He shrugs as if pondering that. "You're right, I could. Let's see . . ." He runs his tongue over his teeth, and the knot in my stomach warns me that I'm going to regret this. "There's the way I make a woman scream when I slide my—"

"Shut up!" He grunts as my fist flies out to punch him in the shoulder.

"Seriously, Irish. Come on. This will be fun!" Ashton's eyes sparkle, and his face beams with genuine excitement. I've never seen him this happy before, and I'm about to agree to anything, including Dr. Stayner's insanity.

Until he asks, "So, do you dream about me?"

My teeth immediately clamp down on my tongue. Hard.

■ ■ ■

"You can let me out in front and I'll just hop out," I say as I realize he's planning on parking.

He frowns. "Oh, no. I'm coming in."

"Oh, is your appointment here?" *Is Ashton sick? Does he need a doctor?*

"No. I have a couple of hours to kill." There's a pause. "I figured I could meet these kids you come all the way out here to see."

"You can't." I feel as if there are two worlds colliding that need to be kept separate.

"Are you ashamed to be seen with me, Irish?"

"No, I mean . . ." I turn to see a hint of hurt in his eyes. *Never.* "They won't just let anyone in, though."

He pulls into a spot. "Don't you worry your pretty little head about that, Irish. They'll let me in."

■ ■ ■

"I, um, I brought someone. I hope—" I stare at Gale blankly. I don't know what to say.

She looks from me to Ashton and she's already shaking her head. Relief ripples through my body. I don't think my emotions can handle a bunch of sick kids and Ashton at the same time.

But then he flashes that sexy crooked smile and those dimples. "Hi, I'm Ashton. I'm actually here on behalf of my father, David Henley of Henley and Associates."

Whatever Gale was going to say fell out of her mouth. "Why, that's fantastic! We're so appreciative of your father's contributions here. It's a pleasure to meet you." Glancing from left to right, she says, "Normally we don't allow visitors in there, but I can let it slide this time."

"Great." *So not great.*

"The twins are eager to see you, Livie."

"I've missed them too." Gesturing at my foot, I add, "I'm sorry about last weekend."

"Oh, no worries. Glad to have you mobile. Have fun!" Waving her stack of folders in front of me, she says, "Back to work for me!" and strolls away in the opposite direction. She glances back once and, checking to see that Ashton has already turned and is walking toward the elevator, she winks at me, mouthing "wow."

I feel my face blanch. Now everyone is going to think we're together.

I catch up to him just as he hits the elevator button. "So you knew that dropping your dad's name would get you in here?"

The charm from a moment ago has vanished, replaced by contempt. "At least it's good for something."

"That's . . . nice of him to donate to the hospital." Based on Gale's knowing his name immediately, he must be a significant contributor.

"Tax savings. And for his image." I look down to see him fingering the belt strap. I can't help myself. I reach up and give his arm a squeeze.

The elevator doors open. Stepping in behind me, Ashton hits the floor button that I call out and murmurs, "It was either that or I take that nurse into a back room for a few minutes and—"

"Ashton!" I slap his forearm and flinch with the impact. Rowing has given him rock-solid everything. "Definitely a strike against your good traits."

"Oh, come on. You don't actually believe I'm serious, do you?" he says with a low chuckle.

"As a red sock on your door . . ."

A pained expression fills his face. "That night was to forget about you. With Connor," he says softly. "And I haven't done anything like that since."

Do I believe him? "Why not?"

Turning to me with a heated gaze, Ashton's hand lifts to cup my chin, his thumb stroking over my lip. "I think you know exactly why not, Irish."

"Are you still with Dana?"

That hoarse tone is back, the one that makes my skin prickle. "What if I say no?"

"I . . . I don't know." I hesitate before asking, "Why did you say we can't work?"

His lips part and I think I'm going to get an answer.

"Your tits look fantastic in that shirt."

Not that answer.

He steps out of the elevator and holds the door while I hobble out, beet-faced. Typical Ashton evading. I bite my tongue and ignore him until we reach the playroom entrance.

A new wave of anxiety hits me, the same tightness in my chest that I feel every time I'm around these kids, only it's amplified now. "Okay, there are a few ground rules before I let you near these sweet little boys."

"Let's hear them."

"One"—I count on my fingers for emphasis—"no talking about death. No engaging in death talk, no hinting at death."

His mouth slants into a tight-lipped frown as he nods. "No worries there."

"Two—don't teach them a bunch of bad words."

"Aside from what they've already learned from you?"

Rolling my eyes, I say, "Three—be nice to them. And don't lie. They're just little boys."

A cloud passes over his face but he doesn't say anything.

I push through the door to find the twins on the floor with their LEGOs. Eric looks up first. Nudging his brother, they scramble to their feet and walk over to meet me. It's been two weeks since I last saw them and I note that they're both moving a touch more languidly, their voices a little less chipper.

"Hey, you guys!" I say as I force the sudden knot of nerves down, hoping the change in them is just the chemo.

"What happened?" Derek asks, his hand gripping my right crutch.

"I tripped and sprained my ankle."

"Is he your boyfriend?" Eric asks, pointing at Ashton.

"Uh, no. He's a friend. This is—"

"You're friends with a boy?" Eric cuts me off.

I glance up at Ashton, thinking about everything that's happened between us. "Yes, I suppose I am."

Ashton leans down and sticks his hand out. "Call me Ace. That's what my friends call me."

They both look up at me in question and I laugh, remembering just how young they really are, before I nudge my head slightly toward Ashton.

Eric takes Ashton's hand first, gesturing him forward like he's got a secret to whisper in his ear. Of course, a five-year-old's whisper might as well be through a megaphone. "What's wrong with you? Livie's really pretty for a girl."

I try not to laugh. Ashton's eyes flicker to me and there's a mischievous twinkle in them. A twinge of panic hits me. Of all the ways he could answer this question . . .

"I've tried, little buddy. But Livie doesn't like me very much."

"She's your friend but she doesn't like you? Why not?" Derek asks, a deep frown creasing his forehead.

Ashton shrugs. "I don't know. I've tried as hard as I can, but . . ." Then his shoulders slouch a bit and his smile falters, playing the role of wounded boy to Academy Award perfection.

The twins cock their heads and stare at me in eerie unison. "Why don't you like him, Livie?" Derek asks.

And I have turned into the villain here.

"Good question. Let's try and figure it out, guys." Ashton leads them over to a kids' table as I catch Diane's attention with a wave. "Gale said it was fine," I call out, pointing at Ashton.

With a wink, she shifts her focus back to her kid, but I don't miss the frequent and curious glances at Ashton. It's the same kind of glance he earned from Gale, and from the nurses along the hall, the female parking attendant, and two doctors . . . one of them male.

I lean my crutches against the wall and gingerly step over to the table where Ashton has already made himself comfortable, his long legs stretched out and his leather jacket lying next to his feet. He pats the chair next to him for me. I take it, not because I want to sit beside him so much as I want to elbow him in the ribs if I have to.

The boys pull two chairs up to face Ashton, and by the serious expressions on their faces, they think they're about to uncover a major problem. "So, boys," Ashton leans forward on his elbows. "Any guesses?"

"Do you like puppies?" Derek asks in a quiet voice.

"Yup."

"Are you strong? Like Superman?"

"I don't know about Superman, but . . . " Ashton flexes his arms and, even through his thin charcoal shirt, I can see the ripples form. "What do you think?"

Both boys reach up to touch his arms and they mouth "wow" at the same time. "Feel his muscles, Livie."

"Oh, no." I wave away, but Ashton is already grabbing my hand and placing it on his bicep. My fingers barely wrap around half of it. "Wow, strong," I agree, rolling my eyes at him, but I can't help the small smile. Or the heat racing up my neck.

"Are you rich?" Eric asks.

Ashton shrugs. "My family is, so I guess I am, too."

"What are you going to be when you grow up?" Derek asks.

"Dude, he's already grown-up!" Eric elbows his brother.

"No, I'm not yet," Ashton says. "I'm still in school. But I'm going to be a pilot."

I frown. *What happened to being a lawyer?*

"Does your breath smell?" Eric asks.

Ashton blows into his hand and inhales. "I don't think so. Irish?"

"No, your breath doesn't smell." I smile, ducking to tuck a strand of hair behind my ear and hide my blush. His mouth tastes like mint and heaven. *Minty heaven.*

"Why do you call her Irish?"

"Because she's Irish, and when she gets drunk, she's got a mean streak in her."

"Ashton!"

The boys start giggling. By the snort of laughter from Diane, I'd say she heard that.

"Honestly." I bury my face in my hands for a moment, which only makes the boys giggle more and Ashton grin more, and soon I'm laughing along with them.

Eventually the questions get more serious. "Do you have a mom and dad?" Eric asks.

Ashton didn't expect that question. I can tell because he falters, and I see his Adam's apple bob up and down as he swallows. "Everyone has a mom and dad."

"Where are they?"

"Uh . . . my dad is at his house and my mom isn't around anymore."

"Did she die?" Eric asks with complete innocence.

A flicker of pain flashes across Ashton's face.

"Remember the deal, boys," I warn with a raised brow.

"I thought that was just our deaths," Derek says solemnly.

"No, it's a blanket rule. It applies to everyone."

"Okay, sorry, Ace," Eric says, hanging his head.

Ashton leans forward and squeezes his shoulder. "Don't you worry about a thing, little man. She's a bit strict with her rules, isn't she?"

Eric rolls his eyes dramatically. "You have no idea."

The boys keep throwing out questions in typical innocent-child style and Ashton keeps answering them. I find out that Ashton's mom was from Spain, which is where he gets his dark eyes and tanned complexion. I find out that he's an only child. I find out that he was born and raised in New York. I'm finding out more about him in this brief interrogation by two curious five-year-olds than I thought possible. Maybe more than most people have ever learned about Ashton Henley.

Finally, Ashton stands and announces, "Sorry to leave, but I have somewhere I need to be. It was real, hanging with you guys." He holds out a hand in a fist-bump.

"Yeah, it was real," Eric mimics casually as he and his brother return the gesture, their fists so tiny next to Ashton's. All three of them turn to look at me, and I realize that I must have made a sappy sound.

Pinching my elbow lightly, Ashton says, "I'll be back in three hours to pick you up by the main entrance, okay?" With that, he's gone.

The rest of the volunteer shift goes downhill quickly. Lola comes in, looking smaller and paler and more feeble than the last time I saw her. Derek whispers to me that she's been coming in less and less. The boys last only another hour before they say that they're not feeling well, twisting my stomach. I spend the rest of the shift with other children—one recuperating from surgery after a car accident, another one there for a rare heart condition.

And I find myself watching the clock for more than one reason.

■ ■ ■

A different guy meets me at the main entrance three hours later. Not the playful, teasing one who shared a miniature table with two sick kids and made them giggle. Not the one who listened with quiet ease while I disclosed my long string of embarrassing, psychiatrist-inspired adventures.

No . . . the guy sitting next to me says barely a word, shares barely a look as we leave the city. I don't know what happened, but something has changed. Something to make his jaw taut and his eyes glaze over. To make him so discontented that my chest aches with the growing tension. More than I already left the hospital with.

I last an hour in silence, gazing out at the darkening skies and the streetlights, tucking my hair behind my ears a dozen times, adjusting and readjusting myself in my seat, before I decide to close my eyes and pretend to sleep, just as we approach the turn-off for Princeton.

"Did you get into the hospital's Ambien supply before I picked you up, Irish?" It's more the sound of his voice than his question that makes my eyes fly open with surprise. I turn to see a tiny smile breaking through that cloud and I heave a sigh of relief.

"Sorry," I mumble. But I'm not. I'm happy to see Ashton more relaxed.

"How was the rest of your volunteer session?"

"Hard. Sometimes I wonder if it will get easier. I love being around kids and I want to help them, but . . ." Tears trickle down my cheeks. "I don't know if I can handle wondering which ones I'm around are going to survive." Ashton is silent as I brush my hand across my cheek and sniffle.

"I wondered about that, back when you told me what you wanted to be," he says quietly. "It takes a special kind of person to be able to sit back and wait for someone to die, especially when you can't stop it from happening."

Is that what happened to you, Ashton? Did you have to watch your mother die? I don't say that out loud. Instead, I say, "I'm not sure that I'm that kind of person." Pausing, I add, "Wow. I've never admitted that out loud before. To anyone."

"Not even your doctor?"

"No! Especially not him. He thinks he has me all figured out," I mutter.

"What do you mean?"

I shake my head. "No way, Ashton. You've already gotten enough out of me for one day."

Strumming his fingertips against the steering wheel, he sighs. "Fine. How were the twins after I left?"

I smile. "They asked if you could come back," I confirm with a chuckle.

A wide smile stretches across his face. "Yeah? They liked me that much?"

I roll my eyes. "I think they liked you more than they like me. Eric said that I must get really angry when I'm Irish if you don't want to be my boyfriend."

A deep, throaty laugh escapes Ashton's lips and my body instantly warms. "What'd you say?"

"Oh, I assured him that I get plenty mad even when I'm not 'Irish' and you're around."

That earns another laugh. "I love it when you don't censor yourself. When you just say what's on your mind and don't worry about it."

"Then you and Stayner would get along well . . ." We pass campus signs, indicating we're not far and my day with Ashton is almost over. I don't know when I'll see him again. The thought hurts.

"That's right. You're supposed to be spilling your guts to me, right?"

My head falls back against the headrest as I mutter, more to myself, "You first."

I didn't really mean anything by it. Ashton is riddled with secrets, but I know they're not going to start trickling out of his mouth anytime soon. Still, I sense the temperature in the car plummet.

"What do you want to know?" His tone is low and quiet. Hesitant, even.

"I—" My voice falters. I start with what I think is an innocent question, my voice as casual as possible. "You told the boys that you want to be a pilot. Why?"

With an exhale, he mutters, "Because you told me not to lie to them."

Okay. "What about being a lawyer?"

"I'll be a lawyer until I can be a pilot." His tone is so calm and quiet that it lulls me into a sense of comfort.

Switching gears, I ask, "What's your favorite memory of your mother?"

There's a slight pause. "I'll pass on that one, Irish." Still calm and quiet, but the cutting edge is there.

I watch him as he begins absently fingering the strap. "How old were you?"

"Eight." The answer comes with a crack. I close my eyes and turn to watch the house lights pass by, hoping they'll replace the vision of the scared little boy that's blazing in my skull.

Ashton's hand curls around mine. "He only lost control the once. The scars, I mean. He never left scars the other times." *The other times.* "The closet was usually his favorite. He'd put me in there for hours. Usually with duct tape, to keep me quiet." I try to suppress the sob with my free hand but I can't, and it comes out in a strange, guttural cry.

We're silent for a moment, but I need to know more about Ashton. Everything. Swallowing the lump in my throat, I ask, "Why do you wear it?"

"Because I'm a fucking prisoner in my life, Irish!" As if that sudden outburst revealed more than he intended, his mouth clamps shut. He releases my hand.

I alternate between furtive glances at him and smoothing the pleats in my skirt, but I don't say anything as he turns into the quiet parking lot. When he pulls into a corner spot, off to the end, I expect him to shut the ignition and jump out, anxious to be rid of me. But he doesn't. He lets the car idle with the radio playing softly as his fingers pinch the bridge of his nose.

"You probably think I'm exaggerating, don't you." His tone is tempered again. I sit still and listen. "I'm living it up, right? This school, the money, the girlfriend . . . this fucking car." He slams his fist on the dashboard angrily. "Poor fucking me, right?" His hands fold at the back of his neck as he leans back to close his eyes. "He's controlling me, Irish. My life. And everything in it. I'm trapped." There's no mistaking the pain in his voice now. It's raw and agonizing, and it squeezes my chest.

I don't have to ask whom he's talking about. I'm sure it's the same person who gave Ashton his scars. I so badly want to ask how he's trapped and why, but I don't want to push him too hard. He might shut down. So instead I whisper, "How can I help?"

"Make me forget." He looks at me. The sadness that I saw in his eyes a week ago is revealing itself again.

"I . . ." I falter. What is he asking me to do? He uses sex to forget, he already suggested that. But I won't . . . I can't . . . Panic is bubbling inside and it must be clear on my face.

"Not that, Irish," he whispers. "I don't want that from you. I won't ever ask for that." He releases his seat belt and then reaches over to undo mine. Taking my hand, he pulls it toward his chest. With no hesitation and enormous relief, I shift in my seat until I can rest it over his heart. It responds immediately, starting to beat faster and harder as his hand presses tightly over mine, warming it.

"Your hand like this? I can't even describe how incredible it feels," he whispers with a wistful smile. I bite my lip as a thrill rushes through my insides, knowing that I'm making him feel this good, that I feel so connected to him.

Resting his head back on his seat and closing his eyes, he quietly asks, "Do you think about me, Irish?"

"Yes." The answer comes out faster than I intended, and I feel the responding skip beneath my fingers.

"A lot?"

I hesitate on that one, trying to swallow my embarrassment.

Cracking one eye to look at me, he murmurs. "You're supposed to just tell me."

"Right." I smile to myself. "Yes." Another skip.

There's a pause, and then he whispers, "I didn't mean to make you cry over me, Irish. The bad stuff was a long time ago. He can't hurt me like that anymore. He has other ways, but . . ."

With a ragged sigh, I offer him a smile. "I'm sorry. I cry a lot. My sister makes fun of me. And I think it was just an emotional day all round. Sometimes it's hard to stop dwelling on the bad stuff."

His lips part as if he's about to respond, but then he closes them. I wonder what he's thinking but I don't ask. I just watch a calm peace pass over his face while his heart still pounds. "Do you want me to help you forget for a while?"

"I . . ." My wide eyes flash to his mouth.

And suddenly he's moving, twisting in his seat and pushing me back gently into mine, telling me to relax before I can even register that my entire body has tensed.

Ashton doesn't hesitate, his mouth claiming mine, his tongue forcing its way in. My chest feels light yet at the same time heavy and my body feels like it's on fire but icy cold. I quickly don't care about anything or anyone else but myself and being with him.

I silently marvel at how his tongue is both delicate and forceful, skillfully sliding and curling around mine. His mouth is just as minty and heavenly and delicious as I remember it being. So delicious that I barely notice my chair reclining. He's set it to a comfortable slant where I'm still sitting but am able to stretch out. Shifting his mouth to my ear to graze the lobe with his tongue, he says in a low, gravelly voice that vibrates through to my core, "I'm going to do something and you can tell me to stop." I inhale sharply as a hand settles on my thigh and begins its ascent. "But I really hope you don't."

I think I know what he wants to do and I can't believe this is happening. Am I going to let this happen? A natural instinct makes me squeeze my knees together for a moment, but then Ashton starts kissing me with a new level of intensity. My knees relax as my body craves his touch, welcoming his hand as it begins slowly rubbing back and forth over my nylons.

I can feel myself respond with each pass and I wonder if Ashton can tell. My hand instinctively moves to the back of his neck, where his dark hair hangs in sexy wisps, to grasp a handful and tug slightly. His kiss deepens even more, his hand moves even faster, and when a tiny moan escapes me, it seems to push him over the edge.

Ashton shifts and reaches down with his other hand. Pinching the seam of my nylons between his fingers, he tugs, and a tearing sound fills the car. Maybe I would have been a little annoyed at that, but I don't have a chance because his hand doesn't waste any time, slipping under the edge of my panties.

I gasp and break free from his mouth to look into his eyes, my body tense and trembling. "I've never—" He stops my words with a kiss.

"I know, Irish. Remember? Jell-O shots are your kryptonite for secrets."

I close my eyes as I groan and press my forehead against his, my cheeks flaming. "I *actually* told you that no one's ever . . . ?" I can't even bring myself to say the words.

As if in answer, Ashton slides one finger in slowly. "No one's ever what, Irish?" he whispers playfully as another finger slides in. My answering moan has his mouth closing over mine again.

In the back of my mind, I'm aware that I'm sitting in the passenger seat of a car in a parking lot. I should be horrified. But

I quickly rationalize that the windows are black and no one is around. Soon, with the way Ashton deftly moves his hand, knowing exactly the right speed and pressure to make my body relax and my thighs fall apart, I realize that the car could be circled by zombies and I wouldn't care.

He doesn't complain at all when I tug at his hair or accidentally bite his lip. By the way his breathing speeds up and his mouth turns more aggressive, I know he's enjoying this. And when I feel the sensation build in my lower belly, Ashton's hand somehow knows to move faster, making me squirm and writhe and rock against it.

"Let me hear it, Irish," he says in a strained whisper, just as my body starts to shudder against his hand. With his mouth pressed against my throat, I cry out in response, my fingernails digging into his bicep as the waves hit me.

"That was fucking hot, Irish," he murmurs into my ear, his forehead pressed against my headrest. I blush as I pull my thighs back together. But he doesn't move his hand away yet and I don't push it away. "Did it help you forget?"

My nervous giggle is the only answer I can give him. Forget? My brain went *blank*. I forgot about my problems, his problems, and the potential zombie apocalypse. If that's what orgasms do, then I can't believe people ever leave their houses. Or cars.

"I guess that's another first for you involving me," he murmurs. *One that I will never forget.*

With one light kiss on my nose, he finally moves his hand to smooth my skirt down to a respectable level. Glancing down pointedly at himself, I hear him say with amusement in his tone, "And for me, too." When he catches my confused expression, he starts chuckling softly. "That's *never* happened."

My eye widen in shock as I drop my gaze to his lap. That only makes the chuckling turn into full-blown laughter.

■ ■ ■

It takes exactly three hours.

Three hours—lying in my bed, staring at the ceiling, my books sitting closed beside me—for the orgasmic wave to pass and for the nausea to set in as I realize what I just allowed to happen. What I *wanted* to happen. What I *don't regret* happening.

And when I answer Connor's call and he apologizes profusely for not taking me to New York, and promises that he'll make it up to me, I just smile into the phone and tell him that it's okay. I wish him good luck with his paper. I think about what a sweet, good guy he is and how much my parents would love him. I think about how I should end things with him, given what I've done.

I hang up the phone.

And I cry.

chapter fifteen

■ ■ ■

THOROUGHBREDS

"What were you thinking?"

"Not much, clearly."

I hear the exasperation in Kacey's voice. "I don't know about you, Livie . . . Sometimes you're as graceful as a one-legged flamingo in a pit of quicksand."

I roll my eyes. Some of the stuff my sister comes up with . . . "It's a mild sprain. It's almost better. I don't even need crutches anymore."

"When did it happen?"

"Three weeks ago now, I think? Maybe four. I'm not sure." Time seems to both drag and fly by lately. All I'm sure of is that I haven't seen Ashton in two weeks, since he walked me to my dorm that night, kissed my cheek good night, and turned away. And I haven't heard from him since I got a text the following morning with the words:

One-time thing. Doesn't change anything. Stay with Connor.

"Three or four weeks and you're only telling me now?" Kacey's tone is a mixture of annoyance and hurt, making a bubble of guilt swell in my throat. She's right. I can't believe I haven't talked to her live in almost a month. I haven't told her about the sprain. I haven't told her about Connor. I certainly haven't told her about Ashton.

"I'm sorry. I got caught up with midterms and stuff."

"How'd they go?"

"Okay, I guess." I've never struggled through exams, or walked into them feeling unprepared. But I left every single one of mine last week with a queasy stomach. I don't know if it's just the jitters from the added pressure. I do know that I spent entirely too much time dwelling on non-school things like what my feelings are for Ashton and what Connor would do if he knew what happened. Would he dump me? Probably. I consider telling him so that he will, because I'm too weak to end it with him. But that could cause problems between Connor and Ashton, and I don't want to do that. They're living together, after all, and I'm the girl in the middle.

And then I'd focus on my irritation with Ashton for ever laying one of his masterfully skilled hands on me. I'd let that irritation fester into full-on anger. Then the leather belt, the scars, the tattoos, and whatever else he's hiding would all culminate into a mess of worry inside my head and heart, dousing my anger, leaving me hurting for him. Desperate to see him again.

And then I'd get angry with myself for wanting to see him, for letting him do what he did, for being too selfish and afraid to end things with Connor. For getting lost in shades of right and wrong instead of sticking to the black and white that I can make sense of.

There's a long pause, and then Kacey asks, "You guess?"

"Yeah. Why?"

"I don't know. You've just never . . . *guessed* before." Another long pause. "What's going on, Livie?"

"Nothing. I'm tired. I haven't slept a lot lately." It's when I'm lying in bed that I seem to think about Ashton the most. Worry about him. Crave him. I've been lying in bed a lot.

"Have you talked to Dr. Stayner recently?"

With a heavy sigh, I admit, "No." Because I'll have to lie to him and I don't want to do that, either. Avoidance is key. *Reagan is onto something.* Checking the clock, I mutter, "I have class in twenty." My English lit class. I don't feel like going. I've only done a quarter of the reading, so I'll be lost anyway. I look at my bed. A nap would feel amazing right now . . .

"Well . . . we miss you, Livie."

I smile sadly, thinking about Storm's growing belly and Mia's science experiments, and nights with my sister on the back deck, overlooking the ocean, and a hollow ache fills my chest. As pretty as the Princeton campus is, it just doesn't compare. "I miss you too."

"Love you, sis."

I'm crawling into my top bunk for that nap when my phone chirps with a text:

Are you in your room? It's Ash.

A thrill rushes through me as I type:

Yes.

The response comes immediately:

I'll walk you to class. See you in a few . . .

What? He's coming here? Now? My wide eyes dart around our room, at Reagan's pile of dirty clothes, at my sweats, at my pale complexion and the rat's nest of black hair reflecting back at me in the mirror. Scrambling, I pull on a pair of jeans and a shirt that

Storm bought me but I've never worn. It's light blue to match my eyes, fitted, and cut in a low V-neck. Because suddenly, I feel the need to tempt Ashton. Then I set to work on my hair, struggling to pull a brush through it. Seriously, I think rats have actually nested in it.

A loud knock on my door makes my heart leap. Peeking at my reflection in the mirror one last time, I quickly smooth on Reagan's sheer lip gloss to add some color to my face. Then, with a deep breath, I walk over to unlock and open the door.

Ashton is standing with his back to me as he scans the hall. When he turns to face me, my stomach flips the way it did the first time I saw those intoxicating dark features. Only the feeling is so much more intense now, because it's coupled with a magnetic pull wrenching at both my body and my heart.

"I thought I'd walk you to class on account of that lame foot," he murmurs with a wry grin, his gaze drifting down and up my frame, unashamed.

"Thanks," I murmur with a shy smile, turning to grab my books and coat from my desk. Truth be told, my foot is almost perfect. But I'm willing to not tell the truth if it means a ten-minute walk with Ashton.

Our conversation is normal, safe. He asks me a few questions about my exams; he answers a few about his. He asks me about the twins. When I see the door to the lecture hall up ahead, my heart sinks. I don't want ten minutes with Ashton. I want ten hours. Ten days. Longer.

But Ashton doesn't leave. He follows me into the lecture hall, down the stairs, straight to the front row, and sits down beside me. I don't question him. I don't say a word. I just watch as he stretches those long legs out, once again encroaching on my space. My body turns toward him this time, welcoming him. Wanting him.

"So how are those redeeming qualities of mine coming along?" he murmurs as the prof walks to the podium with his notes.

I think of the answer I want to give. I finally say, "I'll let you know when I find one."

The professor taps the podium three times, signaling the start of class. Ashton doesn't care, of course. His lips brush my ear as he leans in to whisper, "Do you want me to just tell you?"

I push his face away with my palm, feigning annoyance, the beginnings of the burn in my thighs making me uncomfortable enough to squirm in my seat. Ashton's low chuckle tells me he's noticed and he has a good idea what his proximity is doing to me.

The entire lecture today is on Thomas Hardy and I can't focus on a freaking word with Ashton's cologne swirling in my nose, with his knee bumping into mine, with those skilled fingers of his strumming against the desk. At times I catch him scribbling notes in his book. Notes on what? He's not even in this class.

At one point the prof has turned away from us to take a sip of his water. Ashton tears a sheet out of his book and slides it in front of me without a word. Frowning, I look at it.

I should have known better. I should have waited until after class.

1. I'm brilliant
2. I'm charming
3. I'm hung like a thoroughbred
4. I've stopped all philandering
5. I'm highly skilled, as you've learned the other night.

P.S. Stop staring at my hands. I know what you want me to do with them.

The professor continues his lecture not five feet away from me as blood rushes to my head, to my belly, to my thighs. What is he doing? Why would he write *that* down and pass it to me in the middle of a lecture? The last thing I want to be thinking about while the professor drones on about stupid Thomas Hardy is Ashton and his hands and the other night in the car . . .

A hand squeezes my knee, making me jump in my seat. My elbow reactively flies out and jabs Ashton in the ribs. It's enough to attract the professor's attention. "Is there something you'd like to share with the class?" he asks calmly, regarding us over his glasses.

I give an almost imperceptible shake of my head as seventy-something students lean forward in their seats, their eyes boring into the back of my skull.

That likely would have worked. The prof might have let it go. But then I have to go and cover the note lying on top of my book, as if trying to muffle the indiscretions screaming from it.

I see the professor's eyes fall to it.

My stomach hits the lecture hall floor.

"Notes being passed around in the front row of my lecture. May I?" A weathered hand stretches out toward me and the proof of my scandalous behavior with the guy sitting beside me.

I stare wide-eyed and frozen at that hand as my brain frantically runs through my options. There aren't many. I can't run out of the class because of my foot, so I'm left with either shoving the note into my mouth or stabbing Ashton's expert hand with my pen to cause a diversion. Both will guarantee dismissal from this class; one will include a special jacket and a bonus overnight stay with Dr. Stayner.

So, with a sharp glare in Ashton's direction, I hand the prof the note and pray to God that he doesn't start reading it out loud, because then my diversion tactic may still need to come into play. "Let's see what we have here . . ." The room starts to sway and blur, my ears filling with the rushing sound of blood. I don't doubt that the hall is buzzing with excited whispers, all waiting like spectators at a hanging, but I can't hear a thing. And I don't dare look at Ashton because if he has a smirk on his face, I'll punch him square in it.

"Mr. Henley, I suggest you carry out your conquest attempts outside of my classroom," the prof finally says, shooting Ashton a pointed glare as he crumples the note into a tiny ball and tosses it in the trash. Air leaves my lungs in a rush. *Of course he knows Ashton. Everyone knows Ashton . . .*

Ashton clears his throat as a low murmur grows behind us. "Yes, sir." I can't tell if he's embarrassed or not. I refuse to look at him.

As the professor walks back to the podium, a chorus of disappointment fills the room as students realize they're not going to witness an execution here today. But before he continues on with the lecture, he adds, "And if I were this young lady, I would seriously debate number one."

■ ■ ■

"Do you realize how close you were to having this pen through your hand?" I hold it up for effect as we walk out of the building.

"I was bored. Hardy sucked the first time around, too."

"Well, you didn't have to humiliate me in the middle of a lecture hall, did you?"

"Would you rather I not have come? Truth . . . doctor's orders."

I grit my teeth. Despite everything, I mutter with a smile, "No."

"No, what?"

"No, I'm glad you came."

"I haven't . . . yet."

I slap my book across his arm, blushing furiously. "You're impossible."

"And you're incredible." By the way his breath catches and his dark eyes flash, I don't think Ashton meant to say that out loud.

I have to fight the urge to fall into his chest. I don't fight the words, though. "I missed you."

"I missed you too." There's a long pause. "Irish . . ." His feet slow to a stop and he turns one of his intense, dark Ashton stares on me. My stomach clenches instantly, both eager and terrified of what might come out of his mouth. "Are you going to answer that?"

"What?"

"Your phone." His hand touches my jeans pocket where my phone is tucked. "It's ringing."

As soon as he says it, my ears catch Connor's unique ring tone. "Uh, yeah." I slide it out and look at the screen to see Connor's beaming grin and green eyes. I hit the answer button. "Hey, Connor."

"Hey, babe. I'm running to class but wanted to double-check—you're coming to the race next Saturday, right?"

"Yup, I'll be there for the morning. I have my volunteer shift in the afternoon."

I hear the relief in his voice. "Great. My parents can't wait to meet you."

My stomach does a somersault. "What? You told them about me?" *"Slow and easy" means "meet parents"?*

"Of course. I've got to run. Catch you later." I hear the phone click, leaving me staring at Ashton as he absently kicks the fallen leaves off the path.

When he looks up at me, he frowns. "What?"

I look at my phone and back at him. I hear the tentativeness in my voice as I say, "Connor wants me to meet his parents." I know why I'm telling Ashton. I want to know what *he* thinks about that.

He shrugs, distracting himself with a blond girl walking past. "Hey!" I snap, scowling. "I'm standing right *here!*"

Bowing his head, Ashton sighs. "What do you want me to say, Irish?" Looking up at me with that resigned smile and the thinly veiled hurt that he hides from most, he says, "Meet his parents. It probably makes sense." He pauses, his lips pursed tightly. "You and Connor are together." I hear the unspoken words as if he's screaming them. *You and I are not.*

"What if I wasn't with him? Would it matter to you?" It's the same line that he's used on me a few times. Now it's my turn.

Ashton's hands lift to cradle the back of his neck. He closes his eyes and tilts his head up to the cool blue autumn sky. And I wait, quietly, watching him, my eyes memorizing the curves of his throat and his neck, fighting the urge to reach out and touch his chest, to share that intimate moment with him again.

He drops his arms and his gaze to me, his jaw visibly taut. "I can't give you what you want, Irish." With another heavy sigh, he says, "Do you think you can manage the rest of the way back on your own?"

Biting my bottom lip as the prickly lump forms in my throat, I drop my gaze to my books. "Of course. Thanks, Ashton."

His mouth opens to say something but then stops. I see the imperceptible shake of his head, as if he's warning himself. "See you around." He turns and walks away.

chapter sixteen

...

MEDIOCRE

C minus.

I blink several times, holding it closer to make sure I'm not hallucinating.

I'm not. It's still there, at the top of my chemistry midterm, in all its ugly red glory.

My first college midterm mark and it's almost a D. I've never had anything but an A.

Ever.

I swallow once, twice, three times as nausea fills my body and blood rushes to my ears, my heart beating off-kilter. Maybe I'm not cut out for Princeton. I know I didn't study as hard as I should have, with all the distraction. My father was right. Boys do suck the brains out of smart girls. Either that or I've killed all my smart brain cells with drinking. All that's left are the stupid ones that like to giggle and get felt up—okay, down—in cars.

I rush out the door, past the other exiting students, my legs moving as fast as they can without outright running. Bursting out and into the cool drizzle, I force myself to slow down as a pain twinges in my ankle. I'll reinjure it if I'm not careful.

Without fail, my phone rings. Connor always phones me after this class because he's getting out of his. I don't want to answer it, but I do anyway.

"Hey, babe. What's wrong?"

"I failed my chemistry midterm!" I fight to keep the tears welling in my eyes at bay. I don't want to bawl out here, in the middle of everyone.

"Seriously? You failed?" There's no mistaking the shock in his tone.

"Well . . . almost!" I sputter, my breath ragged.

"Okay. Slow down, Livie," Connor says in a composed voice. "Tell me what happened."

A take a few deep, calming breaths before I whisper, "I got a C minus."

Connor heaves a huge sigh. "You had me concerned there, Livie! Don't worry! I had a few mediocre grades in my first year. It's nothing."

I grit my teeth. *It's not nothing!* I want to scream. It's my first bad grade. Ever. And it's in one of my best subjects! From the tightness in my chest, I'm beginning to suspect that I'm having a mild coronary at the age of eighteen.

"You'll do better next time, Livie. You're smart."

Sucking my bottom lip, I nod into the phone. "Yeah, okay."

"Feel better?"

No. "Sure. Thanks, Connor."

"Okay, good." The phone muffles and I hear Connor shouting to someone on his end. "Need a ride? Yeah . . ." Coming back to me, he says, "I've got to go. We have an extra practice today. Coach threatened anyone who's late with a ten-mile run in the rain."

"Okay."

"Talk to you later, Liv." The phone clicks.

I do not feel better. Not at all. In fact, I somehow feel worse.

I head back to my dorm room with my head down, fighting the tears as the lump in my throat grows. Connor has that automatic confidence in me—like everyone else does. Doesn't he understand that this almost-D is a big deal for me? What if I *can't* do better? What if this is the beginning of the end?

By the time I make it to my room, I don't care who sees my tearstained face. I know I could call Dr. Stayner, but he'll make this about my parents and I don't want to hear his autopilot theories today. I should call Kacey, but . . . I can't. After all she did to help get me here, I don't want to disappoint her.

So I rely on the only thing that I can right now—Reagan's fresh tub of Ben & Jerry's Chocolate Therapy ice cream in the freezer compartment of our mini fridge. My pity party is complete once I change into my pajamas, pull my hair back, and crawl under my covers to stare at the wretched paper lying on the floor. I consider setting it on fire, but I've heard that the smoke alarms are super-sensitive.

There are two more tubs waiting for me when this is done. I've decided I'm going to eat myself to death. I'm halfway through the first tub within five minutes—Reagan's going to kill me—when someone knocks on my door.

I ignore it. Anyone I might want to talk to is at rowing practice. I almost shout, "Go away!" but then the person will know I'm here. So I keep quiet by licking the tablespoon in my hand. The knocking doesn't stop, though. It keeps going and going and going until I'm sure that Dr. Stayner is outside, delivering on his committal promise early.

With a groan, I roll out of bed and stagger over, spoon in mouth and tub in hand, to throw the door open.

It's Ashton.

My mouth falls opens and my spoon flies out. He's got fast reflexes, though, and manages to catch it before it hits the ground.

"What are you doing here?" I note his track pants and shirt. He's supposed to be at practice.

Stepping around me and into my room, he murmurs with a meaningful look at the tub in my hand, "Keeping you from gaining your *frosh fifteen*."

I close the door behind me. "Don't you have practice?"

"Yeah. What are you doing?"

Dragging my feet back toward my bed, I mumble, "I'm eating ice cream in my pajamas in bed. In the dark. Clearly."

Ashton walks over to turn a small desk lamp on, casting a soft, cozy glow to the room. "Connor said you were freaking out about your midterm?"

His words bring me back to reality and my bottom lip begins to wobble. I can't even bring myself to say it. So I simply point at the thing on the floor and let the hideous letter speak for itself.

He leans down to pick it up and my breath hitches as I stare blatantly at his ass. I don't care if he catches me doing it. I may as well add "pervert" underneath "failure" on the list of things that define me.

"Shit, I thought you were supposed to be some super-genius, Irish."

That does it. The tears start streaming down my cheeks in earnest and I can't control them.

"Oh, God. Livie, I'm kidding! Jeez!" Tucking the paper under his arm, two large hands reach up to grab my chin, both thumbs working to gently brush the tears away. "You really do cry a lot."

"You should go," I sob, knowing I'm about to break into ugly-cry mode and I'd rather be buried alive than let Ashton see that.

"Whoa!" Two viselike grips settle on my shoulders. "Hold it. I'm not missing practice so you can kick me out. Come here." He pries the tub of ice cream out of my hand and places it on the dresser. With his hands on my waist, he lifts me into my top bunk. "Get comfortable," he says as he grabs the tub and climbs up the ladder.

"I don't think this will hold both of us," I mumble between blubbers as he crawls in next to me, forcing me closer to the wall.

"You'd be surprised what these bunks will hold." The secretive smile tells me that I don't want the details. So I stay quiet while he pulls the covers up over both of us, adjusts all the pillows so they're under him, and then forces his arm under my head so that I'm tucked in against his side with my head resting on his chest.

He doesn't say a word. He simply lies there quietly, his fingers drawing lazy circles along my back while he gives me a chance to calm down. I close my eyes and listen to the rhythm of his heart—slow and steady and therapeutic.

"I've never had a C minus before. I've never had anything but an A."

"Never?"

"Never. Not one."

"Your sister was right. You are too fucking perfect." I tense at the words. "I'm kidding, Irish." He sighs. "I know you don't believe me but you don't have to be perfect. No one's perfect."

"I'm not, I'm trying to be . . . remarkable," I hear myself murmur.

"What?"

I sigh. "Nothing. Just . . ." *Something my dad used to say.* "What if it doesn't stop here? What if I get bad grade after bad grade? What if I can't get into med school? What will I do then? Who will I be?" I'm starting to get frantic again.

"You'll still be you. And trust me, you'll always be remarkable. Relax."

"I can't!" I burrow my face against his chest. "Have you ever failed anything?"

"No, but that's because I'm brilliant, remember?" His arm squeezes around me to tell me that he's teasing. "I've had a couple of Cs. One D. Bell curves can be a bitch." He scoops a spoonful of melting ice cream out and slides it into his mouth. "Have you gotten any other tests back yet?"

I shake my head against his chest in response.

"How are you feeling about them?"

"Before today, I was a little worried. Now?" My hand finds its way up to wrap around his shoulder, wanting to be closer to him, to sop up this sense of security he's offering me, if only temporarily. "Terrible. Awful. If I did this bad on my best subject, then I definitely failed English."

"Well . . ." Another spoonful goes into his mouth. "Did you do something different preparing for these than in the past? Did you study?"

"Of course I studied," I snap.

"Easy." I hear his hard swallow. "Were you . . . distracted?"

I close my eyes and whisper, "Yes."

There's a long pause before he asks, "By what?"

You. I can't say that. It's not Ashton's fault that my hormones and my heart are wreaking havoc on my brain. "Lots of things." My hand absently shifts down to his chest to settle where the tattoo is. Where the scar is.

Ashton's muscles against my cheek automatically tense. "I told you, I wanted you to forget about that." For a long time, I hear nothing but his heartbeat as my fingers first draw, then rub that spot on his chest, memorizing the ridge. It's enough to lull me into an almost-sleep.

"Dana's dad is a significant client of my father's, and keeping her happy keeps her dad happy." My hand falters for a second at the sound of her name, as guilt slams into my gut. But I force it back in motion as I pace my breathing. "If her dad is happy, then that makes *him* happy. And if he's happy . . ." He says that as if it makes complete sense. All it tells me is that this man—his father—abused him as a small child and still has control over him as a grown man.

Keeping my hand moving slowly, I whisper, "So, you're still with her . . . but not by choice."

"As far as an arranged relationship goes, she's perfect. She's sweet and pretty. And she lives far away." He's numb to it. I hear it. He's acquiescent and numb.

"Does she know about this arrangement?"

A small derisive snort escapes. "She thinks we'll get married. And if—" He clamps his mouth shut. But I think I know where that train of thought was going. If his father wants Ashton to marry her . . . A shiver runs from the base of my neck down my back, around my ribs, into my throat, enveloping me with icy dread. God, what is he holding over Ashton's head?

My body instinctively curls into his, pressing against him. I roll my head just enough to lay a sympathetic kiss against his chest. Or is it more of a relieved kiss? Relieved that I'm not wrecking a happy home because it's all a sham?

"Can't you get away from him?"

"Eventually. It could be months, years. I won't know until I know. I was managing okay, though." He pauses. "And then the most beautiful girl on this planet punched me in the jaw."

A small half-giggle slips out. "You deserved that, Jell-O thief."

The sound of his chuckle vibrates through my body. "I've never had a girl tremble like that for me before while fully dressed, Irish."

"Shut up and give me that ice cream." I lift my body up and reach for the spoon, but his long arm span makes it impossible to reach.

"I think you've done enough damage to yourself for one night."

"I'll be the judge of that. Why are you here and not at practice again?"

"Because I knew there'd be a hot chick with a terrific rack and chocolate ice cream smeared all over her face here."

I freeze. My eyes drop to my shirt. My threadbare white cotton pajama top does nothing to hide the fact that I'm not wearing a bra. And my face? Based on the side of Ashton's shirt, I'd say he's telling the truth. "How bad is it?"

"You know how clowns have lipstick around the outside of their lips . . ."

Ohmigod! I jab my palm into his solar plexus as I move to get up.

His hands around my biceps stop me. "Where do you think you're going?"

"To wash my face!"

In a split second, Ashton has me lying on my back with no effort, my wrists pinned beneath his hands and his weight. "Let me help you with that." He leans down and lets the tip of his tongue run leisurely around the outside of my mouth, beginning at the top, going from left to right, and then the bottom, from left to right, gently lapping up ice cream as he goes.

If there's such thing as a virgin slut, I believe I fit the description.

How did I get myself into this again? I close my eyes, the urge to both giggle and scream at the top of my lungs overpowering. I woke up this morning, as I have every other morning since I last saw Ashton, telling myself to let go, to stop thinking about him and stay the course that I've set out on. The slow-and-easy Connor course.

How, then, do I end up in my bed, struggling not to pant while Ashton licks chocolate ice cream off my face, while I try my own Jedi mind tricks to get a repeat of our night in the car? I haven't said a word to stop him and I could. I could tell him to stop. I could call him a male whore. I could tell him that he's making *me* feel like a whore.

But I don't do any of that because I don't want him to stop.

I let out a tiny whimper as he pulls back slightly. "It's almost better," he murmurs, his breathing shallow. He moves on to my lips, running his tongue along my top lip from left to right, followed by my bottom lip, left to right. I can't help my mouth parting open for him. I can't stop my tongue from automatically sliding out, reaching for him.

That's when he pulls back and looks at me with those sad eyes.

I think I know the answer but I want to hear him say it, so I ask, "Why did you come? The truth."

He swallows. "Because I couldn't stand knowing that you were upset. But . . ." I watch as his eyes close and his head bobs forward. "I can't play this game with you, Irish. I'm going to hurt you."

His light stubble grazes against my palm as I lift his chin up so I can meet his eyes again.

And I ignore.

I ignore his words. I ignore the guilt in my stomach and the screams in my head. I ignore the internal battle I can see going on inside him. I want to forget all the uncertainties growing in my life and make him forget dark closets and tape and belts and his silent prison.

I ignore it all as I slip my hand around the back of his neck and pull him into me to kiss and then trail my tongue along the bottom of his lip. Ashton's breath hitches and I feel the muscles cord beneath my fingers as he hesitates, his hand fisting the pillow beside my head as he fights it.

I don't want him to fight anymore. I'm desperate to see that vulnerable side of him again. I need to feel close to him again. I want to make him feel good. I want *me* to feel good. I want to just let go of . . . everything.

That's what it feels like when I'm with Ashton.

Like I'm letting go.

And that's why I give him a level stare and demand, "Help me forget for a while."

He stops hesitating.

He crashes down into my mouth with an unreserved fierceness. I match it, kissing him like I need the air in his lungs to survive. A part of me is afraid. I feel that deep inside. I don't know what this is going to lead to and I don't know if I'm ready for it.

But I don't think I'll stop it.

It's as if he can read my mind. He breaks free and looks down at me to whisper, "We won't . . . I won't take anything away from you today, Irish. I won't ever do that while I'm not . . . free." I don't miss the fact that he's not using words like "screw" or "fuck" in typical Ashton fashion. Then again, I don't have the typical Ashton here with me anymore. I have the one he hides from everyone else.

I close my eyes as his lips find my throat and I marvel at how they're both soft and forceful. By the time they reach my collarbone, my chest is heaving. Ashton tugs my shirt up and over my head with ease. Tossing it to the floor, he lifts himself up enough that he can stare down at my bare chest, making all the nerves within my breasts tingle. "That morning I woke up in here . . ." His eyes flicker up to catch me watching him before descending again. "I was ready to drop to my knees and beg you to uncover these." A hiss escapes me as he cups and caresses first one and then the other breast, as if memorizing their shape and size and feel. His thumb brushes a hardened nipple and a shudder runs through me. With a small groan, I gasp as Ashton's mouth closes over it, his tongue moving with skill. I can't help but wrap my arms around his head and pull him closer, crying out as his teeth send a sharp thrill straight down to my core.

I've noticed that when I make sounds like that, even unintentionally, Ashton reacts. This time he breaks free long enough to yank his own shirt over his head. The second the shirt's off, his hand is diving beneath me to grasp the back of my pajama bottoms. He pulls them down and off my hips without delay, panties and all. In seconds I'm completely undressed and his mouth is back around my nipple.

I wrap my arms around his head again and rest my head back into the pillow, reveling in the feel of his scorching skin against mine and his erection digging into my thigh. I have the urge to reach down and wrap my hand around it, but it would involve moving and I'm too comfortable right now. So I stay put while I try to imagine what Ashton would feel like inside me. Just the thought has my thighs relaxing and tensing at the same time and wetness beginning to pool.

And that's how Ashton's hand discovers me when it slides down. "Holy fuck, Irish . . ." I hear him mutter, and I tighten my grip of his head against me as my head lolls back and I moan, silently thanking my professor for my shitty chem grade.

"This won't work . . ." Ashton abruptly rolls off the bed.

Panic bubbles. I think I've done something wrong. Is he going to leave me like *this*?

"Sit up, Irish."

I obey, and he lets out a groan as he turns my body and pulls my legs over the side of the bed, pausing to let his eyes drag the length of my frame. "Lean back on your elbows."

I let out a small gasp but I do as asked. I think I know what he's doing. Ashton steps forward, keeping his eyes locked to mine as his hands settle on the tops of my thighs. "The thing about these damn beds . . ." I feel the force against my thigh muscles as Ashton's hands began to push my legs apart. I hold my breath, suddenly petrified.

I know what he's doing and I'm freaking out.

But Ashton's eyes are still locked on mine so I don't resist him. ". . . is that they're not good. . . ." With a quick tug, he has my hips at the edge of the bed. His fingers skate along the length of my legs as he wraps them over his shoulders. He breaks eye contact from me for the first time to start laying kisses along my inner thigh, slowly inching in, his breath sending shivers of anticipation upward. ". . . for things like this."

I gasp as his tongue touches me. At first I'm beyond uncomfortable, exposed like this. I mean, having Ashton's face so intimately *there* is, well, nerve-racking. But it feels . . . amazing. And with his expert tongue and adept fingers working in tandem, I soon start to feel that familiar build, the one where I shut out the world. I let my head dip back and my eyes close and a shaky sigh escape my lips as I try to memorize how incredible this feels. That must be a sign for Ashton, because his mouth becomes more feverish and excited and his hands squeeze my thighs, pulling me closer into him.

When the wave is about to hit me again, I can't help but roll my head back up and look down at him. His eyes are locked on mine with that odd sense of peace behind them.

And it makes me scream out his name.

I'm a limp doll as Ashton shifts my body back onto the bed. He tucks me under the covers and then lifts his arms to rest on the edge. "Don't you want me to . . . ?" I bite my lip as a blush heats my cheeks.

With a secretive smile, he smooths my hair off my forehead. "I've been tied up the last few nights and I'm behind on a paper. I should go work on it." I close my eyes and enjoy the feel of his thumb stroking my cheek, reveling in this deep intimacy forming between Ashton and me. I drift off.

■ ■ ■

Reagan slips in at around eleven that night. I redressed at some point but I'm still lying in bed, my face buried in the pillow that smells like Ashton's cologne, my afternoon with him on mental repeat. I'm holding on to that euphoric afterglow with two gripped hands, desperate to keep the guilt and doubt and confusion from swirling back into my lungs like suffocating black smoke.

"Hey, Reagan. How's it going?"

She flops into her bed. "I got kicked out of the library for being too loud."

I snort. "Too loud at what exactly?" Schoolwork isn't a guaranteed pastime for Reagan at the library, after all.

"Studying by myself. Go figure, right?" I giggle, knowing exactly why. Reagan tends to talk out loud when she's working through her textbooks. I think it's cute, but most people would find it annoying. "If only they knew . . ." There's a pause, and then she casually mentions, "I saw Connor there tonight."

"Oh yeah?" I try to make that light and airy as the *guilty virgin slut* coils tighten around my chest.

The bed frame creaks as Reagan shifts beneath me. "He asked how you were doing. You know, because of a bad midterm mark."

I sigh. "I'm doing . . . better."

"Good."

I pause to take a deep breath. And then I just blurt it out. "I think I'm going to end things with Connor."

"Oh yeah? Maybe you should wait until after the weekend." There's another shift and the sound of tugging sheets, as if Reagan can't get comfortable.

I find it strange that she doesn't ask why, that she doesn't sound at all shocked by my statement. Why not? *I'm* shocked. If I had written down on a piece of paper everything that I thought should comprise the ideal man for me, and then drew a caricature, I'd have a page with Connor on it. "He wants me to meet his parents." How can I do that now? His mother will know! Mothers have radar for these things. She'll out me publicly. It will be the first stoning in Princeton rowing history.

"So meet his parents and then break it off. You're not promising marriage. Otherwise you'll make things really awkward for Connor and yourself the day of the race. It's already going to be awkward."

"Why?"

"Because Dana will be there."

That name . . . it's like a punch to my sternum. "So what if she's there. There's nothing going on between Ashton and me." *Liar! Liar! Liar!*

There's a pause. "Well, that's good, because Ashton's going to be dead by tomorrow anyway."

"What?" Panic bursts.

"He skipped practice tonight. My dad tracked him down. He's probably still out running laps, and it's cold out there."

I'm not sure how I'm supposed to feel about that. Guilty, definitely, because he's being punished for being with me. But . . . my hands press flat against my belly as my heart ruptures with emotion. He knew it would happen and he did it anyway.

Reagan is still talking. "And don't forget there's the Halloween party that night. You don't want to make that super-awkward. It's not like you and Connor are sleeping together yet. . . . right?"

"Right . . . Is Dana going to be there?"

"No, I overheard Ashton saying that she'll be visiting her family in Queens."

I breathe a sigh of relief.

"Anyway, that's my vote. Wait until next week before you dump your pretty boy."

I sigh. "Yeah, I guess." What's another few days of festering guilt? It's a good idea, actually. Punish myself. I deserve it. I roll onto my side, my brain worked into exhaustion. " 'Night, Reagan."

" 'Night, Livie."

There's a pause. "Hey, Livie?" Reagan clears her throat a few times in a way that tells me she's struggling not to burst out in laughter. "Next time can you please hang the sock on the door to warn me?"

■ ■ ■

"They're beautiful," I whisper. I'm curled into a ball on my bed with a bouquet of purple irises in my hand and Connor on my phone. *And I don't deserve them. Or you.*

"I remember you saying you loved irises. They're not in season in the fall, did you know that?"

I smile as the tears trickle down my cheek. Dad used to surprise Mom with bouquets of dark purple irises every spring. Except it wasn't really a surprise because he'd do it every Friday night for, like, five weeks straight—for as long as they were in season. Each time, though, Mom's face would split with a wide grin and she'd fan her face with excitement as if he were proposing to her. Kacey and I used to roll our eyes and mimic Mom's over-the-top reaction.

Now my memory of purple irises will be tied to my treachery.

"I know they're not." That means Connor spent an astronomical amount of money, either on imports or special-grown. "What are they for?"

"Oh . . ." Connor pauses, and I can picture him leaning against the counter in the kitchen. "Just to let you know that I was thinking about you and to not worry about that grade."

I swallow. "Thanks." *That grade*. Since that C minus paper, I've received all of my other midterms back. Cs. All of them except for English lit, which earned a B. The prof even made a note that he liked the way I attacked the complex topic. He made it sound like a B is a good thing. My take on the moral dilemmas faced by the characters in *Wuthering Heights* and their choices was apparently fascinating to him. Maybe it's because I can't seem to get a grasp of my own morals anymore that I can make interesting observations about others' plights. I feel as though I've entered some strange twilight zone where everything I know has been turned upside down. I considered texting Ashton to let him know that I needed more cheering up, but I resisted the urge.

"My parents are looking forward to meeting you tomorrow."

Squeezing my eyes shut tight, I lie, "Same here."

chapter seventeen

■ ■ ■

OCTOBER 31

Dr. Stayner once suggested that all people face a day in their life that defines who they are, that shapes who they will become, that sets them on their path. He said that one day will either guide or haunt them until they take their last breath. I told him he was being dramatic. I told him I didn't believe it. It makes it sound as if a person is a pliable hunk of clay up until that point—just sitting around waiting to be fired, to solidify those curves and creases that hold their identity, their stability. Or their instability.

A highly implausible theory. And that, coming from a medical professional.

Maybe he's right, though.

Looking back on it now, I guess I could agree that my day of firing was the day that my parents died.

And October 31 was the day that shattered the design.

■ ■ ■

"I am getting so drunk tonight!" Reagan announces with her arms held high and her head back, basking in the early-morning sun. She doesn't care that we're standing at a crowded finish line of spectators, waiting for the guys to climb out of their winning boat. Reagan had warned me that this race was a big deal, but I was still surprised to hear that over four hundred boats would be racing today.

"And how is that different from every other weekend?" I tease, pulling my light jacket tight to my body. Three years in Miami temperatures has spoiled me for the crisp northern air that I grew up in. The fact that it's mid-morning and we're down by the river only adds to the chill.

"What do you mean? It's completely different. We have a week off from classes and tonight's party is going to be epic." She jumps up and down excitedly, those adorable dimples under her eyes appearing, her honey-blond hair wagging in a ponytail. "*And* I have the cutest naughty nurse costume." I can only shake my head at her. I've seen it already. It *is* cute and it's certainly naughty. And highly unrealistic. Grant won't know what hit him. "You're dressing up as the naughty schoolgirl, right?"

Apparently the theme for all female costumes must begin with "the naughty"—Grant and Ty's idea. The unfortunate thing is that I'm sure I'll be the oddball if I don't comply. "A schoolgirl, I can manage. Not the naughty part." Reagan saw my pleated skirt—the one I wore the day Ashton drove me to the hospital—and decided to complete the costume for me, coming home with garters, thigh-highs, and red stilettos. I sigh. Truth be told, I don't think I want to go. The sooner this weekend is over with, the sooner I can rid myself of this guilt choking the air out of my lungs. But Reagan doesn't want to hear any of that.

She turns to give me puppy-dog eyes normally reserved for Grant. "Don't you dare bail on me, Livie. It's Halloween!"

"I . . . I don't know. I have this thing and then my volunteer-ing . . ." Not to mention I've barely slept the past four nights, my mind unwilling to shut down, my stomach unable to stop roll-ing. Dread—that's what is ripping me apart. Dread over meeting Connor's parents, dread over seeing Ashton with his sweet and unsuspecting girlfriend.

Dread over seeing Ashton's father.

I don't even know if he'll be here; I never asked. But just the thought makes me sick. There are few things that spawn violence in me. Hurting those I care about is one. Hurting a child is an-other. He's done both. Maybe if I attack Ashton's father, I can avoid meeting Connor's parents altogether?

"Relax!" Reagan says, nudging me with her body. "Say, 'Hi, nice to meet you, ba-bye.' End of story."

"And then what, Reagan? How do I break up with him? It's not like he's done anything wrong that I can use against him." Not like me. A sour taste fills my mouth. I'm going to have to look him in the eye and *hurt* him. Can I avoid that part? It's only been about two months. What's the etiquette? Maybe I could do it through email . . . Kacey would be the right person to ask but, seeing as I've kept my sister in the dark up until now, it will spark an afternoon of questions I'm not ready to face and things I'm not willing to admit having done.

"Livie!" I turn to see Connor in his tight orange-and-white sleeveless top and black shorts—the team uniform—break through the crowd with a wide grin on his face. He's toweling the sweat off his glistening body.

I take a deep, calming breath. *You can do this. Just keep being nice to him.* Just a few more days until I rip his heart out and stomp on it.

"Want a hug?"

I give him a wrinkled-nose smile and curl my shoulder away

from him. That's not fake, actually. A sweaty Connor is far from
appealing. He chuckles and plants a kiss on my forehead instead.
"Okay, later, maybe. What'd you think of the race?"

"It was amazing." I had watched the guys with balled fists as
they rowed in to first place standing—their movements synchro-
nized, powerful, graceful.

"It was." Scanning the sea of heads, he says, "I'll be back soon.
Stay right here. Okay?" A slight frown creases his brow. "You
okay? You seem a little bit off lately."

I immediately force a smile. "I'm good. Just . . . nervous." I lift
to my tiptoes to give him a light peck on the lips.

Those pretty green eyes flash with amusement. "Don't be.
They're going to love you. Stay right here." In many ways, I'm
more worried about that than his mother pointing an accusatory
finger at me while she screams "whore" in front of thousands of
people.

I watch his lean form weave through the crowds.

And then I turn to look for my towering, beautiful man. I
see him almost immediately. He's impossible to miss. His hair
is damp and pushed back, falling at different angles around his
face. His muscles are tight from the recent exertion. A slick sheen
covers his body, as it did Connor's. I realize I wouldn't hesitate for
a second to throw myself at Ashton, though.

He's walking up from the water with a towel around his neck
as he wipes the sweat off. When his head lifts, he catches my eye
and my breath in an instant. I haven't seen him in a few days and
my body instinctively gravitates toward him.

I give him a wide smile and mouth, "Congratulations."

His head bobs once.

And then he turns away and walks toward the pretty blond
waiting at the sidelines with a group of people. I watch Dana
dive into his side, grinning wide. Without hesitation, he puts his

arm around her shoulder and smiles down at her as if there isn't anyone else in the world for him. As if I'm not right here, twenty feet away, watching it all.

Whether real relationship or not, it reminds me that Ashton is not mine. He never was mine.

He probably never will be mine.

The air is temporarily knocked out of my lungs.

Fighting against the sting, keeping the tears from slipping out—tears I have no right to shed—I swallow and turn my attention to the two older couples with them. One I quickly deduce is Dana's parents—she shares too many facial traits with them to be otherwise. I turn my attention to the other couple, to the stylish blond woman of maybe thirty. She's scanning her phone, her expression one of boredom, suggesting she was dragged here and can't wait to leave. Next to her is a well-dressed and attractive older man with gray streaks running through his hair.

"That's Ashton's dad," Reagan whispers to me as I watch him reach out and extend his somewhat stiff arm to Ashton. Ashton immediately takes it, dipping his head as he does so, I notice. As a sign of respect or submission, I'm not sure.

I study the man, looking for signs of the devil hidden within, of the manacle he has clasped around his son's neck. I see nothing. But I know that's meaningless because I've seen the proof. I've seen the scars, the belt, the resignation and pain in Ashton's voice the few times he's let it in. And this man's smile doesn't touch his eyes. I notice that.

I look between him and Dana's father and I wonder how those conversations went. Does Dana's father know his daughter is being used as collateral over Ashton's head?

Reagan's hand rubs my back. "He's a jerk, Livie. A ridiculously hot, brooding jerk that even I'd have a hard time saying no to if he made me scream like that . . ." I have to look away from Ashton as my cheeks flame with the reminder. Through the snippets of teasing, I've quickly deduced that Reagan walked in right at the pinnacle moment. She sighs. "There's nothing worthwhile beneath all that. It's just who he is. He likes the game."

Is she right? *I can't play this game with you, Irish.*

Have I fallen for Ashton's act? Everything in my heart says that the answer is no. But my head . . . This is all such a mess when it doesn't need to be. I have a wonderful guy bringing his parents over to meet me while I fight back tears over a guy who makes me lose all control, all sensibility. Who makes me *hurt.*

"Gidget!" Grant's loud call for Reagan pulls my attention away from my inner turmoil for a second to see him grab her from behind, folding his long, lean arms around her body in a fierce hug.

She squeals and spins around to loop her short arms around his neck. "Stop it! Daddy's somewhere around." She places a kiss on his cheek.

As if on cue, Reagan's dad booms from behind, "Grant!"

Reagan breaks away quickly, her eyes widening for a split second. "Shit," she mumbles, edging away from Grant before Robert's looming stature appears beside him.

Slapping his hand over Grant's shoulder, he says, "Good race, son."

"Thanks, Coach." Grant flashes his trademark goofy grin, but I notice he can't hold Robert's eye, his focus quickly shifting to the crowd.

If Robert notices Grant's nervousness, he doesn't let on. "Ty's looking for you." Pointing to the water, he adds, "Down there." Away from his daughter.

With a salute, Grant spins on his heels and disappears into the crowd.

"Young lady . . . ," Robert starts to say, his brow pulled together in a frown as he regards his tiny daughter.

She throws her arms around his sizeable belly. "Great race, Daddy! I'm going to go find Mom." Like a small child in a crowd, she easily slithers between two people and vanishes before he can utter another word, leaving him shaking his head in her direction. "I wonder how long it's going to take before she admits to me that they're together."

My mouth drops open, my eyes no doubt wide with shock. Is he testing me? Does he want to see if I'll confirm his suspicions?

"Oh, don't tell her I know." Robert's head shakes dismissively. "As long as she thinks I disapprove of Grant, she'll stay with him."

I have to purse my lips tight to keep from bursting out in laughter. I see where Reagan has gained her skills in deception.

"So how did you enjoy the races, Livie?"

"Exciting, sir."

He smiles. "Isn't it? Now I need to work these boys to the bone over the winter so they're ready for the spring season." I hear hollers of "Coach!" from the crowd. He holds up a hand to acknowledge the person as a sigh escapes him. "Never a dull moment on race day . . ." Turning back to me, his smile has been replaced with seriousness. "Before I forget . . ." He reaches into his jacket pocket to pull out a small, plain envelope. "I was hoping I'd run into you here."

Furrowing my brow, I gingerly open it and slip a picture out. It's clearly an old photo, by the quality of the developing. A young couple leans against a tree, the guy's arm slung over the girl's shoulder. She's resting her raven-haired head against his chest as they both smile into the camera.

My breath catches.

It's my parents.

I can't speak for a moment, as my free hand flies to my mouth, as I stare down at the two faces that I remember and yet are so new to me. "Where did you—" My voice breaks off.

"I have boxes upon boxes of old school pictures sitting in my attic. I've been meaning to go through them for years."

I can't speak.

"I thought I might have an old picture of your parents in there but I wasn't sure. It took a good week, sorting through."

"You did this?" I look up at Reagan's dad. "I mean . . ." Tears don't even threaten. They just start spilling out. "Thank you. I don't have any pictures of them in college."

He opens his mouth. I catch the momentary hesitation. "I know, Livie."

My frown lasts only a second before it clicks.

Only one person knew that.

Ashton told him.

"And it wasn't me going through the boxes." His voice is even, his brow arched in a knowing look.

I take a ragged breath. "Ashton?"

After a moment, Robert nods. "He knew it was them right away. It's impossible to miss the resemblance between you and your mother." I look down at it again. It could be me sitting there. *Ashton did this? Ashton spent a week going through someone's dusty pictures, looking for this, not even knowing if it existed. For me?*

"I don't know a lot about that boy, even after three years. He's not big on talking. But something tells me that nothing is quite as it seems with him." His mouth presses into a firm line. "What I do know is what I can see. That he cares greatly about his team-mates, he pushes them to excel, and he'll do anything for them. They all know it and they respect him for it. He's a born leader when he's out on that water. That's why he's captain. I think he could make a fine coach one day. If that's what he wanted to do." A thoughtful look glazes over his eyes. "It's like he . . . lets go of whatever is holding him back on land. Anyhow," Robert says as his eyes fall on me again, "he asked me not to tell you about this. Told me to make up some cockamamie story about stumbling across it." He gives me a wistful smile. "But I thought it was important that you know."

My hands roughly wipe at the tears streaming down my cheeks before one falls and stains the photo. I whisper, "Thank you."

Robert winks. "Now if you'll excuse me, I need to find my wayward daughter and get some photos taken." He ambles away, the crowd parting for him.

The river, the crowds, everything around me has vanished as I stare at the four-by-six in my hands, as I run my fingers along the edges, touching the people within. I'm so lost within the picture that I barely notice Connor's arm slip around my waist.

"You okay?" I have to pry my eyes away from their faces to look up and see that Connor's permanent smile is faltering. "You look a little pale."

"Yeah, I'm just . . ." I take a deep breath, trying to process the intensity of this emotion flooding my heart. *What am I?*

"Are those your parents?" He leans in to get a look at the photo in my hand. "Wow, look at your mom! Where'd you get this?"

I clear my voice. "Reagan's dad."

"Wow, that's nice of him."

"Yeah, nice," I parrot. *No, not nice, Connor. Wonderful, unbelievable, remarkable. That's what this is, Connor. Earth-shattering. My earth. Shattered. The one I knew or thought I knew, blown away.*

Would Connor spend a week straight going through boxes? Delay schoolwork, risk his grades, all for me? That comment Ashton made about being behind on his papers . . . having something tying him up at night. *This* is what he was doing.

All I want to do right now is run to Ashton, to touch him,

to be close to him, to thank him. To let him know how much he means to me.

"Come on." Connor takes my hand, dismissing the entire topic so quickly. As if it's trivial. "Come and meet my parents."

I no longer simply dread meeting Connor's parents; it has now become the absolute last thing I want to do on this planet. But I'm trapped. Swallowing the sudden urge to vomit, I let him lead me through the crowd as I put on the best fake smile that I can produce and pray that any sneers can be chalked up to nerves about meeting them.

He stops in front of an older couple. "Mom, Dad. This"—he gently places a hand on the small of my back—"is Livie."

"Hello, Livie. I'm Jocelyn," Connor's mom says with a broad smile. I note that Connor has her eyes and her hair color. She doesn't have an accent, but I remember him saying she was American. Her eyes quickly appraise me as she offers her hand. It's a harmless and not unpleasant appraisal, and yet I fight the urge to recoil all the same.

Next to her is Connor's father. "Hello, Livie." He sounds just like Connor, and my father, except his accent is thicker. If I weren't ready to bolt out of here like a girl on fire, I'd probably fawn over it. "I'm Connor Senior. We're both so pleased to meet the young woman who finally captured our son's heart."

Captured our son's heart? What happened to "slow and easy"? I glance to see Connor's face flushing.

"Sorry to embarrass you," Connor's dad says, dropping a heavy hand on his son's shoulder. "But it's true."

Connor's thumb slides playfully against my back as anxiety pools in my stomach and creeps into my chest, stifling my ability to breathe. This is bad, bad, bad. This feels all *wrong*.

I put on my best smile. "Your son is a kind man. You must be proud."

"Oh. I can't begin to describe how proud we are of him." Jocelyn beams as she gazes in his direction. "He has a bright future. Even brighter now, with you in it."

Are they insane? I've known him for only two months! My eyes drop down to take in the perfect cardigan and pearl necklace beneath Jocelyn's perfect peacoat and I have a flash of manicured lawns and lapdogs—all these elements that my subconscious has assembled as the ideal life I could share with the main star currently standing next to me. The *only* star, I believed up until now. Who doesn't hide scars with tattoos, who doesn't wear a symbol of his dark childhood on his wrist, who isn't buried in secrets, including how and when his own mother died. Who also wouldn't spend a week looking for a piece of paper that may not exist because he wanted me to have it, not because he wanted me to know he spent a week looking for it.

Right here, standing before me, is the life that I thought my parents wanted for me. The only life I ever saw myself leading. I've found it.

And I need to get the hell away from it. "I'm so sorry, but I have my volunteer shift at the hospital. I need to leave now if I want to catch the train."

"Oh, of course, dear. Connor was telling us that you're planning on med school, right?" Jocelyn nods her head approvingly. "A brilliant student." *Yes, Cs all the way!*

"Okay, guys," Connor says. "You've embarrassed me enough." Leaning in to kiss my cheek, he whispers, "Thanks for coming to see me race today, Livie. You're the best."

With what must be a strained smile and a nod, I turn and get away as quickly as I can without running. My eyes roam the crowd, looking for my beautiful broken star.

But he's gone.

■ ■ ■

"I thought you guys would be excited about Halloween. You know . . . getting dressed up and all." I give Derek's cowboy vest a small tug. He responds with a shrug, pushing a Hot Wheel back and forth with languid movements, his head hanging. I'm afraid to ask how he's feeling.

"They won't let us eat much candy," Eric sulks, sitting cross-legged and fiddling with his pirate eye patch. "And Nurse Gale told me they'd take my sword away if I chased after one more person."

"Hmm. That's probably a good rule."

"What are you dressing up as, Livie?"

"A witch." No way in hell am I explaining to a five-year-old why a schoolgirl could be deemed an appropriate Halloween costume. I can only imagine the questions that would spark. "I have a party to go to tonight," I admit with reluctance.

"Oh." Eric finally takes his eye patch off to inspect it. "We were supposed to have a party today but they canceled it."

"Why'd they do that?"

"Because of Lola."

Lola. Dread runs its icy fingers down my back. There's only one reason I can think of that would make them cancel a party for a bunch of kids who need it more than anything. I don't want to ask. Still, I can't keep the tremble out of my voice. "What about Lola?"

I catch Derek's head shift slightly as he and his brother share a look. When Eric looks up at me again, it's with sad eyes. "I can't tell you because we made that deal."

"Lola—" I clear my throat against the bulge instantly within it, as a strange numbness washes over me.

"Livie, why can't we talk about it? Is it because it makes you so sad?"

Is it because it makes you so sad? His little voice, so innocent and curious. So enlightening. *Good question, Eric.* Was that rule for their benefit or mine? I close my eyes against the rush of tears threatening. *I can't break down in front of them. I can't.*

And then little hands settle on each of my shoulders.

Through blurry eyes, I find each twin standing on either side of me, Derek now watching me with a furrowed brow. "It's okay, Livie," he says in that raspy voice. "It'll be okay." Two five-year-old boys, both suffering from cancer, who just lost a friend, are comforting *me.*

"Yeah. Don't worry. You'll get used to it," Eric adds.

"You'll get used to it." Words that steal the air right out of my lungs and turn my blood cold, as if it froze in my veins. I know it didn't because I'm still alive; my heart is still beating.

All the same, in five words, in one second, something profound just died inside of me.

I swallow and give each of their little hands a squeeze and a kiss. I give them my most heartwarming smile as I say, "Excuse me, boys."

I see my reflection in the glass as I stand and walk toward the playroom door. My movements are slow and steady, almost mechanical, like those of a robot. Turning to the left, I head down the hall toward the public washrooms.

I keep going.

I get on the elevator, I get off of the elevator, I walk past the main desk and out the main entrance.

Out of the hospital.

Away from my autopilot future.

Because I don't ever want to get used to it.

■ ■ ■

Why the hell did I come?

I ask myself this as my stupid red stilettos click up the stairs to the house. I ask myself this as I push past a group of already drunk partiers, one of them trying to cop a feel under my skirt as I pass. I ask myself this as I step into the kitchen to find Reagan perched on the edge of the counter with a slice of lime in one hand, a salt shaker in the other, and Grant's face in her well-exposed cleavage.

Tequila. That's why the hell I came here tonight.

To drown myself in tequila so the thinking stops and the doubts fade and the churning guilt in my stomach stills for one damn night.

And, so I can thank Ashton for the photo and find the nerve to tell him that I think I'm in love with him. Because there is some tiny hope hidden deep in my heart that my saying it will make a difference.

I snatch the shot glass out of Grant's hand before he unburies his face and I down it. The burn is almost intolerable. I steal Reagan's lime to kill the vile taste before I vomit. Of all the things to want to drink . . . *Gah!*

"Livie!" Reagan cries, her hands flailing wildly, scattering salt in every direction. "Look! Livie's here!" A loud cheer of approval fills the kitchen and I automatically blush in response. I have no clue who any of these people are and I highly doubt they care who I am.

"I knew this look would work for you." She wiggles her eyebrows suggestively, her finger jabbing me directly in my left boob. Probably unintentionally. Maybe not.

"How much has she had?" I ask Grant. *Enough not to see that my eyes are still puffy and red from an hour of crying, thankfully.*

"Enough to tell me that if she ever jumped the fence, you'd be good to experiment on," Grant says, handing me another shot. I pound it back immediately, despite knowing I'm going to hate it. I hate this guilty rot inside me more.

"That's right. I did say that! I know what you like . . ." She gives an overexaggerated wink.

"Reagan!" My jaw drops as I look from her to Grant.

He just rolls his eyes, his hands up in the air as if in surrender. I notice for the first time that Grant is in scrubs and he has a name tag on him that reads *Dr. Grant Feel-You-Up Cleaver.* "She didn't explain. I didn't ask." With a mumble, he adds, "I don't want to know what the fuck is going on under this roof."

"Here! Try these. They're delicious!" As usual, Reagan quickly changes to a new topic, this time to a bowl of gummi bears. Sometimes I picture a bunch of squirrels chasing thoughts in her brain like they're nuts. I'm hoping the furry rodents keep their acorns far from Ashton or she's liable to blab, in her state.

With a sigh, and a mutter of thanks, I thrust my hand into the bowl while my eyes scan the kitchen and any other room in my sight, looking for his dark hair while I hold my breath.

"Do you like them?" Reagan chirps as my mouth puckers against the cold, juicy texture in my mouth. *Strange.* "They're full of rum! They're like Jell-O shots!"

New kryptonite. Fantastic. Then again, if I eat enough of these, I'm sure I'll tell Ashton anything and everything without reservation.

"Gidget! Focus!" Grant barks as he's downing another shot. It gives her just enough warning to place the lime between her teeth before he smashes his mouth into hers to suck on it, his hand shifting under her short skirt for good measure.

I turn away from the blatant foreplay. Reagan did threaten payback . . .

"Wow, Livie!" I jump back as a set of glassy green eyes appears five inches from mine.

My heart sinks with disappointment. I was hoping to avoid him tonight. "Hey, Connor."

"I'm Batman tonight, babe," he states as his arms stretch the cape out on either side of him, accidently knocking someone's drink out of his hand in the process. He's oblivious, though, too busy sliding his gaze down the length of my body. "You look great." Arms wrap around my waist to pull me against him. His breath smells like a mix of beer and hard liquor and he's slurring badly. "I mean . . ." Hands landing on each of my ass cheeks with a squeeze makes me jolt. "Really great."

I can't blame him. He's drunk and I'm dressed like most guys' fantasy, so I guess it's to be expected. Still, it makes me squirm away in discomfort, a scowl no doubt on my face. I somehow manage to break free of his grasp and slowly edge away to create some space between us.

"Great, party, huh?" He casts a hand out in the general direction of the crowd and I follow it, taking another small step back.

"Yeah. Looks like it."

"You're a little late to the festivities, though." And . . . he's back in my space, his mouth directly on my ear. Whatever edge two shots of tequila and a mouthful of rum-soaked gummi bears had taken off is back.

I flinch as he yanks one of my pigtails. It gives me the chance to shove him playfully and step around him. "I had a hard day at the hospital." *My future, basically crumbling before my eyes.*

"I'm sure you'll feel better tomorrow." He takes another sip of his beer as his head tilts to the side to get a better angle of my legs. I just shake my head. I know I shouldn't take anything Connor says or does seriously right now because he's drunk, but that was a typical Connor answer, alcohol or not. *You'll be fine. You're smart. You're strong. You're blah, blah, blah.* Such generic and dismissive responses.

I don't know if it's because I saw my future life when I met

his parents or because of Ashton or because I cried the entire
way home from the hospital as my dreams vanished, but I feel
like a fog has lifted and I'm thinking straight for the first time.
Connor is feeling more *wrong* by the minute. He looks perfect
on the outside—smart, sweet, good-looking, charming. He does
cute things like send me flowers and call me throughout the day
to say hello. He's never pushed me into sex or anything aside
from kissing, which, now that I think about it, is just plain weird
for a college guy. Maybe he's gay and I'm the perfect cover for his
parents? Either way, it worked out well, because I've never had
the urge to go farther with him. That in itself should have been
a red flag for me.

No . . . the guy I grew up picturing in my head is definitely
Connor. I just know that I don't belong in the picture with
him.

Ty bursts into the kitchen in his kilt then, causing a com-
motion, one I'm glad for because it forces Connor's ogling eyes
away from my thighs. "Sun!" he booms, his cheeks rosy. "Where
are you, my Sun!" When he spots the slender Asian girl dressed
in what I think is supposed to be a librarian outfit—complete
with a whip in hand—he drops to his knees and starts belting out
the lyrics to "You Are My Sunshine" in an exaggerated Scottish
accent.

The place erupts in an uproar of cheers as Sun blushes. Despite my mood, I can't help but giggle because it's sweet, in a
mortifying way. Then Connor moves in to grab my waist, slurring
into my ear, and my giggle dies.

"Can you believe they're hooking up? What an odd match." I
recoil, but he doesn't notice. "But he said she's a minx in the sack."
What? Who is this guy? I don't like drunk Connor at all.

I'm starting to regret that I ever came. My plan of drowning my sorrows in alcohol is quickly being replaced with my plan to simply get the hell away from Connor. But not before I see Ashton. Just once. "Where's Ashton?" I figure it's a harmless enough question.

"I don't know . . . around." Beer dribbles out of Connor's cup and spills on his costume as he takes a sip. "Or screwing someone upstairs."

I try not to flinch at his words but I can't help it. Just the thought of Ashton doing to anyone else what he did for me makes me cold inside. I hope Connor doesn't notice. "Oh, of course." That answer came out shaky. Suspicious. *Shit.*

Turns out I don't need to worry about Connor noticing anything besides my body parts, as his eyes are now glued to my chest. I wish I could make the shirt less revealing, but Reagan stealthily removed the top buttons this morning. "You're so hot, Livie. How did I find someone so amazing?" I feel his weight shift against me as he half leans, half falls into me, pressing me up against a wall. "You're sweet and pure and perfect. And you're all mine." His mouth drops to my throat. "Sometimes I want to . . ." He leans farther in, pressing his groin against my thigh, squashing my gay theory like a ripe tomato. The hand that's pawing my hair slides down to my breast and starts squeezing it like it's a stress ball—rough and not at all pleasant.

I don't think any amount of tequila will make this feel good.

"I need to use the bathroom," I mumble, squirming out from between him and the wall and dashing out of the kitchen. I can't be here anymore. I can't be near Connor. I want to run home for a shower and forget that just happened.

I need Ashton.

I pull my phone out and send him a quick text. Not waiting for a response, I start searching from room to room, skillfully avoiding Connor twice. I can't find Ashton anywhere, though, and no one has seen him. A quick check of the garage finds his black car.

Ashton is here.

That means he must be in his room.

And he's not answering his texts.

So much for not feeling anything tonight. The dread is back and has increased tenfold, churning in my stomach like a deadly whirlpool of jealousy and hurt and desperation.

I have only two choices—leave and assume that he's upstairs with someone or go upstairs and find out.

With my arms hugging my chest tightly, I climb the stairs, each step bringing me closer to either the pinnacle of a disastrous day or to an ocean of relief. I think that if I find him with another woman, I'll die.

Why am I doing this to myself? *Because you're a masochist.*

I see his door up ahead, closed. There's no red sock or any other indication that someone might be in there.

Still . . .

I don't even need to consciously hold my breath because I've stopped breathing altogether as I put my ear to the door. The softest music is playing, so he's in there, but otherwise . . . silence. No moans or groans or female voices.

Before I can chicken out, I knock lightly.

No answer.

Swallowing, I knock again.

No answer.

I reach down to gently test the doorknob, to find it unlocked.

This is the weirdest feeling I've ever had—blood rushes in my ears as my heart pounds viciously and yet my lungs are still. I know it can't go on forever. I know I'll get dizzy and pass out soon if I don't make a choice.

I have to make a choice. I can turn and leave now—leave this house because I can't deal with Connor—and not see Ashton. Not touch him, not have him help me forget this awful day in a way that only he can.

Or I can open the door and risk seeing him with someone else.

I open the door.

A freshly showered Ashton sits on the edge of his bed in a towel, staring at the floor while one hand fumbles with the belt band. He holds a glass with amber liquid in it.

If I were any more relieved right now, I'd dissolve to the floor. "Hey." I say it as softly as I can, as the gravitational pull toward him takes over.

"Close the door. And lock it. Please. I don't want to see any-one tonight." His voice is low and hollow-sounding. He hasn't even looked up. I don't know what this mood is. I've never seen it before.

I follow his instruction, locking out the house of people, the party, Connor. Everything. Leaving just us.

And then I step closer, slowly, tentatively. Not until I'm three feet away do his dark eyes lift, scanning me from red stilettos and up slowly. He stops at my chest. "You shouldn't be in here," he mutters before taking a sip of his drink.

"Why aren't you downstairs?"

He swishes the liquid around in his glass. "I had a shitty day."

"Me too."

Downing the last of his drink, Ashton places the glass on his nightstand. "Do you want me to help you forget?" A stir in my thighs instantly confirms that my body definitely would appreci-ate that. Brown eyes finally find their way to my face, no hint of amusement in them. Nothing but resigned sadness and a touch of glassiness. "I'm good at that, aren't I." There's a meaning behind those words that I can't fully comprehend.

"I know that picture came from you."

He bows his head.

Now that I'm standing here in front of Ashton, the confusion I've been battling for weeks melts away. For the first time in longer than I can remember, I know exactly what I want. And I have no doubt in my mind that it's right. "I'm going to give you something today, too." I push aside the swirl of butterflies in my stomach, committing fully to what I'm about to do, to what I'm about to give him if he'll take it as I slip out of my heels. I don't know if it's easier or harder with him not watching me, but I undo the four buttons Reagan left me and let the fitted blouse drop to the floor. My fingers make quick work of the buttons on my skirt and let that fall as well.

As if fighting the urge to resist and losing, Ashton's eyes lift to take me in before his face turns away to look at the corner of the room. "Jesus Christ, Irish," he mutters through gritted teeth, his hands squeezing the edge of the mattress, trying to restrain himself. "I won't be able to stop myself."

Reaching back to unhook my bra, I let that fall to the ground in answer. Those stupid garters follow immediately. Soon, I've pulled every last piece of the ridiculous costume off and Ashton's still not looking at me. In fact, his eyes are closed.

I swallow as I reach out to run my fingertip over the bird on his arm, intentionally avoiding the scar. I lean down to place a gentle kiss on it. "Tell me what this means." It's not a question. I'm not giving him a choice.

There's a long pause where he says nothing. "Freedom."

I let my finger skate up to the one on his shoulder. I demand again. "And this? Tell me what it means."

A little louder. "Freedom."

I place a kiss on it in response.

I reach down to pull his towel loose and throw both ends

away. I quietly climb on to straddle his lap. Ashton hasn't touched me yet, but his eyes are now open and taking in my body with a strange expression that I can't read. It's almost like shock or awe, as if he can't believe this is actually happening.

I place my hand over the symbol on his chest, feeling his heart pound beneath. "Freedom?"

His eyes lift to meet mine immediately, his voice more steady, more defiant than before. "Yes."

I don't let that distract me, though, as my hand skates around to where I know the script with my name is. I don't need to ask him what it means because I now know beyond a doubt. He's already told me in so many ways.

He says it without my prompting. "Freedom."

I don't have all the pieces to fix this beautiful, trapped, broken man, but I do have one piece and it's mine to give. For one night, for all nights. For however long he wants it.

Me. Completely.

I know what I have to do next. I don't know how he'll react. Whether this is a good idea or not, I have to do it. Holding his gaze, trying to tell him that it will all be okay with my eyes, I reach for his wrist, for the belt strap, for the snaps that affix it. A flash of panic skitters across his face and his neck muscles cord. It's a moment when I think maybe this is a bad idea. But I grit my teeth against it, using all the anger I have over his father and what he's done to him, what he's still doing to him and, inadvertently, to me, and I rip that damn belt strap off and whip it across the room. "I'm giving you your freedom tonight, Ashton. So fucking take it."

I don't regret a second of it.

Not as he flips me onto my back.

Not as he pushes into my body without hesitation.

Not as I cry out with that moment of pain.

And certainly not as he claims his freedom.

And gives me a part of mine.

■ ■ ■

In the darkness, with the dull sounds of a party dying in the background, Ashton opens the vault just far enough that a memory slips out, unprompted. "She used to sing this song in Spanish." His fingers swirl over my back as I rest my head on his chest, listening to his heartbeat, still in awe of him and me and us together. It was . . . incredible. It feels *right* in a way that nothing else has ever felt right. "I can't remember the words, and to this day I don't know what it meant. I just remember the tune." My cheek vibrates under the low melodic rumble as he begins to hum.

"It's beautiful," I whisper, rolling my face forward to kiss that perfect chest.

"Yeah," he whispers in agreement. His hand slows. "When he put the duct tape over my mouth, I couldn't do anything but hum. So I'd hum for hours. It helped."

For hours.

"That's my favorite memory of my mother."

Lifting to my elbows to take in his face, I see the tears trickling down from the corners of his eyes. I so badly want to ask him what happened to her, but I can't bring myself to do it right now. All I want to do is kiss away his tears.

And help him forget.

■ ■ ■

We've found that if we ignore the knocking, it goes away after a few minutes. It's worked three times already. Now, as I lie in a twisted heap of flesh and soft white sheets with Ashton at noon, sore in ways I've never been sore before, I'm hoping that it will work for a fourth time. Because I don't want to leave these four walls. Within these four walls, he and I have cast away all of our fears, our commitments, our lies. Within these four walls, we both have found our freedom.

"How are you feeling?" Ashton whispers in my ear. "How sore are you?"

"A little bit," I lie.

"Don't lie, Irish. It won't be favorable to you." As if to prove his point, he presses his erection against my back.

I giggle. "Okay, maybe a bit too sore for that."

He sits up and yanks the covers off me completely. Adjusting my legs, he takes his time staring blatantly at my body, the heat in his eyes intensifying by the second. "I want to memorize every square inch of you and have the image branded in my brain and burning hot twenty-four-seven."

"Wouldn't that be distracting?" I tease, but I don't shy away from his scrutiny. I think my body is starting to crave it. It's certainly not as shy around him now, after twelve hours straight of naked Ashton.

Running his large hands up and down the sides of my thighs, he murmurs, "That's the idea, Irish."

"Even my feet?" With a playful giggle, I lift my leg to flick his chin with my toe.

He grabs my foot. With a sly smile, he grips it tight and runs his tongue along the bottom. I clamp my hands over my mouth to keep from howling with laughter as I struggle to break free, but there's no point. He's too strong.

Thankfully he stops that torture, crawling back over to lie on his side next to me, his hand brushing strands of hair off of my face as I let my finger run over the spot where I know my name permanently sits on his body.

"Tell me why you call me Irish."

"Sure but, first things first." His eyebrow arches pointedly.

"God you're stubborn!" I release a heavy sigh. Given that I'm lying naked with the man, I figure I'll humor him to get the truth. Pursing my lips to keep the grin from showing, I mutter, "Fine. I *may* want you."

"May?" He grins at me. "You walked up and practically ripped my toga off as you pulled me down, shouting, 'Kiss me, I'm Irish!'"

I gasp, my hand flying to my mouth as the words trigger the memory of Ashton's shocked expression at that very moment, and the ensuing kiss he laid on my lips. My first *real* kiss. "Ohmigod, you're not lying." My cheeks flame, which only makes Ashton start chuckling.

"And then you just turned around and stormed off to dance." A twinkle skitters through his eyes. "I was going to leave you alone, but after you did that . . ." His thumb rubs my bottom lip affectionately. "No way in hell was this mouth touching anyone else."

I run my fingertip along his defined collarbone as I accept that I started all of this. My unleashed beast somehow knew exactly what she wanted from the very start, long before I could come to terms with it.

Taking my fingertips within his, he kisses each of them, his gaze burning with intensity as it settles on my face. "You do know why I dug through Coach's dusty-ass attic for a week straight, right?"

My heart swells with the mention of that. Of what this sweet guy did for me. I'm not sure exactly why he did it, other than to make me happy. But I know what it meant for me. It helped me see the one thing that I know *I* want, buried amongst a pile of uncertainties.

"Because you're madly in love with me?" I repeat what he said to me that day in class with a teasing wink to let him know that I'm just joking around.

But Ashton doesn't response with a snort or a chuckle or anything close to humor. His expression is a mask of sincerity as he leans in to lay a tiny kiss on my bottom lip. "As long as you know." And then he's kissing me deeply again.

And I instantly fall back into oblivion.

"Maybe I'm not too sore," I manage to get out around his hungry yet gentle lips. With a groan, he shifts his mouth downward along my throat, my chest, my stomach, stirring my need for the tenth, hundredth, thousandth time since we landed in his bed.

And that's when the knocking begins again.

"Ace, open up! I know you're in there." There's a pause. "I can't find Livie. She's not answering her phone."

Shit.

Connor.

I haven't thought of him once. Not once since stepping into this room last night.

"If you don't open this door in two minutes, I'm going to use the damn key."

Ashton and I look at each other, the fire between us doused like a bucket of cold water on a pit of flames.

"Fuck," Ashton mutters under his breath, glancing around. My clothes are strewn everywhere.

We roll off the bed and begin collecting them. Connor may have been drunk, but I think he'll recognize that outfit.

"Here." Ashton hands me my jacket. I thank sweet heaven that I decided on my long black coat last night. It will hide everything but my heels and my black stockings on my way back to my dorm. "Go hide in the bathroom. I'll try to get rid of him," he whispers, kissing me gently.

I scurry in just as we hear Connor fiddling with the lock.

"I'm coming!" Ashton hollers.

Closing and locking the bathroom door quickly, I hold my breath as I quietly begin dressing. I can hear them outside perfectly.

"Jesus, Ashton, cover your junk. I already feel like puking," I hear Connor grumble, and I roll my eyes. Is walking around naked an Ashton thing or a general all-guy thing? "What happened to you last night, man?"

I hear a dresser door slam, and I assume Ashton is pulling on at least a pair of briefs. Even in the present stressful situation, that conjures a visual—one where I'm prying them off him the second Connor is gone. "I wasn't in the mood," I hear Ashton murmur.

"You . . . alone up here?"

"Unfortunately."

"Well, you missed a good party from what I remember. Which isn't much." There's a pause. "I think I fucked up with Livie."

I close my eyes and take a deep breath as anxiety slips through my core. I don't want to be listening to this.

"Oh yeah? That sucks." Ashton is phenomenal at pretending to sound uninterested.

"Yeah, I think I might have come on a bit strong. She left the party early and she's not answering my calls or my texts."

"Just give her time to cool down."

"Yeah, I guess. But I'm going over there to see her today. I need to know things are okay."

They're not, Connor. They never really were. With a small sigh, I accept that I can't hide out in Ashton's room for the rest of my life, though the thought has crossed my mind more than once. I need to finish getting dressed and get back to the dorm so I can end this with Connor.

And he's given me the perfect excuse.

I can blame Connor for the breakup. He pushed me too far.

He knows I want to take things slow and he groped me like a thirteen-year-old boy playing the closet game. This is perfect. Then it won't be my fault. He'll think it's his fault. He'll . . .

Taking a deep breath, I turn to look at the reflection in the mirror—at the woman in black thigh-highs and I-just-lost-my-virginity-and-then-some hair, hiding in a bathroom while her boyfriend is on the other side, worrying about her with his best friend, the dark and broken man whom she has fallen madly in love with. And all this person can think about is how she'll avoid admitting to all wrongdoing.

I don't recognize her at all.

I hear that heavy sigh of Connor's and I know he's rubbing the top of his head. That's Connor. Predictable. "I just . . . I think I'm in love with her."

My body hunches in on itself as if just punched. *Ohmigod.* He just said it. He said it out loud. Somewhere deep in my sub-conscious, I was afraid of this. Now it's real. I think I'm going to be sick. Seriously, I am two seconds away from diving to the porcelain bowl.

This. Will. Crush. Him.

And Connor doesn't deserve to be crushed. He may not be right for me but he doesn't deserve this. Yet no matter what reason I give, whether I blame it on him or me, whether I tell the truth or not, I'm going to hurt him. I have to resign myself to that fact because no matter what, he and I are done.

Ashton's irritated tone surprises me. "You don't love her, Connor. You *think* you do. You barely know her."

My reflection nods her head back at me. She's agreeing with Ashton. *That's right. Connor doesn't know me at all. Not like Ashton knows me.*

"What are you talking about? It's Livie. I mean, how can you *not* love her. She's fucking perfect."

I squeeze my eyes shut. *Too fucking perfect, Connor.* I quietly slide my coat on over myself, pulling it tight to my body, aching for Ashton's warmth.

There's a long pause, and then I hear the bed creak and Ashton's heavy sigh. "Yeah. I'm sure she's fine. You should go and check out the campus, then. Maybe she's at the library."

"Yeah. You're right. Thanks, bro."

The lightest sigh of relief escapes me as I lean back against the wall.

"I'll try her one more time on her phone."

My phone.

Fuck.

I watch the reflection in the mirror of this girl—this foreign woman—go from a slightly pale complexion to stark white as Connor's ring tone sounds faintly from the phone in my purse. My purse, which is sitting on Ashton's nightstand.

It rings and rings and rings. And then it stops.

Dead silence.

Deader than dead. So dead that I could be the last person left in this world.

And then I hear Connor ask slowly, "Why is Livie's purse here?" Connor's voice has taken on a tone that I've never heard before. I don't know how to describe it, but it makes my body suddenly turn cold with dread.

"She swung by to say hi and forgot it, I guess." Ashton's a fantastic liar, but even he can't pull that one off.

The sound of footsteps approaching has me shuffling away from the door.

"Livie?"

I purse my lips tight and clamp my hands over them and close my eyes and stop breathing. And then I count to ten.

"Livie. You need to come out here right now."

I shake my head, and the movement dislodges a stifled moan.

"I can hear you, Livie." After another long pause, he starts pounding on the door, rattling the entire wall. "Open the damn door!"

"Leave her alone, Connor!" Ashton bellows behind him.

It stops the pounding but not the yelling. The yelling only gets more vicious. "Why is she hiding in there? What the fuck did you do to her? Did you . . ." There's a strange jostling sound in the room. "How drunk was she when she came up here, Ash? How drunk?"

"Really drunk."

I glare at the door. *What? No, I wasn't! Why would he say that?* There's another long pause. "Did you force her into anything?"

With a resigned sigh, I hear Ashton say, "Yes. I did."

I feel like someone has just struck a match and stuck it into my ear, hearing words that turn my beautiful, remarkable, unforgettable night with Ashton into a drunken rape story. I instantly know what Ashton is doing. He's making an excuse for me. He's making himself out to be the bad guy. To take all the blame for what I initiated. What I wanted.

I throw the door open and storm out. "I was not drunk and he did not force me into anything!" The words come out in an angry gasp. "He has never forced me. *Never once.*"

The two men turn to face me, the one on the left wearing nothing but track pants and shaking his head in a "why-did-you-come-out-here" way, the one on the right full of shock and barely concealed rage.

"Never once." Connor's tone has evened again, but I don't think it's a sign of him calming. I think it's a sign of him ready to blow. "How many times have there been, Livie? And for how long?"

Now that I've set the record straight—that what Ashton and

I shared was not a crime scene—my anger has vanished, leaving me trembling and unable to speak once more.

"How long!" he repeats in a bark.

"Always!" I burst, wincing as the truth comes out. "Since the first second I met him. Before I met you."

Connor turns to look at his roommate, his best friend, whose eyes haven't left mine, an unreadable expression in them. "Un-fucking-believable. That night with the tattoo . . . You've been fucking her since then?"

"No!" The word flies out of our mouths in unison.

Connor is shaking his head dismissively. "I can't believe you would do this to me. Of all the whores you bring in and out of here . . . you had to turn her into one too."

"Watch it." Ashton's body visibly stiffens and I see his hand clenching, but he stays still.

Connor doesn't seem to care, though. Gritting his teeth, he studies the hardwood for a moment, shaking his head. When he finally looks at me again, I can see the impact of this on his face; his normally bright green eyes are now dull, as if the pilot light has finally been extinguished.

And I'm the one who put it out.

"What happened to taking it slow, Livie? What? You figured you'd jerk me around for a bit while you also screwed around with my best friend?" He turns to yell "My best friend!" with added emphasis.

I'm shaking my head frantically. "It wasn't like that. It just . . . things have changed."

"Oh really?" He steps forward. "What else has changed?"

"Everything!" I cry out, brushing away a sudden tear. "My future. The hospital. Princeton, maybe?" I hadn't realized it until just now, but this place . . . it's all that the catalogues, the websites, the hype promised, and yet it's not what I want. It's not home. It never will be. I want to be back in Miami, with my family. I'm not ready to leave them yet. The only thing that I do want at Princeton is standing silently, his arms crossed over his bare chest, as I spill my guts. "You and I . . . we don't belong together." Connor flinches as if I stuck him, but I keep going. "I'm in love with Ashton. He understands me. I understand him." A quick glance over at Ashton finds his eyes now squeezed tight as if he's in pain.

Something that looks like pity fills Connor's face. "You think you understand him, Livie? Really? You *think* you *know* him?"

I swallow to keep my voice steady. "I don't think. I *know*."

"Do you know how many women he's had in this room? In that bed?" His hand lifts to point toward it for effect. I force my chin up, trying to be strong. I don't want to know. It doesn't matter. He's with me now. "I hope you at least used condoms."

Condoms.

I completely forget. It was just too intense.

The color draining from my face says it all.

Connor dips his head, shaking it with disappointment. "Jesus, Livie. I thought you were smarter than that."

Ashton hasn't said a word. Not a word to defend himself, or us. He stands quietly, watching this entire disaster with sad, resigned eyes.

The three of us stand facing each other in a misshapen triangle, the air between us choking thick and toxic, the lies swirling visibly on the outside while the truth of what Ashton and I have disappears into nothingness.

That's how Dana finds us. "What's going on?"

Honest fear contorts Ashton's face for just a moment before vanishing, leaving his complexion three shades paler. "What are you doing here?"

"I thought I'd surprise you," she says, stepping into the room so carefully that you'd think the floor was riddled with land mines.

Connor crosses his arms over his chest. "Why don't you tell her, Livie? Go on . . . tell her what you just told me." Connor stares at me. Ashton stares at me. And when pretty, sweet Dana steps into the mix, her eyes wide with confusion and fear, she stares at me too, as she reaches up to clutch Ashton's arm.

A sparkle catches my eye.

The solitaire diamond on Dana's left hand. On her ring finger.

The gasp catches in my throat.

When did he propose?

Ashton knows I've seen it, because he closes his eyes and begins absently fumbling with the leather belt strap around his wrist.

It's back on his wrist.

Ashton has put that shackle back on his wrist. Which means he's given up the freedom that I gave him last night.

By the look of dismay on Connor's face, he's also seen the ring and now truly realizes the extent of this betrayal. "Tell her, Livie. Tell her what's going on between you and her future husband, if you think you know him so well."

I don't need to say anything. Dana's face pales. I watch as her eyes take me in from head to toe, then turn to look at the bed, then back to me. Almost recoiling from Ashton's arm, she stumbles back three steps. "Ash?" Her voice trembles as she turns to look at him.

He bows his head, mumbling almost indecipherably, "I made a mistake. Just let me explain."

Bursting into tears, she turns and runs out of the room. Ashton doesn't hesitate for a second. He runs after her as her screams carry through the house.

Turning his back on me. On us. On whatever the hell we were. *A mistake.*

Connor's words are quiet but piercing, soft but deadly, honest but so far from the truth. "You helped shatter two hearts today. You must be proud. Goodbye, Livie." The bedroom door slams behind him.

And I know that there's no reason for me to be here anymore. Not in this house, not in this school. Not in this life that is not *my* life.

I have to let go of everything.

And so I walk away.

I walk away from the voices, the shouts, the disappointment.

I walk away from my deceptions, my mistakes, my regrets.

I walk away from all that I am supposed to be and all that I cannot be.

For all of it is a lie.

chapter eighteen

. . .

LETTING GO

I find them sitting at the kitchen table. Kacey is curled up on Trent's lap with her fingers coiled in his hair, laughing as Dan pokes Storm's swollen belly repeatedly, trying to make the baby respond. She's due in two months now and she's as beautiful as ever.

"Livie?" My sister's watery blue eyes stare at me with a mix of surprise and worry. "I thought you weren't coming home over your break."

I swallow. "Neither did I, but . . . things changed."

"I can see that." She stares pointedly at my outfit. I never did go back to the dorm to change. I simply jumped in a cab to Newark and went on standby for the first available flight out to Miami. It took ten hours, but here I am.

Home.

Where I never should have left to begin with.

No one says a word, but I feel their eyes on my back as I walk over to the pantry. I pull out the bottle of tequila that Storm keeps on the top shelf. For emergencies, she says. "You were right, Kacey." I grab two shot glasses. "You were right all along."

■ ■ ■

"I missed the sound of seagulls," I murmur.

"Wow, you really are fucked up."

With a snort, I fling my hand in Kacey's direction and end up slapping her in the cheek. Last night, with the bottle of tequila and two shot glasses in hand, I had silently walked out the patio door to the deck. Kacey followed me, pulling up a lounge chair next to mine. Without a word, she started pouring shots.

And I started pouring my guts out.

I told my sister everything.

I admitted to every detail of my last two months, right down to the most intimate and embarrassing. Once the truth started flowing, it cascaded out of me in an unstoppable torrent. I'm sure the booze helped, but being around my sister helped more. Kacey just listened. She held my hand and squeezed it tight. She didn't pass judgment, she didn't scream, she didn't cast disappointed sighs and glances or make me feel embarrassed. She *did* scold me for not using a condom, but then quickly admitted that she shouldn't be throwing stones.

She cried with me.

At some point Trent came out to stretch a duvet over us. He didn't say a word, leaving us to our drunken, sobbing stupor. And as the first hints of sun came over the horizon, completely drained of every last emotion, every secret, every lie, I passed out.

"Can I see that picture again?" Kacey asks softly.

I hand her the four-by-six from my purse, so thankful that I had it on me when I left. "I can't believe how young they are here," she murmurs, tracing the lines of the image as I had. I smile to myself. Three years ago, Kacey couldn't even glance in the general direction of our parents' picture.

Waving it at me before she hands it back, she murmurs, "Proof that he cares a great deal about you, Livie. Even if he is a train wreck."

I close my eyes and heave a sigh. "I don't know what to do, Kacey. I can't go back. I mean . . . he's engaged. Or he was." Is he still? I'd received a where-the-hell-are-you text from Reagan earlier. After explaining that I was back in Miami, we shared a few messages, but she had no information for me. Or she didn't want to tell me, other than to say that she hid out in Grant's room all day because there was a lot of screaming and yelling.

That made me start worrying about Ashton more. What if he's not with Dana? What will his father do to him? Will he use whatever he has over his head?

"And he's definitely a train wreck," Kacey repeats. "He needs to clear the tracks before he can move on with anyone, and that includes you."

Just the thought of it stirs an ache in my chest. She's right. Whatever Ashton and I had, I have to let it go. As much as I want to keep trying, to stay close to him while he battles whatever demons he needs to battle, I can't keep doing it. Not like this.

Not with Connor and Dana and . . . *ugh*. The ring. My stomach tightens. This thing between us—love or not—has turned me into a selfish, manipulating idiot who takes what she wants even though it may hurt others. Who kept convincing herself that everything she did was okay because she knew that the man she wanted cared about her.

Who would likely fall back into that trap because it felt so right, despite being so wrong.

"You don't have to go back."

I crack an eyelid to look at her, flinching against the harsh daylight as I do. "What . . . just give up on everything?"

She shrugs. "I wouldn't call it giving up. More like living through trial and error. Or taking a breather. Maybe time away from Ashton and school will put things into perspective. Or maybe they're already in perspective and you just need a little time to let the dust settle."

"Yeah. Maybe." I close my eyes, gratefully absorbing the comfort of being home.

■ ■ ■

"You sure you don't want me to stay home?" Dad asks as he pushes the matted hair off my forehead.

I answer with a sneeze and a groan.

With a heavy sigh, he says, "Okay, that does it. I'm staying."

"No, Daddy." I shake my head, though I'd love nothing more than to have him comfort me. "You should go. I'll just get you sick if you stay here and it's Kacey's big game tonight. She'd be upset if you missed it." Scratch that. My sister would be crushed *if Dad missed it. "I'll be—" My words are cut off by another violent sneeze.*

Handing me a tissue, Dad cringes. "Well, I'm not going to lie to you, kiddo. You're kind of grossing me out right now."

The way he says "kiddo" with his faint Irish brogue makes me giggle.

"Don't worry. I'm grossing myself out right now, plenty," I say between nose blows.

He answers with a chuckle and a pat to my knee. "Just teasing. You'll always be my beautiful little angel, green snot and all." He busies himself arranging the medicine and liquids on my nightstand while I reposition myself. "Mrs. Duggan is in the family room—"

"Ugh! Dad! I don't need a babysitter!"

I see the shift before he utters a word. "Yes you do, Livie. You may act like a thirty-year-old sometimes but you're biologically only eleven, and Child Protective Services frowns upon leaving eleven-year-olds home alone. No arguing," he says briskly, leaning in to place a kiss on top of my head.

My brow knits as I fumble for my remote. Three back-to-back episodes of lions eating gazelles in the wild are too much.

With a sigh and a mutter about his stubborn girls, he stands up and heads toward the door. But he stops and turns back, waiting, his watery blue irises twinkling with his smile. My scowl lasts all of two more seconds before a grin wins out. It's impossible to keep a scowl when my dad smiles at me like that. He just has a way about him.

Dad chuckles softly. "That's my Livie Girl. Make me proud."

He says the same thing every night.

And tonight, just like every other night, I flash him a toothy smile as I answer, "I'll always make you proud, Daddy." I watch him leave, shutting the door quietly behind him.

I wake up to a late-afternoon sky and my last words to my father playing over in my head. Such simple words. A tiny, routine phrase. But in reality, guaranteed to be a lie. I mean, how can anyone commit to something like that? Not every decision you will make is going to be a good one. Some of them will even be disastrous.

I turn and see that the person sitting in the lounger next to me isn't as red-haired or female as the one who was there when I fell asleep.

"Hello, Livie." Dr. Stayner adjusts his hideous two-toned bowling shirt. It almost goes with the Hawaiian boardshorts that no man his age should ever wear. "How do you like my beachwear?"

"Hey, Dr. Stayner. Why are you always right?"

"I tend to be, don't I?"

■ ■ ■

"Thank goodness. I thought I'd have to torch that chair if you didn't shower soon."

I give my sister a playful shove as we walk down the hall toward the kitchen. "So . . . Stayner?"

She shrugs. "I texted him last night to let him know that you finally cracked. I didn't expect him to show up here with a suitcase, though."

Apparently, Dr. Stayner has decided to enjoy a few days in sunny Miami, Florida, at Chez Ryder. Well, Storm insisted that he stay with us, even though that means he takes Kacey's room and she sleeps either with me or at Trent's. I reminded her that it was strange and unprofessional for the family psychiatrist to stay with us. Then she reminded me that everything about Dr. Stayner is strange and unprofessional, so this actually makes sense.

My argument ended there.

And now Dr. Stayner is at our kitchen sink in one of Storm's polka-dot aprons, peeling carrots with Mia's help.

"Do you think eating carrots *really* make you see better or is that just what moms say to make kids eat vegetables?" Mia's at that cute age where she's still quite gullible but is learning to question things.

I lean up against the entranceway with my arms crossed and watch with curiosity.

"What do *you* think, Mia?" Dr. Stayner replies.

She narrows her eyes at him. "I asked you first."

I shake my head and laugh. "Don't bother. She's too smart for you, Stayner."

With a squeal, Mia drops the carrot and runs to dive into my arms in a hug. "Livie! Mom said you were here. Did you see X moving?"

I chuckle. I guess Mia has moved on from the loving nickname "Baby Alien X" to just "X." It works. "No, but I saw Dan poking your mom's belly last night," I say with a wink.

She makes a face. "I hope he's not going to be weird when X is born." The topic quickly changes. "Are you staying for a while?" Her expression is hopeful.

"I don't know, Mia." And it's the truth. I just don't know anything anymore.

■ ■ ■

"What do you think it is?"

Dr. Stayner slurps at the extra-large latte as we sit side by side in lounge chairs on the back deck, watching the early morning joggers pass by. All that coffee can't be good for him. "I can't begin to hazard a guess on that, Livie. He clearly has some issues to sort out. It would *seem* that he uses physical connections with women as a way of coping. It would *seem* that his mother's death is too difficult for him to talk about. It would *seem* that he does care greatly for you." Dr. Stayner sits back in his chair. "And if he grew up with an abusive father, then it is quite possible that he still feels as if he has little control over his life. Maybe he does. But I can tell you that you'll never get an answer that makes sense to you about why it all happened to him. And until he talks about it, it's difficult to help him. And that is why, my dear Livie Girl . . ." I roll my eyes but then smile. For some reason he took a liking to that nickname. "You need to untangle yourself from his mess until you can straighten out yours. Don't forget, your sister and Trent needed the same. It was five months before they reconnected. These things often take time."

I nod slowly. *Five months.* Where will Ashton be in five months? How many women will he "forget" with by then? And can I handle being at Princeton while he works things out? If he's even trying to work things out. My stomach is starting to churn again.

"Livie . . ."

"Sorry."

"I know it's hard, but you need to focus on yourself for a little while. Get this hang-up out of your head that you"—he lifts his fingers in air quotes—"'lied' to your father."

"But . . ." I avert my gaze to my freshly painted toes, care of Storm. "I know what he wanted for me and I'm going against it. How in the world would that make him *proud* of me?"

Dr. Stayner pats my shoulder. "I don't guarantee anything, Livie. Ever. But I will guarantee that your parents would be proud of you and your sister. Beyond proud. You are both simply . . . remarkable."

Remarkable.

"Even though I finally cracked?" I smile sadly, repeating Kacey's words.

He starts chuckling. "You didn't, Livie. I'd like to say that you finally came to a crossroad and just needed some guidance. You're a smart cookie who seems to figure things out. That's all you need sometimes—a little bit of guidance. Not like your sister. Now, *she* cracked." He turns to mouth "wow," and I can't help the snort of laughter that escapes me.

"I think you are going to be just fine with time. Now is the fun part."

I raise my brow in question.

"Figuring out *who* you want to be."

■ ■ ■

I'm used to Dr. Stayner in small doses—one hour per week on the phone, max. So when he leaves after spending several *days* with me, my brain temporarily shuts down like a machine that's overheated. We spent most of that time out on the back deck, discussing all the options I had before me for my education, for my future career aspirations, and for my social life. He never shared his opinions. He said he didn't want to skew my own selection process. The only thing he insisted on is that I embrace ambiguity for a while, that I don't dive into a choice for the sake of making one. He suggested that taking classes without focusing on a major right now à la Reagan isn't a bad idea. Of course, he had to acknowledge that the longer I waffled, the less likely the "stay at Princeton" option would apply, because I'd fail the semester.

I think my biggest fear about going back to Princeton isn't Princeton itself—I've accepted that the school just isn't for me. And I've already called the hospital to inform them that I'm quitting my volunteer position.

My biggest fear is facing Ashton again and my weakness around him. A simple look or touch could pull me back to him and that's not good for either of us. I've walked away once. Will the second time be harder or easier? Or impossible . . .

My life is full of difficult choices and one that's easy—Ashton.

And he's the one choice that I can't have.

chapter nineteen

■■■

CHOICES

I swear Reagan was waiting at the door like an eager pet for the sound of the unlocking mechanism, because the second I step through on Friday night, she barrels into me. "I missed you so much!"

"It's only been two weeks, Reagan," I say with a chuckle, tossing my purse on the desk. I decided to come back to Princeton after all. Not because I particularly feel like this is the place for me, but because I do know that I want an education, and until they either kick me out or I transfer to Miami—which I looked into while back at home—I may as well be here.

Tucking my hair back behind my ear, I ask casually, "So how has everything been?"

Her nose scrunches up. "Same. Don't know. Ashton's staying at my parents' right now and I can't get anything out of my dad. Grant's been staying here a lot because the house isn't much fun right now. Connor is hurt. But he'll be fine, Livie. Seriously. He just needs to get laid." She flops down onto her bed in typical

Reagan fashion—dramatically. "Oh, and Ty sprained his ankle. Dumbass."

I chuckle, but it doesn't loosen the angst inside.

"What's your plan for this weekend?" She hesitates. "Are you going to see him?"

I know who "him" is and it's not Connor. I shake my head. No . . . We need more than two weeks to sort this mess out. It's too new. Too fresh. Too painful to deal with. "Trying to catch up, if there's any hope." I missed a week's worth of classes, including a test. I slowly climb up the rungs to my bed, pushing out all the memories. "And I'm going to visit the boys at the hospital." I have to say goodbye properly, for my own closure.

■ ■ ■

I get a text from Dr. Stayner as I'm taking the train in to the hospital. It has an address, along with the words:

One more task, since you owe me for not completing the last one. Be there at two p.m.

I don't even question him anymore. The man's brilliant. I simply respond with:

Okay.

■ ■ ■

"Hi, Livie." Gale's beaming smile greets me at the front desk. When Kacey told Dr. Stayner that I was back in Miami, he contacted the hospital to let them know, in vague terms, what was happening. When I made the final decision that I would not be continuing on with the volunteer program, he sat with me while I called to let them know. They've been incredible with it all.

"The boys will be so happy to see you."

"How are they?"

She winks. "Go see for yourself."

Walking through the halls doesn't make me as sick as it did before, I notice. I know it's not because I have somehow gotten used to it. It's because I've let go of the idea that this has to be my future.

The twins run to me with energy I haven't seen in a while, clutching my legs and making me giggle.

"Come here!" Each of them grabs hold of a hand. They pull me over to the table. If they were upset that I left so abruptly two weeks ago, they aren't showing it.

"Nurse Gale said you were gone, doing some . . . I don't get what she said. Something about a . . . *soul*? You lost it? And you needed to go find it?" Eric ends that with a quizzical frown.

Soul searching. I chuckle. "Yes. I was."

"Here." Derek pushes forward a stack of papers with drawings on them. "She told us to help you think of all the things you could be when you grow up."

"I *told* her you wanted to be a doctor," Eric interjects with an eye roll. "But she thought it'd be good to give you backup ideas."

Looking at each of them in turn, at their eager little faces, I begin flipping through each sheet, evaluating all of my options.

And I'm laughing harder than I've laughed in a long time.

■ ■ ■

I step out of the cab in front of a large white Victorian house in Newark at exactly two p.m. By the sign out front, it appears to be a nursing home of sorts. A fairly nice one at that, I note as I enter through the front door and into a modest but charming foyer with dark mahogany floors, pastel striped wallpaper, and a floral arrangement sitting on a side table. Across from me is an unattended front desk with a notice directing visitors to a registration book. I sigh as I glance around, looking for a clue as to what I'm supposed to do next. Dr. Stayner gave me no further instruction than to go to this address. Normally he's quite explicit with his demands.

I pull my phone out of my pocket, about to text him for guidance, when a young blond woman in baby blue nurse scrubs strolls by.

With a smile in greeting, she says, "You must be Livie."

I nod.

"He's waiting for you in room 305. Stairs are around the corner, to your left. Third floor and follow the signs."

"Thanks." So Dr. Stayner is here. Why am I not surprised? I open my mouth to ask the nurse what she knows about room 305, but she's gone before I can utter a word.

I follow her directions, taking the staircase to the third floor, the lingering scent of industrial-grade cleaner trailing the entire way. I can't help but notice the eerie quiet as I climb. It only amplifies the creaking steps. Aside from an occasional cough, I hear nothing. I see nothing. It's as if the place is empty. My gut tells me it's far from it.

Following the room numbers on the doors, I watch the progression until I reach my destination. The door is propped open. *Okay, Dr. Stayner. What do you have for me now?* With a deep inhale, I step hesitantly around the corner, expecting to find my graying psychiatrist.

A short, narrow hallway leads into a room that I can't see fully from the doorway. All I can see is the corner ahead and a dark-haired, tanned, beautiful man hunched over in a chair—his elbows on his knees, his hands folded and pressed to his mouth as if he's waiting with trepidation.

My breath hitches.

Ashton is on his feet immediately. His lips part as he stares at me, as if he wants to speak but doesn't know where to begin. "Livie," he finally manages, and then clears his throat. He's never called me Livie before. *Never.* I don't know how that makes me feel.

I'm too shocked to respond. I hadn't expected to see him today. I hadn't prepared myself.

I watch with wide eyes as Ashton takes five quick strides over and seizes my hand, his worried brown eyes locked on mine, a slight tremble in his grip. "Please don't run," he whispers, adding more quietly, more gruffly, "and *please* don't hate me."

That snaps me out of my initial shock but it sends me into another one. Did he honestly think I'd run from him the second I saw him? And how on earth could Ashton ever think that I'd *hate* him?

Whatever is going on, Ashton clearly doesn't comprehend the depth of my feeling for him. Yes, I left two weeks ago. It was something I had to do. For me. But I'm here now and I don't ever *want* to run or walk or *anything* away from Ashton again.

I just pray to God that I won't *have* to.

What the hell is that damn psychiatrist of mine up to now?

Stepping backward, Ashton silently leads me farther into the room until I can see the entire space. It's quaint, simple—with pale yellow paper adorning the walls, crown molding lining the ceiling, and several vine plants suspended before a bay window, soaking up the mid-afternoon sunshine. All of those details vanish, though, as my eyes land on the woman lying in the hospital bed.

A woman with salt-and-pepper hair and a faintly wrinkled face that surely would have been described as beautiful at one time, especially with those full lips. Lips as full as Ashton's.

And it all just . . . clicks.

"This is your mother," I whisper. It's not a question because I know the answer with certainty. I just don't know the mountain of "whys" behind it.

Ashton's hand never slips from mine, his grip never weakens. "Yes."

"She's not dead."

"No, she's not." There's a long pause. "But she *is* gone."

I appraise Ashton's solemn expression for a moment before turning back to the woman. I don't mean to stare, but I do anyway.

Her eyes flicker from my face to Ashton's. "Who . . ." she begins to say, and I can tell she's struggling to form her words, her mouth working the shapes but unable to make the sounds come out. And in her eyes . . . I see nothing but confusion.

"It's Ashton, Mom. This is Livie. I told you about her. We call her Irish."

The woman's gaze roams Ashton's face and then drops down as if to search her memory.

"Who . . ." She tries again. I take two steps forward, as far as Ashton's death grip on my hand will allow me. It's close enough to catch the faint smell of urine that I recognize from the seniors homes with patients who have lost all bladder control.

As if giving up on figuring either of us out, the woman's head rolls to the side and she simply stares out the window.

"Let's get some air," Ashton whispers, pulling me with him as he walks to a little radio on the side table. He turns on an Etta James disc and adjusts the volume up a bit. I don't say anything as he leads me out of her room, closing the door softly behind him. We head down the hallway and a different set of stairs in silence, one that leads out to the home's backyard garden, a sizeable property with bare oak trees and small paths weaving through the flower beds, long since prepared for winter. I suspect this is a lovely respite for residents in warmer weather. Now, though, with the weak November sun and a bite in the air, I shudder.

Taking a seat on a bench, Ashton doesn't hesitate to pull me onto his lap and wrap his arms around my body as if to shelter me from the cold. And I don't hesitate to let him, because I crave his warmth for more than one reason. Even if I shouldn't.

This is exactly what I was afraid of.

I don't know what's right anymore. All I know is that Ashton's mother is alive and Dr. Stayner sent me here, no doubt to learn the truth. How Dr. Stayner knew . . . I'll figure that out later.

I close my eyes and inhale, absorbing Ashton's heavenly scent. Being so close to him after our night together is even harder than I imagined it would be. I feel as if I'm standing at the edge of a cliff and the storm of emotions threatens to push me off—pain and confusion and love and desire. I can feel that gravitational pull, that urge to curl into his body, to slide my hand over his chest, to kiss him, to make myself believe that he's mine. He's not mine, though. He's not even *his* yet.

"Why, Ashton? Why lie about her death?" Why . . . *everything*?

"I didn't lie. I just didn't correct you when you assumed she was dead."

The word "Why" is on my lips again, but he speaks before I can say it. "It was easier than admitting my mother doesn't re-member who I am. That every day I woke up hoping that it was the day she died so I could be free of my screwed-up life. So I could be at peace."

I close my eyes to stave off the tears. *Peace*. Now I understand what that strange look was, the night that Ashton found out about my parents' death. He was wishing the same for himself. Heaving a deep breath, I whisper, "You need to tell me. Every-thing."

"I'm going to, Irish. Everything." Ashton's head tips back as he pauses to collect his thoughts. His chest pushes out against mine as he takes a deep breath. I can almost see the weight lifting off his shoulders as he lets himself speak freely for the first time. "My mother has late-stage Alzheimer's. She developed it very early—earlier than most."

An instant lump forms in my throat.

"She had me when she was in her early forties. Unplanned and highly unexpected. And unwanted by my father. He . . . isn't one to share. That apparently included my mother's affections." He pauses to give me a sad smile. "My mother modeled for years in Europe before meeting my dad and moving to America. I have some of her magazine covers. I'll show you them one day. She was stunning. I mean drop-dead gorgeous."

I lift a hand to touch his jawline. "Why doesn't that surprise me?"

He closes his eyes and leans into my fingers momentarily before continuing. "When she met my dad, she had no interest in having kids either, so it worked out well. They were married for fifteen years before I was born. Fifteen years of bliss before I ruined everything, according to my father." He says that last part with an indifferent shrug, but I know he's far from indifferent. I can see the pain thinly veiled in those brown irises.

Even though I know that I shouldn't, I press my hand against his chest.

Ashton's hand closes over it and he squeezes his eyes shut. "I thought I'd never feel you do that again," he whispers.

I give him a moment before I gently push. "Keep talking." But I leave my hand where it is, resting against his now racing heart.

Ashton's lips curve into a small grimace. When his eyes open, he blinks against a glassy sheen. Just the idea of Ashton crying wrenches at my insides. I struggle to keep myself composed. "I still remember the day my mom and I sat at the kitchen table with a batch of cookies that I helped her bake. I was seven. She pinched my cheeks and told me that I was a blessing in disguise, that she didn't realize what she was missing until the day she found out she was going to have me. She said that something finally clicked inside her. Some maternal switch that made her *want* me more than anything else in the world. She told me that I made her and my dad so very happy." That's when the single tear finally slips down his cheek. "She had no idea, Irish. *No idea* what he was doing to me," he whispers, his eyes closing once again as he takes a deep, calming breath.

I brush the tear off his cheek but not before it spurs a dozen of my own, tears that I quickly wipe away because I don't want to derail the conversation. "When did it start?"

Clearing his throat, Ashton goes on, pushing the door wide open to show me his skeletons without reservation. Finally. "I was almost six the first time he locked me in a closet. Before that, I never saw him much. He worked long hours and avoided me the rest of the time. It didn't really matter. My mom doted on me constantly. She was an expressive woman. Endless hugs and kisses. I remember her friends joking that she would smother me to death with love." His brow furrows. "Looking back on it now, that must have bothered my dad. A lot. He had had her undivided attention before that, and . . ." Ashton's voice turns bitter. "One day, something changed. He started staying home when my mom had plans—a baby shower, or a party with her friends. He used those days to stick me in a closet with a strip of duct tape over my mouth. He'd leave me in there for hours, hungry and crying. Said he didn't want to hear or see me. That I shouldn't be alive. That I'd ruined their lives."

I can't understand how Ashton is so calm, how his heart keeps its steady rhythm, because I, despite all of my resolve to keep my composure, have melted into a blubbering mess as the visual of that little dark-eyed boy—not much bigger than Eric or Derek—curled in the closet burns bright in my mind again. I struggle to speak with the sharp lump in my throat. "And you didn't say anything?"

Ashton's palm wipes away some of my tears. "A few months earlier, I had accidentally let our Pomeranian out the front door. He ran right into traffic . . . My mom cried for weeks over that dog. Dad said he'd tell her that I *intentionally* let it run out the door, that I was a wicked little boy that did bad things to animals. I was terrified that she'd believe him . . ." He shrugs. "What the hell did I know? I was only six." There's a pause. "It was about a month before my eighth birthday when my mom started forget-ting dates, and names, and appointments. She did it occasionally before that but it started getting really bad." His Adam's apple bobs with a big swallow. "Within a year they diagnosed her. That's the day . . ." Inhaling deeply through his nose, he rubs the belt on his wrist. The one that's still there, still confining him. His constant reminder. "He never used a belt on me before that. I don't think he knew how hard he could hit before breaking skin. And he was mad. So mad at me. He blamed me for everything. He said the pregnancy did this to her, that the hormones had started wrecking her brain the day I was born." Ashton absently scratches his forearm, where one of his scars hides. "He told me not to tell her what happened or the stress of it would make her get worse, faster. So I lied. I told her I got the cuts screwing around on my bike. After that, I lied to her about everything. The bruises on my ribs when he punched me, the welts when he hit me with the belt again, the bump on my forehead the night he shoved me into the door frame. I got so used to lying, and my mother's health was deteriorating so quickly that what he was doing to me became . . . insignificant. I got used to it.

"He stopped hitting me the day we moved my mom into a

high-end research and treatment facility. I was fourteen. At the time, I still held out hope that she might get better, that the treatment would reverse or stall the disease. She still laughed at my jokes and sang that song in Spanish . . . She was still in there, *somewhere*. I had to hope that we could buy enough time until they found a cure." Ashton's head dips. "That was the first day my mom asked me who I was. And when he came at me that night . . . I knocked him flat on his back. I was a big kid. I told him to go ahead and hit me as hard as he could. I didn't care anymore. But he didn't. He never laid a hand on me again."

With a resigned sigh, Ashton gazes up at my face as he brushes the never-ending stream of tears from my cheeks with his thumbs. "He found a better way to punish me for breathing. I just didn't realize exactly what it was at the time. He sold our house and moved us across the city after that, for no reason other than to remove me from the life I knew, forcing me to change schools, to leave my friends. He could have shipped me off to boarding school and washed his hands of me as a responsibility, but he didn't. Instead, he started dictating who I would speak to, who I would date, what sports I would play." With a snort, Ashton mutters, "He's actually the one who demanded I join crew. Kind of ironic, given that rowing is the one thing that I love to do . . . Anyway, one night when I was fifteen, he came home from work unexpectedly to find my unapproved girlfriend and me fu—" Dark eyes flash to my face as my back stiffens. "Sorry . . . messing around. He called her a whore and kicked her out of the house. I snapped. I had him off the ground, ready to pound the shit out of him." Ashton's arms tense around my body as he holds me close to him. "That's when he started using my mother against me."

I feel my brow furrowing with confusion.

"He threw around numbers—the price of keeping her in her

expensive facility, how much it would cost if she survived another ten years. Said that he was beginning to question the point of it. She wasn't going to get better, so why waste money." Ashton's tongue slides over his teeth. "A waste of money. That's what the love of his life became to him. He hadn't gone to see her since the day he put her there. His wedding ring was long gone.

"I didn't want to believe that. I couldn't just give up on her. She was all I had and he knew it. So he made my choice very simple—I could either live the life he permitted me to live or her last few years would be spent in some shithole, waiting to die. He even found newspaper clippings, examples of horror stories from those kinds of places—neglect, assault . . . That's the day I realized how much my dad despised me for being born. And I knew he'd follow through with his threat."

I release the air I've been holding. So this is what has been hanging over Ashton's head all this time.

His mother.

"So I gave in. Over the years, I've kept quietly accepting his demands." With a snort, Ashton mutters, "The worst part? I could never really complain. I mean, look at my life! I'm going to Princeton, I have money, a car, a guaranteed job at one of the most prominent law firms in the country. It's not like he's *torturing* me. He's just . . ." Ashton heaves a sigh. "He just took away my freedom to choose how I live."

"Well, forcing you to marry someone is something to complain about," I mutter bitterly.

Ashton's head bows, his voice turning gruff. "That was the worst day of my life. I'm so sorry you had to go through that. And I'm sorry I didn't tell you about the engagement."

"Look at me," I demand, lifting Ashton's face with a finger under his chin. I want so badly to kiss him right now but I can't cross that line. Not until I know . . . "What happened with Dana?

Where do things stand?" *Is the wedding still on? Is what we're doing right now, sitting here together, wrong?*

Those gorgeous brown eyes take in my features for a moment before continuing. "Three years ago, I was at the firm's summer golf tournament, playing with my dad, when a new client introduced himself and his daughter to me. She was there, playing with him. That's how Dana and I met. I guess Dana's dad mentioned something about how much he'd love his daughter to be with a guy like me . . ." Ashton's neck muscles cord. "Dad saw an opportunity. Dana's father had given the firm only a portion of his businesses while three other law firms represented the rest. Getting 'in' with Dana's dad was a huge financial win for the firm. Worth tens of millions, maybe more. So I was instructed to make Dana love me." Ashton's arms shift to pull me tight to his chest as he buries his face against my collarbone, making my pulse begin to race. He keeps talking, though. "She was pretty and blond and really sweet. I never felt anything *real* for her but I couldn't complain about having a girlfriend like her. Plus she lived across the country most of the year, going to school, so it's not like she cramped my lifestyle. Not until you came along." I resist the urge to lean down. It would be so easy . . . just a little shift and my mouth could be on his.

"Three weeks ago, my dad called me and told me to propose. Dating Dana had secured a larger portion of her dad's business. He figured marrying her would secure him the rest. I refused. The next day, I got the call from the facility with questions about my mother's impending transfer to a nursing home in Philadelphia. I was barely off the phone when I got an email from my father with at least a dozen reports of neglect at this place. Even a sexual assault case that got thrown out of court on a technicality. The sick bastard was waiting and ready for it." Ashton's chest lifts and falls against me in a resigned sigh. "I had no choice. When he handed me the ring two weeks ago, after the race, I asked Dana to marry me. I told her she was the love of my life. I couldn't risk her saying no. I was going to convince her to have a long engagement, until I finished law school. I just needed to hold out until my mother died and then I could break it off." The self-loathing in his voice is unmistakable. He hates himself for it.

I struggle to wrap my head around this entire situation but I can't. I can't make sense of it. How could a man hate his own child this much? How could he find satisfaction in dominating another person's life so completely? Ashton's dad is sick. Just thinking about how such cruelty could be packaged in a sharp suit and successful career twists my stomach. I don't care what dark demons lie in Ashton's father's past to make him like this. The person that I am will never find an acceptable answer for all that man has done.

I gently push against Ashton's shoulder, enough to see his face again, and a few tears streaking his cheek. I search his features while his eyes rest on my mouth for a long moment. "When you came to my room that night and . . ." He swallows, his forehead furrowing. "I wanted to tell you. I should have told you before we . . ." Ashton's expression twists in pain. "I'm so sorry. I knew I'd end up hurting you and I let it happen anyway."

I won't let him punish himself for another second about that night. "I don't regret it, Ashton," I answer truthfully, giving him a small, reassuring smile. If there is one mistake I will never regret for the rest of my life, it is Ashton Henley. "So, what now?" I hesitate before asking, "What happened with Dana?"

"She screamed and cried a lot. And then she said that if I promised to never let it happen again, she'd forgive me."

Coils tighten around my stomach. Ashton is still engaged. His father still controls him. And I shouldn't be here, getting this close to him. Shutting my eyes against the harsh reality, I sigh and whisper, "Okay."

In a gruff voice, struggling to contain emotion, Ashton whispers, "Look at me, Irish."

It's through a haze of tears that I see his tiny smile, and I frown in confusion. Raising a hand to pinch my chin, Ashton pulls me into a soft kiss. It's closemouthed and it doesn't last long, but it leaves me breathless all the same. And all the more confused.

Ashton whispers. "I said, 'No.'"

"But . . ." I turn to take in his mother's home. "He'll transfer her from here to that awful place . . ."

"This is a new place, Irish. I moved my mom here a week ago." A strange grin transforms Ashton's face—a mixture of elation and relief and giddiness. It only amplifies his suddenly teary eyes.

"I don't . . . I don't get it." My heart has gone from breaking into pieces to now galloping and skipping over beats with anticipation. I know that he's hinting at something profound but I don't know what and I *need* to, now. "Tell me what's going on, Ashton."

His expression turns somber. "I ended things with Dana. I realized that my life wasn't the only one being ruined in this mess anymore." A flash of pain crosses his eyes with a memory. "I saw the empty look on your face when you walked down the stairs and out the door that day. It destroyed me. After that, I did the only thing I could do. I went to see Coach. He's . . . I've always envied Reagan for having a dad like that. Well, Coach cracked a bottle of Hennessy and I told him *everything*." His words bring me back to my night of confession with Kacey and tequila. It's kind of funny that we were doing the exact same thing at the exact same time . . . "Coach demanded that I stay with them for a few days until we could sort things out. Sure enough, my phone was ringing off the hook on Monday morning, my dad telling me to fix it with Dana or else. I bought myself some time, telling him that I was trying. Meanwhile, Coach and I started contacting friends of his—lawyers, doctors, Princeton alumni—looking for a way around my dad's legal control over my mother, a way to get her somewhere safe. It didn't look like we were going to get anywhere. I was sure I was trapped." A wry smirk touches his lips. "And then Dr. Stayner showed up on Coach's doorstep four days later."

My eyes widen with shock. "What? How?" Four days later . . . That means he literally left me in Miami and flew to New Jersey.

"Apparently he tracked down Coach, figuring he'd find me that way."

Of course. "I . . ." I heave a sigh, feeling guilty for divulging so much of Ashton's personal life. "I'm sorry. I told him things about you when I was in Miami. I needed to get it all out. I didn't ever think he would come here." *Why didn't I think he would do that?*

Ashton shushes me with a finger against my lips. "It's okay. Really. It's . . . more than okay. In fact, it has made *everything* okay." Ashton's head shakes as he laughs. "That guy is something else. He has a way of getting information out of you—you know you're being interrogated but in a friendly way. I've never seen Coach defer to anyone like he did with Stayner."

Rolling my eyes, I can't help but giggle. "I know exactly what you mean."

"In four hours—no lie, Irish, *four hours*—the guy had a full rundown of my past and my situation. He made a bunch of phone calls to colleagues." Nodding his head toward the house, Ashton explains, "The director of this place is a very good friend of his. He lined up a room." He smiles sadly. "They don't think she has too much longer now. Maybe another year or two. Her old place was nicer, but it didn't make sense for her to be there anymore, with the expensive treatment and therapy. Nothing is going to bring her back. I've accepted that. She just needs a place where she's safe and comfortable. She needs peace now."

"Stunned" cannot adequately describe how I feel right now. I am bursting with emotion—a volcanic mixture of happiness and sadness and adoration—adoration for that insane doctor of mine who has somehow brought another person that I love back to me. I don't bother to wipe the fresh set of tears as I frown, still working to make sense of everything.

"But how did you get her moved? How did your dad—"

Ashton's burst of laughter cuts my words off. "Oh, Irish. That's the best part." He wipes a tear that runs down his nose as his gaze drifts off somewhere, thoughtful for a moment. "It's shocking what some people are willing to do when they know they can get away with it. It's even more shocking what they'll do when they find out that they can't. My dad's been getting away with abusing me for sixteen years. And the day after Stayner arrived, he, I, and Coach drove right to my dad's office to end it. I've never been more scared in my life. But the fact that I wasn't alone in this anymore . . ." Ashton's voice cracks, and my heart cracks with it.

I pull him against me, squeezing my arms as tight as I can. I want to hear the rest. I need to. But for just a moment, I need to hold Ashton close to me as I come to terms with all of this. I may have lost my parents years ago, but I've had memories of a loving childhood to battle against the loss. Ashton has carried nothing but darkness and loathing. And the burden of protecting a woman who doesn't even remember the little boy she once smothered with love.

"My dad is a powerful man. He's not used to anyone telling him what to do. So when Stayner strolled into his office—uninvited—and took a seat in my dad's chair . . ." Ashton chuckles softly. "It was like something out of a movie. Stayner calmly laid out the facts—

the abuse, the manipulation, the downright scandalous blackmail. He didn't dwell on it, he didn't curse, or yell, or anything. He made sure that my father was fully aware of what he knew, what Coach knew. And then Stayner placed a note with this address on it on his desk and informed my dad that a room had been secured, that we would be transferring my mother here, that *he* would be maintaining the bills, and that she was not to leave this facility until the day she left her body."

My mouth has fallen open as I try to picture the scene. "What happened? What'd he say?"

Ashton's lip curls upward slightly. "He tried throwing some legal shit at Stayner, threats of a lawsuit, of getting his license revoked. Stayner smiled at him. Smiled and painted a very enlightening picture of what would happen if Dana's dad found out why his daughter's heart is shattered, how it would likely be much worse than simply losing him as a powerful client. That, added to the fact that I still had those emails about the nursing home—proof of his intentional malice toward his wife—well, it would be enough to damage that pristine image he's worked so hard to uphold. Maybe enough to keep a good lawyer friend of Stayner's busy for a few years. A friend with a penchant for taking on tough pro bono cases that he's notorious for winning. Stayner dropped a name and my dad's face went white. I guess there are more intimidating lawyers in New York than David Henley."

He pauses. "We left after that. I turned my back on my father and walked out. I haven't seen him since."

"So . . ." I point to the house in amazement. "He did what Stayner told him to do? Just like that?"

A curious frown touches Ashton's face. "Not exactly . . . The transfer did happen. They picked my mom up two days later and moved her in here. And then four days ago, a courier dropped off a bunch of paperwork with a letter of intent. My father is signing over power of attorney to me. I will have control of my mother's well-being and her estate. It has all of her financial records. Remember, I told you she was a model, right?"

I nod, and he continues. "She had a lot of her own money. When she found out she was sick, she made sure it was set up to cover her care. She made sure there was money to cover everything since the beginning. It had never even come out of *his* pocket."

"So, he's just . . . letting you go?"

With a slow nod, Ashton says, "The one condition is that I sign a nondisclosure agreement about my . . . relationship with him. Our history, about Dana. Everything. I sign that and he guarantees that I will never hear from or see him again."

The look on my face must ask the question because he confirms, "I'm going to sign it. I don't care. It's in the past. All I care about is what's sitting in front of me right now." Ashton's hand slides down to my thigh to pull me closer against him, his voice raw with emotion. "I can't ever undo all of the mistakes that I made with you, all the lies I told, all the ways that I hurt you. But . . . can we please just"—he grits his jaw—"somehow *forget* all of that and start over?"

This is really happening. I'm actually here, sitting with Ashton—the one thing I know that I want—and it may finally be *right*.

Almost.

"No," slips from my mouth.

I see Ashton flinch against the single word as he fights against the tears welling in his eyes. "I'll do anything, Irish. Anything."

My fingers slip to his wrist, to that awful thing that I know is still there.

I don't even have to say a word and he knows, sliding the sleeve of his coat up to uncover the glaring reminder of his abuse.

He stares at it for a long moment. "My dad threw this belt out after that night. Trying to get rid of the bloody evidence, I guess," he says softly. "But I found it in the trash and hid it in my room for years. The day I covered my scars with my tattoos was the same day I had this cuff made from a piece of the belt. My constant reminder that my mother needed me to hang on." Glancing up at a window on the third floor—his mother's, no doubt—he smiles wistfully. My heart melts as I watch his fingers deftly unsnap the band. Sliding me off his lap to stand, he takes a few steps away and then, with what appears to be all the strength in his body, he throws the last piece of his father's control over him into the mass of trees.

He turns his back on it, a pleading look in those gorgeous brown eyes of his, mixed with that heat that buckles my knees.

Taking a step into him, I press my hand against his racing heart and close my eyes, memorizing the feel of this moment.

The moment I make a choice for me and only me.

A choice that is right because it is right for *me*.

The smile escapes me before I can give him my last stipulation . . .

Ashton has never been a patient guy. I guess he sees the smile and takes it as my acceptance. His mouth instantly crashes into mine in an all-consuming kiss that weakens my knees and explodes my heart.

I manage to break free from his mouth. "Wait! Two more things."

He's breathing heavily, his brow furrowed as he gazes down at my face with confusion. "What else is there? You want my clothes too?" With an arched brow, he adds, "I'll gladly give them to you when we get somewhere a little bit warmer, Irish. In fact, I insist."

Shaking my head, I whisper, "I want you to get help. You need to talk to someone about all of this. Deal with it."

Ashton smirks. "Don't worry, I already have Stayner all over my ass. I have a feeling I'll be taking up your ten a.m. slot on Saturdays."

Relief pours out of me in an exhale. If there's anyone I trust with Ashton's well-being, it's Dr. Stayner. "Good."

With a small peck on my lips, he murmurs, "And that other thing?"

I swallow. "You said you wanted to forget everything. But . . . I don't want you to ever forget a thing that happened between us. Ever."

The most gentle of smiles passes over Ashton's face. "Irish, if there's one thing I've never been able to forget, it's a single second with you."

■■■

EPILOGUE

"You know, I haven't had cheesecake in almost a year," I murmur, dragging my fork along my plate as I watch the June sun setting over Miami Beach from the comfort of my lounge chair. "I don't think I like it anymore."

"I'll eat it, then," Kacey mutters, one step from licking her plate clean. "Or Storm will. I swear she puts back fifty thousand calories a day feeding that hog of a child." As if baby Emily heard the magic word from her bouncy chair in the kitchen, the hungry wails begin. Again. Emily was born in early January, immediately affixing herself to Storm's nipples and fighting to stay ever since. Things have not been easy for Storm, but she's handling it with all the patience and love that you could ever expect from her.

With me back home, it's given her a bit of respite. Emily is even taking a bottle from me now. Storm calls me her lucky charm.

I stayed to finish the year at Princeton after all, even managing to pull my overall average up to a solid B. It's ironic that my English lit final mark ended up being one of my strongest of that first semester, given it was also the most difficult course for me.

Ashton was definitely a motivating factor in my choice to stay. Once all the confusion, the pressure, and the lies were gone, I was left with nothing but choices. Small, large, easy, hard—all of them mine to make. For me.

I started with the easy ones. Like choosing to be where I could see Ashton whenever I wanted. That was a no-brainer. He had less than a year to go for a Princeton degree and he decided that he wanted to see it through, regardless of his reason for being there in the first place. Plus he was committed to his role as crew captain through the spring season.

Eventually Connor, Ashton, and I reconciled. It didn't take long for Connor to see that I wasn't just another one-night stand for his best friend. Connor started dating the blond girl—Julia—who'd approached him that night at the eating club. We even went on a double date. It was weird, but by the end of the night, I think it helped our friendship. From the looks I catch Connor giving me every now and then, I know his feelings for me haven't completely disappeared. I hope with time, he'll see that we weren't right for each other.

Ashton moved back into the house at the beginning of the spring semester. I stayed over a lot. That was also weird at first, but Ashton quickly made me forget about my nerves . . . and anything else that didn't involve him.

One of the harder decisions I had to make was whether or not to stay at Princeton beyond that first year. I'd applied for a transfer to Miami and, not surprisingly, it was accepted. There was nothing keeping me in New Jersey anymore, except Ashton. He would be done that year but his mother was still in New Jersey, and Reagan's dad had offered him a position as assistant coach while he figured things out. I toiled over my own decision for weeks, not sure what would make *me* happiest.

Then one night, as I was lying in bed and outlining his Celtic symbol with my fingertip, Ashton told me he was following me to Miami if I chose to go. He had even started looking into hospices down there with Stayner's help. Robert confirmed that the assistant coaching job would always be there for him.

That suddenly made my hard decision *really* easy. Which made me know that it was the right one.

I wanted to go home.

And I wanted to bring Ashton with me.

The sliding door opens behind us and two strong hands clamp over my shoulders. "You never told me it was so damn hot in Miami," my gorgeous man grumbles, leaning down to steal the mouthful of cake off my fork, following it with a kiss on my lips. I squeal as drops of sweat land on my face.

My eyes drift over the sheen coating his bare chest. Ashton has taken to evening jogs without a shirt since moving down here, and it's doing very bad things to my hormones on a nightly basis.

"The kid'll get used to it," I hear Trent mutter from behind as he steps out of the house, also sweaty and shirtless, with a towel around his neck. There's about an eight-year difference between Ashton and Trent but their maturity levels seem to be equal, because they get along perfectly. I'm not sure yet what that says about either of them.

"What is this—the sweaty guy convention?" With a blanket over her shoulder to discreetly hide the baby latched to her boob, Storm joins us, followed closely by a third shirtless, sweaty man— Ben. And just like that, the deck has come alive with people.

"You're too fast, Princeton," the rugged blond mutters, high-fiving Ashton.

I smile at the nickname. Everyone has taken an instant liking to Ashton. Including the small group of women passing by on the beach. It's the same group every night. They've discovered that if they swing past our house at this time in the evening, they're likely to find fit, half-naked men lingering out on the back deck. That Kacey, Storm, and I are usually sitting here too is a minor inconvenience . . .

"Hello!" Kacey waves dramatically at them as she does every night, clearly enjoying the fact that her man is being drooled over. She points at Trent. "He's five hundred for two hours!" Swinging her hand Ashton's way, she adds, "Seven-fifty for him because he's young. You should hear how he makes my sister scream!"

"Kacey!" I snap, but it's too late. Everyone's laughing and my cheeks are burning. Ashton bends down to plant a kiss on my neck, as if that will distract me from my mortification. As much as I've come out of my sexually repressed shell, so to speak, I still like to keep what's private . . . private. Ashton respects that and he doesn't tease me as much as they do. But he can't resist when the rest of them get into it. They seem to have so much more material on me now, thanks to my welcome-home party, complete with too many Jell-O shots and thin walls.

"What about me? Am I not worth some coin, Madame Kacey?" Ben's hands are held out in question, a mock look of insult on his attractive features.

"*I'll* pay *them* five hundred to get you out of my hair for one night," Kacey moans. But she follows it immediately with a wink.

"I can take a hint. I'm heading over to Penny's for a beer, anyway. Hey, Princeton, you sure you don't want me to hook you up with a job? Good money, lots of—"

"No, thank you!" I answer before Ashton can. There's no way in hell my beautiful Mediterranean underwear model is working in a strip club. I don't have my sister's self-confidence.

Ashton shrugs and then, with a lascivious smile in my direction, says, "I'm good here. I've got my hands full with this one."

"I think she might be worse than her sister," Trent adds wryly.

Another round of laughter heats my cheeks. "How about you go fill your hands with a long shower, by yourself?" I retort, slapping his hard stomach for emphasis. And then I realize what I've implied and I'm burying my face in my hands as they all burst out in laughter. Again.

Truth be told, Ashton is in no rush to find a job. We didn't end up moving his mother to Miami after all. She died peacefully in late April, just before exams. I was with Ashton the morning that he got the call. I held him close to me as he cried quietly—tears of both sadness and relief, I think.

There's enough money left to buy Ashton some time while he figures things out. He's not rich by any means but it's enough for the short term. Storm insisted that he move in with us, so he's not burdened with rent. He's signed up for flight lessons already, and is deciding for the first time what he wants to do with his life. I think he's savoring every second of the process.

Looking back over the past year, I can't believe how Ashton and I came from such different family situations—mine a place of love, his a place of pain—and yet we ended up in exactly the same spot at exactly the same time: learning how to make our own choices.

The only thing both of us seem to agree on is that we want each other there every step of the way.

I know, in my gut, that med school is not the right path for me, regardless of my academic capability. I kept in touch with the children's hospital until I knew that Eric and Derek had finished their chemo and were released. And then I laid that part of my life to rest. I'm giving serious consideration to social work.

While it won't be easy—some of those kids face situations worse than what Ashton faced—I know that I want to help children in a meaningful way. So Dr. Stayner has lined up some volunteer work at a foster care center to see if it's something my fragile nature can handle. And if it's not? Well . . .

Life's all about trial and error.

Dr. Stayner and I talk frequently. Dr. Stayner and Ashton talk even more frequently. Stayner jokes that he's our household shrink. I've told him he should just move in with us. I'm still searching for the right way to express the adoration that I feel for the man and all that he has done for us. All that he continues to do for us.

Giving him my firstborn child is starting to sound like a reasonable option.

"When are your friends coming down, Livie?" Storm asks as she adjusts her top. Emily's chubby cheeks finally make an appearance from behind the flannel curtain, with a contented burp.

"Tomorrow afternoon." The guys and Reagan are flying in for a few days.

They were shocked when they found out that Ashton's mom had been alive all this time, but they simply stood by their friend that day in late April and then celebrated her life with him at Tiger Inn until the wee hours of the morning. While Ashton can never disclose all of the details because of his agreement with his father, I think the guys have come to realize that their captain's life was far from the ideal exterior.

And Reagan? Well, aside from the three-week-long pout I had to deal with when I told her I wasn't coming back in the fall, Reagan has been the best roommate and friend I could ever ask for. She's still madly in love with Grant. Maybe enough to tame her wild streak.

"All right! So we're getting lit tomorrow night," Ben exclaims, clapping his hands together. He bends down to kiss Emily on her cheek.

"You stink!" Storm pushes him away with a giggle and a crinkled nose.

"On that note . . ." Ben lays a sloppy kiss on Storm's forehead and then heads into the house with a holler of "Goodbye!"

Trent stretches his long, muscular arms over his head. "The Grill tonight?"

"Yes! I need a night out!" Storm exclaims, a sudden frenzied look in her eyes. Like she's a caged animal. She kind of is. "Dan's going to be home in an hour and then me and these milk bags are ditching this joint. Lemme go empty them." She's gone with Emily in a split second to pump.

The guys follow, arguing about who gets first shower, leaving Kacey and me alone on the deck once again.

We sit silently for a long moment, as I listen to the seagulls and watch the calming waves roll in. "You know it's been almost a year since that night?" God, everything feels so different! I'm still me. And yet I've changed so much.

"Huh." Kacey pauses as she scoops my plate out of my hand. "You mean since the night I told you that you're completely fucked up?" I see the tiny curl of amusement in her lips as she polishes off the last chunk of my cake.

"Yeah, that's the one." I stretch my arms back and nestle them behind my head.

And I smile.

ACKNOWLEDGMENTS

It is nothing short of a miracle to figure out what your dream job is and then actually be able to live it. I am still in shock that this is now my life. I have many people to thank for it.

First and foremost, to my readers. Some of you have been with me since *Anathema* and many of you have just discovered me with *Ten Tiny Breaths*. All of you are cherished. It is because you pick up my books, appreciate my style, and share my name with your friends and family, that I am here today.

To the fantastic bloggers of the world—some of the most passionate readers I've ever met—I would not be writing this acknowledgments page without you. Not a chance. A special thanks to Aestas Book Blog, Autumn Review, Maryse's Book Blog, Shh Mom's Reading, Three Chicks and Their Books, Tsk Tsk What to Read, Natasha Is a Book Junkie, and The Sub Club. An extra-special thanks to Mandy at I Read Indie Books, for your *TTB* review. I think the pack mule won readers over. I could easily list a hundred blogs here. You have all been truly amazing.

To Heather Self—an amazing writer, blogger, and friend. Thank you for your mad naming skills, lavender-infused vodka, and your infectious positive attitude. Expect that Canadia will show up on your Texas doorstep one day. Be ready.

To Courtney Cole—thank you for reading *OTL* when you

were staring down the barrel of your own deadline. I lurve your words on my cover. Absolutely lurve them.

To Kelly Simmon of Inkslinger PR—and so the journey continues. You have become so much more than a phenomenal publicist to me. You are truly a friend. I expect nothing but great things to come for you.

To Stacey Donaghy of Corvisiero Literary Agency—where do I begin with you? I still tell my husband to this day that I am brilliant because I signed with you. Okay, maybe I don't say that. I think it's more along the lines of, I'm the luckiest writer out there to have an agent like you. Thank you for dropping everything to come to my aid at the eleventh hour, for your constant encouragement, and for believing in me in the first place. And for not letting me kill off all of my characters in a Red Bull–induced rage.

To Sarah Cantin—I want to steal you and put you in my pocket and carry you everywhere with me. You are a dream editor. So positive, so supportive, so willing to help. I get excited every time I see your name appear in my email inbox. I am thrilled to have you in my corner.

To Marya Stansky—for your insight into Princeton eating clubs. Thank you for enduring my random questions and giving me tons of great material to work with.

To my publisher, Judith Curr, and the team at Atria Books: Ben Lee, Valerie Vennix, Kimberly Goldstein, and Alysha Bullock, for your outstanding work getting this book into the hands of readers. I can't even begin to explain how perfect the cover is for Livie.

To my husband—thank you for a month of daddy day care so I could hide in my cave to get this book finished for my deadline. One day I will learn to cook again.

To my kids—because they are the cutest, sweetest little devils on earth.

ABOUT THE AUTHOR

K.A. Tucker published her first book at the age of six with the help of her elementary school librarian and a box of crayons. Today, she remains a voracious reader, and resides outside of Toronto with her husband, two beautiful girls, and an exhausting brood of four-legged creatures.

Turn the page for a sneak peak at
K.A. Tucker's novel:

FOUR SECONDS TO LOSE

a novel

Available April 2014 from Atria Paperback

I believe some people are inherently evil.
I believe guilt is a powerful motivator.
I believe redemption is something you can strive for but never
    fully achieve.
I believe second chances exist only in dreams, never in reality.
I believe you don't have years, or months, or weeks to impact a
    person's life.
You have seconds.
Seconds to win them over,
And seconds to lose them.

—Cain

chapter one

■ ■ ■

CAIN

10 years ago

Blood drops decorate the dusty gray concrete like an abstract piece of art. The stocky brute facing me—his bottom lip split open, an angry cut across his cheekbone—can account for some of that. But given the colossal beating I'm taking at the hands of this recently paroled rapist, most of that blood is probably mine.

Holding my left elbow tight against the ribs that he just splintered with a series of powerful blows, I struggle not to wince as my feet shuffle back toward the ropes of the makeshift ring. Screams and shouts bombard me from all angles, echoing through the underground parking lot of the downtown business building. Normally I have a decent crowd of rich bitches throwing their names, numbers, and "pretty boy" comments at me. Not tonight, though. All of these people took the twenty-to-one odds against me and they're no doubt picturing sandy beaches and shiny BMWs.

Hell, *I* almost bet against me. But, there's not a person in the world that I trust with that kind of money to place it for me. Except maybe Nate. But he's fourteen and a known associate of mine, so I might as well have painted a target on his head if I sent him to the bookie.

"Come on, pansy ass!" Jones bellows, slamming his meaty fists together, a wicked grin on his face.

I remain silent as Nate splashes my face with cool water and I swig some back, trying to rinse the coppery taste out of my mouth. I've heard this guy likes to draw his beatings out, so I'm not worried about him charging me like a bull. I *am* worried about the crowd shoving me in, though. I can feel their impatience swelling in the air over my pause. They want to see my skull hit the ground. Now. This is *real* underground fighting. The kind that brings the high-rolling criminal element and thrill-seekers together like family at Christmas. There are no weight classes here. No drug tests. No rules. No true refereeing. The match doesn't end until one fighter's broken body is collected off the ground.

Not exactly the world a loving father would introduce his son into. But I don't have a loving father. I have a mean wanna-be-mobster prick of a dad, who—after pounding on me enough to teach me how to hold my own and harden my muscles beyond their years—decided he could make some real cash by throwing me into L.A.'s illegal fighting scene. At the age of seventeen, when my body wasn't even fully developed but was solid on account of the grueling workouts my dad insisted on. I can't say that I went unwillingly. I've even enjoyed it, most times. It's always my dad's face I'm bashing in, his bones I'm snapping, every time I raise my fists.

Every time I pulverize my opponent.

And now, at nineteen years old, I've ended up fighting for my life in the upper echelon of this illicit world. I could win *big* on this one with what I put down. Or I could end up in a body bag. As I gaze at the goon in front of me—steroid-enhanced pecs twitching with anticipation, ugly veins protruding from his neck, his face a hideous mess of blood and ink—I accept that I probably won't be the last one standing here, tonight. I'm a fucking moron for showing up to this fight. Jones is probably high on meth. Nothing short of two shots of fentanyl is going to bring the animal to his knees, and I don't have elephant tranquilizers in my back pocket.

"Zee!" Nate's voice cracks behind me, using my fighter name. I glance over my shoulder at the scrawny kid in my corner. My only reliable confidante, the one by my side through every single fight. He's holding his cell phone to his ear, his ebony skin turned a sickly ashen tinge. "Somethin' big is going down at Wilcox." *Wilcox. My parents' street.* Nate's wide molasses eyes flicker to my waiting opponent before returning to my mangled face.

"They fighting again?" I ask. It wouldn't be the first time.

Nate's head shakes slowly, somberly. "Nah, something different. Benny saw two guys show up about twenty minutes ago." Benny's a fifteen-year-old kid who lives across the street from my parents and goes to Nate's school with him. He's a shithead, but he worships Nate because Nate is connected to me.

"For him or her?" As disturbing as the question is, it's valid. Both of my parents took entrepreneurial paths down the wrong side of morality—my dad venturing into the drug trade, my mother running a quaint bookkeeping business/ brothel out of my late grandmother's house. And now one of them has clearly pissed someone off enough to track them down on their doorstep.

Normally, I wouldn't give a shit. I'd be ecstatic. Maybe, if my dad pissed off the right people, they'd get rid of my problem for me. Only it's one in the morning on a Tuesday, and Lizzy, my sixteen-year-old sister, *could* be asleep in her bed. And, if these guys came looking for money and my dad goes to the hollowed-out armchair to pay them off, he's going to find it empty.

Because I stole every last bill earlier today to put down on this fight.

A new visual blazes in my head. One of these guys collecting their payment on Lizzy.

That's all it takes for my adrenaline to kick in. The crippling pain in my side instantly vanishes as I look at my opponent through new eyes. If I bury the odometer needle, I can get to their house in under fifteen minutes. It may be enough time. It may not. This goon is the only thing stopping me from leaving *right now*.

"Nate, tell Benny to call the cops."

I toss my water bottle to the ground and charge forward.

It's over so fast, no one watching seems to know what the hell happened. Silence fills the vast parking lot as everyone waits for Jones to get up. Everyone except me. I know he's not getting up for a while. I felt the bones crack as his head snapped to the side with the venomous blows that I delivered in quick succession.

He still hasn't moved as my peeling tires screech up the underground ramp.

■ ■ ■

"Stay here," I bark at Nate as I pull my GTO to a stop in the middle of the street. I'm not sure how I didn't crash, given that one eye is swollen shut. I jump out, running past the crowd of curious onlookers, toward the throng of emergency vehicles and police officers, lights flashing, cops running with radios in their hands. They couldn't have beaten us by more than ten minutes.

It takes four police officers, a gun aimed at my forehead, and a set of handcuffs to stop me. They won't let me go in. They won't answer the one damn question I ask over and over again. *Is Lizzy okay?* Instead, they hammer me with an onslaught of words that don't register, that I don't care to acknowledge.

"What happened to you, son?"

"Who did this to you, son?"

"You need medical attention."

"How do you know the occupants of this home?"

"Where have you been since midnight until your arrival here?"

Despite my warning, Nate ventures out of my car and somehow slips through the police tape. Like a silent shadow, he waits with me as a young paramedic tapes the gash above my eyebrow and informs me that I have three broken ribs.

I barely hear her as I watch a parade march in and out of my parents' front door.

As I watch the coroner show up.

The beginning of dawn lights the sky when one . . . two . . . three gurneys finally roll out.

All topped with black bags.

"I'm sorry for your loss, son," a stocky police officer with a gruff voice offers. I didn't catch his name. I don't care about his name. "Things like this shouldn't happen."

He's right. They shouldn't. Lizzy shouldn't have been there in the first place. If I hadn't given up on her, if I hadn't kicked her out of my apartment, she wouldn't have.

I could have saved her.

But now I'm too late.

■ ■ ■

Present Day

"What do you mean you can't deliver until *after* the weekend?" Despite every effort to keep my cool, my tone is biting.

"Sir, I'm sorry. As I've already explained, we're experiencing labor shortages. We're working as fast as we can to cover orders. We're sorry for the inconvenience," the customer service rep recites evenly, sounding like she has said it a hundred times today. Because I'm sure she has.

Pinching the bridge of my nose to dull the sudden headache forming, I fight the urge to slam the receiver against the desk. This conversation is a complete waste of time. It's the same one I've had every day for two weeks. "Tell your management that 'inconvenient' isn't the right word." I hang up before she has a chance to spew the prewritten response for that.

With a groan, I lean back in my leather chair and fold my arms behind my head. I survey the walls of my office—lined floor-to-ceiling with shelves, doubling as supply room overflow. Five weeks of abnormally busy nights at Penny's coupled with sporadic beer deliveries means I'm out of our top brands for the coming weekend. That means I'll have to spend yet another Saturday night explaining to customers why being out of Heineken doesn't entitle them to a free lap dance.

I hate this business, some days.

Lately, I hate this business *all* days.

Cracking open a fresh bottle of high-end Rémy Martin, I pour the deep golden liquid into my tumbler. It's my vice—a glass before the club opens to take the edge off and one to close the place down. Unfortunately, the edge doesn't come off so easily anymore and I find myself topping up the glass a lot. It's a good thing our hours are limited or I'd have a drinking problem. At two hundred bucks a bottle, I'd also have a money problem.

My office door cracks open just as the comforting burn slides down my throat.

"Cain?" Nate's deep voice rumbles a second before his six-foot-six, 280-pound frame eases through the doorway. I'm still in awe of how that twiggy little kid turned into the giant now standing before me, almost overnight, too. It shouldn't surprise me, though, given that I was the one footing the steep grocery bill through his teenage growth spurts. "Just got a text from Cherry. She's sick."

"She texted *you*?"

He nods slowly, his dark eyes never leaving mine.

"That's the third time she's called in sick in two weeks."

"Yup," he agrees, and I know his thoughts are on the same wavelength as mine. No one knows me better than Nate. In fact, no one *really* knows me *but* Nate.

Cherry has worked for me for three and a half years. She has the immune system of a shark. The last time she started missing shifts because she was "sick," we found her battered and strung out on blow, thanks to her douchebag boyfriend.

"Do you think he's back?"

I shove my fingers through my hair, gritting my teeth with rising frustration. "He'd be the world's biggest moron if he is, after what happened the last time." Nate put him in the hospital with a broken femur and two dislocated shoulders as a warning. I have to think that was an effective deterrent.

"Unless Cherry invited him over."

I roll my eyes. She's a good girl with low self-esteem and terrible taste in men. Though I'd be surprised, I wouldn't put it past her. I've seen it happen before. Many times.

"I think I'll just swing by her place to make sure this isn't something more than a bug or . . . chick issues." Nate grabs his keys from the rack.

With a sigh, I grumble, "Thanks Nate." We've helped her stay clean and idiot-boyfriend free for a year. The last thing I want to see is a repeat. "And, here." I pull a twenty-dollar bill out of my wallet and toss it across my desk. "Her kid loves Big Macs."

Nate scowls at my money, leaving it where it lays. I should know better. "And if he's there?"

"If he's back in the picture . . ." I run my tongue over my teeth. "Don't do anything . . . yet. Call me. Immediately."

With a lazy salute, Nate exits my office, leaving me with my elbows on my desk and my folded hands against my clenched mouth, wondering what I'm going to do if Cherry has taken a turn for the worse. I can't fire her. Not when she needs our help. But . . . *fuck*. If we have to go through this with her *again* . . .

And I had to convince Delyla to go back to counseling just last week because she started cutting again. And two weeks before that, we were rushing Marisa to the hospital with complications after the back-street abortion that her asshole boyfriend convinced her to undergo. She hasn't even made it back to work yet. And the week before that—

A knock on my door only seconds later makes my temper flare unexpectedly. "What!"

Ginger's face pokes in.

Taking a deep breath, I gesture her in with a "sorry," silently chastising myself for barking at her.

"Hey, Cain, my friend is coming in to meet you tonight," she reminds me in that low, husky voice suitable for phone sex companies. The customers here love it. They love everything else about her, too, including those naturally large breasts and that sharp-witted tongue. "Remember? The one I mentioned earlier this week."

I groan. I *completely* forgot. Ginger sprung it on me last Friday as I was refereeing an argument between Kinsley and China in the hallway. I never did agree to meet with this person but I didn't say no. Ginger is clearly taking advantage of that. "Right. And she wants a job as what again? A dancer?"

Ginger's head bobs up and down, her wild short hair—colored in chunks of platinum blond, honey, and pink—in styled disarray. "I think you'll like her, Cain. She's . . . different."

"Different, how?"

Ginger's hot pink lips twist. "Hard to explain. You'll see when you meet her. You'll like her."

My hand finds its way to the back of my neck, trying to rub the permanent tension out. It won't work. Weekly trips to a massage therapist do nothing for the kind of knots this place creates. "It's not about liking her, Ginger. It's about being overstaffed. I don't need any more dancers or bartenders right now." Given Penny's reputation, this place has basically become the crème de la crème of adult entertainment clubs. I don't take walk-ins or random applications. Employment is by referral only and turnover is low. Aside from Kinsley, I haven't hired anyone new in almost a year. Too many dancers means catfights over money.

"I know, Cain, but . . . I think you're *really* going to like her." Ginger has been bartending for me for years, longer than anyone else. I trust her opinion of people. The three others she recommended turned out to be outstanding employees who are now on healthy life paths, leading far away from the sex trade business. Hell, she's the one who introduced me to Storm—my shining success story!

After a long pause, I ask, "And her preferences? Is she . . .? Not that it matters, of course."

Teal-green cat eyes sparkle as she smiles at me. "I'm pretty sure she's into dudes. Haven't seen the proof yet, but that's what my vibe tells me. Unfortunate for me . . ." I've come to truly appreciate Ginger's sexual orientation. There's never been that awkward moment with her, where she's decided that I would welcome her hand on my cock. She's one of the *very* few female employees I can say that about. It's one of the reasons why I get along with her so well.

"Her name?"

"Charlie."

"Real or stage?"

She shrugs. "Real, I think. 'Charlie' is the only name she's ever given me."

I pause to take another sip of my drink. "You vetted her?" Ginger knows the requirements. No track marks. No pimps. No prostitution. I have zero tolerance for drugs and prostitution. I'd get shut down in a heartbeat if the cops caught on, and too many people rely on Penny's to let that happen. Plus, there's no need for it here. I make sure the girls can rake in the money safely, without selling the last shreds of their dignity.

Her curt nod answers me.

"Experience?"

"Vegas. She had a couple of interviews here, including one at Sin City." Ginger's brow arches meaningfully. "You know what Rick makes them do."

I lean back in my chair. Yeah, I've heard what Rick's requirements are for getting and keeping a job in his club. The fact that the guy's a fat, sweaty tub of hair doesn't help. "She didn't comply?"

Ginger giggles. "She barely made it out of there without puking, from what she told me."

I nod slowly. That definitely earns her a few points with me. I want to help out every woman who feels she needs to take her clothes off to survive but I'm only one man, and not every woman is strong enough to avoid the pitfalls of this industry.

I've seen too many of them fall fast.

And trying to catch them over and over again is so very exhausting.

Taking in Ginger's exotically beautiful face, I finally ask the big question. "What's her deal, Ginger? Why strip?" With a finger, I slowly trace the rim of my glass. There's usually a good reason. Or a bad reason, depending on how you look at it. As far as ratios of completely normal to fucked-up employees go, the numbers generally weigh in heavy for the latter. "High school dropout with no future? History of abuse? Douchebag boyfriend wanting extra cash? Daddy issues? Or is she just looking for attention?"

Ginger's head tilts as she murmurs in a dry tone, "Jaded much?"

I throw my hands up in the air. "You're the exception, Ginger. You know that." Since the day Ginger walked into my office—on her eighteenth birthday—I've never had to worry about her. She comes from a stable, abuse-free home and she has never even batted an eye at the stage. Her purpose is straightforward and honest: save enough money to open an inn in Napa Valley. With the kind of money she rakes in here, I'd say she's getting close to that dream.

After a pause, she shrugs. "All I know is she wants to make good money. But she seems to have her head on straight, since she didn't take the other jobs."

Because she probably figured out she'd be sucking cock in the private room . . . With a deep exhale and my hand pressed against my forehead, rubbing the frown smooth, I mutter, "All right. We'll see." *Am I really going to do this right now? What if she's another Cherry? Or Marisa? Or China? Or Shaylen? Or—*

"Great. Thanks, Cain." She pauses, her curvy frame—dressed in cut-off shorts and a tank top for setting up the bar—leaning against the door frame. "You okay? You seem . . . worn out lately."

Worn out. That's a good way to describe it. Worn out by week after week, month after month of brazen customers, everyday ownership issues, and employees who can't seem to straighten out their lives without someone running interference. Throw in police attention—because they assume, based on my past and my current business, that I'm following in the footsteps of my parents—and you've summarized my life for the past decade.

It's enough to make any rational person quit.

And I have considered quitting. I've considered selling Penny's and walking away. And then I look at my employees' faces—the ones who I know *will* end up at a place like Sin City without me—and the metal teeth of the trap around my chest dig in tighter.

I can't abandon them. Not yet. If I could just get this lot out and safe, without adding any more problems to my plate, I could live out my life somewhere quietly. A remote beach in Fiji is sounding pretty damn good.

None of those thoughts ever gets spoken out loud, though. "Just haven't been sleeping well," I say to Ginger, pulling on the fake smile that I've mastered. It's beginning to feel like a suffocating iron mask.

By the way Ginger's brow pulls together, I know she doesn't believe me. "Okay, well, you know you always have my ears if you want 'em," she offers, grinning playfully as she rolls her hips and winks. "And *nothing* else."

Her soft laughter follows her out the door, temporarily lifting my dour mood as I set to preparing payroll for the small army of dancers, security, kitchen, and wait staff I have under my employ. Serge—a forty-eight-year-old retired Italian opera singer—manages my kitchen as if it were his own, but I handle everything else.

Unfortunately, the dour mood returns with a vengeance twenty minutes later when Nate's call comes through. "His blue Dodge is here."

My fist slams down against the desk, rattling everything. "You're kidding me, right?" I take a moment to gain control of the rage bubbling inside me. Nate doesn't bother to answer. The two of us have always had an easy back-and-forth banter, but he knows what not to joke with me about. Fuckheads taking advantage of women is one of those things.

"You want me to go in?" Nate offers.

"No, wait outside. If he's back, he's probably carrying." As stupid as this guy is, he must have learned after the last time. "I'm on my way. Don't go inside, Nate." I throw that last warning in with a stern voice. I couldn't bear to lose Nate over this. I shouldn't even have let him get involved. I should have made him go to college and lead a normal life. But I didn't, because he's all I have and I like having him around.

I'm out of my seat and crouched in the corner in seconds, dialing the safe combination. My fingers wrap tightly around the biting steel of my Glock. I despise myself for touching it. It represents violence, illegality . . . the life and the choices that I've left behind, that I would never let consume me again. But if it means keeping Nate and Cherry and her eight-year-old son—the one who dialed my number on Cherry's cell phone for help when he found his mother unconscious on the couch the last time—safe, then I will jam the barrel right into the scumbag's temple.

I'm about to slip on the holster when the door creaks open. "Cain?"

I need to start locking my damn office door again, I tell myself. Stifling a curse, I slide the gun back into the safe and stand, struggling to keep the venom from my voice as I growl, "Ginger, you really need to learn—" *How to knock* is how that sentence is supposed to end.

But instead it ends in a sharp hiss, as I find myself staring at my past.

At Penny.